THE RED PRESIDENT

Also by Martin Gross

THE BRAIN WATCHERS
THE DOCTORS
THE PSYCHOLOGICAL SOCIETY

The RED President

MARTIN GROSS

Doubleday & Company, Inc.
Garden City, New York
1987

Library of Congress Cataloging-in-Publication Data

Gross, Martin L. (Martin Louis), 1925–
  The red president.

  I. Title.
PS3557.R587R4 1987   813'.54   86-13496
ISBN 0-385-23490-2

For my wife, Anita,
and my daughters, Ellen and Jane.

And for the man of all times,
Thomas Jefferson.

ACKNOWLEDGMENTS

This is a work of fiction, but the research needed to accurately explain the defense establishments of both the United States and the Soviet Union required the help of several individuals and agencies. I would like to thank the public affairs sections of the Defense Department, the Air Force, the Air Force Association, the U. S. Army, the U. S. Navy, the Defense Nuclear Agency, and the officials of several specialized organizations, including the American Defense Preparedness Association and the American Security Council.

For help in making the environment of the CIA, and its sworn adversary, the KGB, more realistic, my appreciation goes to several retired career CIA officials, who should not, however, be held responsible for any fictional license of the author.

At Doubleday, I need to thank Sam Vaughan, former editor-in-chief, for his faith in this project; Jim Moser, for his work and skill; and Patrick Filley, another encouraging editor.

A special note of gratitude to my agent, John Hawkins, and to my writing colleagues who read the work in progress, sometimes ad infinitum, and offered always valuable suggestions: Peter Meyer, Stephen Fenichell, Robert T. Crowley, Frank Van Riper, and Sidney Offit. And to those others who contributed, in their own way: Nancy Hahnfeldt, Betsy Hulick, and Muriel Hyland.

MARTIN L. GROSS,
1986

"The American struggles against the obstacles that nature opposes to him; the adversaries of the Russian are men. The former combats the wilderness and savage life; the latter, civilization with all its arms. The conquests of the American are therefore gained by the plowshare; those of the Russian by the sword. . . .

"The principal instrument of the former is freedom; of the latter, servitude. Their starting point is different; yet each of them seems marked out by the will of Heaven to sway the destinies of half the globe."

ALEXIS DE TOCQUEVILLE,
1835

THE RED PRESIDENT

Prologue

January 21, The Day After Inauguration

The President knew it was early, perhaps too early, but he couldn't wait. He had slept as long as possible, the covers holding him intact against the cold, peering out occasionally at the January frost mottling the second-floor windows of the White House.

The digital clock alongside his bed in the family quarters read 5:45 A.M. There was no need to wait any longer, to delay as he first had, waking almost every hour during the night, staring at the intricate Federal molding on the ceiling, then moving restlessly about the room, chastising himself for his impatience.

He had desperately wanted to get to the Oval Office yesterday, but the typed agenda thrust on him had devoured every minute. The inaugural swearing in and the parade, ceremonies in the East Room, then the round of inaugural balls had been satisfying yet peculiarly frustrating. His hands ached to hold a presidential pen, to lift a telephone of authority.

By six-forty he was dressed and moving toward the Oval Office. The small private elevator took the President down to the ground floor where two Secret Service men followed discreetly as he walked the connecting corridor toward the Executive West Wing.

"Good morning, Mr. President."

The guard's greeting at the threshold of the office brought a cheery nod from the President, now unable to repress his feelings. He was stirred by the title, democracy's approximation of nobility.

It was quiet before the maelstrom he knew would soon usher in this first business day of his administration. Except for the guards, he was alone.

The President moved cautiously across the room, his eyes halting momentarily on the presidential seal woven into the carpet. The eagle seemed to be studying him. He smiled at the thought, then lowered himself into the chair behind the antique Civil War desk, once the property of Lincoln's War Secretary, Edwin Stanton.

Surveying the historic office, which had served every President since Teddy Roosevelt, he experienced surprise. It was smaller than he remembered it from the times he had come, political hat in hand, to visit the previous Chief Executive.

Tentatively, then with more confidence, he started around the room, his steps respectfully soft. A piece at a time, his fingertips touched the furniture—the colonial wing chairs, the built-in scallop-shelled bookcases, the bulky carved mahogany desk, the drop-leaf table against the tall window between himself and the Rose Garden, even the console of the three television sets.

The touching was a child's compulsion. But it seemed to make the dream more real. Yes, he was truly the President of the United States.

He had never revealed his entire vision of a new, surely better, America. Much of it had to be secret. But one thing he swore to himself. The Cold War that had plagued the nation for almost fifty years would soon be over.

The intercom ring startled the President.

"Who's there?" he asked.

"It's me, Mr. President. May I come in?"

His administrative secretary, a small, spare woman, fortyish, entered the office as the President stood.

"Good morning, Mr. President. Welcome to the White House," she said, taking in the bright yellow and white room, sharing the morning's discovery. "We are here? Aren't we?"

"Yes, and probably too early." The President paused. "What time is it?"

"Exactly seven-one."

"What time does that make it in Moscow?"

"One minute after three in the afternoon. Why?"

"Perfect timing. Forget the teletype hot line. Get me the General Secretary at the Kremlin on the phone, personally."

"Are you sure, Mr. President?"

"Quite sure."

His eyes scanned the far wall, settling on the Rembrandt Peale portrait of Thomas Jefferson. What would old Tom think? Would he understand the need for change in an unsafe world?

His thoughts were interrupted by his secretary's voice issuing from the intercom.

"Mr. President. I have Moscow on the line."

Book One

Chapter 1

In July, Six Months Earlier

The desolate stretch of fifty miles between Baker and the Nevada border was Tom Ward's target zone.

As he drove across the great California desert on Interstate 15, the July heat careened upward in massive drafts, disturbing his visibility. Ward had rented the Ciera at the Los Angeles airport, driving it hard for an hour, then two, until at San Bernardino he exited the enormous Los Angeles basin, climbing the San Gabriel Mountains that husbanded its moisture, then into the desert beyond. He was headed toward Victorville, Barstow, Baker, and on, in the direction of Las Vegas.

California was a virgin landscape for Ward, but he nodded knowingly as he peered through the sandy haze at the road signs and man-made features, all of which had been projected onto his brain with sickening repetition. Now as he scanned the bleak, tanned horizon, he was searching ahead not for his memorized cues but for a dark speck on the side of the roadway.

A man.

The search was not fruitful. The road was littered in places, the occasional droppings of civilization marring the emptiness. But there was no human castoff. He continued to drive for miles without sighting a person, then, with a sudden sharpness, he pulled the car off the highway and onto the shoulder.

From a small airline bag on the back seat, Ward removed a pair of scissors and stripped the dull metal sheath from each glistening blade. He twisted the scissors at its common center, splitting it in two. His hands now held two rapier-sharp knives, one of which disappeared into each jacket pocket.

The car was well past Baker, approaching Nevada, but there was still no man. At the sign of WELCOME to the state of legal prostitution and gambling, Ward put the Ciera into an abrupt U-turn and crossed illegally over the wide brown grass divide to the other side of the highway.

It was Monday, 6:30 P.M. local California time, the sun drifting lower in the sky as he moved through the barren foothills of Clark Mountain, retracing his route through the Mojave back toward Los Angeles.

Behind the wheel, Ward was the impeccable rental-car client, the American businessman, traveling light with the single airline bag. Ward adjusted the sunglasses on the bridge of his pointed nose. It overlooked a pale but not sickly face, which contrasted sharply with his straight, resinous black head of hair.

The clothes were suited to the car, if somewhat better. Conventional but finely cut. The gray worsted, wide pin-stripe suit with a pale pink oxford shirt and claret and blue rep tie were surely more Eastern than California.

He drove into the stillness for another ten minutes before he saw the man. Ahead about a quarter of a mile, he was walking with his head bent, apparently in a torpor brought on by the heat.

Ward slowed. The hitchhiker was dressed in cheap clothes, a T-shirt and worn slacks, with the ubiquitous American sun shield, a baseball cap, atop his head. He was young, probably in his thirties, wearing a bushy, untrimmed brown beard, of medium build and about the same size as Ward, five feet eleven. A classic American drifter, Ward guessed.

As the car approached, the man suddenly came awake, enthusiastically waving for Ward to stop. He pulled over and rolled down the window.

"I'm going to L.A.," Ward called out. "Want a lift?"

"Great," the man answered, wasting no time moving in front alongside him. "Yesus. It's nice in here. I don't think I could've took another minute in that sun. Thanks, mister."

Ward smiled in return. "You going to L.A.?"

The hitchhiker nodded. "Yeh. I got a lift at the casino on the Nevada border, but the guy was so drunk I was afraid. I got out here."

"Where'd you come from, Las Vegas?"

"No." The man laughed. "I can't afford that kind of shit. I'm trying to make it all the way from Maryland to L.A. on ninety dollars. I come this far, and I got twelve dollars left. I started out with a knapsack but somebody stole it off me in Nevada."

Ward continued to probe the drifter's provenance. "I suppose you left the wife and kids back home, to first see if you make it out here?"

"Naw. I got nobody back home. Always been on my own—lumberjack, car washer, whatever. Fellows say I'm some kind of a character, that I could act in Hollywood if'n I wanted. I'm goin' to give it a try."

Ward knew he had his man. He drove a while longer, then jerked spasmodically at the accelerator until the car came to an agonized stop on the shoulder.

"What's the matter?" the man asked.

"Don't know. But I've got an extra can of gas and some tools in the trunk. Do you know anything about engines?"

He had asked the right question. Within seconds the man was running his hands expertly under the hood, searching intuitively for any break in the link of power.

Ward moved quickly, retrieving a five-gallon gas can from the trunk and the small airline bag from the back seat, bringing both up front where the man was working. With the two stiletto blades now in hand, he circled silently behind the hitchhiker, who was still bent over, intent on the engine. Pressing one knife against the flesh of the man's neck, the other into his side, Ward sternly whispered his instructions.

"Stand up slowly, and don't try to turn around. If you try anything, both these blades will go in deep. Do as you're told and I'll try to make everything painless."

The hitchhiker's eyes froze, an amalgam of fear and incomprehension.

"Mister, this is crazy! You're the dude with the fancy clothes and the car. What the hell do you want with me?"

"Pick up the gas can and the bag. Turn around slowly and start walking into the desert." Ward's voice was unemotional, the tone one of studied indifference. "Just go at an even pace and don't talk."

Together, the strange duo—a slim, urbane, impressively dressed, clean-shaven man and a bearded drifter at loose ends with life—marched into the desert, wending between the cacti, kicking up the dry waterless soil. After ten minutes Ward ordered the hitchhiker to stop.

"All right. This is far enough. No one can see us here. Take off all your clothes and throw them in a pile in front of you."

"Jesus, Mother of Mary!" The hitchhiker's cry of relief filled the desert. "So you're one of those guys. You just want to play a little. Sure."

His tone was now absent of fear. "You didn't need those damn knives. All you had to do was pay me something. But please . . . leave me be afterward."

"Stop the chatter. You're getting on my nerves," Ward said, his impatience breaking through. "Just take your clothes off, slowly."

With the knives still threatening, the man obediently disrobed, standing strangely nude in the desert. From the airline bag Ward removed a full set of clothes, none American in design or cut, and tossed them at the man's feet.

"Put these on," Ward ordered. He could see the fear return to the eyes of the hitchhiker—no longer sure why he had been singled out for this bizarre desert ritual.

As soon as the man was dressed Ward reached into his own pocket and took out a clear plastic identification badge, the type used at conventions. It simply read, "Stanislaw T. Wynoski, Warsaw Institute of Genetics and Breeding."

"Pin this on your jacket," he told the confused hitchhiker.

Ward went to his pocket again, but this time he removed a wallet, whose identification card carried the same Polish name, "Wynoski." With two fingers he delicately extracted a flat wafer the size of a nickel and pried off the plastic skin. Pressing the knife convincingly at the man's throat, Ward moved the cyanide tablet in front of his face.

"Open your mouth," he barked. "This won't hurt at all."

Instead, the man reacted by reflex, clenching his teeth like a vise. Ward responded by jabbing the knife into the man's throat a millimeter, drawing some blood, waiting for the right moment. The instant the jaw slackened in pain, Ward wrenched it apart with two hands and thrust the wafer of potassium cyanide, four times the minimum lethal dose, deep inside. The man first gagged, then, unable to retch up the pill, violently snapped his mouth shut on Ward's finger.

"You bastard!" Ward shrieked as a spurt of his own blood issued into the sand.

But he pushed back his pain and watched as the hitchhiker's breath came in rapid, convulsive motions, the lungs gasping for air. The man clutched his stomach, his chest, then at his throat, softly screeching a death call, turning blue as if the oxygen was being driven from his entire body—as it was. Within a minute he had tumbled to the ground, his body curled into a lifeless mass.

Moving rapidly to complete his assignment, Ward wrapped a handkerchief around his bleeding finger, then threw the clothes into the airline bag. A dozen feet from the dead man he placed the wallet in the sand.

Unlocking the cap on the gas can, Ward carefully poured all five gallons over the body, which soon reeked with the stench of gas stations everywhere. He stepped back three paces, took a match from his pocket, then hesitated. Ward had practiced on the carcass of a dead wolf, but this corpse was human.

The scratch against the sole of his shoe caught and Ward released the lit missile from his hand in a slow arc, watching as it hit the wet body and burst into flame. Staring into the fire storm, he was surprised how rapidly it began to consume the flesh of the innocent wayfarer.

Ward retreated a few feet to avoid the heat, then bent over, his head facing the warm sands, and vomited.

Chapter 2

At 7 A.M. that Monday, Sam Withers expectantly left his bed and climbed the stairs to the attic of his two-bedroom home in suburban Maryland, all he could afford on his $39,000 government salary.

Twisting his frame into the tight overhead space, Withers lifted out his wife's hatbox. For four years he had been putting documents into it, a disciplined one at a time. Now he emptied the cardboard container and placed everything in a white, rectangular plastic picnic thermos he had found, abandoned, alongside it.

By eight-thirty Withers was at Langley, first entering the Northwest Federal Credit Union, the CIA bank, where he withdrew $3000, a third of his liquid assets. Mad money in case nothing else worked.

Prudence, Withers reminded himself. All morning he stayed close to his desk at the Agency, sitting in his second-floor office staring at the thermos. It was an innocent-looking companion for a sweltering July day, but Sam knew it held all of his compulsions.

"Going on a picnic, Sam?" Molly Sandoz, the pool secretary, asked. Sam only nodded and smiled.

Despite his small physique—five feet six and perhaps a hundred and thirty pounds—Withers dominated his surroundings with his intense dark green eyes. A prematurely gray-streaked crew cut added to his aura, that of a lean, nervous fox.

Withers couldn't keep his eyes off the thermos. No longer was it safe to procrastinate. If he didn't act, events would inexorably pass him by, he was convinced. But his mind moved in and out of decision. Who could be trusted in this warren of convoluted mirrors?

Sam had considered confiding everything, but he knew the idea was mad. Al Springs, the Agency director, was *nashi*, as the Soviets called it. Ours, real, trustworthy. But who knew about the others? The Administration had tried to plug it, but Langley was still a sieve, sometimes even a conduit, to Moscow. A handful of mundane KGB plants had been spotted in the mid-1980s, but the upper-echelon mole, or moles, Sam was certain, reported only to the Center or to the Politburo itself. Some had probably already gracefully retired to the Gulf Coast of Florida on their U.S. federal pensions.

Leaning over his dictating machine, Withers recorded a brief message, pocketing the cassette. He lifted his phone and dialed a local number.

"Could you have a cab at Langley, front entrance, in five minutes? Name is Withers."

Smiling at Ms. Sandoz, Sam moved out into the corridor of the seven-story mammoth, the same height, he mused, as the Soviet KGB headquarters in Teplyy Stan, in the woods outside Moscow. The decision to leave pained, but as long as he remained at Langley the file was impotent.

Withers took the elevator up to the seventh floor and walked toward the director's office, pleased that it was lunchtime, the best cover for any movement.

"Barbara, just a small thing," Sam said to the secretary, a heavy-set peach-complected blonde, as he placed the cassette in her open hand. "Could you give this to Mr. Springs as soon as he returns from lunch? Tell him it's from me. Real important. Okay?"

Withers was soon moving across the inlaid marble insignia of an eagle, shield, and eight-pointed star on the floor of the main lobby. He walked out into the sun, his car abandoned in the parking lot.

"Enjoy yourself, Mr. Withers," the guard said as Sam moved toward the cab, swinging the thermos with as much nonchalance as he could muster.

☆ ☆ ☆

"How long will you be staying with us, Dr. . . . Braun?"

The clerk at the Washington Mall Hotel was seated on a worn leather stool, staring up at Sam Withers.

"I really don't know. Why?"

"I'm sorry, sir. But our policy is cash in advance."

The hotel clerk, a surprisingly neat young man with a silver collar pin, was unused to a Dr., even a supposed D.D.S., registering in this raunchy hostelry on lower Massachusetts Avenue, not far from the Capitol, an area where identities on registration are traditionally vague.

Withers extracted three tens out of his wallet for the night's lodging. "I don't expect any phone calls, so try not to bother me. Okay?"

For the next few hours the room was his sanctuary. He tried to rest but indecision was pricking at him. Withers sat in a 1950s chrome chair and pondered his possibilities. He decided to follow instinct and go public. It was a violation of his code, an insult to his obsession with secrecy. But there was no choice. Time was a virulent enemy.

Who would be his collaborator? It would have to be someone like himself, a partisan warrior depressed about the nation's security.

Withers strained, mentally checking, then crossing off names, struggling for a short list, until he came to that of Jack Granick, the nationally syndicated newspaper columnist who lived in a small Potomac River village. Of course, he congratulated himself. The ideal composite of reliability and isolation.

Granick had never been connected to the Administration, but Withers would sooner trust him with matters of national import than expose them to the Washington bureaucracy—with its garrulous, its timid, its politically untrustworthy, and worse.

Withers opened the thermos and moved its contents into the lining of his jacket, pinning it securely in place. He abandoned the empty container in the bathroom and at 5 P.M. walked into the near-barren lobby, grinned at the young clerk, and left the hotel.

On the street, Sam quickly located a pay phone. "Mary darling.

This is Sam. I won't be home tonight. It's not exactly official business, but it's important."

"What is it, Sam? Is there trouble?" his wife asked, the sound of her soft tears a warning that she had already been questioned by the Agency.

"No, Mary. I'm fine. But I may have to be away awhile. Don't worry. I love you. I'll keep in touch." Withers was promising, but it was clear that his home line was no longer open.

From the booth Withers could see that he was not alone. Someone parked in a car across the street had followed him. By squinting, Sam could make out Davie Hopper, a new face in counterintelligence, a kid who had just finished his "tradecraft" sessions and survival training at the Farm, the Agency's rugged acres at Camp Peary near Williamsburg.

Hopper probably had orders to pick him up. Sam went to the back room of his head, to his early training, to find a strategy to shake the kid. Walking was the answer. Hopper was tied to his car, or at least thought he was.

Sam grinned at Hopper before taking his wiry frame into a fast pace, almost a trot, toward the Metro subway stop at Union Station. By the time Hopper realized Withers' goal and had joined the foot race, Withers had descended the long escalator into the cavernous, waffle-roofed station.

He inserted his prepaid commuter Farecard into the computer turnstile and moved onto the platform. The Red Line train from Silver Spring was approaching from the northeast end of the system. Withers jumped on. As the train was leaving, Hopper was still fumbling to extract a ticket from the machine.

The smooth train took Sam to the Metro Center, where he changed for the Orange Line to Rosslyn, exiting at the glass and concrete village of office towers on the Virginia side of the Potomac, across from Georgetown.

He approached a cabby near the station. "Do you know where River Falls is?"

"Sure. But it's about twelve miles. You'll have to figure about seventy-five dollars."

"Okay. Take me to Waterview Road, No. 14," Withers said, shaking his head at the rising cost of his compulsions.

At 6 P.M., Sam arrived at the river-front village. Minutes later he banged the brass knocker of Granick's black, weather-worn door.

"Sam Withers?" Granick asked at the threshold, surprised to see the CIA man make such open contact. "What the hell are you doing here? Did they finally kick you out of the Agency? About time." Granick's enormous jowls moved in unison with his laughter.

"No, Jack. But I've left. Can I come in?"

At that, Granick's body, perhaps three hundred pounds of pleasant fat, moved aside, surprisingly catlike, forcing the door open wider for Withers.

Sam could see that the inside of the small 1840 home was in the same disrepair as the exterior, where the wooden Greek Revival columns no longer rose at the perpendicular and the peeling paint seemed almost original. The decor of the living room was musty Victorian, with an occasional exposed couch spring. Everywhere there were books and periodicals, stacked aimlessly, with still more piles on the floor. Traversing the room was itself an achievement.

"Jesus, you look pained, Sam. What's up?" Granick asked, still surprised at this sudden appearance.

Withers looked at him silently, a sign that he would explain at his own pace.

"Some coffee first?" Granick asked.

As Granick mixed the contents of a jar of instant, Withers slit open his jacket lining and removed the file, including a single cassette.

"Jack, I don't expect you to believe everything you read or hear, but take my word for it, it's all checked out," Withers said, laying the report on Granick's ample lap. "Please don't get any coffee on it. It's the only one, and it's too dangerous to make an uncontrolled copy."

Granick reached for the four-page summary, read it rapidly, then examined some of the photos, registering first surprise, then alarm. He listened to the cassette for a few minutes, then shut it off in disgust.

"Never would I have believed it." Granick's expression was doleful. "It's the best sleeper job I've ever seen. It's scary, Sam."

Granick stared at the material again, then struggled his large body off the couch and paced the coffee-stained rug.

"Sam, this is bad news. Who have you showed it to so far?"

"No one. I don't know who to trust, Jack. I gave Springs a cassette that I was leaving with my file, but I didn't say who it involved. I was torn between trying someone at the White House and taking it public. Then I thought of you. You've got an audience in the millions—

the kind of people who would understand. I'd like you to blow the whole thing sky high."

Granick's full cheeks shook vigorously side to side.

"No, Sam. You were right not to show it to the Agency. My guess is that the Administration is no help either. Aside from security leaks, it's probably too hot for them to handle politically. But me publish it? No. My reputation is too conservative. The media would call it another sleazy Joe McCarthy trick. What we need is an establishment person we can trust. . . ."

Granick halted in mid-thought. "I think I know what to do, Sam. If you'll let me take it."

As the columnist outlined his plan, Withers' bony face took on a curious look, his gray crew cut now shaded almost white in the sketchy light of the old river house. He stared at Granick for an instant, then nodded, unsurely.

"Don't worry, Sam. Leave it to me," Granick said.

His voice was laced with confidence, but his gentle face was betraying exactly the opposite.

Chapter 3

Douglas McDowell was feeling more than the oppressive Washington summer heat. At his desk in the network's L Street headquarters it struck him, with a pull at his intestines, that he had only an hour before air time.

Just turned thirty-four, the youthful commentator had been chosen as the sole mediator for this last televised debate of the seven Democratic presidential candidates, and the thought of probing the possible next President, like a matador teasing a bull, was gnawing away at his usual seamlessness.

McDowell leaned into his leather chair, his fingers straining through his carrot-red hair.

"Meg, I'm going to take ten. Please wake me," he called into the intercom.

His head had just touched the backrest when his assistant, Meg Larsen, appeared, walking light-footed. The tall, comely woman, perhaps five years his junior, stood over the reclining McDowell, his eyes already shut, and touched his shoulder lightly.

"Doug, I know this is no time to bother you, but that columnist, Jack Granick, is waiting outside. He's yelling that he's got to see you before air time. He knows you're going on soon but says that if you won't see him you'll regret it . . ." Meg slowed, embarrassed at what she was about to say, ". . . for the rest of your life."

Doug opened his eyes and stared at his assistant, unbelieving. "What are you talking about? I'm exhausted. I've got to go downstairs, get made up, get everything ready in forty minutes to handle a presidential debate by myself, and you want me to see some rightwing kook who's been insulting me for years. Get him out of here."

Meg obediently backed off a few paces and stopped. Turning, she faced McDowell again, her eyes displaying fear.

"Doug, I know it sounds crazy, but I've never seen anyone act so strange. Granick's ranting that it's the biggest story of his life and he wants to give it to you. I'm afraid he's going to push me around if I don't let him in."

"Push you? I'll kill the creep. Where's he now? Outside?"

As Meg nodded, Doug moved protectively alongside her, walking toward the reception area, his head pulsing in anger. "What a lousy time for this to happen," he muttered, his audience no one in particular.

McDowell's first view of Granick shocked him. The columnist was sprawled back into the pillows of the couch, his obese body spread directionless, arms akimbo, staring intently ahead. His jacket was two sizes too small for his enormous girth and his shirt collar struggled, unsuccessfully, to surround his mastodon neck. Granick's slick, straight black hair, looking as if it had not been combed in days, hung in an uneven cascade over the forehead of his round face. Everything about him was unruly, except his eyes. As soon as McDowell entered the room they riveted on him.

"And what the hell do you want?" McDowell was almost screaming.

Granick lifted his body off the couch and approached McDowell like a supplicant.

"It's a matter of life and death, Doug. I know you don't like me but, believe me, I'm not crazy. A little distraught now, but not crazy. Let's talk in your office. Just five minutes, that's all I need."

The columnist grasped McDowell's sleeve and tugged on it, breaking into a child's faint, pleading smile.

"Now. Please. It's got to be before the debate."

McDowell tried to look away, but Granick's sense of urgency was being transmitted. He knew that Granick hated his political guts and would not be begging unless he needed help desperately. The columnist was a right-wing fanatic—the coming political theologian of the Neanderthals, Doug had heard. But he couldn't believe that Granick was perverted enough to invent a ploy to disrupt him just before the Democratic presidential debate.

"All right, I'll give you five minutes. But if your story is not earthshaking, I swear I'll clobber you next week, right on network television. Now let's hear whatever it is that's turned you into a madman."

Chapter 4

The class of 210 Russians, Czechs, East Germans, Poles, even one Englishman, were beginning their last day of training at the Foreign Intelligence School near the village of Yurlova in the Moscow woods when the phone rang in the student barracks.

"Captain Peter Stefanovich Semanski."

Devronich, adjutant to Colonel Lev Orlov, the head of Active Measures, American Section, was on the line.

He eliminated the amenities. "Semanski, I am sending a driver for you. The director wants to see you in his office. Please be ready in forty minutes."

The call was not from the Lubyanka in Moscow. The First Chief Directorate of the KGB responsible for foreign espionage had since moved out of the old Stalinist prison on Dzerzhinsky Square, only a few blocks from the Kremlin, to the new Center, a modern Finnish-designed headquarters in a forest fifteen miles southwest of Moscow near what had been the village of Teplyy Stan.

Exactly forty minutes after the phone call, the black Chaika—Semanski thought perhaps Orlov's own car—pulled up in the courtyard of the school. The ride to the Center, Semanski's first, was through the outer Moscow suburbs, spottily developed except for an occasional new apartment block and clusters of small *izby*, the traditional Russian log cabins.

The countryside was populated with enormous evergreen trees which Semanski found depressing. So unlike the softer vista of his Polish homeland, with its light as incandescent as that of France, or the beautiful deciduously wooded areas of Connecticut which he remembered from his youth.

Russia was forbidding. A nation of coffee-gray clouds and dulled expressions. Perhaps it suited the Russians, but he could live elsewhere. Then he reminded himself that, despite its shortcomings, Russia was the mother nation of socialism. Semanski enjoyed the West, with its frivolity and sense of self. But he couldn't understand a system based on personal economic competition—insecurity that surely aggravated the capitalist stomach, perhaps even its soul.

The Chaika, Russian for "seagull," soon deserted the main highway and turned onto a narrow road until it came to a sign: WATER CONSERVATION DISTRICT. Semanski smiled at the subterfuge. They drove another third of a mile to an area closed in with a cyclone fence topped with barbed wire, an enclave policed by soldiers whose uniforms bore the blue lapel flashes and trouser stripes of the KGB Guards Division.

"Who have you come to see, Comrade Captain?" asked a young noncommissioned officer.

"Colonel Orlov. American Section."

Semanski noticed the guard's eyes react. Even in this heart of the KGB apparatus, *Amerika*, the name of the enemy, was pronounced with awe. Because Semanski had once lived in the despised nation, he too had *klass*, he presumed.

"Surely, Captain. One second, only."

The sergeant inspected the Chaika briefly, then waved it on toward the main road, which ran only four hundred yards, ending at a modern seven-story glass and aluminum building in the shape of a three-pointed star. Trim, he thought, if out of place in this near-virgin forest.

Semanski moved alone into the hushed marble foyer, dominated by a large bronze bust honoring Felix Edmundovich Dzerzhinsky, the mild-mannered first director of the Cheka, the secret police chief who had loyally murdered millions for Stalin.

As he approached the bust, Semanski pulled his foot back just in time, nearly crushing the fresh flowers at its base. He shrugged. No shrine would ever be raised to him. He was Polish, not Russian, a vital failing in the new empire.

"Peter Stefanovich!"

He turned to face a small man, perhaps five feet two, moving energetically across the marble floor.

"Always a pleasure, Captain Semanski."

It was Colonel Lev Orlov, now straining his short arms half a foot upward to squeeze Semanski's shoulder blade as a sign of greeting. His enthusiasm for Semanski, whom he had met only once before, was overflowing.

"Please come. I'm on the fourth floor."

Upstairs, as Orlov moved his guest hurriedly into an upholstered armchair, Semanski surveyed his host, a fortyish, owl-faced man, disguised by a perpetual, peculiarly frightening grin. Then he scanned the room, tastefully furnished in the blond woods of Scandinavian modern. The head of Active Measures, American Section, was apparently in an exalted category.

"Some mineral water or lemonade, Captain?" Orlov asked.

Semanski could see that the buffet top, an improvised bar, was strikingly void of vodka, part of the KGB's new spartan image.

"I'll never forget that speech you gave on American political parties," the colonel began. "I steal portions of it whenever I can. It impresses everyone."

The "speech," Semanski remembered, was actually an informal conversation at Yurlova, following a symposium on American politics hosted by Georgi Arbatov's Institute of U.S.A. and Canada. Semanski had added his own comments on the Republican and Democratic party realignments after the two Reagan victories.

His elders had listened attentively, particularly when Orlov reminded them that, from the ages of ten to fifteen, Semanski had lived in New York City, where his father, Stefan Semanski, had been first secretary at the Polish Consulate on Madison Avenue and Thirty-seventh Street.

"Captain. You're unsurpassed in speaking and writing English," Orlov continued. "But I'm a practical man. Your tours for the Polish SB as a consular official were impressive. In Stockholm, we watched your infiltration of the Social Democratic Party with our agents. And Beirut. No one is going to credit you with the American withdrawal" —Orlov chuckled—"but I've heard of the influential people you recruited there as well."

Semanski returned the smile, his mind pacing ahead. What would be required of him now?

"You have heard of made-over men. Illegals?" Orlov asked.

Semanski nodded.

"We have almost a thousand throughout the world. Some have even become citizens of their new countries." Orlov hesitated. "Do you like the idea?"

"Yes, Comrade Colonel."

Semanski knew his answer had to be positive, but he brightened, preferring the life of a "made-over man" to still more consular duties, always juggling public diplomacy while running agents. It offered unpredictability, the romantic, perhaps neurotic satisfaction which he guessed had drawn him to the SB in the beginning.

"Captain, now that your training is complete, we've asked for you to be assigned to us rather than send you back to Warsaw. I hope you don't mind being KGB?"

"Colonel, I presume it's meant as a promotion."

"Exactly, Semanski. You're going to America, to your adopted homeland, on a sensitive political mission. To tell you too much would only inhibit you. You will enter the country as a Polish geneticist attending a conference in Los Angeles, under the name of Stanislaw Wynoski. Learn what you can about genetics so that you don't embarrass yourself. But you need not be an expert. Follow Day One and Day Two scenarios, which are in this folder, marked Oval Red. Later on, as things progress, you will know everything. Good luck."

So his assignment was America after all. As Semanski left the modern building and moved toward his Chaika, scenes from youth tunneled out of his mind. It had been eighteen years, but the adolescent memories were still rich.

Had the five years in Manhattan dripped any capitalist dissent into his ideological veins? He thought not, except that those times were memorable. It was, of course, blind innocence. He knew nothing of politics then. His obsessions were jazz, the New York Yankees, and American girls, whose early favors had taught him well.

But he had since learned that there were rewards greater than money and individuality. Purpose.

Still he would have to be wary. If for no other reason than that the prospect of going back was not entirely unpleasant.

☆ ☆ ☆

Semanski had been in California only two days, but he was not disappointed.

He had arrived in Beverly Hills on Sunday, and now, on Monday afternoon, he could already feel the impact of the palm trees, the balmy air, the unhurried but determined manner in which the citizens pursued their capitalism in this physical paradise.

It was plainly Gomorrah, a city of selfishness, conceit, and narcissism. But he couldn't help but admire the ease with which the daily business—whether asking for a towel at the Beverly Hills Hotel pool or seeking directions to Santa Monica Boulevard—was accomplished.

The lubricant was obviously money, obscene amounts of it. Still he weighed the superficial grace of Beverly Hills against the grief regularly encountered in Moscow, or even Warsaw, in getting on with one's existence. Of course, this was a life without reason, except for the accumulation of the strange accouterments he had seen for sale on Rodeo Drive.

Semanski thought of his own clothes. Could some gap in his staged appearance trigger betrayal? As he glanced at the scientists in the ballroom of the Beverly Hills Hotel, he relaxed. His outfit seemed to fit in: a poorly cut corduroy jacket, chino pants an inch too long, a loud rainbow-hued striped shirt. The shoes were a cross of short army boots and Clark spacers. He laughed. In all, the ideal outfit for a junior Polish scientist.

"Wynoski?" The voice was very American. Semanski stared up at a tall, bony figure, bending over, somewhat patronizingly, he thought, to examine his nameplate. The American almost brushed against his newly acquired bulging waistline, which gave the disguised Semanski a prematurely middle-aged appearance, one strengthened by an untrimmed brown mustache and beard.

From photographs he had studied in Moscow, Semanski knew the man was Dr. Clyde McCormick, the Lion of Berkeley.

"Hello. Didn't I just see you with Pitok?" McCormick asked.

"Yes, Dr. McCormick. I am Dr. Pitok's second assistant. He will be giving the lecture on viral and bacterial transmission of gene anomalies."

The answer had been memorized, but even as he said it, Semanski feared he was transparent. He was delivering his English sentences laboriously, stressing all the wrong syllables, straining to meticulously suppress the one skill that would give him away: his flawless American speech.

McCormick grinned at the young assistant. "Pitok's never mentioned you, but I'm glad to see that he has support troops. By the way, this is Larry Carver from our State Department, an emissary of good will, I presume, from the host country."

Carver, a tall sandy-haired man, stood impassively alongside McCormick.

"I am pleased to make your acquaintance," Semanski said in the same mock Polish-English, eyeing the outline of Carver's massive build and square jaw. Were this Warsaw or Moscow, he would swear that Carver was SB, the Polish *Sluzba Bezpieczenstwa*, or the Soviet KGB. But in America, he knew, there was always the possibility that the amiable hulk was actually from State.

Semanski contemplated the opportunity. In a few minutes the group would be dissolving into smaller seminars. Glancing furtively around, he spotted Pitok in a heated conversation with an outspoken Hungarian geneticist.

"Please," Semanski begged of the two Americans, "I have more notes for Pitok's lecture. Excuse."

He moved swiftly across the room. "Pitok," Semanski said, spiriting the scientist out of anyone's earshot, his tone firm, not that of an assistant to a leading academician.

"As the room empties, walk casually with me to the elevator. Make some small talk, then say that you will meet me later at the seminar. Understand?"

The two men strolled out together, passing Carver and McCormick, who seemed to be staring intently at Semanski. It's only my Russian paranoia, picked up by adoption, he thought as they moved by the smiling Americans.

But at the elevator Semanski scanned the lobby and decided that his first intuition was correct. From behind the registration desk a round-faced man in his late twenties—FBI and Irish-American, he guessed—was straining to watch him. The bell captain, a tall black man with a bulge near the armpits of his uniform, also seemed inordinately interested in the two geneticists from Poland.

Behind the registration desk, Semanski could see the clerk leaning over to rub the aching balls of his stocking feet. "I'm sorry, ma'am, not a chance for a bungalow, or any room. We have a waiting list a half mile long."

Semanski listened, then moved swiftly into the emptying elevator.

"Good, Dr. Pitok," he called out loudly in response to the scientist. "I'll meet you later at the seminar."

☆ ☆ ☆

"Why such a fuss?" the bellman, Saunders, queried his colleague, Martin Rourke, once they had rendezvoused in the manager's office. "Carver is here from CIA counterintelligence, there's us, a wired cab waiting outside, and a continuous 16mm film being shot from the pink palace across the way. What do they think? That Wynoski's going to steal a gene?"

"All I know," Rourke responded, "is that our man in the Polish UN delegation passed a note: 'Wynoski—L.A.—KGB.' It escapes me what a Polock posing as a scientist is doing working for the Soviets in Beverly Hills. But I'm sure we'll find out."

☆ ☆ ☆

In room 327, Semanski removed his Polish-made clothes, revealing the padding that had transformed his true slim runner's figure into Wynoski's portly profile. Not unlike a baseball catcher's chest protector, the harness began at the breastbone and budded out a full five inches at the waist, receding back at the crotch. It was held up like a woman's brassiere, with straps over the shoulder.

Semanski opened a small plug in the upper corner of the device. Within seconds it was reduced to a small square of plastic.

In the bathroom he pulled at two hidden burr snaps at his temple, lifting the curly brown wig, then ruffled his own dark hair to regain its resilience. Semanski began to shave off the beard and mustache, a natural disguise dyed to match the false hair. Dipping his fingertips into his eye sockets, he removed the blue contact lenses that had covered his own brown pupils.

Now slimmer, clean-shaven, black-haired, and brown-eyed, he moved back into the bedroom to complete the transformation. From an East German hanging bag he took out the gray suit, plain-topped black shoes, pink oxford button-down shirt, and rep tie, an outfit purchased in New York and stored in Moscow for the occasion.

Semanski was fully dressed when he heard the latch turn on the hotel door. Racing to his suitcase, he instinctively combed through it for a gun. There was none, he remembered. This mission had made the possession of a firearm inadvisable, even dangerous.

He lurched for his toilet kit and extracted the stainless steel scissors, rapidly converting them into the rapier knives. With one in each hand, he approached the door.

"Shall I come back later?" It was a female voice. "Do you need any towels?"

Semanski was embarrassed by his momentary loss of control.

"No, it's not necessary," he answered the maid. "I have plenty of them."

The lines had come out in faultless colloquial English, but he quickly covered in stumbling Polishese. "No problem. Thanks much."

He couldn't afford another such interruption. From the hanging bag Semanski removed a small airline valise and placed Wynoski's discarded clothes and the fat padding into it, along with the folded hanging case itself. His fingernails neatly separated the LOT Polish airline decal from the body of the small suitcase, crushed it in his fist, then flushed it away in the toilet.

Semanski studied himself in the bathroom mirror. The view was pleasing but would be out of place in either Warsaw or Moscow, except in the highest echelons. Why had Orlov required such a fashionable image for this assignment?

Semanski stared at his reflection again. Did he conform to his own vision of an American? he wondered. Though his nose was somewhat long and pointed, it was not excessive. The eyes were small and the mouth thin, but definite. His jaw strong, his hair black, straight, and prominent. Yes, Semanski concluded, I could be American, of Irish, Polish, or even Anglo origin.

He was surely moving too slowly. Turning over his toilet kit, Semanski unscrewed the four brass pods, exposing an inner lining. With a penknife he slashed the plastic and gingerly inserted his fingers, searching.

There it was. A thin leather case holding two documents that would grant him the beginnings of an American identity. A driver's license showing him wearing the same suit he had on. Semanski nodded approvingly. The license was from the Motor Vehicle Service in Washington, D.C.

His address was in the 4000 area of Massachusetts Avenue. Alongside the driver's license was a tagged key. Apartment 11A. From his Yurlova seminar, he knew he was being quartered in the exclusive northwest area of brick homes, embassies, and high rises. He was gratified they had chosen a civilized city, perhaps the most civilized in

America. From East European diplomats Semanski had heard that Washington supported a gracious lifestyle, financed, of course, by the federal establishment, one of the most generous economies in the world.

Americans are strange, he mused. It required so little subterfuge to assume a new identity. No fingerprints had been taken of him when he first came to America as a child, nor was he fingerprinted now as he entered the country as Stanislaw Wynoski.

Semanski studied the second document, an American Express card, on which was embossed his new American "moniker," as his fellow students at the UN school in New York used to say.

THOMAS R. WARD

He turned the name over. Tom. Tom Ward. A promising beginning for Oval Red, whatever that involved.

But before he could board his plane to Washington under his new identity, Semanski knew that he had to perform an onerous duty—to first scour the California desert for a substitute.

To create a charred corpse to take Stanislaw Wynoski's place.

Chapter 5

Jack Granick inhaled, struggling to regain his composure. The obese columnist was winded even though it was only a fifty-foot walk from the network waiting room to Doug McDowell's office.

"Okay, Granick, spit it out. What's the life-and-death situation?" McDowell demanded when the two men were seated facing each other. One a slightly swarthy, black-haired mass, his face displaying palpable threat. The other, a tall, lean, freckled, normally contained redhead, straining to hold back his irritation.

Granick raised the worn attaché case onto his lap and stroked the scuffed leather, almost as if it were a puppy.

"It's all in here, McDowell. You know that I hate your head-up-your-ass liberalism, but I still think you're a good newsman. What I have is explosive, but it needs your establishment reputation. I'm willing to give it to you—exclusively. But I want you to promise me something first."

McDowell sprang upright in his chair.

"Let's get something straight from the beginning, Granick. I'm promising you nothing. You've got only four minutes left. If you have something to say, say it—now."

McDowell could feel the pressure. Milt Samuels, president of network news, had thrown this job onto him too casually, he was afraid. Moderating the presidential debate was a step up in McDowell's plan to become the youngest of network news anchors. But McDowell was an outspoken liberal commentator and Samuels was billing him as Mr. Neutral. Though it troubled him, he intended to fulfill Milt's assignment. Exactly.

The presidential primaries had been inconclusive. No Democrat had won enough delegates for a first-ballot nomination and the climax had to wait three weeks until the party massed, like a giant soccer contest, in the new Javits convention center on Eleventh Avenue in New York. Meanwhile, Samuels expected millions of viewers to tune in this last televised debate.

Now, an hour before air time, Granick had barged in, disrupting his careful equilibrium.

"All right, Doug. For . . . get the promises," Granick agreed, the short stammer betraying his anxiety. "But do me one favor. Look at the material before the debate. Then just ask one of the candidates— you'll know who—a few questions. I promise it'll change the whole race on the spot."

McDowell eyed Granick suspiciously. Was he trying to ensnare him in some wild scheme to enhance the Republican candidate? But McDowell knew that Granick was a professional, and no fool. He would have to live with the network for years.

"Okay, Granick. Let's hear what's so urgent," McDowell repeated, his annoyance gaining.

"Doug, no matter what some of my friends think, I know you're not a lefty sympathizer," Granick began. "That's why I'm here. To tell you that our republic is in danger."

Granick's eyes blinked erratically, then steadied as he continued.

"McDowell, one of the Democratic candidates you're going to question tonight is a traitor. Not a pinko. But a secret Communist. A real dyed-in-the-wool Red."

Granick didn't wait for McDowell to respond. "I've got the goods on him here in this briefcase," he said, tapping the leather with small fingers that were out of place attached to his over-large body. "Look at it now, then give it to your network's best reporters to check out. If they agree it's true—and they will—I want you to use your on-air commentary this week to denounce the son of a bitch, to expose him for what he really is. . . ."

He halted in mid-sentence as McDowell slowly rose from the desk chair, his small blue eyes tightly drawn, his tall, spare frame over-shadowing the heavy columnist.

The words were forcing a childhood nightmare back to life. Mc-Dowell could see his mother standing over his bed, tearful, retelling how his father had lost his job as an assistant professor of history for refusing to sign a school loyalty oath during the McCarthy era. Three years later, a melancholy man trudging the streets selling printing, he had suffered a heart attack and died.

McDowell stood facing Granick, his red-flecked skin flushed into blotches.

"Look, Granick. I'm going to try to be polite with you. Why don't you just take your Joe McCarthy shit and get the hell out of here while I still have some patience? Okay?"

Granick stared at McDowell, unbelieving.

"But, Doug, all I want you to do is read it . . ." Granick stammered, his right arm flailing.

As Granick started up again, intent on convincing the commentator, his hand swung wildly in front of him, cracking against a silver water pitcher, a prime symbol of network status. Abruptly the canister fell over, the water racing indiscriminately across the desk.

"Damn it!" McDowell shrieked, staring at his soaked debate notes. He looked up at Granick, all reserve now gone.

"You fat fascist bastard!" McDowell shouted across the desk. "Get out of here before I kill you! You come in here with your crazy stories about Communists and expect me to fall over and kiss your Nazi ass. Now this—just before the debate. Get out. Out!"

McDowell leaned over and lifted a squash racket from a nearby chair, brandishing it in the direction of Granick, who, horrified at what his proposal had triggered, moved his large body out of the way with surprising agility.

"Meg!" Doug yelled into the intercom. "Get him out of here before I'm arrested for murder! Get anybody. But get rid of him!"

Granick was now cowering near the door, weaving almost comically, like a punch-drunk fighter, futilely trying to present as small a target as possible. He blinked uncontrollably and, with a voice only slightly louder than his usual whisper, assailed the commentator.

"You can scream all you want, McDowell. But no 1960s piety is going to erase your responsibility. I won't give you the file, or the name, but you're involved—right up to your asshole. You know one of the candidates is a Red and you're not doing a damn thing about it. Don't worry, I'll take my wares elsewhere, where people are not ashamed to be patriots."

With that, Granick clutched the worn attaché case to his bosom and stormed out.

Seconds later, Meg responded to McDowell's call and rushed into his office.

She found McDowell standing, frozen into a stiffened posture behind his desk—the squash racket still outstretched, aimed accusingly at a Granick who was no longer there.

Chapter 6

"Director. The President is waiting. He understands that you *have* to see him."

It was the raspy, authoritative voice of Emily Bachrach, the fiftyish private secretary who ferociously guarded the Chief Executive against a world she viewed mainly as a conspiracy to destroy his time and temper.

The President was working late at eight thirty-three that Monday evening. Springs was three minutes late, which only heightened his anxiety.

The director looked unlike any caricature of an Agency chief. Of average height, with a nondescript Anglo face and a demeanor to match, he appeared more like a history teacher at Choate, which had been his father's lot. His suits were presentable, but clearly off the discount racks of roadside Virginia.

On his $75,000 salary, with two children in college, Springs had to remind his wealthy administration colleagues that he was lucky Langley provided him an inexpensive lunch—the meager American equivalent of the lavish weekly Kremlin *payoki*, the fancy food ration given his Moscow opposite number, along with an elegant, virtually rent-free pre-Revolutionary apartment in the Lenin Hills.

It was, Springs thought disconsolately, a symbol of the relative respect afforded espionage in the two nations.

"Mr. President. The CIA director is here," Bachrach said through the open door.

"Come in, Al. I'll be right with you."

As the President arranged his papers before retiring to the family quarters, Springs waited, thinking how radically the power of the Agency vacillated with each occupant of this office. This administration was friendly, but he still quaked at the decimation of the 1970s, when Watergate, congressional investigations of CIA excesses, and rumors that the Agency was involved in the assassinations of JFK, Martin Luther King, and Bobby Kennedy had turned much of the public against covert action. To Springs, it was still the mother's milk of intelligence.

That era had produced its share of hysteria, and he was glad it was over. Or at least he hoped it was.

Springs was unsettled by this evening mission. A victim of Agency purges himself, he had been sacked in the 1970s along with hundreds of veteran agents. Since his return to Langley, he had mollified the White House by keeping maverick actions under control. No more Watergates, the President had warned, particularly in these last six months of his administration.

"Al, what's going on at Langley?" the President finally asked, looking up from his papers. "You've gotten me curious."

The President took his tall frame, now heavier at the hips, and moved across to the fireplace, where Springs sat facing him.

"It's about one of my people, Mr. President," the director began. "I'm afraid they sometimes get too enthusiastic—and into things they shouldn't be in."

"What kind of things, Al?"

"This time it's the stickiest. Domestic politics. I just learned that one of my best men in counterintelligence has been checking out a Democratic presidential candidate. The officer's name is Withers, Sam Withers. And I think he's hit a mother lode."

Springs sensed that he had captured the President's attention.

"Well, what's he found? Even if he wasn't supposed to?"

"It's as bad as you can get, sir. He believes that one of the seven

Democrats . . . Well, I really don't know how to put it—is a—Communist."

The President shuttered his eyes. Only months before the end of his successful administration, he was hearing a disturbing rhythm.

"One of the candidates a Communist? Al, we don't want another damn Watergate, do we? The media already think we're a bunch of paranoiacs.

"This man—Withers," the President continued. "Does he 'believe' or actually 'know' that this Democrat is a Red?"

Springs couldn't equivocate. He had opened an anxious wound in American politics.

"Yes, sir. He's sure that one of the Democratic candidates is a Communist."

"Does he know which Democrat?"

"Yes, sir. Apparently. But he's refused to name him right now."

"Al, be patient with me. I'm just trying to get this straight. Is this candidate a member of the Communist Party?"

"No, sir. No establishment leftist would join the American Communist Party. His name would turn up on an FBI computer fifteen minutes later. No, I know Withers. He's a thorough professional. What he means is that this person—whoever he is—is a secret Marxist-Leninist. Someone opposed to our form of government, someone sympathetic to the Soviet Union, someone who probably has close connections with Castro or the Soviets, or both. One of those seven is going to get the Democratic nomination."

Springs hesitated. "And since you're not running, he—or she—could be sitting in your chair six months from now."

"Al, I assume you have supporting evidence. Or is this just somebody's crazy hunch?"

Springs could sense his sure poise crumbling.

"Sir, I assure you that the proof exists. The man who compiled it is one of our best."

"So what has he shown you?"

"That's the trouble. Withers is gone, and his documentation with him."

"Gone? What do you mean, gone?" the president erupted. "Where to?"

Springs cast his eyes down at the rug. "Unfortunately, I have no idea. He just left me a cassette and walked out of the building. Right in the middle of the day. We checked his home. There's no trace of him."

The President turned mute, but only for seconds.

"Al, if anyone else walked in here with a tale of a Red in the Democratic Party, I'd throw him out. But I'm relying on your track record. First off, we're not going to have another Joe McCarthy witch hunt. If we make an open accusation of Communism, even with documentation, the press will label us smear artists. With the backlash and sympathy votes, we'll lose the next election. And by the time the truth is sorted out it'll be too late. Just as if Watergate had broken against Nixon before November instead of after."

The President waited, seeking emphasis. "Al, I want you to find Withers right away. I don't care how. Get the documentation and hide it. If you don't, some eager idiot in the Administration will splash it all over the headlines. It's taken thirty years to get over the Joe McCarthy backlash. We can't afford to lose another generation to the other side. If you find Withers soon, hold him incommunicado until the Democratic convention is over. If either of the nominees— for president or vice-president—is not involved, we'll forget the whole thing. At least for now.

"But if one of them is Withers' man we'll talk again. Meanwhile, use all the resources of the CIA, but not the FBI—this is not an official investigation—to find Withers. Let me know as soon as you get anything."

The President rose as he finished his last word.

"Mr. President. Consider it done."

The CIA director turned, grateful to be exiting the room.

Chapter 7

On his return to the River Falls home that Monday evening, Granick was still trembling from the confrontation with McDowell. His plan had backfired badly. The only consolation was that McDowell had not seen the file on the Communist candidate, which now lay in the same bruised briefcase on the living-room floor amidst an unsorted pile of conservative and academic journals.

"What the hell did you expect of a network newsman like McDowell?" Withers asked as they talked in the river house living room.

"I know, Sam," Granick groaned in response, the disappointment with McDowell and himself spread across his pudgy features. "But I figured he'd listen, and he's got such a large audience . . ."

Granick walked aimlessly up and down the room as he spoke, but after a while he could no longer handle his self-flagellation.

"Sam, I'm going out to relax. Don't worry. I won't be long. We'll figure out the next step as soon as I get back."

The columnist had no true form of exercise. Walking his cumbersome frame more than a hundred feet was a torturous experience. His body only seemed to be at peace when sitting, which eventually bored him, or when floating, which Granick could do for hours on end.

Not floating directly on water, for Granick could not swim a stroke. Floating was something he did on his small dinghy, anchored at the foot of the shallow incline that ran some sixty feet from his house down to the Potomac. River Falls was one of the few places one could boat on the upper Potomac, which had become a national trust. At R.F., as the natives called it, a viaduct crossed over the old Chesapeake & Ohio Canal, letting the local boaters move out onto the open river.

Now, seated on the ledge of the upstairs window facing the water, Withers could see Granick in the strong moonlight. His body filled an abnormally large portion of the small boat, his head back on an overstuffed pillow, his eyes staring upward into the nothingness of the warm night. One hand was lazily placed on the tiller as the boat drifted with the soft current.

From that distance, he could not see Granick's expression, but the limp nature of his body suggested that Granick's face was lit by a smile, freed from the obsessive political thoughts that dominated his hours on land.

The river was empty at that point, except for a small motor launch which moved cautiously upstream and slowly came to a stop not more than thirty feet from Granick's boat. As Withers watched, first with curiosity, then with horror, a dark figure—he could make out the shape of a wet-suited frogman—jumped from the boat into the river.

The splash startled Granick out of his reverie. The frogman swam rapidly toward the dinghy, then arose from the water in a faint arc and dove under the small boat.

Within seconds the dinghy tipped over, forcing Granick's three-hundred-pound body into the river with a resounding splash, his hands flailing hopelessly for support on the watery surface.

"Sam! I'm drowning. Help! Help me!"

Withers jumped at the sound of Granick's scream, but in that instant his instincts were torn. Sam leaned out over the window ledge, his hands poised for a monumental leap to the lawn and a race to Granick's side in the river.

But in the cone of his mind's eye the briefcase—projected as if in the spotlight of his retina—kept flashing off and on between the frightening sight of Granick's body slipping into the water.

He started his move to join Granick, then he leaned backward away from the ledge as if to retrieve the briefcase. Then forward again, in what seemed like a half dozen alternate movements within the instant.

But the self-tussle was soon academic. The frogman had emerged from under the boat and was swimming deliberately toward Granick, who screamed each time his head emerged from the water. A black-gloved hand rose from the deep and pressed itself down on Granick's head, forcing him underwater.

Withers stood transfixed, helplessly watching the murder of his friend. Then he lurched down the narrow stairs to rescue the only thing left.

He picked up the briefcase on the run and fled out the back door of the house, across the lawn to the adjacent woods. As he moved out the back, he could hear someone kick open the front door, then several heavy footsteps thrashing about quickly in the living room. One of the two men—could they be Agency, or was it KGB?—raced through the house and out the back, following rapidly after Withers.

Would they dare fire at him and rouse the closest neighbor, about three hundred yards away? His answer came in the form of a shot that passed within inches of his head just as he entered the woods.

Withers pumped his one free hand, balancing himself as he ran, trying to hold the briefcase tightly yet not lose forward momentum. His slim frame was ideal for running, and the ex-George Washington University quarter-miler wasted nothing in propelling himself forward. There were no more gunshots. Withers was a difficult target in the semidarkened woods. He was confident he could outrun the man, but he kept up his pace.

Sam soon stood at the edge of a wide brook studded with rocks and small white-water caps. From the bank, it looked treacherously deep, perhaps five or six feet. But Withers had waded across it several times while hiking in these woods with Mary when Granick—he flinched at the thought—was out floating.

The brook was actually only two and a half feet high at its crest. Sam was across it in minutes, determinedly holding the briefcase aloft as he reached the other side.

He kept running, then after a hundred yards stopped and looked back at his pursuers. Through a break in the trees Withers could see a solitary figure, pistol still in hand, testing the brook. The gunman placed his foot into the white water, and as it sank over his calf he pulled it out in disgust. He issued an epithet whose language or content Sam couldn't make out, then turned away and started to walk back toward River Falls.

Sam continued through the woods and within ten minutes exited onto an old, semipaved state road. He knew his way around physically, but otherwise he was disoriented. Besides Granick, was there anyone he could trust?

The Agency was out. Hopper was proof that they were looking to take him in, along with the file. And now he had attracted the unwanted attention of the KGB. But how did they know about him and the briefcase? Besides Granick, McDowell was the other person who had been told. Was the newscaster one of them?

Only one person could help him now. John "The Baptist" Davidson, his former chief at counterintelligence. The old spy, feared, loved, and trusted by some, suspiciously eccentric to others, was his best chance. The Baptist was the only one at Langley who had approached the lofty ideals of a counterespionage man, manipulating paranoia and deception into sweet revelation. He had preached the gospel no one wanted to hear—that the Agency, even at the highest levels, was heavily infiltrated by Americans working for the KGB, put in place from university recruitment onward.

Withers considered no one more loyal to his country. Paranoid, yes. Davidson even saw Communists in some progressive Republican politicians. But disloyal, no.

Davidson was now in bureaucratic exile. Implausibly, he had left Langley under a cloud. After Watergate, during one of the Agency's metamorphoses, Davidson had been purged—secretly accused of being the Soviet mole who had infiltrated the ranks a quarter century before—and forced into retirement without formal charges.

But he, Springs, and everyone who served with the Baptist knew it was a scapegoat operation. A cover-up for the director's inability to find the real mole. Or worse, to disguise the culpability of those at, or near, the top.

Yes, John the Baptist, the sly old bastard, was his hope of sanctuary.

Davidson lived on the route to Leesburg, Virginia, seventeen miles from River Falls. Sam couldn't risk having anyone—a cabby or a driver offering him a ride—later help trace his route and objective. He couldn't call Davidson to pick him up. Even though this administration was better disposed, Davidson's phone was probably being tapped by the Agency.

There was only one secure way. He had to walk to Davidson's home. It was now after 9 P.M. If he walked all night, unseen, he could arrive at Davidson's farm at about three in the morning. He had no idea what his reaction would be, but there was no place else to go.

With that decision, Sam turned in the direction of Leesburg, swung the briefcase up and down a few times to exercise his arm, and moved his small body forward into the night.

Chapter 8

Moments later, in downtown Washington, Doug McDowell settled into the moderator's chair at the L Street studio and ran his fingers over his partially salvaged notes. It was fifteen minutes before air time, 9:30 P.M., EDT.

He had his debate material virtually memorized, which was just as well. His mind was unfocusing, moving involuntarily back to the ugly confrontation with Granick. Son-of-a-bitch slander peddler. Why did he have to crash in at such a crucial time?

The last of the candidates, Governor Marc Daniels of Illinois, arrived and was rushed into make-up. He needed little cosmetic help. Of average height and a touch stocky, the self-made agri-millionaire had a fatherly smile and a ruddy, lineless face, the product of fifty-six years that were viceless, except for compulsive ambition.

A relative novice in politics, Daniels was already the party favorite. In his one term in the statehouse, he had blocked farm foreclosures and protected thousands of jobs being eroded by imports. Not eloquent, or brilliant, he exuded a sense of caring.

Minutes before air time, McDowell sat in front of the seven candidates and a small, select audience and began his warm-up.

"Please introduce yourselves, one at a time, so that we can get voice levels. I know you've done this more times than I have. But indulge me anyway."

The candidates smiled, then began from left to right.

"I'm Senator Katy Meredith of Oklahoma. I'd like to run as a person, but you press people insist that I'm the woman candidate. So I accept. It's better than nothing."

The male candidates looked uneasy. The tall, fiftyish former college president had attracted 680 delegates, more than any female politician in history, and was regularly mentioned for the number two spot, now the accepted—almost sexual—position for female politicians.

"Oh," Meredith interjected. "Should any of you want me to play Katharine Hepburn to your Spencer Tracy, I am not available for VP. The White House or nothing."

McDowell was pleased. They were making news and the debate hadn't even begun. He needed good news. The altercation with Jack Granick had left him emotionally sapped. Just keep your eyes on this ball game, he warned himself. Forget Granick and his fascist bullshit.

But the image of the columnist's fingers pressing against him, the brown eyes with their Slavic, slightly slanted cast, was fixed in McDowell's consciousness.

Could one of these seven really be a Communist? God, the word had been so abused. But, from Granick's intensity, McDowell knew the columnist was talking not about a "leftist" or even a "fellow traveler" but, as he had said, a traitor in American political garb.

The next speaker was the only black candidate. The bull-necked, silver-haired politician spoke in perfect tones, covering his deep Southern farm origins.

"I'm Congressman Clarence Jackson Rawlins, 16th District—the black Mecca, Harlem. We blacks now cast almost one in four Democratic votes. The ethnics have left the party. Women pay lip service to our feminist slogans and only we are steadfast. You've been warned before, but all we hear is that blacks have no place to go. Four more years and I promise we'll find someplace."

The audience stirred.

As McDowell stared at the next candidate, Democratic Senator

Angus Delafield of North Dakota, he thought of Granick. Delafield, too, had taken up the national security banner. The former Air Force brigadier general, who had earned a DFC in World War II as a young bomber pilot, then a dozen more medals in Korea and Vietnam, was dressed in Midwest browns, his craggy face as weather-worn as the Scottish moors of his ancestors. His hair was gray, but full, almost a young man's pompadour placed incongruously atop his lined face.

"My name is Delafield," he began, "Angus 'The Bull,' they call me. Why? Because I'm the only one on this stage smart enough to know that the Russians are planning our demise. But enough of that chit-chat. Let's get on with the debate."

Some of the other candidates laughed nervously, finding Delafield not only an embarrassment but a reminder of better times. More than one Democratic Party leader was convinced that victory would elude them again in November unless they recognized the appeal of Delafield's message.

Hawk versus dove was becoming the dominant campaign theme, McDowell could see. The Democratic candidates had embraced varying shades of opinion. The doves were for nuclear freeze and the elimination of not only the MX but the Stealth bomber and the Star Wars antimissile defense, the first unit of which was already deployed in space. The mobile Midgetman missile threatened to ignite the controversy even further.

The hawks, led by Delafield, had tagged their opponents as "peaceniks," casting them as the architects of the party's humiliating losses in recent presidential contests.

Daniels was not laughing with the others, McDowell noticed. He was anxious to hear how the governor would handle the battle between dove and hawk and still hold his edge in the divided party.

Granick's face, with the black lock of hair falling aimlessly before his eyes, conjured itself up again. For an instant McDowell saw each candidate with a vision dictated by Granick's paranoia. Which of the seven was the Communist? Was it Meredith, or Daniels, or Rawlins, or maybe even Delafield, a Red masquerading in the costume of patriots?

He was still tussling, unsuccessfully, with the subject of patriotism, McDowell recognized. It had its place, but he usually found its protestations vulgar, Texan-like braggadocio. He had been brought up in two eras of American paranoia—McCarthyism and Watergate—and had learned to connect them. Though too young to remember Joe

McCarthy, his generation had been schooled in its excesses, especially the undocumented accusation of Communism, of which his father had been a victim.

Watergate was his own. While a student reporter at the University of Oregon, he had watched his lifestyle heroes, Bernstein and Woodward, shake reactionary foundations. It seemed only natural that the war against neofascism, not Communism, was tied to his generation. The real-world villains were the Stroessners, Marcoses, and Pinochets, even the ghosts of Franco and Chiang Kai-shek. Each sign of resistance to fascism, anywhere, ennobled his spirit.

Communism itself? He had no zeal for that kind of radicalism. In fact, he tried not to think about it. There was some good in their spread of education and health, as in Cuba. But the ideology was a foreign problem, not an American one. So why become so perturbed, as did people like Delafield—and Granick?

In a quick sweep of the stage, McDowell concluded that the most liberal, perhaps even left, member of the group was Senator Brock Sommerville of Massachusetts. The thin, almost frail former Harvard professor of international relations, a board member of the Council on Foreign Relations, had entered the race late. Only 60 delegates, mainly from Massachusetts, were pledged to him, but Sommerville had awed the intellectual community and much of the serious media.

"My name is Brock Sommerville," the senator began, unconsciously adjusting his navy bow tie, then the bridge of his dull gold-framed spectacles. "I hold no brief for the Soviet Union, although I must say that, for a nation with so short a history of Western culture, it often acts more reasonable than we do. In any case, I am offering myself as the nominee for a simple reason: to save civilization."

McDowell smiled at the arrogance. Daniels was next. The other candidates were respectfully silent as he offered a moderate view of defense and foreign policy, with something for everybody. It was a good tightrope act, McDowell thought, but no guarantee that it would land the political acrobat on his feet.

As the next candidate, Jed Hankins, rose, some young people in the audience sent out finger whistles. At age thirty-nine, the junior senator from Virginia was the youngest candidate for President in either party.

Hankins was a tall, angular, handsome man whom some considered Lincolnesque, if one accepted the Gregory Peck image of the Civil War President. At least six feet three, Hankins boasted a head of luxuriant wavy brown hair. The wealthiest of the candidates, Hankins was the heir to a near-billion-dollar meat-packing fortune. The rich bachelor's romantic exploits filled the supermarket tabloids as did news of his stable of racing horses.

With his formula of "More Peace, More Prosperity," Hankins had shaped a following among the boomers. "My name is Jed—Jedidiah Breckinridge Hankins," he began. "Jedidiah, my father used to remind me, means 'beloved of God' in Hebrew. But this year I'll settle for being the favorite of everyone who's thirty-nine years old." His supporters roared.

The last candidate, Hawley Briggs, former three-time governor of Arkansas, was only in his early sixties, but time had eclipsed his style. Briggs dressed like a traveling hardware salesman and looked like everybody's grandfather.

"Just let me say," Briggs opened, "that the little guy with a wife, and a baby, and a mortgage too damn big for his paycheck, and a pickup truck that needs a new transmission—well, he's been hosed by the Republicans for a hundred years. And lately he's been getting it from his own party. I intend, the Lord willin', to fix all that in the White House."

The short speech evoked sincere belly laughs. McDowell noted to interview the canny Southerner at the convention.

"Fuck Granick," McDowell whispered to himself. For a moment he feared that the word had actually issued into the microphone.

Where's his damn Communist? Rawlins? Maybe, but who would blame him after fifty years of broken promises to the American blacks? Hankins? One of the richest men in America? Briggs? He would bet his VCR that he was the soul of rural America. Sommerville? Who the hell knew anything about professors?

Granick, that damn rightist bastard, had him doubting his own political sensibilities. He would not lightly forgive him.

But there was no one to forgive.

At 9:25 P.M., five minutes before the actual debate, McDowell left the auditorium, seeking a short break. He walked into the newsroom next door and up to the AP news wire, chattering away its catalogue of mayhem. As McDowell leaned over the teletype his eyes focused on the first item to greet him.

TONIGHT, AT NINE-TWENTY, THE BODY OF NATIONALLY SYNDICATED CONSERVATIVE COLUMNIST JACK GRANICK WAS RECOVERED FROM THE

UPPER POTOMAC RIVER, WHERE IT HAD CRASHED OVER THE FALLS.
DROWNING APPEARS TO BE THE CAUSE OF DEATH. HIS SMALL DINGHY,
OVERTURNED AND EMPTY, WAS STOPPED JUST BEFORE THE DESCENT.
POLICE ARE INVESTIGATING THE POSSIBILITY OF FOUL PLAY.

McDowell flinched. Granick dead? Was it truly an accident? Or
what? He could still see the fear in the columnist's eyes. God, he had
refused Granick on moral grounds, but now he applauded his decision. Would he too be dead—maybe at the orders of one of his seven
TV guests—if he had accepted Granick's offer to expose the Red candidate?"

Unsteadily, McDowell moved back into the auditorium, the stakes
now higher. McDowell could hear the director's voice in his earpiece.
"Doug, five, four, three, two, one. On camera."

The actual on-air debate started an instant later, with Senator Delafield waving a red-covered paperback over his head. "This book is
several years old," Delafield began. "It's the 1985 edition of *Soviet
Military Power* put out by the Defense Department. Listen.

" 'The Soviet SS-18 . . . force currently deployed has the capability to destroy more than 80 percent of U.S. ICBM silos using two
nuclear warheads each.' "

"Oh, come off it, Angus," Sommerville interrupted, straining in his
chair. "You're promoting your new holocaust again. Where do you
get these crazy ideas?"

"As I was saying—have we improved our security since?" Delafield
continued, ignoring Sommerville. "Well, this other book is the newest
edition of *Soviet Military Power*. Hear this.

" 'The 50 MXs at Warren Air Force Base, Colorado, are capable of
destroying the hardest Soviet sites. But their numbers are so small,
and without mobility, that it is impossible to guarantee'—and listen
carefully—'that any American land-based missiles will survive a Soviet strike from SS-24s and mobile SS-25s.' "

"Angus, can't you throttle that voice of doom?" Sommerville interrupted again. "I can already hear you pitching for that little mobile
Midgetman. I've listened to you war spokesmen for thirty years now,
going back to Jack Kennedy. It's high time somebody championed
peace," Sommerville concluded, pronouncing the word as "pace" in
his thirteen-generation-old Boston accent.

McDowell was pleased that the debate was heating up for Governor Marc Daniels and Senator Jed Hankins, champions of two gener-

ations and two styles. Daniels was ahead in the delegate count, with
Jed Hankins second and Katy Meredith not far behind. Daniels
couldn't afford to resent the woman candidate, but he saw Hankins as
the spoiler, a millionaire kid too grandiose for his own talents.

"I really don't know what you're talking about," Daniels replied to
Hankins' charge that he had "no real military or foreign policy."

Daniels looked sharply into the television camera. "I've made my
position clear. I want a strong America, one ready to fight, but determined not to. Doesn't that make sense?"

McDowell recognized that Star Wars was the cutting edge of the
debate. One unit of the nuclear-triggered X-ray laser antiballistic device was already operational.

"Governor, if you were President, would you add the second Star
Wars unit in January as planned, or would you do away with the
whole program?" McDowell asked.

Daniels took on the look of a cornered politician.

"Doug, I don't like an arms race in the heavens, but a lot depends
on the true Soviet attitude toward disarming. And I won't really
know that, will I, until I get into the White House?"

"Just more Tweedledum and Tweedledee," Hankins said, moving
aggressively into the argument. "Governor Daniels sounds like the
Republican candidate—willing to spend trillions on nuclear technology when a simple missile can destroy us all. Meanwhile our men
can't stay in conventional combat more than thirty days because
we're putting the money into $300-million bombers and unneeded
missiles. Incidentally, I've just written a book on the subject—*A New
Military for a New World*—and I commend it to you."

McDowell glanced at Daniels, who was fidgeting anxiously as the
young candidate attacked him from the right and the left. Hankins
was talking about both military expansion and limits on the military
in the same breath. And, McDowell thought, he seemed to be getting
away with it.

As the debate came to a close, Hankins walked across the stage to
offer his hand to Daniels, but the flush-faced governor rose, turned
his back, and moved into the wings.

McDowell was happy he had gotten through the hour. Wasn't it
only coincidence that Granick had died right after making his wild
claim? Stories about Reds in high office were among the oldest of
Washington saws, invariably out of the mouths of conservative fanat-
ics like Jack Granick.

But, he reminded himself, they didn't drown moments later. Did they?

The newsman packed up his papers and walked toward the exit, his mind riddled with unhappy confusion.

Chapter 9

Withers had been walking for three hours on the hard, dark road, heading against the traffic on VA 7, Leesburg Pike, drawing the bright car headlights into his eyes. The briefcase, filled with only the file, now tugged incessantly at his arm.

It was after midnight, early Tuesday morning, and he had covered less than half the distance. The seventeen-mile expedition to Davidson's house was proving more painful than he had expected.

Never had he felt such loneliness. The damning information he carried was known to no one. Granick had read it, but he was dead. He was now the sole caretaker, a job he had thrust upon himself. But Sam had little choice. He was sought by both sides in the Cold War, a target of the KGB and the CIA, each for different reasons. Springs had already called on police friends to pick him up on any charge, from vagrancy to stealing state secrets, he was sure.

The walk continued, one tortured step after another, until, at the ten-mile mark, Sam stopped and squatted cross-legged on the ground. Pulling off his tight dress shoes, he futilely massaged the soles of the bruised feet, swollen from pushing out against the taut leather.

Withers tilted toward the stars, addressing himself in a small voice, almost a wail.

"God. Is it worth it?"

The question was rhetorical. Patriotism as a repayment for freedom had been a family credo. Love of country and Love of God, insisted his late father, a career army warrant officer, were the only antidotes to the modern disease of materialism, which had infected Americans and Russians alike.

Sam despised everything Communist, as had his father, a malaria victim in Vietnam. But those who worked for the Soviets out of conviction had some saving grace, he conceded. Withers hated Americans who served the KGB for money. What perversion. Little danger to him. He had never made much money, even escaped the temptation of judging one's life by the dollar sign. On this, he supposed, he agreed with the Communists. But otherwise the tyranny of Red fascism repelled him.

There was no choice but to continue on Leesburg Pike. Placing one lacerated foot after another, he forced himself forward on the harsh shoulder of the road.

Yes, he was sure of it. Ahead was a police car, probably searching for him. The car was not flashing, but the lighted knob at the top of the vehicle was telltale. Withers ran off the shoulder and pressed his body tightly into the tall, uncut grass. The police car approached—he thought he saw it slow down—but it moved on past him.

By 2 A.M., Withers had exhausted every physical resource. He couldn't go another step. Then he remembered his watch. The elaborate wristclock had an alarm. With twenty measured minutes of rest, he might have the strength to cover the last miles. Otherwise, he would sleep for hours in the grass and risk arrest.

Pulling a dead branch with a puff of leaves over as a pillow, Sam lay down, set his alarm for 2:20 A.M., and was asleep as his head reclined toward the ground.

It was a sound decision. When Withers woke, he could walk, however unsteadily. He developed a waddle, shuffling from side to side like a pelican, avoiding pressure on his feet.

For the next half hour, as Sam passed several dairy farms, he sharpened his eyes for Davidson's place. At three-fifteen in the morning, about three miles out of Leesburg, directly off the pike, he saw it.

Davidson's farm, a small, gentleman's dairy operation, was ahead a few hundred yards. The full moon was now obscured by clouds and he could barely make out the outlines of the main house as he turned onto the driveway. The sign, which was enveloped in darkness, he knew by heart.

Over the painting of a smiling calf, it simply read: DAVIDSON'S COWS. It was one of John's jokes on society.

Withers didn't know how to approach the house at such an ungodly hour. Was there a watchdog? He had forgotten. Could he just walk up to the front door and ring the bell until he woke Davidson? That simple strategy seemed best.

He moved down the long gravel driveway to the door of the farmhouse—circa 1800, he guessed, from the Federal fanlight. Sam placed his finger on the buzzer, closing his eyes from the embarrassment of what he was about to do.

Withers rang the bell, off and on, for two minutes, but there was no answer. He was about to turn toward the back of the house to throw a pebble at an upstairs window when he froze.

A piece of cold steel was pressed into the back of his head. It was, he could feel, the snout nose of an army .45, a weapon designed to carve a massive, final hole.

"Is there anything I can do to help you?" It was the dulcet voice of John Davidson. "You didn't have to ring so loudly. I wake easily, you know."

"John, it's me, Sam Withers. Please put that gun away and invite me in. I'm near death."

Davidson whirled Withers' body around to face him, the gun still targeting his head.

"By God, it is you. What the hell are you doing here? And at three-thirty in the morning? Couldn't you call first?"

"John, things are bad. I couldn't call. They're looking for me and I figured you might be tapped. I have to talk to you. Can we please go in?"

In the house, Withers was soon engulfed in an overstuffed colonial armchair, a blanket over his chilled body, his worn feet immersed in warm water and Epsom salts, a hot toddy with cinnamon, a Davidson special, in his hand.

The older CIA man first explained his little surprise. He had a sonar perimeter around his entire property. Whenever anything as sizable as a human body crossed the line, it rang loudly at his bed. Before Withers had approached the front door Davidson was out by the side of the house waiting to see who had come to call at this peculiar hour.

As the two men sat by the fire, Withers explained everything that had taken place since he left Langley earlier that day, including Granick's murder. He could see Davidson's dark eyes flare with interest as he approached the subject of the briefcase.

"John, I won't spoil it for you. Open it up and read it yourself. It'll justify all your paranoia."

Withers recounted the origin of the file, which had begun three years before, during a routine FBI surveillance of a Soviet diplomat suspected of being KGB. A photograph was taken of the Russian with the Democratic candidate, showing them having lunch in a small colonial eatery in Fredericksburg, Virginia, thirty-five miles from the capital, ten miles outside the travel limit for Soviet diplomats.

"My friend at the FBI turned the picture over to me, gratis. I knew it really didn't mean too much," Withers admitted. "But it was after that that I began my investigation."

Davidson opened the case and laid the file bare on a small table by his armchair. The sixty-eight-year-old retired spy's thin visage, high cheekbones, and deep-set eyes gave him a hypnotic aura, not unlike that of a Shakespearean actor. The parallel was strengthened by his wavy silver hair.

He was no dandy, more the tweedy Virginia gentleman, usually dressed in a gray herringbone three-piece suit. Until tonight, Sam had never seen him wear anything else, summer or winter, and it was rumored that it was either his only suit or one of a clone of three or four that he rotated to fool his friends. He had the look of an old alumnus of Princeton, where he had edited a fledgling intellectual magazine, *Papyri*, before entering World War II, and eventually the Office of Strategic Services under Dulles in Switzerland.

Davidson adjusted his glasses on his classical nose and picked up the file, reading page by page, staring at the photos, saying nothing for almost five minutes. When he finished, Davidson placed it down and looked at Withers.

"Sam, it's a nightmare. He's fooled a lot of people, including me. I've disagreed with him on many issues, but I never suspected this. Reckless charges have been made against several prominent people—Kissinger, McGovern, even, as you know, me. But this is real."

Davidson's traditional aplomb seemed shaken.

"You were right in getting off the street and bringing it to me. I'm glad McDowell refused to put it on the air. The screams of outrage from the left would be heavy—even more than from the other side. McDowell would have been called a smear artist, the purveyor of sleazy, trumped-up documents. It would make a bigger stink than Watergate. It's my guess that Springs thinks the same way. He's probably got half the Agency out looking for you now—to squelch the file."

"John, I still don't think that makes any sense. Why not call a spade a spade? Why so damn bashful?" Withers asked.

"Sam, the old Joe McCarthy era is still poisoning the arena. We lost some of the best people in the last generation because of the 'Red-baiting' backlash. We can't afford that again. Leave the file with me, Sam. Trust me. I'll use it, the best way, at the right time."

Withers felt relieved, assured that his all-night trek was not wasted. He felt safe, even content, in this old farmhouse.

Davidson was plainly Sam's idol. He knew of Allen Dulles, but John was a living victor in the old espionage wars of the 1950s and the 1960s. Davidson had infiltrated the KGB hierarchy with Alexei Martinov, a secret worshiper in the Russian Baptist Church—hence the origin of John's own nickname.

Then he had pulled the wire. He had smuggled Martinov into the American Embassy in Vienna, then back to America. After fifteen years in Dzerzhinsky Square, Martinov's brain was saturated with the files of Soviet agents in America and Western Europe. From his defection to Davidson, the Russians lost seven illegals, several KGB members of the UN, and numerous Soviet officials expelled from embassies around the world.

After that, Davidson was hallowed in suburban Langley. That is, until he was scarred in the internecine Agency wars of the 1970s, which Davidson's side had lost. He was the first victim, retribution for his snide accusations of either insufficient zeal or disloyalty. And among the longtime Soviet plants in the Agency, it was an unexpected chance to get even for all his victories in the Cold War.

Little wonder that in the presence of the old spy Withers felt secure.

But it was short-lived. It was Davidson himself who punctured Sam's comfortable fantasy.

"Sam, you can't stay here more than a few hours. By 8 A.M. there's going to be an unmarked Agency car at my door with a polite request that I tell them whether I've seen or heard from you in the last day. If they think I'm lying they'll strong-arm me and search the place. No, you've got to go."

Withers' face turned ashen.

"Go? Where? In the next few hours?"

He could hardly walk another step. Could he have mistaken Davidson's concern—or even his loyalty?

"No, Sam, don't worry. I'm not throwing you out into the cold. Ever since you walked in here I've been planning our next move. I think I have it. If you're up to it."

Withers nodded blind agreement.

"I've kept a safe house, a small beach place, on the Outer Banks of

North Carolina for years. I've used it from time to time to hide a few people, whom I sent down there as renters. The house is in the name of Robert Doherty. That's supposed to be me, but no one has ever seen me. I do all my business by mail through an agent.

"You're going to be Doherty instead of me. I've kept a whole set of ID for an emergency. I've got a spare car—an old '75 Ford—with North Carolina plates. Take three hours' sleep, then drive straight through Virginia to the house. Don't stop for any reason. When you get there, just check in by phone with the rental agent. His name is Jason Muller. Tell him you're Doherty. Keep a low profile. There's a general store there that'll deliver anything. Wait until I call you from an outside phone. Don't call me. They tap this phone at will with a new high-tech device at Langley."

A smile, the first he had allowed himself all night, moved across Withers' face.

"Don't worry, John. I'll like being Mr. Doherty. Just do me one favor. Call my wife anonymously and tell her that I'm okay."

Chapter 10

By the time the CIA men assigned to keep the Withers home under surveillance arrived on Tuesday morning, it was too late.

Mary Withers was found dead in her own kitchen, her face up, her eyes focused in fear on the ceiling. The telephone next to the sink was hanging loose by its cord, the buzzing of a phone-off-the-hook now silent.

"Get Springs on the other phone," James Barber, the older officer, yelled to Hopper, who stood white-faced, tears forming on his collegiate cheeks. "Tell him we've got one big mess on our hands. Ask if we should call the police."

Hopper raced to the phone. "Director Springs. This is Hopper. I have some bad news. We're in Sam's home and Mrs. Withers is dead. Yes, sir. It was murder. No bullet or knife wounds. There are repeated blows on the back of her neck. Looks like the work of experts. Must have snapped her neck. Pretty messy thing."

He listened to Springs's frustration. "Yes, sir, we saw something.

Just as we came up to the house, a white van was leaving. No. I couldn't make out the license plate. They moved out too quickly.

"Should we call the police? Okay. We'll stay here and leave the body as is and put everything in your hands. Yes, sir, I understand."

"What the hell is he talking about?" Barber yelled after Hopper had hung up. "Leave the body where it is? Has the director flipped out?"

Hopper shook his head. "It seems we've walked into something too big for us. Springs doesn't want a word out to the police or the press. They're sending an unmarked ambulance and arranging a private burial. Withers—wherever the hell he is—is not to know about it either. God, that poor guy. I wonder what he's up to? Whatever it is, it's going to be too much for him now."

☆ ☆ ☆

At the Soviet Embassy in Washington earlier that morning, Nikolai Baneyev, Colonel, KGB, the *Komitet Gosudarstvennoi Bezopasnosti*, Committee for State Security, and the KGB *rezident* at this key post, stared painfully at the message from Moscow.

Baneyev, a man of forty-five, stood out physically in Washington diplomatic society, where he masqueraded as the embassy's cultural attaché. His upper torso was heavily muscled, but his thin face was exotic—with high, Tartar cheekbones, a virtually bald scalp, and an almost feminine milky-white skin. A long nose began at the ridge of his brow and hooked late in its passage downward.

The colonel was worried. Four years of effort had gone into developing a leading American politician as an ideological ally. He might even be considered an agent in place. Baneyev was banking on his man rising all the way to the Oval Office, and now one insignificant CIA man, acting on his own, threatened to destroy his plans.

The message from Orlov had just arrived by diplomatic pouch at the new Soviet Embassy on upper Wisconsin Avenue. Baneyev had decoded it personally.

A Polish KGB agent, Captain Peter Semanski, operating as an illegal under the name Tom Ward, would be arriving from California today to join Walter Rausch's unit and take tactical command of Oval Red, the message revealed. Orlov had stressed that Baneyev was to be doubly cautious about security. Even the Soviet ambassador was to be excluded from any knowledge of the operation, which was not safe in talkative, even stupidly garrulous diplomatic circles, Russian or otherwise.

Baneyev reread his assignment. He didn't need Moscow to remind him what had to be done. Security on Oval Red had already been violated. He had tried to mend it, with mixed results. A member of Walter Rausch's local Washington apparatus had led them to Granick, who in turn had brought them to the original leak, Withers at the CIA.

Granick had been taken care of, but Withers had escaped. Moscow had now ordered that Withers and his incriminating file be found. He was to be permanently silenced. Baneyev was not to be delicate, only efficient.

The colonel rose from a comfortable armchair in his three-bedroom apartment atop the high rise overlooking the ten-acre Soviet compound at Wisconsin Avenue and Tunlaw Road. With the dispatch in hand, he walked downhill to a main embassy building, a sizable portion of which was reserved for his KGB operations.

From his birch-paneled office Baneyev called for his assistant, Sergeant Alexei Teshovich, a spare, bespectacled clerk with steel-rimmed glasses.

"Teshovich," the colonel began, "a CIA counterintelligence man, Sam Withers, has disappeared with information that could incriminate an important friend of ours in Washington. We must find him. Our only lead is his wife. Send some people to convince her to cooperate. But be careful. The Agency is probably watching the house."

Teshovich, Baneyev knew, was capable of organizing such forays, even though he would be useless in a physical conflict. His mind worked in espionage fantasies, a trait that was invaluable for operating in the open Washington arena, what the KGB called "accessible."

Baneyev had finished, but Teshovich stood unsmiling in front of the desk.

"Yes?" Baneyev asked. "Is there anything else I need to say?"

"No, sir, but I have a thought that might be valuable."

"Yes?"

"From what you tell me, Withers has disappeared with the information you want," Teshovich said. "He's obviously acting rationally and will only produce what he has at the right time—to our detriment. We need to make him act irrationally. Do something that would induce him to come out in the open, available to us."

Baneyev listened, finding no flaw in the argument.

"Good thinking. How do we accomplish that?"

"Very simple, sir. We arrange for his wife to have an accident. A fatal one. Once she is found, the Agency may try to keep it out of the press. But when the time is right, we can leak it ourselves. We have friends in Washington. When Withers hears the news, I guarantee you all his professional training will mean nothing. He will be seeking revenge and be back among us. Very soon."

Baneyev peered at his sergeant. Brilliant, he confessed. Soon he would have to grant Alexei a superior rating, but he would make it clear that the young man has grandiose illusions about himself. He could not afford an enemy in Teshovich, but neither need he propel him ahead too rapidly. Yes, brilliant. A touch frightening, but brilliant nonetheless.

"Yes, Alex. Good. Do it. Don't involve me in the details. Just let me know when it's done."

☆ ☆ ☆

It was done at the instant John Davidson had called anonymously to let Mary know that Sam Withers was safe.

Mary picked up the phone, and as Davidson started to say, "Mrs. Withers, I have a message for you," he could hear a gruff, accented voice in the background.

"Give me that phone. I told you not to answer it."

Then Davidson heard what sounded like a sharp blow being delivered, then another. After a moment he heard only the maddening buzz of a disconnected phone.

He had to know what was happening at the Withers house. Boldness was the only reasonable approach. Davidson dialed the Agency number in Langley—703-482-1100—and asked for the director's office.

"Who shall I say is calling?" the operator asked.

"Just tell him it's John Davidson. He knows me."

"Oh yes, sir. Mr. Davidson. Good to hear your voice again. I'll try to get him right on."

Springs took the call immediately. "John. The Agency's not the same without you. What's up?"

"Al, I have no time. Something's going on. I heard from the scuttlebutt that Sam Withers was missing. I just called the house to ask Mary if she had any news of him. I heard someone there. He seemed to be hitting Mary. Then the phone disconnected. Could you have your men check it out?"

"Hold on, John. We have two men in a car with a radio close by. I'll call them."

The wait was only three and a half minutes, but it felt interminable. Davidson had not gotten Withers into this, but he felt responsible. God, could Mary have been hurt badly? And why? She knew nothing. That was implicit at the Agency. Wives of deep-cover and counterintelligence men were kept ignorant of their work for that very reason.

"John. I have bad news." It was Springs back on the phone. "Our men went into the house. Mary is dead. Someone beat her repeatedly about the neck. God, why would anybody do such a thing?"

Springs slowed, his composure shaken.

"John, I can't tell you anything about this now, but I need a favor. Could you keep it quiet? We want it under wraps until we get some information that Sam has. It's essential to national security."

Davidson was strangely indecisive. He trusted Springs, but he couldn't reveal the truth about the Withers file. The Soviet mole was probably still at Langley, inhabiting a high position in the hierarchy. And if he promised Springs silence about Mary's death, what could he tell Withers? Sam deserved to know.

He pondered while Springs held the phone. Actually it might be best not to reveal the tragedy to Withers. If Sam knew, he would break his incognito and come back, raging. No, it was too early to act.

"Al, I'll go along with you, for now. But I suspect something big's afoot and I want to help out. Will you call me in before it breaks?"

"John. I can't promise, but we may need you on this one. Meanwhile, thanks. I'm sorry about Mary."

Chapter 11

COLUMNIST FOUND DEAD IN POTOMAC
House Ransacked. Murder Suspected

The headline bounded off the page of the usually sedate journal. So it was murder, after all. McDowell was still not convinced by Granick's tale, but what motive could there be other than the columnist's claim that he knew the identity of a Communist among the seven candidates?

Nothing seemed to be missing from the house, the newspaper account stated. Granick's only valuables were rare first editions of W. M. Thackeray and Samuel Johnson, which had not been taken. What the police and reporters were unaware of, McDowell knew, was the existence of Granick's briefcase. Which probably was missing.

What did Meg think? She had been there when Granick arrived, with that crazed expression.

"Meg, could you come in?" McDowell called into the intercom.

"In a minute, Doug. There's someone here from the River Falls sheriff's office. Should I send him in?"

A young deputy, gangly, about twenty-five, in plainclothes, was soon seated opposite McDowell, displaying his badge.

"Just a couple of questions, Mr. McDowell. Someone at the network saw Jack Granick come into the building around eight, eight-thirty last night. The watchman says he came up to see you. Is that true?"

McDowell was worried that his discomfort was showing. Was he somehow involved in a double crime—a murder and some variant of political conspiracy? But what about this kid cop in front of him? Would it make sense to pass on Granick's political rumor, for which he had no name, no proof, and a dead informant?

"Yes, Officer. He came to see me about eight-twenty, about an hour before the televised debate."

"What did he want?"

"Just a journalistic request. Jack was a real conservative and didn't like some of the Democratic candidates. He wanted me to ask a few nasty political questions during the debate."

"What did you tell him?"

"I brushed him off. I told him I was just the moderator, not an inquisitor."

"What happened then?"

"Nothing. He was disappointed, but he left. I suppose he went home."

After the interview, McDowell sat at his desk and interrogated himself. Did he feel guilty about not bringing up the Communist business? No. He had no evidence and, unlike Granick, he wasn't in the smearing business. Besides, he had learned there was little gain, either professionally or socially, among his media peers in being actively anti-Communist.

Moments later Meg came in and sat on the couch facing Doug. He fastened on her. Perhaps twenty-eight or twenty-nine, he surmised, surprised at his ignorance of someone he had worked with for months. McDowell digested Meg in a glance, as if for the first time. From her long auburn hair combed in an old-fashioned sweep, her hazel eyes and petite nose, down to her particularly long legs. The mouth was full. Not obviously sensuous, but inviting.

Meg always dressed traditionally, he had noticed. Perhaps too tasteful for an office. So unlike the other assistants, who were fastidiously sloppy, even to worn sneakers. Meg's dresses were often silk and form-fitting, with a gold Patek watch circling her wrist. McDowell first assumed she was dressed for a date, but it proved to be a daily ritual, which he found not unrewarding.

She is very attractive, he thought. Just as quickly, McDowell reminded himself to be cautious. Meg would be incensed if he regarded her more as a woman than as a coworker, whatever the truth.

He did respect her opinion. Meg had a rapid, intuitive sense that often bested his own plodding, crypto-intellectual approach.

"Meg, you know about Granick's death last night?"

"Yes," she said, looking at him sadly. "Wasn't that horrible? That poor man was so distraught, and now he's dead. Why would anyone want to kill him? Although I must say he looked really alarmed."

"Did you know why he came here?" McDowell asked, hoping not to involve her more than she was.

"Well, I suppose I shouldn't. But, to tell you the truth, I could hear part of the conversation through the door. Especially when you were screaming at him."

Meg abruptly covered her mouth. "Oh, I didn't mean you were rude, Doug. But I heard him telling you something—well, pretty strong—about one of the candidates. That he was left-wing, to put it mildly."

"Did you tell that to the police officer?" Doug asked.

"No. I figured that was your business. To tell him if you wanted to."

"Meg, what do you think? Could that be the reason Granick was killed?"

McDowell could see Meg study him, almost motherly, as if to protect him from his boyish apprehensions.

"No, Doug. I can't believe either thing. That the Democrats would have a Communist among their presidential candidates. Or that Mr.

Granick would be killed because he knew who it was. Maybe I'm just old-fashioned about politics, but I hate to think such skulduggery goes on."

McDowell could feel his tension ease. "Thanks for your opinion, Meg." His gaze was now almost affectionate. "You know I value it."

She was probably right, McDowell decided as Meg left the office. But he couldn't shake the other possibility. Could the damn Neanderthal have been onto something?

Who could help him out of the painful confusion?

Only one person's counsel on matters of national security was always candid, and available to him. He was retired but still a fountainhead. It was off the record, but McDowell had found it uncannily reliable over the years.

John the Baptist. He would know if Granick's tale and his death made any sense.

McDowell depressed the intercom button.

"Meg. Get me the Cosmos Club. Tell them I want to speak to Mr. Davidson. Mr. John Davidson."

Chapter 12

Colonel Lev Andreievich Orlov leaned his miniature frame against the leather backing, propping his short legs on the raised stool of the Chaika. He reached up and switched on the compact East German overhead light. The chauffeur, who understood that these were Orlov's best moments to meditate, maintained silence.

Orlov was pleased, with everything. He had dispatched Semanski to America only a few days before and had already received a report from Colonel Baneyev in Washington assuring him that, except for the Withers problem, things were progressing smoothly.

So was his personal life, which centered on the comfort that went with his rank. As always, his body was impeccably garbed in soft woolens made by Kransky, a masterful Jewish tailor in Moscow. Orlov rewarded him with foreign currency coupons, which were then happily exchanged for Western goods at the *beriozka* store across from the Kremlin.

The other payment was intangible but more valuable. Orlov was Kransky's protector in the world of unofficial Soviet anti-Semitism. Kransky's daughter had used Orlov's connections to enter Moscow State University despite the punitive Jewish quota. When Kransky's wife suffered a stroke, a bed magically opened at a Kremlin-connected hospital, saving her not only the ignominy of daily bribes to get her sheets changed, but from the staphylococcus that infects the common Moscow hospital wards like frost on an early winter sill. Status—not money, as in America—was survival in Soviet Russia, Orlov had long realized.

The relationship between Orlov and his tailor spawned rumors that the colonel, whose internal passport was stamped "Russian," had once been a Jew. He laughed. Orlov was only an eighth Jewish on his maternal side, but he enjoyed the ethnic gossipmongering, a favorite conversation piece in often bored Moscow.

That Tuesday morning, Orlov's car left the Center at Teplyy Stan and drove through the outer suburbs to Route M14, a modern road south and west of Moscow, one of the highways that exited into the ring roads girdling the capital. After ten miles, the Chaika moved onto Leninsky Prospekt and the city center. Orlov looked out just as the car crossed the Moskva River and entered directly onto the giant terrace of Russia—Red Square.

It was an open plaza, a street, a stone-paved roadway. The square itself held only four buildings, including St. Basil's, Lenin's tomb, and the glass-roofed GUM department store, once a czarist mall of small shops. All else, from churches to the Czar's former palace, was behind the tall, crenellated Kremlin walls. Some buildings were public. Others, like the seat of the Soviet government, were accessible only to the Orlovs of Russia.

The car moved slowly past St. Basil's toward Spassky Gate, just before the tomb of Lenin. Above them was the giant clock, a Russian version of Big Ben, the symbol of the Soviet Union on national television. Two red lights on the tower wall warned the Chaika to stop.

"Your papers, please." The KGB guard moved his head toward the rear of the black sedan. He studied the documents, then surveyed Orlov, who sat with a detached, superior expression. The guard returned the papers.

"Thank you, Comrade Colonel Orlov. You may go in."

The Chaika drove through Spassky, then to the right onto a narrow road directly behind the Kremlin wall. There it was. Invisible to

strollers on Red Square was the Presidium, a three-story, ocher and
white classical structure built in the 1930s. It was here that the General Secretary of the Communist Party worked, where the Politburo
met every Thursday afternoon at 3 P.M., where decisions were shaped
that caused the West daily anxiety.

Orlov evaluated the security. Could a capitalist madman storm the
General Secretary's office and assassinate him? He thought not. The
men at Spassky were only lightly armed, but as he drove on Orlov
saw half-hidden soldiers with heavier arms on alert.

He was pleased that the KGB was not confronted with Washington's security problems. When he first heard that the public
toured White House rooms below the President's living quarters,
Orlov didn't believe it. Then he visited Washington and saw that it
was true. Reports of the man who wandered into the President's dining room confirmed his instincts about the childishness of the American government and their people. But it was that immaturity, of
course, that made his entire operation possible.

At the Kremlin, only officials were permitted to enter the Presidium or the nearby green-domed Council of Ministers Building.
Equally forbidden was Communists' Street, with its rows of government bureaus. A white line, backed by armed guards, enforced the
stricture.

But the Presidium Building, the site of the General Secretary's
office, was special. Officially, it was a nonbuilding. Photos of it almost
never appeared in the Soviet press or in guidebooks published in the
West. Orlov was amused that one American volume published a
Kremlin map but eliminated the existence of the Presidium alto-
gether. He laughed. That was true security.

Orlov's sense of self-importance heightened as he mounted the
steps. When he entered the meeting room at the rear of the second
floor, the Politburo members were already gossiping, drinking mineral water, staring out the large windows overlooking the Church of
the Twelve Apostles.

"Colonel Orlov. Punctual, as always." It was Grigori Vassilin, his
boss and the fourth head of the KGB since Andropov. Vassilin, a tall
man in his seventies with a military bearing and a chiseled face
topped by a white crew cut, turned to his colleagues.

"Comrades. Our guest is here. Could we assemble?"

The baize-covered table, laden with bottles of Georgian mineral
water, silver ball-point pens, and white pads, was large enough to

hold all fifteen members of the Politburo, but only five had been invited.

Vassilin, seated next to Orlov, spoke first.

"Comrades. Colonel Orlov, the head of the Active Measures unit in the American Section, has a plan. It is far from conventional, but I think promising. Please give him your attention."

The table was headed by the General Secretary of the Communist Party. Seated next to him was the aging President of the nation. The others included the Defense Minister, then Vassilin, and the working secretary of the Central Committee, a stringy thirty-six-year-old enthusiast named Alexei Luchovsky, who functioned like an American presidential assistant.

Orlov looked about, somewhat edgily. He need not have. He was respected at the Kremlin level, even if his elaborate plans for the subversion of American society were always initially greeted with skepticism. Vassilin had been told that the Politburo members enjoyed his presentations, much as one would a private story conference in Hollywood, at least in the days of Goldwyn.

His creative yarns about subverting America from within— whether academia, foundations, the media, the CIA, Congress, the military, or the executive bureaucracy—seemed like exotic fiction. And no matter how often Orlov converted his grandiose scenarios into reality, it continued to amaze his superiors.

To this, Orlov pleaded humility. The credit, he insisted, was all America's. No other nation, he maintained, was so anxious to distort and scourge itself, struggle not only to make Orlov's scenarios become real but to give them endings favorable to the Soviets.

Orlov began directly.

"Chairman. Comrades. I call this project Oval Red. It is a plan to place someone totally sympathetic to us in the American White House—as President of the United States."

The table rustle signaled that Orlov had begun well.

"Yes. Comrade Orlov." It was Luchovsky. "Please continue."

"Some of our people thought America ripe for revolution during the late sixties. It was poor thinking. Such protests are easily absorbed by the American system. Reforms are made and it is all forgotten, or used commercially in the next generation."

The Defense Minister leaned forward, his face registering confusion. "But, Colonel, if rebellion wasn't possible then, how can you expect to put a 'sympathetic' man—as you call him—into the White House now? The country is much more conservative. No?"

"Yes, Comrade Minister. But it finally occurred to us that the only way to take over a democracy is to get people on our side to win elections. At first we thought in European terms, in radical movements. Again it was a mistake. America has a two-party system—one slightly left of center, the other slightly right. There is no room for anything else. The Progressive Party, in which we had a hand in 1948, was an abysmal failure. It is not possible to get Americans to elect an openly leftist candidate. But the answer was there, in front of us all the time."

"And what is that?" Luchovsky asked, his look sharpening.

"Simply to have our man infiltrate the Democratic Party, then take the nomination for President or Vice-President."

"But how? Why would the party bosses permit such a thing?" It was the Defense Minister again, obviously intrigued.

"Comrade Minister. Times have changed. The political machines are weak. The nomination once went to the favorites of the bosses and veteran legislators—people like FDR and Johnson," Orlov explained. "Today the primary elections rule. They are run by the states. As Americans say, it is a 'crazy quilt' that no one really understands—tailor-made to nominate a man who would never make it through regular party channels."

Orlov produced copies of a one-page document, distributing it around the table.

"If you look at the sheet, it shows—state by state—the presidential primary votes cast for Democratic nominees. It is astounding. George McGovern took the Democratic nomination for President in 1972 with less than four million votes. That's out of over forty-five million registered Democrats. Jimmy Carter—a virtual unknown in the party and the nation—became the candidate in 1976 with less than six million votes. They may not have been ideal for us, but you see the point. The American political parties can be taken over through their own primaries."

Orlov paused. "But no one can gain the White House with an openly radical candidate. Our only hope is someone with an apparently moderate view, with liberal, but acceptable, patriotic leanings. That person can win the presidency for himself."

He waited another instant, striving for maximum drama.

"And for us."

The members moved. The General Secretary, who had been silent, now focused on Orlov, his intelligent eyes taking on a skeptical cast.

"Comrade Colonel. May I play devil's advocate? What good would it do us if the Democratic candidate is another 'moderate'—as you say —like Truman, or Johnson or Kennedy? They were the worst warmongers of the century."

"Comrade Secretary. I said 'apparently' moderate. We have a prominent Democratic politician who is one of us," Orlov answered, straining not to appear too prideful. "He has been in place for three years and is now an announced candidate for the nomination. This person has a national reputation for liberalism, yet with a clever conservative touch that keeps him from being suspect.

"We have—tentatively—put Oval Red into motion. It would not be wise to use our regular American agents, so I have sent a superlative operative, a young man who grew up in New York City, back to America to make contact with the principal at the right moment and become our confidential courier. He doesn't yet know his true assignment, but he is being put into position."

The room hushed. The Defense Minister was the first to speak out of the silence.

"Comrade Orlov. This is a most ambitious plan. But frankly, does it have any chance of success?"

"I don't want to lead anyone astray," Orlov said, his tone now subdued, even modest. This, he knew, was the moment to underplay his scheme, to hedge the chance that the Withers file—still out there and uncontrolled—would turn up and destroy Oval Red.

"There are six other candidates seeking the Democratic nomination. Then there will be the Republican opponent in November. As I've learned, anything can happen in an American election. As they say, it's a 'long shot,' but I can't proceed any further without your permission. Successful or not, our involvement in an American presidential election carries enormous international risk. So, Comrade Chairman, comrades . . . tell me. What is your disposition?"

The Chairman nodded to the aging President, as if to appoint him surrogate. The President began cautiously.

"Colonel Orlov, there is no denying the danger of discovery—and potential embarrassment. But we have not come this far in defeating America politically without great risks. Even if it is a 'long shot,' as you say, the rewards are enormous. I believe I speak for us all, Lev Andreievich. Move ahead. But . . ."

The President's delay was calculated. "Display one vital touch of restraint. Let your people know about Oval Red, but withhold the name of our candidate until the last moment. Too early an interference by us in the regular American political process could have ugly ramifications. Is that clear?"

As Orlov nodded agreement, the glacial expression of the old Bolshevik softened. "And, Colonel. Should Oval Red come to fruition, the Order of Lenin could be yours."

The Politburo members rose, now quietly chatting about what they had heard. The diminutive colonel nodded and moved softly out of the room, followed by his mentor, Vassilin.

"Lev Andreievich, we have promised much." The KGB chief had to lower his arms to cradle Orlov's shoulders. "It's time to make good."

Chapter 13

Tom Ward, airline valise in hand, deplaned at Washington's National Airport on Tuesday afternoon, the stench of burning flesh just fading from his nostrils. He had never killed a man. What was the sensation? Indelible or fleeting? Punishing or stimulating? Ward felt surprisingly calm. He had thrown up, but that was from revulsion at the sight of a flaming body, not guilt, he was sure.

Was he morally crippled in becoming involved in *mokroye dyelo*, or "wet business," as the KGB called murder? He thought not. The years of training had led inexorably to that day. He could already feel the incident becoming logged in an inaccessible region of his mind.

California had been isolated from both America and Europe by palm trees, but as his taxi drove from National Airport into Washington, Ward remembered New York with its extravagant pulse. The capital was quieter, but still reminiscent.

The cab moved up Massachusetts Avenue, past dozens of mansions converted into embassies. At the 4000 area, there it was. A luxury apartment house with marble-faced entrance, a dream of capitalist extravagance.

"Can I help you?" the house doorman, the unofficial American equivalent of the KGB, asked. In America, he had heard, it was the house staff he would have to watch out for—and take care of—more than any Washington bureaucrat.

"I'm a new tenant. Tom Ward. Apartment 11A. Could you get the super?"

He was taken aback by the apartment house superintendent, a short, middle-aged man named Vladimir Radofsky. From his name and accent, Ward guessed that the superintendent was a Russian Jew, probably a recent émigré to the United States. He checked his surprise as Radofsky showed him through the spacious two-bedroom apartment, including a small terrace.

"I come from Russia," Radofsky told Ward, who restrained a sudden impulse to speak to the man in his native tongue. "I'm only the super here, but I have an apartment in this building too. You wouldn't know, but there's nothing like this in the whole rotten Soviet Union. God bless America," the super recited, as if crossing himself.

Ward's smile was gracious. "I wouldn't know about Russia, but it's a nice apartment. Thanks for getting it in shape."

Quietly, he placed a twenty-dollar bill in Radofsky's hand. The super looked at the money, returning the smile.

"Like I said, God bless America."

Ward toured the apartment by himself, astonished at the blatant luxuries of American life. Why, he wondered, were Americans so superior in the materialistic world? Ward presumed it was simple greed. Or could it be a new spirituality? Every man a king. That, he was certain, would be a truly successful religion.

The phone rang sharply. It could be only one person, his Washington control. The voice on the other end spoke perfect English, but in an accent tinged with German.

"Walter Rausch calling," Ward heard. "Was the trip to Las Vegas profitable?" It was the code sentence, delivered precisely as rehearsed in Yurlova. "Welcome. I'll drop up to see you. Five minutes be okay?"

Ward delivered his half of the identity message without emotion.

"Yes, I broke the bank at Las Vegas. All of ten dollars' worth." Then, with guarded enthusiasm, "Sure, come right up."

Exactly five minutes later the bell rang.

The figure in the doorway was a tall and stolid-looking man in his forties with somewhat long, stringy dark blond hair. Except for his hair length, he was a caricature of German middle-class respectability, dressed like the successful American businessman he had become. His eyes were small and Germanic, frozen on the surface. Ward stared, suspecting there was hidden, perhaps repressed warmth at their core. But he wouldn't count on it.

"Welcome to the U.S.A.," Rausch greeted Ward.

The two men entered the living room where, as they sat and chatted, Ward periodically stared at the blank walls.

"Don't worry about security," Rausch reassured him. "One of our technicians swept the apartment this morning. It's absolutely clean. You'll also be happy to know everything went off perfectly in California. The body in the desert was found by the Highway Patrol. Someone from the Polish Consulate in Chicago flew out and identified the body. There are no suspects and Stanislaw Wynoski has been declared dead. Tom Ward has been born in his place."

"That's good," Ward said.

He excused himself and recovered the airline bag from the bedroom, removing the toilet kit and scissors, leaving the folded hanging bag and the pitiful clothes of the desert corpse.

"Give it to me," Rausch said. "I'll 'deep-six' it in the Potomac."

Ward was relieved that Rausch seemed a cut above the usual KGB type, as he was that the tiresome reminders of the desert incident would soon be gone. His mind turned to his assignment.

"I've traveled over twelve thousand miles and killed a man to get here. What am I expected to do?" he asked Rausch.

"Your first job is to memorize a complete legend of your new life. We've made it airtight."

Ward sensed that Rausch was sidestepping the question.

Instead, he told Ward about himself, describing a provenance any KGB man would envy. Born in Weimar, now East Germany, Rausch had joined the *MfS*, the *Ministerium für Staatssicherheit*, the East German Secret Police, directly out of the university. After training in East Germany and Moscow, he had "fled" to West Berlin, posing as a refugee. With seed capital secretly provided by the KGB, Rausch had built a documentary film company.

He was transferred to KGB service and sent to Canada as an immigrant. Rausch loved Toronto, where he was a respected member of the Canadian Conservative Party. After six years he emigrated to the United States and settled in Washington, where he opened Doric Films. Rausch became an American citizen in 1980 but stayed politically neutral, producing documentaries for both parties.

Ward listened, impressed with the sophistication of the American KGB operation. But he could no longer restrain himself.

"What will I be doing here? What's my assignment?" Ward asked again.

"You know that Ironman is your code name?"

"Yes. Orlov told me that at Teplyy Stan."

"Did he give you any hint of your work here?"

"None at all. Except for my two-day scenario, which I finished. I expected you to tell me everything."

"I can't tell you everything, but what I do know is extraordinary. Tom, you've been given the most important mission in the history of the American apparatus. You know the code name, Oval Red?"

Ward nodded.

"What it means is that we have a chance to place one of our people in the White House—right in the Oval Office."

"At what level?" Ward asked. "An executive assistant to the President? An important staff man? Like Gunter Guillaume, the Center agent who was AA to Willy Brandt?"

"No."

"What then?" Ward was confused.

"The President himself."

Ward stared at Rausch, incredulous.

"The President himself?"

"Yes. I just picked up this message from Baneyev at one of our drops, outside Reston. Here, read it yourself."

A word at a time, Ward took in the decoded cable from Teplyy Stan.

OVAL RED

TOM WARD, CODE NAME IRONMAN, WILL ARRIVE IN WASHINGTON TODAY TO BEGIN OVAL RED. A MAJOR DEMOCRATIC CANDIDATE FOR PRESIDENT IS TOTALLY SYMPATHETIC TO OUR CAUSE. IRONMAN IS TO HELP CANDIDACY WHERE FEASIBLE AND UNDETECTABLE, AND REVEAL HIMSELF TO CANDIDATE AT TIME OF HIS OWN DISCRETION. IRONMAN IS TO BE SOLE CONTACT BETWEEN CENTER AND CANDIDATE, PRESENTLY, AND IN EVENT OF HIGH ELECTED OFFICE. IRONMAN IS TO REPORT THROUGH R. IDENTITY OF CANDIDATE TO BE REVEALED LATER, AS REQUIRED. THIS IS MOST IMPORTANT ASSIGNMENT GIVEN YOUR UNIT. DO NOT FAIL. ORLOV.

A potential American President totally disposed to the Soviet ideal? God, what an espionage coup, Ward thought. The concept chilled him. Did the message mean that the candidate was a Marxist-Leninist or, as the media used to say, just a "fellow traveler"?

No, Orlov had not meant that. "Totally sympathetic" was the key phrase. The Democratic politician was one of them.

"That's incredible, Walter." Ward had used Rausch's Christian name for the first time. It had come out naturally and Rausch apparently didn't mind.

"Is it really possible," Ward asked, "that an American presidential candidate is an agent in place?"

"I don't know if he considers himself an agent. But Orlov's cable was clear. Like you, I'm overwhelmed."

"Do you think it'll be long before we know which candidate it is?"

"No. With the convention coming up, we should be hearing soon. There's only one problem. A renegade CIA man, Sam Withers, compiled a complete file on our man, then secretly left the Agency. Even our own people at Langley have no idea where he, or the file, is. But there's nothing you can do about that now. You've got to get ready for Oval Red."

Rausch hesitated. "Tom, Moscow tells me you're very talented. Not only in writing and politics, but in the manipulation of people. That's good, because your first job involves making friends in high circles, particularly in the Democratic Party."

"But where do I start? I have no contacts in Washington."

"Don't worry. We do. In fact, we have an immediate opportunity. My company, Doric Films, is producing a documentary film for the Democratic Party convention in New York. Much of the shooting is done, but we need a complete narrative script."

"Will I be doing the writing?"

"Yes, you can start immediately. In the process, you'll meet the main Democratic Party politicians. And socially, we have many friends in Washington. I'm hosting a party at my place Thursday night. It will give you a good start on Oval Red, whoever our man is."

"Will I personally be in touch with the *rezident* at the Soviet Embassy?" Ward asked, speaking of the chief KGB officer in Washington, someone with powers possessed by no mere Foreign Ministry bureaucrat.

"No, absolutely not. You are not to go near the embassy." Rausch's tone was firm. "Leave all the contact work to me. I handle four drops in the Reston area—where I pick up material from Baneyev at the embassy and leave whatever I have for him. But you must steer clear of all that. You're to be a clean-cut, charming young American with no political ties or strong ideological beliefs."

As they spoke, Rausch filled Ward in on the Soviet Embassy operation in Washington. Even in Moscow, Ward had heard about the extraordinary new building, opened only the year before.

In the old Soviet Embassy on 16th Street, Rausch explained, the KGB *rezident* was convinced that the FBI and the CIA were violating the secrecy of their radio transmissions to Moscow. The decision was made to build a new, secure embassy. The American government had cooperated by foolishly giving the Russians one of the highest points of land in Washington.

"It's called Mount Alto—three hundred and fifty feet above sea level, a large ten-acre piece of land near the intersection of Wisconsin and Massachusetts, not far from this apartment," Rausch explained. "First we built a nine-story apartment house, then a school and a gymnasium. Last year we moved the embassy there too. It's like a private city, fenced in and secure."

The new Soviet Embassy was ideal for electronic espionage, Rausch proudly told his colleague.

"Because of our high position, we have a straight line of electronic sight to the White House, the Defense Department, the State Department, most embassies, even the Congress and the CIA at Langley. We can listen in on most government phone conversations, even those from business offices and homes. Media, too, when we want to."

Ward was surprised. "Don't the Americans have an electronic defense?"

"Only secure phones, but they cost a fortune. Just the other day, CIA Director Springs was complaining that he needs thousands of them just to protect only the most vital communications."

Ward was intrigued by the American naiveté. "Can they do the same against us in Moscow?"

"No. During détente, they gave us their best piece of land and we gave them our worst—a parcel in downtown Moscow stuck between several buildings. It has almost no electronic access."

Ward was becoming optimistic about the work of an agent in this eccentric city of Washington. He picked up the folder of his life legend and glanced at it.

"I see I'm working at your place, Doric Films on K Street. Should I begin tomorrow morning?"

"Yes. We can talk about our next step in Oval Red."

Rausch rose. "Tom, please go through the legend and find out exactly who you are. Baneyev's invented a pretty interesting American."

Ward said his good nights and was soon on the bed, shoes off, reading the dossier of Thomas R. Ward, fascinated by his new self.

Chapter 14

Sam Withers had never swum so much in his life.

The beach and the ocean on the Outer Banks of North Carolina were the best medicine for isolation, the harsh waves keeping him from going mad.

Davidson had called an hour before, from a pay phone in the District.

"John, I don't know about this waiting," Sam had said. "What if the bastard locks up the nomination before we act?"

"Don't worry, Sam. I'll move quickly if and when the time comes. Just stay put. Okay?"

"You're the boss, John. But please keep on top of it. We can't afford to lose this one."

Sam slowed. "How's Mary?" he asked.

Withers missed his wife, his best, perhaps his only, friend—willing to put up with his monastic Agency existence and his repetitive tirades against the enemy.

"Have you spoken to Mary?" Sam repeated when Davidson failed to respond.

Davidson's throat contracted at the sound of her name. Only a crude noise left his mouth.

"John. You okay?"

"Oh, I'm fine, Sam," Davidson finally responded, disguising the pain. "And Mary's fine too. She sends her love."

"Good. Send her mine. I miss her." Sam hung up.

The swimming filled part of his days. During the rest, Sam read

and listened to music. On an old phonograph, he played World War II
vintage 78s. That day, his nimble fingers beat a tattoo to the percus-
sion of Benny Goodman's "Sing, Sing, Sing." Then Withers recalled
seeing cassettes and a portable Panasonic in a cabinet. He crossed the
room and searched through it for more oldies. One cassette remained
in his hand, bouncing repeatedly, apparently aimlessly, up and down
against his palm.

Sam hadn't examined the label, but it represented some elusive
thought trying to drill a hole in his memory. But what?

For no apparent reason, it started to unravel in his mind. He remembered another cassette, the one that held the incriminating taped
conversations of the Democratic candidate. He could hear himself
telling Granick:

"Jack. Wait until you listen to this. Like you said, a real sleeper."

It was clear. Granick's was the last place he had seen that cassette.
He couldn't recall Davidson ever holding or listening to it. Their
most convincing evidence against the Red candidate was missing.

Could it still be in the riverside house? Or was it already in the
hands of Baneyev?

Davidson had insisted he stay put, but Sam felt he had no choice
but to leave the sanctuary.

It was dusk, five hours later, when Withers arrived in River Falls in
the old Ford. He drove past 14 Waterview Road. No one was in sight.
Sam noticed a brass padlock on the front door, but he had no intention of using that entrance. After cautiously parking down the road,
Withers cut through a small wood and walked along the Potomac
banks, coming into Granick's river lawn from behind the house. The
padlock, Sam guessed, wouldn't be duplicated on the door to the
wooden porch, its screening pocked by age.

He was right. Withers took out a key Granick had given him and
entered the house, now mustier than ever. The coffee stains on the
rug by Granick's chair were still visible in the faint light. Sam walked
around the room, first aimlessly poking between the books and the
bound volumes of old *Harper's* and *Atlantic* dating back to the 1930s,
which seemed almost contemporary in this setting. He searched
through the random artifacts, hoping that chance would reward him.
But there was no cassette.

Withers sat on the couch, his body tilted to avoid the exposed
springs, staring across the room. What would the columnist have
done with the cassette after listening to it? Other than place it back in

the briefcase? His eyes halted for a moment on the tall country pine cabinet in which Granick kept the cassettes for opera, his other obsession. Granick's absent-mindedness was legendary. Was it possible?

Sam rummaged through the cabinet. Apparently nothing had been disturbed. First *Aïda*, then the more obscure *L'Italiana in Algeri*, then between *Don Giovanni* and *The Daughter of the Regiment* he noticed something. His hands moved back through the operas. There it was. A small unmarked cassette, whose dialogue was more shocking than any staged libretto.

Withers moved quickly out the side door, locking it after him. With the cassette secure in his pocket, he started across the soft lawn, back toward his Ford.

☆ ☆ ☆

Boris Mikhailovich Genshikov, a foot soldier in the army of Colonel Baneyev, was tired of sitting his life away in a car, or walking up and down the road near Granick's house in River Falls—as boring as his native village near Rechysta in Byelorussia—searching for someone who never came.

Did they really expect Withers? The less he questioned, the happier his days, he had learned. When in the car, he listened to black soul music on station WKYS-FM, tapping his foot in a clumsy approximation of the beat.

Today had been impossible. Hot and humid. It must have reached a hundred degrees, and he couldn't use the air conditioning. Running the engine would draw too much attention. He was pleased that he would be leaving in only a few minutes, at 7:30 P.M.

The worst assignments, he pouted, were saved for him. And because he was a peasant's son they ridiculed his failure to understand the niceties of the West.

Sergeant Teshovich, for one, had been bothering him lately.

"Genshikov, you look like a goon. What kind of clothes are those for someone living in America? I could spot you as KGB anywhere."

He had bought new shirts and pants, even a tie. But Colonel Baneyev laughed at his combinations. "With that Slavic head, it makes no difference. Genshikov, you still look like a *krestianin.* Peasant."

Then Baneyev laughed again, his voice tinged with sadism. "*Muzhik,*" he said, employing the insult for those who labored by brute strength.

They loved to harass him, but when real work, like taking care of the enemies of the Motherland, was needed, they weren't bashful about calling on him. Like killing nice ladies in their own kitchens. Would Baneyev soil his milky hands with such mischief? Never.

Now, at the end of another boring day, Genshikov was walking back to his car to meet his replacement when he saw someone get into an old Ford. He only noticed because of the North Carolina plates. Then, as he stared, the car started up and moved past him slowly.

He recognized the man at wheel. His face was a duplicate of the photo of Sam Withers, features that had been registered in his brain. The CIA man had returned to visit his dead friend after all.

Genshikov wrote down the license plate, which Teshovich could check through a contact in the Washington Motor Vehicle Service. But now he had to keep up with Withers. He started the engine of his new blue Oldsmobile, then began the chase, with no idea of where he was going or how far.

Chapter 15

The apartment intercom was ringing.

"Yes," he told the doorman. "I'll be right down."

Captain Peter Semanski—alias Tom Ward—had been in Washington only a few days, but he could already see that this capital, like Moscow, produced little except government and gossip. He expected to take naturally to both.

Rausch's chauffeur was waiting to take him to the Georgetown house where Walter had arranged a gala to celebrate the documentary and to introduce Ward to Washington.

Semanski had digested the fictitious legend Baneyev had created for him. Tom Ward was a foundling, born in a small Minnesota town at St. Olaf's School, one of the colonel's useful American institutions. The orphanage and its records had burned and Ward's birth could not be traced. He had supposedly been taken in and raised by a wealthy American expatriate family, Mr. and Mrs. Farring Jessups, nominally Republicans, but actually longtime Communist Party members.

From Minnesota, Tom had ostensibly been taken to the Jessups' home in Geneva, Switzerland, where he was educated by tutors. In Europe, the man called Ward was a free-lance film writer, a credential supported by producers the Center could count on. A contact in the U. S. Passport Office had fabricated a passport in Ward's name, but, he noticed, it had not been given to him—only pictured in the legend document.

He was now to make his first public appearance as Tom Ward.

Minutes after the intercom rang, Ward was in the chauffeured Mercedes, driving through the streets before passing over to Georgetown, a "village" that entranced Washingtonians no matter how long they lived there.

"Could you turn onto N Street?" Ward asked the driver. "I'd like to see the JFK house."

The driver slowed at 3307 N, the simple three-story Georgian home occupied by President and Mrs. Kennedy when he was a young senator. The car advanced a few blocks farther, then turned the corner onto a row of fine houses. Rausch's was a large, authentic black and white clapboard colonial. Outside, two giant lanterns flickered in the summer night like old London. The street was layered with chauffeured limousines, their drivers awaiting their capitalist-politician masters inside.

Rausch's lifestyle is reminiscent of that of Victor Louis, Ward mused, thinking of the mysterious Moscow journalist with prime contacts in the West who enjoys an existence of almost czarist splendor in a city of base mediocrity. Here's Rausch, a longtime KGB agent, who's not only respectable by American standards but living parasitically off both the Communist and the capitalist worlds. Life is more than irony, Ward concluded.

As he mounted the steps, he wondered whether Peter Semanski could pass among the sophisticated Georgetownians, who had surely met every shade of political agent and poseur.

He was dazzled by his first sight. In the hallway a willowy woman dressed in a white brocade gown with a black silk sash, her dark hair piled meticulously atop her head, was moving toward the door just as Ward entered. He looked at her, then at what seemed like a geometric apparition.

The foyer floor was a checkerboard of black and white marble squares, its center a five-pointed star. The woman, perhaps thirty, walked toward the center of the design, then stopped. Her pale, powdered complexion, the white gown, and her black hair and sash mimicked the stark configuration.

The woman burst into a luminous smile.

"Mr. Tom Ward. Am I right?"

"How would you know my name?"

"Easy. Two ways. One, I lie and tell you I'm psychic, which I might be anyway. And, two, just as the last limousine pulled up, Walter Rausch told me it was his—that he had you picked up at the apartment. So I put one and one together and figured the next man under sixty who walks through this door is Tom Ward. Rausch tells me I have to meet you."

Her beauty was obvious, but it was the cast of her almost chinawhite skin and her chocolate eyes he admired, an indefinable look of quality. Her features were sharp and distinct. Not Russian, which often were not so fine, but those of some princess from a long-vanished Central European monarchy.

"My name is Leslie Fanning," she said. "I'm the assistant to Governor Marc Daniels. Come inside and meet everybody."

In the tour of the room, Les—as everyone called her—introduced him to ambassadors, senators, congressmen, lobbyists. But Ward's eyes were focused across the room, on a face that was unsettlingly familiar. Larry Carver, the "State Department" man from Beverly Hills, was there, holding court.

Les pulled at Ward's sleeve, propelling him toward Carver. "Tom, I want you to meet somebody."

She made the introductions. "Tom Ward. Newly arrived in Washington. This is Larry Carver, a Washington party standby. Handsome, smart, and diplomatic. He's supposed to be in the State Department, but I think he's really CIA. Larry—Tom is working with us, writing the narrative for our convention documentary. He's a real talent, I understand."

Carver laughed.

"It's always a pleasure to meet any friend of Les's. But I guarantee you, Mr. Ward, the closest I've come to the CIA is reading spy novels. I hope you like Washington. Where are you from?"

Ward felt his first stirrings of discomfort. Carver was staring at him with professional intensity.

"Been living out of the country. All over Europe, doing film work. Geneva and elsewhere," Ward replied.

"I know Geneva well," Carver said with enthusiasm. "Was stationed at our consulate there for a year. We'll have to compare notes. *Eh bien?*"

Ward felt only relatively secure about Geneva. Last year he had spent five weeks there, at the Polish Mission to the United Nations on Chemin de l'Ancienne Route. Had the SB sent him intentionally? He didn't know the Swiss city intimately, but well enough, he expected, to escape a major gaffe. His French? He had studied in America and in Poland, and practiced it in Beirut. It was fluent, with only the slightest trace of an American accent, logical for someone who had first come to Geneva as a teenager.

"*Certainement,*" Ward said, hoping to exit that conversation.

Carver continued his scrutiny of Ward for a moment, then dropped the gaze. Ward was relieved. Stanislaw Wynoski seemed a century away.

"Ward?" It was Carver again, working on an afterthought. Tom looked up, apprehensive.

"Yes?"

"Did you spend much time at the Richelieu Bar? Great hangout? Ha?"

Ward couldn't recall the place. Was he being tested on locale? He should have boned up more thoroughly on Geneva, but who expected an American, maybe CIA, with that background at his first entry?

"Carver. I take it you're a real bar man," Ward said, sidestepping the question as he moved away.

Was there a Richelieu Bar hangout in Geneva at all? Had he already injured his legend?

Ward directed Les to a small couch against the wall. As they sat, he decided that she was delightful, listening more to Les's nuances than her words, watching her lips move excitedly as she spoke, casting a glance at her bosom cleavage.

Les was an ethnic "mutt" from Denver, he learned. The paternal granddaughter of a Hungarian prospector who never found gold and a Czech grandmother who raised ten children on nothing. Les's own father had worked the silver mines until he died young.

Her mother, daughter of an Irish immigrant, was stone poor until she remarried Michael Fanning, a department store owner who gave his only stepdaughter, Leslie, the best. From poverty to wealth in three generations. The American dream, Les proudly told him.

As Ward told Les his manufactured life story, which seemed to entrance her, his mind kept returning to his exchange with Carver.

He would have to check out the Richelieu. Meanwhile, he needed to focus on Les Fanning.

"What exactly do you do for Governor Daniels?" Ward asked.

"Well, Mrs. Daniels—Sally—prefers staying home on the farm with the kids. So I've sort of been appointed the governor's assistant, traveling companion, hostess, friend. Sometimes even mother," Les explained candidly.

Ward's professional curiosity was aroused. Was she trying to confide in him? He assayed this woman and her slightly slanted eyes. Beautiful she was. Clever and charming. But, he wondered, was she Daniels' mistress as well?

She seemed to be inside his mind. "Yes, I suppose I'm everything—except the governor's mistress," Les added.

Ward was unexpectedly distracted by someone standing over them. From his photographs, he could make out Governor Marc Daniels.

"Who's the victim?" Daniels asked Les as he bent toward the seated couple.

"Oh, Marc. I want you to meet someone. This is Tom Ward. Tom, this is my boss, Governor Marc Daniels of Illinois."

"Pleasure to meet you, Governor." Ward's arm stretched toward Daniels. "I'm with Doric Films, Walter Rausch's outfit. I've been writing the narrative for the new Democratic documentary."

"Oh? I've read the script outline. It's good stuff. Why don't you two move over and let me sit down? You can flirt later on."

Ward was exhilarated. His efforts for Oval Red were beginning sooner than he thought.

"How does your campaign look, Governor? I listened to the debate on the radio the other night and thought you did well."

"Thanks. I'm ahead—1400 delegates to less than 900 for Hankins, and about 680 for Katy Meredith. But it's frustrating. I need another 550 votes, otherwise either Hankins or Meredith could become serious contenders. Hankins talks peace to his boomers, but I don't believe he understands the Russians at all."

Ward's antenna was alerted.

"How do you see the enemy, Governor Daniels?" he asked.

"I believe they're paranoid, Tom. Dangerously so. The Soviets want only two things—world conquest and peace. We have to handle them like they're psychotic, never forcing them to face their own reality. They pretend to have the same goals of world harmony as we do. I say, let them. Once the pretense is broken, the danger begins."

Ward had never heard the Cold War explained in psychiatric terms. It was partly true, but Daniels was apparently another American who didn't understand how much subversion, how much blood, how much money, went into destroying their enemies—without a major war.

That was the key that eluded the West, Ward was sure. The constant, unspoken Soviet threat of war was their method of avoiding the war and winning it. The Americans had written a best-selling book—*Winning Through Intimidation*—about the technique. Weren't they aware that the Russians had penned the bible on it long before that?

"Didn't I tell you how brilliant he was?" Les offered, kissing Daniels on the cheek. "Don't be jealous, Tom. He'll make a great President. But he's happily married."

"Some kind of girl, Ward," Daniels responded. "I couldn't be in politics without her. As smart as she is pretty. A species of one."

With that comment, the candidate excused himself to circulate.

It was getting late, but Ward's first night in Washington society had produced substantial assets, particularly Les Fanning. He couldn't let the opportunity evaporate.

"Les, would it be all right if I took you home? I can borrow Walter's limousine or escort you in your own car. What do you say?"

Ward could sense Les studying him. He hoped she would find something sincere in his expression yet be unable to decipher the cynicism at its edges.

"My car will do, Tom," Les finally replied, leading him by hand toward the marble foyer.

As he opened the door, Ward's glance caught the eye of Larry Carver, who was also about to leave.

For all the night's success, Ward felt the jolt of an emotion he despised. Simple fear. Had he jeopardized Oval Red his first time out?

Chapter 16

It was midnight when Withers arrived back at the small beach house, sitting solitary on the crest of a dune, its slatted wooden deck jutting like a prow over the sand. He was tired after a total of ten hours in the old Ford. Tomorrow he would think how best to get the cassette to Davidson. Now he would mimic Granick and place it in his own music file, close to Benny Goodman, for safekeeping.

Each night Withers went through a short security routine. He double-locked the front door and closed the window jams. The switch for the burglar alarm, a Dictograph system activated when a door or window was forced, would be set last. First he would check the outside.

As Sam flicked the switch for the floodlights, the beams transformed the beach and the ocean waves into a chrome portrait. They were lit bright as day, but not from above as would the sun. More like a moon—actually five full moons—transmitting its light eerily only onto the object below.

Withers walked onto the wooden deck, peering over the railing out to sea. For a minute he watched the wave caps hitting the floodlit night. Then he turned, reentered the house, closed the door, and shut off the outside lights. He double-locked the deck doors and activated the alarm.

"How do you say it, American? After the cow has left the barn. No?"

Sam whirled instantly, his face only inches from the black barrel of a Luger aimed at his head.

"What the hell! How'd you get in here? Who are you?"

"Too many questions, Agent Withers. I am the man with the gun. Remember? How did I get in here? I followed you from Granick's. I was hiding in the sand, under the deck. While you were admiring your beautiful ocean, I climbed up and just walked in. Withers, I think you are a *muzhik*. No?"

Withers ignored the insult. His mind sized up the man, obviously KGB, as a brute, perhaps twice his own weight.

"You know you're not supposed to be in this area," Withers bluffed. "Your diplomatic immunity doesn't stretch to North Carolina. I could have you arrested. Why don't you just give me the gun, and we'll forget the whole thing. Okay?"

Genshikov smiled sadistically. His free hand left his side and, like a bullwhip, smashed across Withers' bony jaw. Withers fell to the wooden floor, his skin bleeding.

"That's the only immunity I need, CIA. You be a nice boy and get up. We're making another trip, back to Washington. You'll have plenty of room in the Oldsmobile trunk. No?"

Genshikov poked the gun barrel into Withers' face. "Now turn around and walk quietly out the front door."

Sam moved toward the door and was about to unlock it when the gun pressed harder into the back of his head.

"Stand still, CIA. I saw you set that alarm button. Now go back and release it. If the alarm goes off, your head goes with it. Understand? I am not so dumb, Withers."

Sam unset the alarm. The two men, one ruddy-faced and massive, the other small and lithe, walked out onto the dark, sandy driveway. Withers' mind turned over rapidly, seeking a strategy.

"KGB. You forgot something. Don't you want the file? Isn't that why Baneyev sent you to watch for me at Granick's? You can take me back, but they really don't want me. I'd just be another dead CIA man. They want the file."

Genshikov froze in place, confused by the crosscurrents of ideas Withers was throwing out. Teshovich had only told him to watch the Granick house and report who came by. In Withers' case, of course, he was to take him. The sergeant had said nothing about bringing back a file, but he knew that Withers was right. That's what they were crazily searching for.

It would make him a Hero of Socialist Labor. With that red rosette, he could get tickets to any hockey game in Minsk, probably Moscow as well. Even Baneyev would have to act with respect.

"You have the file, CIA?"

"Of course I have the file. What do you think this is all about?"

"Where is it?"

"On the beach."

Genshikov leaned over, smashing his calloused palm across Withers' face. Sam staggered from the blow.

"You are mad, CIA. An important piece of paper on the sand? Do you think I'm stupid?" He pressed the gun firmer into Ward's head.

"No. Not loose. It's in Granick's briefcase. I have it buried in the sand down by the ocean. No one comes here except me. It's the best hiding place."

More waves of thought, each one more upsetting to Genshikov than the last. The simplest thing would be to take the CIA man back in the trunk of his car and dump him in the embassy courtyard on Wisconsin Avenue. Let Teshovich worry his smart head over what to do next. But what if Withers were to tell Baneyev that the file was buried here in North Carolina and that Genshikov had refused to bring it back?

"All right, Withers. Take me to the file. But one bad try to fool me, and you are dead. File or no file. Get it?"

Sam picked his way back along the wooden path alongside the house, then up the dune. The large man behind was stumbling to avoid the tall grass that kept the hill of sand from eroding. First up the six-foot dune, then down the other side, with just enough light from the moon sliver to guide their way. The beach was deep at this point, and the two men trudged on. The giant stumbled and cursed in Russian, but the gun never relaxed in his hand.

"So, when do we reach it, CIA? Is there still more beach?"

"In a second. Here's the place right over here. You can see I have it marked with a beer can. I can also tell that it's right because it's sixty feet from the high-tide mark and exactly in front of my glass doors."

The KGB man turned his head quickly and tried to surmise if the dimensions were right. He guessed they were.

"Okay. Now start digging, Withers. Get the damn file, quick so we can go home." The beach had an unfamiliar feel for the inland Byelo-russian.

The burly man stood guard with his gun aimed at Withers, who was now crouched, his agile knees bent, his hand starting to scoop out the night-cooled beach.

He dug as Genshikov looked on, the impatience spread across his Slavic features. Once again Sam filled his two hands with sand, but this time he bounced his knees slowly up and down to coil his body.

As Genshikov's eyes moved away for an instant, Withers sprang upward, a small leopard casting sand into Genshikov's face.

The Russian was stiffened in surprise.

"Sukin syn! Son of a bitch!" Genshikov screamed in both languages, desperately rubbing the sand from his eyes, his mouth now frothing with the beach kernels.

Sam leaped up and propelled his body against the confused Genshikov, twisting the gun out of his weakened grip. As the weapon fell to the ground, both men lurched for it, but Withers' speed brought it up first. Lying on his side, Sam saw Genshikov about to leap. The gun went off in Withers' hand, the sound echoing only faintly over the roar of the waves.

Withers looked up into the bewildered expression on Genshikov's face as the bullet pierced the Russian's forehead like a clean arrow.

Sam got up and stood over the dead KGB man. *"Muzbik,"* he said. "Robert Doherty" could not afford a dead body on his beach front. Sam had to dispose of Genshikov and the Oldsmobile.

Withers knew he couldn't lift the massive corpse for more than a moment. Instead, he dragged the dead weight all the way, from near the ocean line across the sands. The dune was his nemesis. Inch by inch, he pulled the body up the incline. Not much different than building a pyramid in the desert, he imagined. The draining job took over an hour.

When he reached the car, Sam virtually crawled under the dead KGB man. A little at a time, he placed the body securely across his back, then lifted it by rising slowly off his knees. Once half standing, he arched his back, tightening his muscles like a spring. Then he flipped Genshikov through the open door onto the driver's seat.

Withers entered the car on the passenger side and put on the ignition. He pushed Genshikov's body toward the door, stretching over to negotiate the wheel and gas pedal from the passenger's side. Awkwardly, he drove the car slowly down the beach road, then turned inland toward the Sound. Sam went past several vacant lots, then saw one that would do. It was flat and dry and only marshy at the water's edge.

With the Olds in first gear, he moved across the land cautiously, stopping the car a few feet from the Sound. The Olds sat uneasily in a strip of mushy ground sprouting tall reeds.

Sam kept the engine idling and, with the emergency brake on, scoured about for a sizable rock, which he forced down on the accelerator pedal. Taking Genshikov's gun out of his pocket, he wiped off his own fingerprints, then pressed the Luger into the right hand of the corpse, turning the fingers into the correct firing position.

Now handling the Olds from the outside, standing next to the driver's seat, Sam placed the transmission in first gear and released the brake. The car moved, at first hesitantly, then picked up speed as it drove itself into the Sound, gurgling as it went.

Sam watched it sink beneath the water, then he turned and moved out onto the main road.

There was no way Genshikov could have made contact with the embassy on the trip down. Withers could only hope that the body, which would surely lead Baneyev to the Outer Banks, and to him, would not surface soon. At least the cassette was safe, stored alongside Benny Goodman's best.

There was nothing more he could do, except hope that Davidson was right in holding off. That the Red bastard would fail at the convention.

Withers kicked his foot aimlessly at some loose sand and began his solitary night walk back to the safe house.

Chapter 17

The Cosmos Club on Massachusetts Avenue was only a five-minute cab ride from the network office, but Doug McDowell feared it was a waste of time. It was a hot July afternoon and Davidson might be on his Leesburg farm rather than at the Cosmos for his weekly holding of court for the press and assorted intellectuals.

Davidson had agreed to see him on Friday morning, if he was in town. It was worth the chance. Not only was the riddle of Granick's death nettling him, but he had become personally uncomfortable with Granick's charge of sedition. Why? Did he feel on trial?

McDowell couldn't help it. It was as if Granick had accused him instead of some unnamed presidential candidate. McDowell had always resented the not so subtle implications of the right that liberals were less than patriotic. Granick's charge had only heightened that resentment. The whole thing was unsettling.

Maybe the old spy would have something useful to say.

The Cosmos was housed in a gray stone French turn-of-the-century Gothic mansion, once the home of the late Sumner Welles, patrician undersecretary of state during the Cordell Hull days.

Intellect, not affluence, was the admission pass to Cosmos membership. Washingtonians gossiped that money went to the Metropolitan Club, brains to Cosmos. Of course, Washington talent was increasingly learning how to cash in with New York publishers. But not Davidson. He had begun and ended his career in the CIA without exploiting his reputation. But that didn't diminish the stream of the curious who came by to pick at the memory of the veteran operative.

John the Baptist must be well over sixty-five, McDowell thought. He admired the way Davidson had fought back after resigning under a cloud as the supposed Soviet mole. He had reminded the news me-

dia that some of the top CIA men who had accused him of disloyalty
had since left the Agency and become active in the nuclear freeze and
anti-Star Wars movements. Who, indeed, was the mole? he asked.

McDowell thought Davidson was sometimes paranoid about national security. But he couldn't believe that the Baptist, however mis-
guided, could have been a Soviet servant.

Moments after McDowell's taxi drove up at the circular driveway
of the Cosmos, he was greeted by a retainer.

"Your name, sir?"

"Doug McDowell. I've come to speak with Mr. John Davidson—if
he's here. He knows me."

In a few minutes McDowell was led to the second-floor library, a
somewhat darkened, wood-paneled chamber. Davidson, book in hand,
was seated in a far corner in a leather wing chair, looking much a part
of the furnishings.

"McDowell, how nice of you to come."

Davidson's subdued tone was loud enough for McDowell, but he
could not be overheard by the few people on the far side of the room.
Privacy was important in the restrained world of the Cosmos.

"You're the first caller today," Davidson continued. "Sometimes—
in fact every week—I'm afraid that no one will remember John Davidson. Or think me important enough to talk with anymore. Then
I'll just be an old, retired bureaucrat. Sit down. What's on your
mind?"

The arrogant old bastard. As long as he occupied that wing chair
the parade of visitors would continue, unabated, McDowell knew.
Davidson had served six presidents and ten directors of the CIA, and
in his head he carried stories of Cold War intrigue that would make
all other memoirs—if he were to publish his, which he wouldn't—
bloodless by comparison.

Davidson sat there securely, looking feline, dressed in his three-
piece gray herringbone tweeds. With his hawkish face, he looked like
an aging actor considering his next line in the unwritten political
plays of the Western world.

"Mr. Davidson," McDowell began respectfully. "I'm driving myself crazy trying to figure out if I'm part of a bad dream or in the
middle of an intrigue that's too big for me. I need your help."

Davidson's expression sharpened as McDowell poured out the
story of Granick's visit. When the newsman had finished, Davidson
asked only one question.

"Did Granick identify the person named in the file?"

"No. He never got the chance. I threw him out first. Mr. Davidson, is there any possible truth in the whole thing? Could a Communist secretly infiltrate a major political party and become a candidate for President? Or is that just more conservative hogwash?"

☆   ☆   ☆

Davidson was uneasy. He presumed he was talking to the only person, besides Withers, who knew that Granick had once held the secret now hidden in the smokehouse of his Leesburg farm.

There was no need to tell McDowell anything about the file. But he could share political speculations, perhaps even influence him. Mc-Dowell could be a powerful ally in the Inner Cold War of Washington.

"Doug, I have no personal knowledge of the situation," Davidson lied. "But I can tell you—off the record—that we always had a few mavericks in the Agency who played around with domestic politics even though it was off limits. They may have come up with something. I really don't know."

McDowell seemed disappointed, which Davidson quickly read off his face.

"But why would you disbelieve it to begin with, Doug?" Davidson asked, hoping to draw out the commentator.

"I'm a liberal, Mr. Davidson. You know that. We're targets ourselves—all that talk of the media being soft on Russia and tough on our own government. Normally, I'd never have trusted Granick on anything about Communism. He was too right-wing, too obsessive. But, frankly, I was frightened by his murder. It seems like too much of a coincidence."

"Why wouldn't you trust Granick on anything about Communism? Don't you fear the Soviets as much as he did?" Davidson's manner was almost coy.

McDowell was nonplussed. "I suppose. But being a liberal gives me a different outlook on the Cold War. Don't you think there's room for disagreement?"

"I'm sure there is, Doug. But if you think being liberal gives you leeway on the Soviet Union, or on a strong defense, how do you account for Truman and JFK and Johnson?" Davidson asked. "Nobody doubted they were liberals. But all three were hawks against the

Russians. The Communists even called them warmongers. Am I right?"

☆ ☆ ☆

McDowell felt stymied. He could sense that the exploration had gotten past Granick and the file. Again, he felt on trial, one in which he was both prosecutor and defense attorney. But he was no Communist—far from it. So why was he resisting Davidson's argument? McDowell asked himself.

Was he afraid of being anti-Communist? The answer was revealing. Yes, he was afraid. But why? Who could penalize him for such a conventional idea?

That was the penalty, McDowell now realized. The fear that anti-Communism was conventional, a cage he had tried to escape by fleeing small-town provincialism of his youth. He thought of the enormous reward that escape had brought him. More, really, than he believed his mind, or his talents, deserved. To join the masses in their hatred of Communism would only label him as an anti-, or, at the very least, a non-, intellectual—not appreciably different from the people he was supposedly educating on the air.

Was he afraid to reveal his ordinariness to his peers, who really controlled his success? Perhaps even his self-esteem.

McDowell could see the old spy smile, a hint that he was husbanding a secret.

"Doug, you keep saying that you're a liberal. 'Liberal' is only a word, but it's become a tricky one. What would you say if I told you that the Communists have carried on a worldwide intellectual war based on that one word?"

McDowell nodded. He didn't have to agree with the Baptist. Davidson's reputation for anti-Communist paranoia didn't spring overnight from the primal ooze. But it wouldn't hurt to hear his diagnosis. At times like these, McDowell felt academically deficient. He covered well on television, but he feared that the front was less reliable in the company of the Davidsons of the world.

"Doug, in the fifties and early sixties I was called a liberal, working against Communism internationally," Davidson said, his tone confidential. "What they now call a hawk. But nobody doubted that I was a liberal. In fact, the left used to curse me. How? By calling me a liberal. It was then a bad word in the left lexicon. They called themselves leftists, radicals, Marxists. Whatever. The enemy was either capitalists, reactionaries, or liberals.

"But the more they cursed the liberals, the more of us there were. They were loosing the word war and the left wasn't used to that. When Orwell was in the Communist Party he was repulsed because they took over words like 'peace' when they meant 'Communist war.' "

"So why didn't they do the same thing with 'liberal' right away?" McDowell asked, enjoying the engagement of Davidson's mind.

"I think the word had become too dirty for them," Davidson smiled. "But about the mid-1960s they got smart. Instead of insulting people like me as being liberals, the left took the word for themselves. They became the 'liberals.' "

McDowell was intent. He had never heard the argument.

"Go on, Mr. Davidson."

"Well, what happened to us real anti-Communist liberals?" Davidson asked rhetorically. "We were now called hawks, or conservatives. Doug, my politics never changed. Just the words. I think it was all pulled off by a young Georgi Arbatov in the Soviet Union's U.S.A. Institute. He tied an honored word to being soft on Communism. It was brilliant—the great semantic trick of our time. And it worked."

McDowell rapidly tried to sift through the argument, to find a riposte, or even a clever query. But he came up blank.

"But to get to your first question, Doug," Davidson continued. "Could a Communist secretly infiltrate a major political party today and get the presidential nomination? The answer is yes. It would make infinite sense for a Communist to disguise himself as a liberal with a messianic peace message that played to the fear of the people. Yes, he could even get elected President of the United States. I hope that doesn't frighten you, but I think it's the truth."

The idea of a secret Red in the White House did frighten McDowell. But his own safety was a more pressing concern. He could visualize the bloated, overlarge body of Jack Granick floating lifelessly in the Potomac. McDowell began to sweat, despite the air-conditioned comfort of the Cosmos. He was trying to push away the thought when Davidson offered a parting word.

"And, Doug, if I were you, I wouldn't mention Granick's claim to anyone. With me, you're quite safe. Come to see me any time, particularly if you have some new information. But otherwise I would keep

my mouth strictly shut. It could be dangerous for you. Very dangerous."

Davidson's expression, which had been severe, suddenly softened.
"But, Doug, don't let me scare you too much, either. I spent all my
years in counterintelligence. It's a paranoid business, and we all have
that occupational disease."

Davidson extended his hand. "By the way, you did a great job on
that last televised debate. Now that I think back on it, I wonder
which of the candidates Granick was warning us about? See you."

As McDowell rose, his legs performed unsteadily. He paced himself slowly toward the door, which was opened by the retainer.

"Can I help you, sir? You look a little peaked."

The newsman smiled wanly. "I wish you could," he said, then
moved out onto Massachusetts Avenue and into the blinding sunlight
of a Washington July day.

Chapter 18

Ward woke in his apartment the morning after the Georgetown party
and riffled through the Geneva guidebooks Rausch had supplied with
his legend. There was no popular hangout called Le Richelieu. Carver's local trivia question was almost surely a trap.

Otherwise the evening had been a strategic success. After the party
he had spent a fruitful hour with Les Fanning in her brownstone
apartment on New Hampshire Avenue, talking about the campaign
and each other. Her connection to the Democratic Party hierarchy,
particularly front runner Daniels, perhaps Orlov's man, was invaluable.

As for the Geneva gaffe, Ward expected some unrewarding ramifi-
cation. It came sooner than expected.

"Your taxi's waiting outside," the doorman said as Ward moved
through the apartment house lobby a half hour later on his way to
work.

As the cab left the curb, a gray Ford Tempo pulled into the lane
and moved in behind the taxi. Ward swiveled his neck. Through the

rear window he could make out a familiar, large face. It was Larry Carver.

Ward leaned back into the seat, confused. Hadn't Carver—he now had to assume he was CIA—learned his tradecraft better than that? Making such an obvious tail, employing neither an unknown agent nor a personal disguise?

But why? Did a documentary film writer with a wounded legend merit such attention from counterintelligence?

When the obvious struck, more kinetically than expected, he realized he had been avoiding the possibility. Could the American have spotted traces of Stanislaw Wynoski, now deceased, in the transformed physiognomy of Thomas R. Ward?

Ward couldn't imagine how, but the thought pricked at him as the Tempo shadowed the rear of his taxi. Carver was so open, as if the surveillance were a child's carnival ride rather than one of the depressing businesses of the Cold War. What was going on? The amateurishness had to be purposeful. But to what end?

When Ward arrived at K Street, he couldn't swear to it, but he thought he saw Carver flash a quick wave of recognition as the Ford pulled away into the heavy rush hour traffic.

Chapter 19

Doug McDowell was torn. Davidson's warning to keep his mouth shut was well taken, but neither could he let the mystery die. If he snooped around, discreetly, perhaps he wouldn't have to join Granick in the District morgue. That is, if he really believed that the columnist's death was a political penalty.

Samuels had asked for some "perspective" pieces for the Democratic convention, now less than two weeks away. They were an ideal cover.

McDowell traveled to the Hill by cab, stopping at the marble mausoleum, the $150-million Philip A. Hart Senate Office Building on Constitution Avenue, where Senator Jed Hankins had his offices.

"What can I do for you, McDowell?"

Bill Fenton, Hankins' AA—administrative assistant—was surprised by the unannounced visit. "We're busy as hell getting ready for the convention. But I can spare a few minutes—if it's important."

McDowell knew Fenton as probably the most astute staffer on Capitol Hill, one of a hundred AAs, or "junior senators." Though not elected by the people, they earned almost as much as their bosses and wielded near-equal power. With senators tied down by political commitments, their places are often taken, virtually everywhere except on the Senate floor, by their alter egos. Of whom Fenton was a model.

With his perpetually unsmiling face, tortoise-rimmed glasses, pinched features, stern expression, and blue serge suit—even on this sweltering July day—Fenton struck McDowell as more fundamentalist preacher than politician. McDowell knew that the AA was a graduate of a Baptist seminary in his home state of Alabama, but he obviously preferred the moral arena of politics, with its chance for larger jousts with God, to the simple sparring of a rural ministry.

"Yes, Bill, it's important," McDowell assured him. "It's about the network convention coverage. Do you have anything special that might make a good feature?" McDowell's pause was deliberate. "I'll tell you what I'd really like. Some controversy. Some tough talk about your opposition."

"There is one thing, Doug," Fenton responded, seeming eager to contribute. "Jed's going to push the military preparedness issue. Governor Daniels likes to pretend he's balanced on defense, but we think it's all a smoke screen. When it comes to spending money on the real hardware—ships, tanks, new divisions—he's out to lunch. All he ever talks about is missiles and Star Wars. High-tech weapons which we'll never use."

"Why do you think Daniels talks that way?" McDowell was pleased that Fenton was opening up.

As Fenton contemplated, McDowell could see behind the spectacle lenses to his alert pupils. Maybe even farther back to the swirling cortical cells. Like other media people, he was in awe of Fenton's fertile brain, an unnatural canniness which he envied, but which sometimes frightened him.

"I can't say for sure, Doug," Fenton finally answered. "But it worries me. I don't think Daniels can be trusted as President. Either to make peace with the Soviets on a realistic basis or"—Fenton halted for an instant—"or to make our conventional defenses modern enough to dissuade Russia from war. I'm not really questioning his patriotism. But . . . well . . . maybe I am. I don't know."

Fenton finished with a satisfied grin. "I don't suppose there's a story there, but I thought I'd tell you anyway."

McDowell left more confused than ever. Was Fenton really implying that Daniels was less than patriotic? Had he stumbled on something useful?

Over the next hours McDowell reached several of the candidates or their aides. All answered his questions, but McDowell was no less frustrated. Where did he get the notion that a covert Communist plan to infiltrate the Democratic Party would surface in open conversation? How naive could he be?

The Metro was the easiest route from the Hill to the Daniels' headquarters on K Street. McDowell entered the subway at the Capitol South station and approached the computer to buy a Farecard. He was reaching into his pocket for a dollar bill when he felt a rude nudge in his back.

Someone was trying to force his way toward the machine. He turned to face a bearlike man in a colored T-shirt—unshaven in days, his face wearing a smirk.

"Sorry," the man said. "We're all a hurry. Right?"

McDowell didn't respond, just bought his ticket and moved through the turnstile and down to the platform. The station was clogged with House and Senate employees on their way home. McDowell stood near the front of the platform, waiting for the train, mentally sketching his interview with Daniels. Would it be wise to repeat Fenton's veiled charge?

He didn't appreciate the crowds piling up behind him. McDowell was trying to hold his position near the front so that he could board quickly, when out of the darkness he could make out the train emerging from the rail cavern, its light brightening as it moved silently in on rubber wheels.

As it approached the station, McDowell prepared himself, inching carefully forward.

When the lead train was only fifty feet away, McDowell was startled by a sharp jab in the small of his back. It propelled him forward almost a foot until he stopped, uncomfortably close to the edge. But before he could swivel his head to see who, or what, was responsible, he was hit again.

This time he could feel the powerful thrust of two large hands wedged between his shoulder blades.

"Watch out! Watch out!" someone screamed.

It was an instant of panic. He could feel his body now angled off the horizon, his feet leaving the ground in a free fall toward the lip of the concrete platform. Out of a corner of his moving eye, he could make out the front of the train coming toward his falling body—on a collision trajectory.

Only inches more to death, his mind calculated. An ignominious conclusion for a young man on the rise.

He was saying good-bye in that millisecond when suddenly an arm —he remembered the patch of black hair covering it—shot under his body as it fell, braking, then girdling it. Before he knew what was happening, the arm was joined by another and McDowell was pulled, like a stretched rubber band, back onto the platform. Less than a second before the train passed.

"What the hell were you doing so near the edge of the platform?" the Samaritan said. "You sure came close to killing yourself. Real lucky I grabbed you. Jesus."

McDowell was now seated cross-legged on the Metro floor, his breath irregular, the heart almost audible, peering up at his Samaritan. It was the same unshaven man who had pushed him at the fare machine.

"That was close," McDowell said between breaths. "Thanks for saving me."

The smile of the bearlike man was pasted on. Should he be thanking him? Or charging him with attempted murder?

"That's all right, Mr. McDowell. I recognized you from the TV. Jesus. If I was you, I'd stick to broadcasting and forget running around Washington on the Metro. That's for guys like me."

With that, the man moved into the open train, leaving McDowell on the ground. He sat for a minute before being helped to his feet by bystanders.

Instead of going to Daniels' headquarters, McDowell returned to the network on the next train. Was the Metro "accident" some kind of warning? he wondered. If so, it was perversely producing the opposite effect. What was happening to him? Could he be experiencing hallucinations of physical bravery? Perhaps. But, except for Meg, he would still keep his mouth shut about Granick while he pursued any leads.

At L Street, McDowell told Meg the story of the Metro incident.

"Doug, I'm sure the whole thing's a coincidence," Meg reassured him. "I think Granick's driving you nuts from the grave. Can't you forget that crazy man?"

She was probably right, McDowell thought. But his need to know was now obsessive, and despite Meg's skepticism, he decided to enlist her help.

"Meg, I'm going to do a separate network segment on each of the candidates. Real person-to-person stuff, at their homes. I'll take Daniels. Would you like to do one? It could be a good break for you. Right on camera."

Meg brightened. "Gee, Doug, that's great. Yes, I'd like to interview Hankins. He's an exciting candidate—and a bachelor. When do you want me to start?"

"I understand he's at his place in Virginia right now. Why not set it up?"

McDowell waited, somewhat embarrassed.

"Meg. I know how you feel about the Granick business, but I'd like you to do me a favor. When you're out at Hankins Farms, could you keep your eyes and ears open? Maybe learn something that would point me in the right direction? Okay?"

Meg's look at McDowell was one of near reproach.

"I think you've gone bananas, Doug. But sure. Why not? I'll call you soonest if I learn anything."

Chapter 20

Meg Larsen was no ordinary newsgirl and she knew it. She worshiped beauty and money, and the thought of meeting Hankins at his fabled estate was setting off pleasing fantasies in her mind. Never had she been confronted with so much wealth and power in one person.

She had been primping for an hour in the Silver Spring condominium apartment, rising early in her bedroom, its walls covered with flowered chintz. She laid out her best summer frock, a coral gauzelike silk that displayed her figure, and a long string of oversized pearls. Moving quickly to dress, Meg was soon in her blue Jaguar to begin the drive to Hankins Farms, the senator's 700-acre horse breeding station in the rolling northwestern countryside of Virginia.

Ninety minutes later Meg drove up the *grande allée* of tall oaks, expecting an antebellum mansion at the end of the driveway. She was not disappointed. Hankins' great-grandfather, the original Jedidiah Hankins, had built Homestead in 1877, a pillared three-story mansion only once removed from pre-Sherman Atlanta.

As Meg approached the gravel courtyard she could see a tall man in blue denim waiting on a bay.

"Hi, Miss Larsen. Is that you?"

It was Senator Jed Hankins, seemingly spontaneous, greeting her on horseback. A clever pol, she thought. Hankins dismounted and they walked together onto the mansion's colonnade entrance.

"It's too much, right?" Hankins asked, the embarrassment of riches on his face. Meg felt no such emotion, only envy for someone who lived like a Renaissance prince in a prosaic era.

"Senator, by thirty-nine you should be used to your money," Meg answered. "Why not enjoy it? I know the public does."

Hankins laughed. "I suppose it's a problem everyone would like to have."

After his father had died two years before, Meg recalled, Hankins' financial disclosure showed a net worth of $278 million, which some analysts felt was understated.

The camera crew had already set up in the elegant marble-floored sunroom.

"Senator Hankins. What makes a superrich man like you get so involved in liberal politics?" Meg began the interview as the video tape rolled. "What are you trying to prove?"

"Nothing, Miss Larsen."

Meg could see the annoyance develop at the borders of his mouth.

"A lot of poor people are archconservatives and so are my rich neighbors. I'm just a liberal politician who worries about the people who can't pay their heating bills and are afraid of nuclear holocaust. Could we forget about my bank account—for once?"

Hankins was now more confident, showing the opposite side of his self-consciousness.

"How do you see our relations with the Soviet Union, Senator?"

"They scare the hell out of me. Every day in the Senate we wrestle with the Cold War. I'm convinced we're all going to die in a nuclear war unless we change."

Hankins' pause was polished. "I'd like to propose a deal with the Soviet Union. That we both allot one percent of our defense budgets to feed an African nation. That's a better use for money than all our missiles. Don't you think?"

Meg glanced at the camera crew, who were fastened on the senator. Hankins had good magic, she could see, playing both sides of the street. The rich playboy and the concerned statesman.

The ten minutes of questioning went quickly.

"Why don't I give you a tour of the place?" Hankins asked when the interview was over. "You can have your camera people follow and photograph the happy couple."

Meg carefully avoided the personal comment. "Sure. Doug would like that. Show us the way."

They visited the track where one-year-olds were being fussed over by their racing trainers, then to the Grand Pavilion, the ritual heart of the farm—an enormous structure with a striped cloth roof. Meg could imagine the lavish receptions held for winning horses, family weddings, even political galas to impress the rural voters.

Their last stop was the breeding shed, where future Hankins Farms champions were conceived.

"Why don't we take a look?" Hankins asked ingenuously. "Just as long as the cameras don't roll."

At the end of a barnlike structure, Meg could see a mare struggling as men placed a blanket over her back and tied up her left front leg with a stout belt.

"We do that to protect both the mare and the stud," Hankins explained. "Otherwise, she might kick him when he mounts. It's better for the mare to relax and enjoy it."

"But does she enjoy it under these circumstances?" Meg asked, her tone provocative.

"I don't know. Now you've asked me a political question, Meg. Whenever I debate women's rights, I'm told women enjoy making love as much as men. Is that true?"

Meg looked at him with mock annoyance. "Senator, let's stick to horses."

At that moment the stallion, a twelve-year-old chestnut, a cousin of Studs Lonigan, Hankins' own prize thoroughbred, was brought up behind the mare. The stud lifted his front legs and mounted her rear, breathing heavily. Meg could see him forcing his penis—which to her looked surprisingly like the human organ, if several times the size—into the mare's vagina. Once in, the stud pushed his 1200 pounds onto the mare's backside with each purposeful thrust, moving rhythmically in and out for about three minutes, making grunting, horselike sounds. Then, suddenly, the stud came into the mare with a fury.

The attendant gave the stud a moment to rest before leading him away, his job completed.

Meg's face was flushed as much in excitement as embarrassment. "My God, that was something to see," she finally commented.

She could sense Hankins reacting as well.

"I hope it's been a good day for you," Hankins said as they walked toward her car. "I don't know the professional ethics, but I am a bachelor. Do you think we could see each other for dinner sometime?"

Bowing low to enter her Jaguar, Meg peered up.

"I'd love to, Senator. But I must warn you. I don't go for that business of tying up a woman's legs."

Meg smiled enigmatically, then turned the ignition. As she drove up the *allée*, she could make out Hankins standing there, his mouth almost agape.

☆ ☆ ☆

A mile down the road, Meg located a phone booth outside a gas station. She parked, sifting through her purse for enough coins to call the District. The experience had left her suffused with energy. She couldn't wait to report in.

Meg dialed the Washington 202 area code, then the number. Impatiently she waited for the ring. First one, then two. Finally a voice at the other end. It was not the polished diction of Doug McDowell but a thin voice with a trace of a German accent.

"Hello. May I speak?" Meg asked nervously.

"Yes," the voice answered. "It is clear."

"Walter. I'm calling from outside Hankins Farms." Meg was almost breathless in her enthusiasm. "I spent all morning with Hankins. He's someone we have to start cultivating. Rich and naive. And very promising. He could become President. If not this time, then next. I think I'll be seeing him socially. Let me know if there's anything special I must learn."

"Good," Walter Rausch answered. "You've done well. Go home and take it easy. I'll speak with you tomorrow. And, Meg . . ." He hesitated. "I'll see if I can get you a small bonus. Maybe a couple of thousand."

☆ ☆ ☆

Rausch hung up, confident he had been right to encourage Larsen. She had become a solid arm of his Washington apparatus. Meg had already led them to Granick, whom Baneyev had killed. And Granick had brought them to Withers, who was still loose.

She had now made a possibly intimate contact with a candidate for the presidency of the United States. Who knew? Hankins might even be the man of Oval Red.

The young woman was confirming the new equation of espionage. Mercenary Americans like her, without ideology, were proving the most trustworthy of KGB agents. The power of money in America, Rausch thought. The absolute power of money.

Chapter 21

John Davidson was surprised by the early morning phone ring. It was still not 8 A.M.

"Yes, who is this?" he asked, a bit surly, he was ashamed.

"John, sorry to call so early. This is Al at Langley."

"Al Springs? What a surprise." Davidson paused. "I presume we're being recorded for posterity, Mr. Director."

"No, I gave orders. The line's clean. John, you offered to help out on the Mary Withers killing. We're sure it was Baneyev, but part of a larger operation. We hadn't a clue, but one of our people in Vienna tells us Orlov has sent an illegal to Washington on some big project. We don't know who or what, but I think it's tied to the Withers file."

"I'm glad you've got a lead, Al. But how can I help?"

"John, Sam's the key. If we can find him and the file, we'd know what the hell is going on."

The line turned silent for an instant. "John, you two were an unholy duo. Don't you have any idea where Sam is?"

It was not easy to rebuff Springs, an old compatriot in the CIA wars.

"Al, I'd love to help out, but I haven't spoken to Withers for ages," Davidson dissembled. "I fear retirement has taken hold too well."

Davidson could sense the disappointment at the other end. "Al," he continued. "On that illegal—are you following up?"

"Yes, John. I've put Larry Carver on it. A relatively new man. I understand he had a lead. He hasn't told us anything yet, but I expect something concrete soon."

"Can he be trusted?"

"I sure hope so. So far, his record's excellent. He took out a double in San Francisco, a Czech working in Silicon Valley. And, John . . . Please keep your eyes open for Sam. We need him badly."

The director allowed himself a moment's contemplation. "John, we all miss you here. Damn it. We do."

"Al, the feeling is mutual. We had a few glory days, didn't we?"

Chapter 22

Why was Carver toying with him? Was there a leak on Oval Red?

If Carver wanted to play, Ward decided, he would reciprocate. He would let himself be followed in the open. Then *mokroye dyelo.* Simply kill Carver. Time had narrowed his alternatives. The Democratic convention was less than ten days away.

Soon after he woke in the Massachusetts Avenue apartment, Ward stripped the dull sheaths from the scissors and placed the rapier knives into his suit pockets. A rented Buick Skylark was waiting when he emerged from the building. He searched about but there was no Ford Tempo in sight. Ward feared an absent Carver even more than his presence.

He started down Massachusetts Avenue, somewhat disappointed, but at the first traffic light Carver's large image appeared in the rear-view mirror. He had sharply swerved the Tempo and pulled up at the rear bumper of the small Buick.

Ward smiled at the audaciousness of the Langley man. The most eccentric surveillance he had ever seen. Crossing the bridge, Ward headed into Virginia, glancing back periodically. The Tempo was still behind, the two cars seemingly attached by an invisible string.

On the Beltway, Ward headed north out of Washington, then onto Route 270, driving for an hour until the metropolis faded and the land

took on the isolated look of the hilly, wooded country of northwestern Maryland. Ward exited the highway, using his right directional
blinkers to alert Carver. To the west, the land became less populated,
until ahead Ward could see dirt roads branching off. He abruptly
turned onto one of them. In a small clearing in a wood he stopped the
Skylark. Not a home or a person was visible.

The two cars were now parked fifty feet apart, both men behind
the wheel, judging, waiting.

It was Carver who made the initial move. With his arms not quite
raised, but dangling far enough from his body to suggest a gesture of
peace, he came out of the Tempo and walked up against a tree.

Ward knew it was his turn. With one hand grasping the blade in his
pocket, he advanced toward Carver, halting a dozen feet short.

"What's up, Carver?" Ward asked. "Ever since we met at Rausch's
party, you've been following me. Why?"

"That shouldn't be any surprise. I spotted you right away, Ward.
You're Wynoski—Stanislaw Wynoski, the chubby Polish geneticist."

Ward's face displayed shock. All the Center's obfuscation in Beverly Hills had been futile.

"How the hell did you know that, Carver? Damn it, how did you
connect Tom Ward with Wynoski?"

"It was easy, Ward. First, I played the Richelieu trick on you at the
party. When you avoided the question, I suspected something."

"But surely that couldn't give you a hint about Wynoski."

"No, but then I listened to your voice."

"My voice? Carver, you never heard my real voice in Beverly Hills.
I was speaking with a phony Polish accent, and higher than usual.
How could you spot that?"

"It wasn't that delivery I heard. Remember the maid. She's with
the Agency. When you talked to her through the door, you forgot
yourself for a moment and spoke normally. She was carrying a mini-
recorder. I listened to the tape over and over, memorizing your voice,
figuring you might become an illegal. When I heard you speak at
Rausch's party, I knew you were Wynoski."

Ward was experiencing confusion.

"If you knew I was Wynoski, why didn't you have the FBI pick me
up? I don't get it."

Carver didn't respond immediately. He started toward Ward, his
smile knowing.

Ward waited for the CIA man to attempt the arrest he had once delayed, for whatever reason. Carver was now less than ten feet away and still moving, one hand sweeping toward his inside jacket pocket.

Ward discarded indecision. He leaped, grasping the CIA man's neck in a wrestler's grip, the scissor-knife suddenly at the carotid artery.

"Don't move, Carver. Or you're dead. I don't know why you walked into this trap, but it's your last—and worst—piece of tradecraft."

Carver's eyes registered everything.

"Ward," he breathed through the tight grasp. "Hold off. We Americans are not that stupid. Like you said, I could've taken you in any time. But I followed you openly so you'd make this move—bring me to a private place of your choosing. Before you do anything rash, I've got to show you something."

Carver stared up at Ward's resolute face.

"Can I take my hand out of my pocket now? I've got a picture to show you."

Forcing the knife in, rupturing that main artery, was the surest end to this encounter. But Ward's curiosity had been piqued. He hoped it wouldn't cost him.

"All right, Carver, but easy does it. Take the hand out slowly. If something other than a picture emerges, it's all over. *Capisce?*"

Carver nodded painfully, slowly offering the snapshot to Ward's vision.

Ward could make out some medieval buildings. It looked like a village in Germany or Austria. There were two men in business suits standing together. Carver on the left, and another man, with a peculiarly thin, pale face perched over a heavily muscled torso, on the right. It was Colonel Baneyev, the Washington KGB *rezident.*

"What are you doing with Baneyev?" Ward asked, startled. "What's going on?"

"That's why I followed you, Ward. To tell you that you're safe. I'm part of Baneyev's apparatus."

Ward waited, uncertain.

"Why should I believe a CIA man who wants to save his neck?"

"I don't blame you, Ward, but I can prove everything. I'm an American, but I've been with Baneyev ever since college, when he recruited me and had me infiltrate the Agency. Like the Russians say, I'm *nashi.* If you relax your knife, I can give you my bona fides."

Ward had come to eliminate a CIA threat and was now being told
he had a compatriot serving as a double for the KGB.

"Sure as hell I'm not going to trust you, Carver. But I don't want to
kill one of my own people either. Let's move to that rock. I'll keep the
knife in your side while you answer some questions. I hope they're
good."

Carver nodded and the two men moved, Ward still cautious.

"All right, Carver. First off, who's my control?"

"Jesus, Ward. You know I wouldn't know that—CIA or KGB. Each
man to his own box."

"Good. But if you want to live, you have to answer this one. Do
you know Orlov?"

"Colonel Orlov at the Center? I don't know him personally. How
would I? But Baneyev has mentioned him. Seems quite impressed.
Little guy, about five-three. He's at Teplyy Stan. Right?"

"Carver, you're either *nashi* or a damn good CIA man. Which is it?"

"Come off it, Ward. You know I wouldn't have trusted you in the
damn Maryland hills alone if I wasn't for real."

Carver's eyes were suddenly hopeful. "I know how to convince
you."

"How?" Ward was almost enjoying the exchange.

"You're Polish—not Russian—aren't you? From Warsaw? Right?"

Ward was initially impressed, then he remembered.

"That's not much of a feat, Carver. You heard me speak Polish to
Dr. Pitok in Beverly Hills. Warsaw? Who isn't in Poland?"

The CIA man's face was suddenly bathed in confidence.

"True. But I also know who you really are. Captain Peter Semanski, SB Serial 0-958-489."

As Ward heard the sound of his name, he first tensed, then felt the
knife involuntarily relax in his hands.

"How the hell would you know that, Carver? What's the story? Are
you involved in my mission?"

"No, but last week Baneyev asked me to find out if the CIA had any
computer information on a Captain Peter Semanski. I got out your
file—we had something on you from Beirut—and sent it to him by
microdot. I just put two and two together. If you're a new Polish
illegal and Baneyev was worried what CI had on you, Ward—who
was Wynoski—could well be Semanski. Right?"

Ward started to laugh, the desperate nature of his work tickling a
macabre side of his spirit.

"Carver. You're pretty good. Yes, I believe you now. I suppose I did right away. Nobody but a double or an idiot would have tailed me that way. You had to be inviting me to rendezvous."

Ward stopped. "I'm glad you're on our side." He placed the knife back in his pocket, but out of survival habit his hand stayed curled around its steel hilt.

"Can you tell me what you're here for, Semanski?" Carver asked.

Ward looked at him disapprovingly. "No. If that's the only reason you chased me down, you've wasted your time."

"I understand. I have no need to know. No, the reason I forced this rendezvous was because you goofed on Geneva. I didn't want you to worry, and I knew you'd consider a bit of 'wet business' unless you knew the truth. I couldn't turn you in, so if I was going to save my skin I had to play the game I did. Right?"

Ward smiled. "Right, Carver. But I must tell you that you scared the life out of me."

"No more than me, Semanski. No more than me."

As the two men started toward their cars, a thought diverted Ward.

"Carver, do you know a CIA man named Sam Withers? He's not my assignment, but it's hanging over my head."

"Sure. He's in counterintelligence with me. Or at least was. A few weeks ago he flew the coop. Scuttlebutt says he took an important file with him. But nobody knows what or why."

"I have almost all the answers to that, Carver. But I could use some help in finding Withers. Any ideas?"

"I don't know, Semanski. Sam's a real soldier. And a canny damn fox. I wouldn't have any idea where he's hiding, but if I get anything I'll start tailing you again. We can meet here. Okay?"

"Thanks." Ward moved toward his rented Buick. As he was about to lower himself into the seat, he was pricked by an unsettling idea.

"Carver. Since you're on our side, why would you try to trick me on Geneva to begin with? Wouldn't it have been easier just to produce your bona fides, without all this? Or . . ." Ward was caressing the rapier blade.

"Or what?" Carver asked.

"Or maybe you really are an Agency man, tricking me to learn my identity and mission."

"Semanski, now you're smoking it," Carver said. "You know as well as I that I'm *nashi.*"

As the word exited his mouth, Carver's hand darted toward his inside pocket. Simultaneously, he leaped, stomach first, to the ground, his body prone in the dirt.

Ward reacted instinctively, leaping at Carver's hand, which was coming uncoiled, revealing a revolver raised almost high enough to fire. As Carver was about to pull the trigger, Ward's rapier reached the outstretched arm, the knife ripping through the tendons, the gun immediately limp in a bleeding fist.

"*Nashi*, are you?"

Ward's voice was contemptuous as he retrieved the gun out of the dirt and raised it over Carver's head.

"I must say, Carver, you did one hell of a job."

Ward fired the single shot into Carver's skull, the noise resounding like a car backfire in the otherwise mute Maryland countryside.

Chapter 23

Twenty-five hundred miles away, San Bernardino Detective Sergeant Pete Fuller sat in his office in the downtown county courthouse on that miserable summer day, the temperature approaching a hundred, his beefy hands toying with a dossier.

"Wynoski, Stanislaw T., Polish National," read the label on the manila cover.

Fuller's eyes were drawn to it, over and over. Almost a month had passed since the California Highway Patrol found the charred body in the Mojave Desert and turned the case over to him in the sheriff's office. "San Berdu," as the old-timers called the burgeoning town, was the gateway to the desert, the seat of the nation's largest county, stretching across almost twenty thousand square miles of sand to the Nevada border.

The murder had been covered by the neighboring Los Angeles papers in sensational detail. Why, everyone wondered, had a supposed Polish scientist attending a convention at the Beverly Hills Hotel been kidnapped and murdered in the desert? And his body burned?

No one wondered as much as Fuller. Tall and tomato-faced, the homicide squad veteran was more a caricature of a Texas Ranger than an urban California detective. He had none of the answers, but the bizarre nature of the case intrigued him.

Since there were no suspects, his superiors had decided that it was probably just another random, aberrational California murder. Fuller had accepted that script, but only because he had no other answer.

But now, obsessed with the mystery, he was less inclined to accept it. Not that he had any new evidence. The FBI file on Wynoski had said that he was probably a KGB agent but, with the subject dead, the FBI had closed the case.

Fuller had no witnesses, not even a theory. All he had was his dossier. He had studied it for tedious hour after hour, searching for a discrepancy. Then on that searing day in San Bernardino, heat that can make that inland part of California onerous even to the native born, Fuller noticed something. Maybe valuable, maybe not. One word stood out from the others. FBI agent Martin Rourke had described Wynoski as broad around the middle—or "portly."

How did that compare with the actual corpse? Fuller knew that the shape of charred remains cannot be taken as fully reliable. Yet he remembered the moment he had first looked at the body, much of which had been saved, probably after the gasoline burned off in the desert air. The burned clothes clung to the remaining muscles and bones in what seemed to be straight proportions from the chest to the waist. There was no "portly" stomach bulge evident.

The official theory of a random crime was based on one simple assumption. That Wynoski was Wynoski. But what if the burned corpse belonged to someone else? And the real Wynoski was still alive?

Fuller was afraid he had made a colossal error on the ID. Instead of asking the Polish government to supply dental films of Wynoski, he had sent the X rays of the corpse's teeth to the Polish Consulate in Chicago. It was Wynoski, the answer came back. Sure, but the ID was meaningless if the consulate was part of some unknown plot. There was nothing Fuller could do about it now.

The "portly" lead from the FBI excited him, but Fuller needed expert counsel. He drove to the County Hospital, where he pushed open the door of Deputy Coroner Mike Prestor.

"Can you spare a minute, Doc?" Fuller asked. The room was cluttered with exhibits and anatomical charts, lining not only the walls but set up on spare tables, including an old bridge fold-up. Prestor had been a deputy coroner for almost twenty years and his forensic skills were respected, even by colleagues in the arrogant big-sister city of Los Angeles.

"I've got an idea on that Wynoski killing," Fuller told the medical examiner, who was bent over a microscope, his remaining rim of hair facing Fuller.

"What's going on, Pete? I've never seen you so taken by a case," Prestor commented, looking up from his work.

"Well, I admit it's driving me a little nuts, Doc. But maybe I've come up with something."

In his deliberate manner, Fuller explained his theory that Wynoski dead might not have been the same person as Wynoski alive.

"Is it possible my hunch is right, Doc?"

"You can never be sure with burned corpses, Pete," the deputy coroner equivocated. "Let me take a look at the case record."

Fuller stood over his shoulder, lip-reading the report, but the medical jargon escaped him.

"Well, what do you think, Doc?" Fuller asked when the file was finally closed.

"You may be onto something, Pete. The report shows that the fire didn't destroy the body wall. The stomach muscles in front of the abdomen were mainly intact. The muscle sheets were thick, the sign of good tone, like in a young man who was in shape. There were no signs of excess fatty tissue around the center. I'd say that your corpse didn't have a spare tire when he was alive. I'm pretty sure that the guy was not—how did the FBI agent say it?—'portly.' "

Prestor put down the file. "Does that help you, Pete?"

"You bet," Fuller responded.

The homicide detective returned to his office, encouraged but confused. If it wasn't Wynoski who was murdered in the desert, how did the real Wynoski get out—or get taken out—of the Beverly Hills Hotel without being seen by the FBI agents or their elaborate film surveillance? The FBI had played the footage repeatedly, with no sign of Wynoski exiting, either alone or with the abductors.

Fuller dialed the FBI office in L.A. "Rourke? This is Fuller, San Bernardino Homicide. Hi. I'm going through the Wynoski file for the eightieth time, and I finally have an idea. Maybe you can help out."

"What is it, Fuller?"

"About your movies. Instead of trying to spot Wynoski, why not concentrate instead on anyone going out of the Beverly Hills who isn't shown coming in? It could be someone in disguise, either Wynoski or his kidnapper. What do you think?"

"Sounds like a good idea, Fuller," Rourke responded. "But it's academic. As far as the FBI is concerned, Wynoski's dead. And your idea will cost a hell of a lot of dough. Did you ever watch two days of film, including infrared, looking for one solitary bozo who came out but didn't come in? I'd love to help out, but it depends on how important they think it is upstairs. I'll let you know."

Fuller knew he would have to wait until he heard from Rourke. The only other possibility was the cop's eternal pal, serendipity—that something unanticipated would turn up which would lead the case of the desert murderer even an inch away from Beverly Hills or the California desert.

Chapter 24

The sunlight etching the New York Hilton hotel window on Friday morning woke Tom Ward, blinking at the new day. He turned over and rubbed Leslie Fanning's back, toying with the sharp edges of the vertebrae pushing through her milky skin.

"What time is it, darling?"

It was Leslie, who had woken, not from Ward's massage, but from the same insistent sunlight. They had forgotten to close the curtain when they hurriedly fell into his hotel bed the night before.

Both had come to New York from Washington for the Democratic convention, which was to open at the huge convention center on Eleventh Avenue on Monday evening. Les was there to work with Daniels in this last push for delegates. Ward was supposedly there to help Rausch supervise the documentary, but he was actually in New York to be in place when the identity of Oval Red was revealed. It had to be imminent.

In these last preconvention days, Les and Ward had turned a flirtation into an affair of the heart. After Rausch's party in Georgetown, Ward had called and arranged a dinner date, hoping to carefully probe her vulnerabilities.

They had met at the Daniels for President headquarters on 15th and K. His first surmise was that she was a different woman. Instead of coolly elegant, she was tired and irritated, her long dark hair tied in a pony tail, her mascara streaked. But she was still strikingly feminine even though harassed, softly ordering several people about simultaneously.

At dinner, Les talked about Daniels, then about herself, gradually releasing her anxieties. Ward listened, searching for the psychological imperfections, the raw material of his craft. She seemed less "frazzled," as she called it, but still with an edge of female vulnerability, a seismic flaw Ward found personally attractive. And professionally useful.

"Tom, in everyday life, it seems I can abide almost anyone. I suppose I'm just the tolerant type. But I'm a stickler when it comes to men," Les confessed as the evening progressed. "I'm already over thirty and I haven't really been in love. Do you think there's something wrong with me?"

Ward's laugh was genuine. "No, not at all. You're just a discriminating person."

"Oh, don't misunderstand me. A lot of men have found me attractive," Les said, her eyes focused on Ward. "But eventually they all disappoint me. They're either too cold or too brittle or, if they're warm, they're not smart enough. I suppose I'm searching for something that doesn't exist."

In the hurried days, and nights that followed, Ward had tried to become that something. He used every excuse to see Les regularly and was pleased by the rapidly blossoming relationship, in and out of bed.

Chemistry had moved Les, first to admiration for this confident and bright lover, then to affection.

"Whatever it is, he's filling a vacuum in my life," Les told Governor Daniels, who had given his blessings to the match. He liked the young man, he told his assistant. An astute mind, as he viewed it. And a gentleman.

Les and Ward had come up to New York together. Ward had taken a hotel room for himself, but Les was one of the Daniels party staying —at least officially—in the Triplex Suite at the Palace Hotel on Madison Avenue. The governor had leased the elaborate $1650-a-day layout as repayment to his staff, who had been working on the presidential campaign for two years.

The previous evening, until the early morning hours, Ward and Les had celebrated the showing of the documentary rushes to Democratic Party officials. Afterward, it was a gala for only two, at the Rainbow Room, but they had gone formal. Ward had rented a tux and Les—who had forgotten to bring a gown—wore one borrowed from a Manhattan girl friend.

"Do you still love me after my dancing on your toes all night?" Les asked that morning in the Hilton, her head resting lazily on Ward's shoulder.

"Darling, you dance fine. And yes, I still love you. You do everything fine. Too good for me."

Ward reflected that never had he pretended so little.

The evening had been nostalgic for Ward, moved by the jazz, as he called the 1940s swing he had come to enjoy as a young man in New York, then in Poland. He had played down his appreciation of the night for fear Les would be suspicious of his enthusiasm. But she had no reason to believe he was other than what he appeared to be.

Les's face suddenly appeared troubled. "What's wrong, darling?" Ward asked.

"Tom, I was just thinking about Larry Carver. Remember how I kidded him about being CIA? I suppose I was right. Did you hear that he was found dead, shot in the head in the Maryland woods? They have no idea why or by who. But my guess is that it was somebody from the other side—you know, maybe the KGB."

"No, I hadn't heard, Les," Ward feigned with some effort. "That's horrible. Seemed like a nice enough guy. Remember, we were sharing some talk about Geneva. He had been stationed there."

So Carver had been found. But, from what Les said, there was little to lead them out of those isolated woods.

"You know, darling, I have to confess something." Les spoke up. "I had you pegged as CIA as well. That night at Walter's, when you and Carver were talking, I sensed that you knew each other—so I supposed. And, don't misunderstand me, I respect your work as a film writer, but you somehow impressed me as more. Or let's say different. But now, with Carver killed, I hope my suspicions were stupid."

Ward stared at Les, unbelieving, unsettled. He was dealing with a sharpened intuition such as he seldom observed in professional intelligence people. What had he done to alert her inner senses? Probably nothing. Just a primitive knowing, one he had to dispel immediately.

"Whoa, Les. Your imagination is running riot. First off, you have Carver as CIA just because he was murdered. Other people do get killed, you know. And now me. No, honey, I'm sorry to disappoint you, but I'm just as prosaic as I look. And still only a writer. You don't have to worry about my getting killed in the woods, or anywhere. I'll die a natural death in my bed, a bored, and boring, old man."

Les laughed heartily, mainly at herself. "I suppose I was taken by the gory glamour of the whole thing. Tom, I'm glad you're not CIA or anything. But boring? Never, darling." She leaned over to kiss his forehead.

Ward hesitated for only an instant, then moved toward Les to divert the conversation. He softly kissed her, then found he couldn't restrain himself even though they had made love only seven hours before. Ward's mouth traveled down Les's body, kissing the extended nipples, reddish, clear skin that accented her breasts.

"The answer is yes even if you haven't formally asked," Les said. Ward moved his hand between Les's long legs and touched her gingerly. "I said yes, darling. We don't need any preliminaries."

Ward had started to laugh when he stopped abruptly. It was the phone. He had forgotten to turn off the ring. Resigned, he reached for the receiver.

"Yes, who is it?" he asked, annoyed.

"It's me—Walter Rausch. Tom, I'm downstairs in the coffee shop of your hotel. I hate to bother you so early, but it is urgent. Could you get dressed and meet me here in ten minutes? I repeat, urgent."

Ward was about to complain, but he was talking to a dead line.

"Les, honey. Walter is downstairs and he insists we go over some last-minute items on the documentary. I was hoping to beg off, but he hung up on me."

"Don't worry, Tom. I'm big enough to know that work comes first," Les said, then stopped in mid-breath.

"Oh, dear. Governor Daniels has two appointments later this morning. I've got to get back to the Palace Hotel headquarters. Let's leave together. Why don't you take the bathroom first?"

Tom stole a furtive glance at Les's nude body and carried the picture with him into the bathroom. As he shaved, he surveyed his own image, including his inner senses. He looked the same. The only concrete change was the fashionable American haircut. But finding the touchstones of reality was increasingly difficult.

The sense of Poland and Russia, all his SB and KGB training, even the incidents in the desert and with Carver, seemed real. As Peter

Semanski, he had prepared for them since university days in Warsaw. But these weeks in Washington and now in New York, with Les, Daniels, the film, the celebrating, the heady sense of interaction with American politicians, the first hints of independent action, were less than concrete.

These moments seemed made to tantalize him. Only, he knew, to be withdrawn at the caprice of someone in Moscow. Now, what did Rausch want of him? Was this pleasurable, if unreal, pattern to be broken? And replaced by what?

Tom reentered the bedroom and was surprised to see Les fully dressed, wearing her black satin evening gown.

"Yes, darling, this is all I brought with me. I'll get dressed again when I get back to my hotel. Meanwhile, do you mind going downstairs with a hussy who's obviously just shacked up?"

Ward was ready in moments and the two descended to the lobby. Anxious to hear Walter's urgent message, Tom perfunctorily kissed Les good-bye.

In the coffee shop, Rausch was waiting for him at an isolated table in the corner, reading the morning *Times*. Tom sat down silently, sensing Rausch's impatience.

"Tom, please let's skip the pleasantries. I have some exciting news from our people. I picked it up at the Reston drop early this morning and came right to New York on the shuttle."

Rausch reached deliberately into his inside pocket and took out the dispatch. He handed it to Ward.

Ward digested it, then went back and read it again.

It was only two lines. The name of the Democratic candidate and his code name.

"My God." Tom had impetuously spoken out loud, then checked himself.

My God, he repeated, now silently. Ward inhaled a short stabilizing breath as he read the name again. He flushed. Not from any impending danger, but from the realization of the awesomeness of his assignment. For him, for the two nations involved, even for the unknowing rest of the world. The short dispatch simply said:

SENATOR JEDIDIAH B. HANKINS, VIRGINIA.
CODE NAME YEARLING.

Ward and Rausch sat mute for a moment.

Hankins? Tom thought to himself. Why not? He won't be the first rich American to feel the knife pierce of guilt. Each takes a different route of expiation. Some in religion, even in Christian rebirth, others in mild political liberalism, or in ecology. And still others, like the Cantabrigians of the 1930s, by seeking comfort with their side.

Whatever, the news was not just useful, he decided. It was the kind of extra finger on the scales of history that would make the revolution inevitable and democracy a grand illusion.

"So what do you think? Are you stunned by it all?" Rausch asked.

Ward looked at his KGB colleague, thoughtfully.

"Yes. Stunned. And excited."

The younger man picked up his coffee cup and offered it as a toast. Rausch responded, lifting his.

"To victory."

"To victory."

Chapter 25

Ward sat in the coffee shop immobile for a few seconds, staring at Rausch, contemplating the news, his assignment turning over in his mind, his compulsions racing. He now had the identity of Oval Red, but in three days the convention would open and he had no coherent strategy. Making direct contact with Senator Hankins was too dangerous at this juncture, he decided. Any break in his cover could bring Yearling down as well. He might be expendable, but the candidate was not.

Neither Rausch nor the Center had insisted he play power broker, but his immediate mission was obvious. Carver and his threat were gone. Baneyev's men at Langley had confirmed that Carver had not revealed anything about Semanski before he was killed. Ward could now concentrate on moving delegates to Hankins, if possible. The balloting would begin on Wednesday night.

"Walter, I've got to make quick contact with someone dependable, an important American politician I can rely on," Ward said. "Do you know anybody?"

As Rausch weighed the question, Ward rapidly assessed the risk. If the supposed ally were predictably left, but still patriotic, he might alert the FBI or CIA counterintelligence. But the properly sympatico politician would not only agree with his world view but be willing to close an educated eye to his KGB origins.

Mobilizing his Yurlova training, Ward mentally ran down the roster of Americans who might be sympathetic. Congressman Terry Maynard, a young progressive from California, headed the short list. Not only was he an outspoken Pentagon opponent and early nay sayer on Midgetman and Star Wars, he had been among the first to fight the Administration on both economic and military aid to all Central America and the new Philippine administration.

"Walter, what do you think of Congressman Terry Maynard?" Ward asked without waiting for Rausch to respond to his first query.

Rausch smiled in instant recognition.

"Great idea, Tom. He's a good man. Devoted to peace. We've even become friends."

"Walter, I'd like to meet Maynard right away. What if I play producer for Doric and shoot a segment on him for the documentary? Today, if possible. How does that sound?"

"Fine, Tom. Terry's become a member of the House Armed Services Committee. It wouldn't hurt to cultivate him some more."

"Where can I find him?" Ward asked.

"He's in the old Cannon House Office Building. I'll call him down there, then arrange a soundman and cameraman for you. You can take the shuttle and meet them at the House building. How does that sound?"

"Good, Walter. Thanks."

That afternoon, after a hurried trip to Washington, Ward mounted the steps of the Cannon Building with his two-man crew, struck by still another pseudo-Grecian palace of democracy with its doors open to anyone. Nothing like the Kremlin's lined-off Communists' Street. He laughed.

The interior of the Cannon Building was out of a Currier and Ives print. Built in 1908, it was named after Congressman Joseph "Uncle Joe" Gurney Cannon, the powerful conservative Speaker of the House under both Teddy Roosevelt and Taft.

"Welcome to the legislative stockyards." Maynard greeted Ward in his outer office, cluttered with old wooden bookcases serving as makeshift cubicle walls. "I understand you want to take my picture for the convention film, Mr. Ward. Shoot away."

They moved into his private office, furnished in government-issue desks polished to disguise the nicks of time. Ward smiled at the contrast between the man and the setting. Maynard was over six feet tall and the blondest American he had ever seen. Yet his skin was tanned deep bronze, as if, Ward guessed, he had just finished two weeks of surfing. Maynard was wearing a sports shirt, open almost to his navel, chino slacks, and Nike sneakers. His features were pure California—Anglo-Saxon and refined by thirty-five years of orange juice and sunshine.

Ward interviewed Maynard as the cameras ground, but the ringing phone kept interrupting the film session.

With his sneakers indelicately poised on the desk, Maynard fielded a half dozen calls in the next few minutes.

"Ricky? Don't be foolish. Forget the idea of an amendment on the Midgetman missile bill," Maynard was saying. "Let's defeat this one outright, now. So the party once liked the mobile Midgetman gimmick. That's when it was theory. Now it's real. It's time to cut it down. Okay?"

Ward noticed that most of the calls had to do with defense appropriations. Maynard seemed to be orchestrating the potent extreme end of the defense opposition. So far, he hadn't guessed wrong on this congressman.

When the filming was finished, Maynard pulled Ward aside.

"Tom. I'm going down to the floor. Why don't we chat a little in the Democratic cloakroom?"

Maynard was seeking something, perhaps a privileged spot in the documentary, Ward sensed. No better way to cement their relationship.

The crewmen returned to Doric while Tom and Maynard took the elevator to the basement, where they walked the tunnel for a short distance before picking up one of the subway shuttle cars that scoot underground between the Capitol and four of the six Senate and House office buildings, connecting the Hill in an interlocking political metropolis.

At the House, Maynard showed Ward the floor of the chamber, then took him to the House Democratic cloakroom, one of four underpublicized "clubs" for members of both houses and both parties.

"Some coffee?" the Californian asked. They walked to the snack bar, then sat in two ample leather armchairs.

"So you work for Walter?" Maynard opened. "He speaks highly of you."

"Well, I enjoy the work and he seems like a nice fellow."

"Yes. I like him, and his politics too," Maynard said. "He came here from Germany, through Canada, you know. Doesn't share the paranoia of most Americans about Russia."

Maynard's look at Ward was sharp. "I hope you don't mind my asking, but how about you? Do you agree with Walter?"

Ward smiled back insincerely. Was Maynard merely a contact or actually part of Walter's apparatus? He assumed it was the former. Otherwise, Walter wouldn't have raised the possibility of "cultivating" the congressman. On the other hand, the identity of his agents was not something Walter would share, even with him. In either case, his confidence that Maynard was a potential ally was rising.

"Congressman, I'm not particularly political, but I suppose the world will get blown up if both superpowers keep arming. One of them has to stop, sooner or later."

"Good thinking." Maynard grinned approvingly. "Now I feel better about asking you a favor. Tom, that Midgetman mobile missile is provocative and has to be blocked. You shot a few minutes of me talking about it. Could you use it in the film—maybe with a scary background shot of the damn missile? Okay?"

Ward now knew why this cloakroom huddle.

"I think that can be arranged, Terry."

"That's wonderful, Tom. Now, is there anything I can do for you?"

The cue was inviting. "As a matter of fact, there is, Terry."

"What is it, Tom? Don't be bashful."

"Terry, I assume you don't know much about me—except that I'm working with Walter. If you don't mind, I'd like to keep it that way. But I can tell you that I have a vested interest in seeing a peace candidate win the Democratic nomination next week—as I'm sure you do. Well, I have a man who's absolutely dedicated to world peace."

Maynard peered at Ward quizzically.

"Tom, you just said you weren't political. Just worked with Walter. What's the real scoop?" Maynard laughed lightly, his white teeth glaring. "Are you really just a scriptwriter? Or what?"

"Congressman, please. I'd like you to listen to what I'm saying without pressing me. Afterward, talk to Walter. I don't know what more he'll tell you, except what I have—that we're both interested in a peace candidate getting the nomination."

Ward felt as if he had been conscripted into a chess match, feigning, covering. Intuitively, he was confident Maynard knew more about Rausch than he let on. Thus, by inference, about him. He had played this game before with Moslem politicians in Beirut. Not a word was said about the KGB, but they understood.

"You've gotten me real curious, Ward. Or whoever you are. Who's your candidate?"

Ward decided on directness.

"Jed Hankins."

"Hankins? Really?" Maynard's surprise sounded genuine. "I know Jed pretty well. I like his man, Fenton. Good thinker. But Hankins? He's okay. I suppose he's a progressive, but he's always playing both sides of the street—drives me crazy from the Senate with his harping on conventional arms. Who needs any of that crap? It just fuels another war."

Maynard's look was contemplative. "Hankins?" he repeated. "Does Walter know about this?"

"About Hankins? Yes, but I have carte blanche, and he'll back me up completely. Does that help?"

Maynard's boyish expression had vanished, a mature cast overtaking his perfect features.

"Yes, that does help, Tom. What do you want me to do?"

"Do you have any delegates to throw to Hankins?" Ward asked.

"Tom, we have a lot. About 350, pledged to a half dozen different candidates. Our plan is to wait until after the first ballot. If there's no immediate winner, we'll organize them for a candidate of our own. Maybe even a dark horse. Now are you telling me that Hankins is our peace candidate?"

"Exactly right, Congressman. I'd like you to call the senator right away and talk things over. I think you'll be pleased by him."

"Tom, I'm promising nothing. But I'll speak with Hankins as soon as I get to New York tomorrow. At least I'll listen to what he has to say. I never thought of Hankins as a real peace candidate. . . . But . . ."

Maynard rose to shake Ward's hand.

"And, Tom, thanks for that plug against the Midgetman. That creepy little missile could destroy any real chance we have for peace."

Chapter 26

As the airliner left the Los Angeles International Airport behind, San Bernardino Sergeant Pete Fuller considered how strange it was that he was flying to Washington, D.C.

Just the afternoon before, he had been approached by a staff patrolman with a readout in hand. "Sergeant, something just came across the National Law Enforcement teletype. It's from Washington, D.C., and it might fit that Polish case—you know, the desert murder."

Indeed it did fit. Two miles below the Arlington Memorial Bridge crossing from Washington to Virginia, a small airline-type bag had been found ensnarled in a dead tree on the Potomac. When the D.C. police opened it, they were amused, and puzzled. Inside was what looked like a catcher's chest pad but was not. They thought it unusual enough to place a description on the national wire.

"D.C. This is Detective Sergeant Pete Fuller. I'm calling from San Bernardino, California."

Fuller had gotten on the phone minutes after he saw the report. Could it be the item that would substantiate his theory that the body of Wynoski, so identified and buried, was actually not his?

"Could you hold the stuff picked up in the river? Please don't tamper with it. It might be material evidence in a murder case here. Right. I'll be in Washington tomorrow. Thanks."

Fuller had made Flight 76, American Airlines, out of Los Angeles International at 8:45 A.M. On board, he examined his motivation. What was propelling him across the nation in search of a clue that might only be a child's toy?

He was obviously exhilarated by the case. A suspected KGB man found charred in the Mojave was challenging enough, but there was the added possibility that the body was someone else's. The case conjured up pleasing images of recognition. Ten years a sergeant was not without local rewards, but he had never made the big-city headlines like his friends in L.A., whose gory rape-killing cases filled the tabloid sheets.

Fuller wouldn't kid himself. He also liked the idea of tracking down a spy. Not just for the publicity. He was personally pissed by the news stories showing the KGB running circles around Americans.

From Dulles International, Fuller went by cab to police headquarters on Indiana Avenue. He was greeted by Deputy Inspector Josh Greenway, who accompanied him to a long aluminum table on which he had laid out the almost shapeless vinyl airline bag.

"Somebody deep-sixed it in the Potomac, figuring the current would wash it out to sea, but it stuck on a dead tree branch and a curious kid brought it in," the D.C. officer explained. "We thought nothing of it until we found that padded thing inside. There it is, over there." Greenway was pointing to the device on the other side of the table.

Fuller picked up the strange padding, first turning it over, examining it, then lifting it up against his own body, placing his arms through the brassiere-like harness.

"I'll be damned," Fuller exclaimed. "The thing actually works. Look here. It gives me a tire right around my middle."

To himself, Fuller noted that the unique contraption was probably what made Wynoski appear "portly," as the FBI had said. The real Wynoski—whoever he was—surely had a slim figure, not unlike the torched victim.

"Was there anything else in the valise?" Fuller asked.

"Two things. One is the remains of a hanging bag, some foreign make. The other is a set of rags that look like they come off some bum."

Fuller opened the airline bag and looked inside. The Potomac waters had made a mess of the inner surface, but as he concentrated on the scrambled contents, something jumped out at him. At the base of the bag there were grains of sand. Either from a beach or—the thought struck him—a desert.

He asked Greenway for an envelope and scooped up a pinch of the sand. The lab guys back home would analyze it.

The small bag was unusual, he decided. It was an exact model of those sold by the airlines, but it had no logo. But as Fuller studied the valise, he could make out the unreadable impressions of a decal that had been removed. Perhaps the lab people could decipher that mystery as well.

A probable scenario was unfolding. Wynoski had either disguised himself or, more probably, removed the elaborate disguise that had become Wynoski, including the ingenious fat padding. He had put on a second suit which he had brought with him in the hanging bag, then taken the prefixed decal—maybe the Polish airline LOT—off the small valise, and placed the hanging bag along with Wynoski's discarded clothes and ID into the suitcase.

The slimmer, transformed Wynoski then simply walked out of the Beverly Hills Hotel.

What happened after that was only speculation, but Wynoski had probably picked up a hitchhiker in the desert and killed and torched him, leaving the body to pose as his. Judging from the fact that the items were fished out of the Potomac, Wynoski—under some assumed name—could be here in Washington.

His next step was to contact Rourke again. Now perhaps the men "upstairs" at the FBI, as Rourke had put it, would agree to study every millimeter of the exit films from the Beverly Hills Hotel.

"What's it all about, Fuller?" Greenway asked, his curiosity piqued by the strange contraption.

"Can't tell yet, Inspector. But it could be valuable in that desert murder I told you about. I'll let you know as soon as we have something."

Fuller thanked Greenway, scooped up the evidence, and placed it in a large plastic bag he had brought along.

Serendipity had done its job. Now it was up to the FBI.

Chapter 27

"Jed. We've got to do something," Senator Hankins could hear his AA, Bill Fenton, telling him. "If we don't look like we're moving, Daniels will steamroll us on the first ballot."

Fenton and Hankins were in the library of the Italianate stone townhouse on East Seventy-third Street that Hankins had rented, at an exorbitant price, for the convention week. It was Saturday afternoon, two days before the official opening of the convention.

Hankins was uncommonly depressed. He could feel his plan of moving America into the Marxist orbit slipping, precipitously. He ached for the presidency—couldn't let go of the dream. With himself in the Oval Office, America, a land of natural richness, not Russia, would become the true test of the superiority of the ideas of Marx and Lenin.

"You're right, Bill. And our meeting this morning with Congressman Rawlins was a disaster," Hankins said disconsolately. "He doesn't give a damn about all my civil rights legislation. To him, I'm just a rich white Southern son of a bitch who's toadying to the urban middle class. I'll bet he even thinks I'm antiblack."

The meeting with Congressman Rawlins had been as inconclusive as those with Senators Meredith and Delafield. Sommerville's 60 votes would probably come along, but that wasn't nearly enough.

Sometimes Hankins wished he could tell the world of his true political heart and stop this perpetual disguise. He could even visualize himself as a guerrilla with Fidel in the Sierra Maestra of Cuba, but fighting a secret war with brains instead of guns. When the final history of American Communist heroes was written, those whose weapon was politics—including the politics of stealth—would be as venerated as any brave soldier, he was sure.

Why? he asked himself. Why, with all his wealth, was he involved in such a clandestine political scheme? Purpose was all he could think of. The power? Surely, he envied every occupant of the Oval Office. Even John Kennedy had confessed that his favorite tune was "Hail to the Chief."

But it was not the fame or the deference he sought. People gave him that anyway, with his millions. What he craved was Purpose, to bring enlightenment to millions of Americans suffocating under the shallow desire to be rich. That would give him a reason for living, other than the banal trappings of wealth.

"What can we do, Bill? Any ideas?" Hankins finally asked his AA.

He could see Fenton turn pensive.

"I think I know the answer, Jed." Fenton smiled reticently, a signal that he felt intellectually victorious.

"What is it, Bill?"

"Our best hope is Terry Maynard. I've heard he's secretly organizing peace delegates all over the country. I was hoping to get a lot of them on the second ballot, but we can't wait. It could be Daniels on the first. We've got to talk to Maynard now. Somehow convince him to release them to us—before the voting begins."

"But is that legal? How can we get his people on the first ballot when they were elected pledged to other candidates?" Hankins asked.

"Jed, don't you remember? We helped change the party rules years ago. A delegate can vote his conscience on the floor any time, no matter who he was pledged to in the primaries."

Hankins' eyes displayed surprise, then recollection. "Yes, you're right, Bill. But there's still a problem. Probably a big one. Maynard likes some of my ideas, but he's never been sure if I'm progressive enough. Any money for the Pentagon is too much for his people."

Hankins hesitated, his stare at Fenton thoughtful. "I don't think I can level with Terry completely, but I'll give it a shot. Bill, get me Maynard on the phone."

Fenton flinched. Hankins knew his aide despised playing boy Friday, but he watched silently as Fenton dialed the number anyway.

☆ ☆ ☆

The phone rang in the Plaza suite. Congressman Maynard, dressed in tennis shorts and a striped Polo shirt, took the call while stretched out on the couch.

"Terry, this is Jed Hankins."

Maynard was surprised. Would Hankins believe the old saw that he was—really—just about to call him? Had Tom Ward already alerted Hankins, or was it just coincidence?

"How's the campaign going, Jed?" Maynard asked.

"It could be better, Terry. That's why I'm calling. I know we've had our differences, but I've always felt we were basically on the same wavelength. Bill and I expect we'll be getting some of your people on the second ballot. But, Terry, I need them right now."

"What exactly are you looking for, Jed?"

"I need your delegates to break their pledges before the first ballot and announce for me. It'll create an electric wave on the convention floor."

Before the Californian could respond, Hankins pushed again.

"Terry, I know other candidates talk peace, but you can count on me for true friendship with the Soviets. That's right—a real partnership, not a Cold War. An end to giant missile programs. Finis to our stupid attempts to stop people's movements in the Third World, especially Latin America and the Mideast."

Maynard was absorbing it all. Everything Hankins was saying corroborated what Tom Ward had told him.

"I read you, Jed," Maynard said. "But you've confused me with all that gobbledygook about conventional arms. What's that all about?"

☆ ☆ ☆

In the townhouse, at his end of the line, Hankins knew it was time to make his position clear, for the first time, if only to Maynard.

"Terry, just think about it this way. Conventional arms aren't going to do much good in a real global nuclear war—or even a blackmail showdown. And money spent there isn't going toward those murderous missiles. Am I coming through?"

"I read you, Jed. I can see your heart's in the right place," Maynard responded. "We're all politicians. Not everything we think is for public consumption. And not everything we say in Congress is the gospel. Right?"

The conversation was going better than Hankins had expected.

"How many delegates do you have?" Hankins asked.

"About 350."

"Terry, this may be the only shot you'll ever have to put a peace-minded candidate into the White House. I don't think it's a time to equivocate. Do you?"

Hankins stopped, husbanding the sweet carrot he had held in reserve.

"And, Terry. If I make it, you're my prime candidate for the number two spot. You'd make a great VP."

Hankins could hear a deliberate silence from Maynard. Then the congressman spoke up, sharply.

"Jed. I've thought it over. You're right. It's now or never. At least for four more years. The answer is yes. I'll get on the horn right now. I can't promise, but I think I can get 325 out of the 350."

"That's great, Terry. See you at the convention," Hankins concluded, hanging up the phone.

From Fenton's smile, Hankins could see that he had deduced the conversation.

"Congratulations, Jed," Fenton said, jubilant. "We're still in the fight."

Hankins looked somewhat perplexed.

"What's wrong?" Fenton asked. "I thought everything went fine."

"It went great. But that's what surprises me. It was as if Maynard knew what was inside my head. Almost like he was expecting my call. Well, maybe I'm more transparent to people on our side than I thought. Or I'm just a persuasive politician. In any case, it's great news."

"Jed, now we've got to get it on national television." Fenton's voice was charged with uncharacteristic enthusiasm. "It could snowball and make the undecided delegates think twice about going over to Daniels."

"You're right, Bill. And I know just who to call. I promise you that by the time the convention opens Monday night it'll be all over the floor. Like a political brush fire."

Chapter 28

"Meg? Meg Larsen? Yes, this is an old friend. Jed Hankins."

She was surprised, having given up on the senator calling her as his presidential star rose. And at this hour, 11 A.M. on Sunday morning?

"Senator, what a pleasure. What can I do for you?"

"I'm sorry I haven't called before, Meg. The campaign has killed my social life." Hankins' voice was rich in timbre. "McDowell's office told me where you were. I've got a great story for you."

"A story? Good. How do I get it?"

Meg's journalistic career had been accelerating since the Hankins Farms interview. Milt Samuels himself, she had heard, was encouraging McDowell to use her more on camera.

"It's yours exclusively—if you come up. I've rented a townhouse for convention week," Hankins said. "Yes. Right now. It's at 616 E. Seventy-third Street, between Madison and Fifth. See you."

The call complete, Meg darted exuberantly around her Waldorf suite, changing her costume, striving for the surest, most impressive combinations. Always, she was thrilled by the pulsating touch of things beautiful, particularly by the subtle scent that surrounded the expensive.

Raised in poverty in South Boston, Meg's scholarship to Boston University had taught her one thing. It was that well-connected girls from Great Neck and Bala Cynwyd, scheming from seventeen on to victimize a gynecologist or a lawyer, were happier in their prideful ignorance than she, with all her intelligence and taste, and her frustrated dreams of the grand life.

No man of substance had yet volunteered to make it real, but

Rausch was providing a beginning. Meg had concocted a cover story to explain her new wealth. She had become a spurious Beacon Hill heiress, the beneficiary of an aunt she had befriended in her dotage.

It was supposedly that money, reputedly over a million—not the Soviet largesse—that had paid for the Jaguar, vacations in Baden-Baden, and the smartly furnished, three-bedroom condominium in Silver Spring.

For Meg, spying was a matter of economics. She saw herself as a capitalist of purity, with no politics except money. During the last two years the Soviet Embassy, through Rausch, had paid her $155,000, happily tax-free, with the promise of more.

Meg recalled the day she had met Rausch socially. After a short, insincere courtship, she knew his motives were not love or even sex. And he learned that she couldn't live in the manner she wanted on her network income. At first Rausch had used a "false flag" recruitment, implying that he was from MOSSAD, the Israeli Secret Service. But when he realized that Meg didn't care who the client was, he told her the truth. Meg had suspected he was KGB anyway.

With her television network front, Meg made easy contact with government officials, just as she had with Hankins. The senator was good business, maybe even the next President. And despite internal denials, she found the man attractive. How much? Perhaps she would soon learn more.

"Meg. Welcome." Hankins greeted Larsen in the upstairs drawing room, a large overfurnished chamber with vestiges of nineteenth-century charm.

"Senator. We have to cut this out. Every time we meet, it's in some mansion or other. I'm just folks."

Hankins kissed Meg on the cheek, handing her a drink of iced wine and club soda.

"Come sit over here. I've got a great story for you. It's all yours if you want it."

Larsen scribbled shorthand notes as Hankins related the details of his peace delegate coup, omitting any mention of Terry Maynard, presenting it as the natural movement of like-minded people to his campaign.

"Meg. I think we're talking about 350 votes. It'll be a whole new horse race."

"That's a great story, Senator. I'll talk to my boss, Doug McDowell.

I'm sure he'll love it. There's nothing better than making the presidential race hotter."

The interview over, Hankins accompanied Meg to the door. They stood self-consciously, Meg wondering if the senator had invited her solely in the name of good politics. They were silent for a moment, both uncomfortable at the thought of parting so abruptly.

"You've been here only a short while, Meg. Is there some way I can delay you?" Hankins asked. "Give you another drink? Show you my scrapbook? Or whatever?"

Meg mocked a pensive stance. "Let me think, Senator. I tell you what. Things are slow at Eleventh Avenue. I'll stay awhile, and you can show me your etchings—or anything."

Within fifteen minutes Hankins and Larsen were in bed, where the tensions of a year of running for President seemed to wash away.

"You had all this planned the minute you walked in. Didn't you?" Hankins said, his head luxuriating on Meg's bosom.

"I could say the same thing about you, Senator. And besides, those are female secrets. But I can tell you that my mother wanted me to marry the richest man in America. And my father wanted me to marry the President. Maybe I can please them both at the same time. Whatdyethink?"

Hankins lifted his head to laugh. "I'm hardly the marrying type, nor the richest. Or even a presidential nominee. But there's nothing like a scheming woman for my taste. Particularly one as luscious as you."

Meg pressed her lips against Hankins', then kissed his hand, his chest. She leaned into the pillow, pulling the side of his head over to whisper in his ear.

"I don't want anyone to overhear us. I keep thinking about the stud and the mare in your breeding shed. Remember we talked about whether she enjoyed it or not. I'd like to find out. But, please, without tying up my legs."

With that, Larsen pulled away the covers and raised herself onto her hands and knees. She turned so that her soft nude rear was facing Hankins, her auburn hair falling back over her shoulders. Meg craned her neck to peer back at Jed, who was transfixed in pleasure.

"Whenever the stud is ready," she said.

Chapter 29

Colonel Baneyev knew it was time.

It was early Sunday morning in the Wisconsin Avenue compound of the Soviet Embassy, a day before the opening of the Democratic National Convention. He was pleased that Oval Red was in motion. Ironman had been given the identity of Yearling, but the Withers file was still out there, a potential destroyer of everything.

Three weeks had passed since Withers' disappearance. Baneyev, who had been waiting for the opportune moment to release the news of Mary Withers' death, sensed it was now. The convention was the logical place for Withers to emerge once he was flushed out. The site of the Red candidate, the source of his agony.

"Sergeant Teshovich!"

The stoic aide was soon in front of the colonel's desk.

"It's time to follow up on your plan," Baneyev ordered. "I want Withers in our hands within a few days. Get a message to Rausch. Tell him we want national media exposure of Mary Withers' death. And soon."

Teshovich beamed.

"Yes, Comrade Colonel. Rausch has been alerted. We'll make swift contact."

"Good. Any word on Genshikov?"

Teshovich had obviously sifted through all the possibilities.

"I'm sure he's dead, Comrade Colonel. It doesn't sound like an official CIA job. They wouldn't waste it on that peasant. More like a free-lance. My guess, Colonel, is that it was Withers."

"All the more reason to smoke him out now. Please get on it, Alexei."

Chapter 30

Meg pushed through the convention crowd, bruising her elbow against the Wyoming state stanchion. She apologized, even to those who had kicked her in the maddening desire to circulate. The delegates were loud and unruly, as always on the opening night of convention.

"Little lady, you're going to skin your shins on my spurs," one delegate hollered, whipping his cowboy hat in the air. As Meg tripped over outstretched boots, the delegates caught her just before she fell into a crowd of eager Westerners.

It was Monday evening at 7 P.M. in the Jacob K. Javits Convention Center in New York, the start of the largest political confab in history. Some 13,000 people, including 7864 delegates and alternates, and thousands of newsmen, assorted hangers-on, and anyone with enough guile to secure a ticket, filled the grandstands and the mammoth floor —the size of two football fields. Above, like aircraft carrier decks cantilevered outward, were the ornate media booths, including that of Meg's own network.

Democratic expectations were high. The Republican incumbent could no longer run, and perhaps, after a long presidential drought, nature might provide, the party faithful prayed.

Meg found her way to the stairs of the network booth, where she could see Doug McDowell's red-topped head peering out.

Doug had his job and she had hers. Meg had already given McDowell the Hankins "peace delegate" story. But the assignment that paid the mortgage on her Silver Spring condo was Rausch's. She was to get word of Mary Withers' death on the air. Meg had done her homework. Now if only McDowell would use the item in his hourly newsbreak between the segments of convention coverage. If necessary, she would cajole him.

"Meg, for God's sake. Where have you been?" Doug asked as she entered the booth, a touch of pique in his voice. "You're supposed to coordinate the stories. Things are beginning to happen."

McDowell handed her a note from the reporter who had just interviewed Fenton on Hankins' new delegate strength.

"I think you've brought in something big, Meg. Look at this."

"In a second, Doug. I have another item. Not exactly the convention, but it's politically related and it's got real intrigue."

Meg was talking to him straightforwardly, but her voice carried a seductive undertone.

"All right. Let me see it." McDowell read it in a sweep. "Where'd you get this? Very interesting."

"I got the tip from an anonymous caller, a clerk at the CIA. It seems one of their men, Sam Withers, is missing and his wife is dead. I gave it to Cavanaugh and it checked out. A neighbor saw an unmarked van at the Withers house. There's been no funeral, but the undertaker finally talked. It seems Mary Withers was murdered in her kitchen, from blows around the neck. Sounds like a real thriller."

"Good work! I'll use it right after my commentary," McDowell responded. "I've never trusted the damn CIA. If we gave them their head, everybody would be spying on everybody else, like in Russia. Thanks, Meg. Now, please look at my interview with Bill Fenton. We may have the scoop of the convention."

☆ ☆ ☆

Sam Withers' television set was tuned to the convention coverage. He had been watching more as the small beach house started to move in on him.

It had been three weeks since he arrived and two since the Genshikov affair. Withers was feeling better about the whole operation. He had the missing cassette, but Davidson had called, telling him to hold on to it. Hankins seemed to be out of the running for President, with Daniels far ahead in the delegate vote. Withers was confident he had done his duty, whether it was appreciated or not.

He poured himself a scotch and water, then sat on the mildewed wicker couch. McDowell was suddenly on screen, highly energized.

"Tonight, we'll see the beginnings of the jousting for delegates," the newsman began. "Remember, it takes 1967 votes to win. Earlier today, Governor Marc Daniels was well ahead with 1400 votes, and looked to be the easy winner.

"But in the last five hours something dramatic has been taking place behind the scenes. It's all based on a strange party rule. Delegates elected for one candidate are not bound to respect the voters.

They can change their minds and vote for anyone, even on the first ballot. That's just what's happening on the floor right now. Jed Hankins, the number two contender with 875 votes, has been rapidly picking up desertions from each of the other candidates—what he calls 'peace delegates.'

"They're coming in from every delegation, including the black and women's groups. Daniels has even seen fifty of his own people leave. He's now down to 1350 and Hankins has gone up to 1200. No one knows who is coordinating it, or how, but the race may not be as handily in Daniels' pocket as everyone thought."

McDowell offered a concluding note.

"Tomorrow, Tuesday night, at 10 P.M., the challenger, Jed Hankins, will address the convention for fifteen minutes—one of seven candidates to do so under an unprecedented plan announced today by the Democratic National Committee. Some people are saying it's part of a 'Stop Daniels' move started by Hankins' friends on the committee. Whatever the truth, it has spiced up the race for the Democratic nomination. This is Douglas McDowell."

Withers listened, incredulous. Hankins, the lousy Red, catching up and once again a threat? And addressing the convention tomorrow night?

Except for a slim electronic thread, Sam felt disconnected from Davidson and the world. Then he remembered the obvious. Should the worst happen, should Hankins get the nomination, Davidson would surely move into action immediately. Let it rest. Davidson, not he, was now commander.

Sam rose from the couch and approached the bar to freshen his scotch. His back was turned when he thought he heard his name being called out. The word "Withers" seemed to be coming from the television set. Was he hallucinating? The ocean waves had said it. No?

He turned abruptly to confront the source. Would it dare say it again?

But this time he saw a picture. His eyes focused on the frame and he could only try to interpret what was going on. It was a photo of his wife's face. Was it cut from their wedding picture? It was on the screen on national television. What was going on? Had he lost his link to reality?

Then, a syllable at a time, like words in slow motion, he heard the announcer's voice, as if in a child's nightmare.

"Mary Withers, wife of CIA agent Sam Withers, was found murdered in their suburban Maryland home. The CIA refuses to acknowledge the fact, or the whereabouts of Mr. Withers . . . but . . ."

Withers stared at the screen, the words now blotted out. His mind catapulted back in time, to the moment he had begun the file on Hankins. Now returning to this instant, then forward into a black oblivion.

"No, no!" Sam screamed, racing to the door that blocked the ocean winds from the room. He tried to open it, but his unresponsive fingers couldn't grasp the lock. The drink fell to the floor out of a paralyzed hand. Then his body dropped slowly, where he lay, defeated, in a pool of scotch on the wooden planks of the beach house.

Mary. Mary. Why you? Why did they do it? Why . . . ?

His sobbing was uncontrollable, the guilt of leaving Mary alone this time, and all those years, ripping at him. He had failed her in every way. Now his political compulsions had set the stage for her death.

Withers lay there for almost five minutes, his hair matted with sweat, the smell of acrid tears and scotch in his nostrils, his heart deadened with final pain. He rose slowly from the floor and turned off the television set.

Upstairs, in the attic. That's the place Davidson must keep his guns, or at least one security weapon. Yes, it was as essential as extra water in the desert. He was sorry now that he hadn't kept Genshikov's Luger.

Withers found a ladder and climbed into the small attic over the kitchen, probing with a flashlight. He opened every package, every cardboard container, but there was no gun. Then it struck him. He knew Davidson's mind. The toolbox.

The large wooden box was padlocked, with no key. He had no time to find it. Withers took the ax propped against the wall and, swinging up toward the attic rafters, brought it down menacingly on the top of the box. It split into parts. Inside, his hands moved quickly. He could feel the cold skin of a Beretta automatic, with silencer.

Sam was about to take the Beretta when his fingers touched the edges of another gun, one he had seen pictured but had never held. It was a Glock 25, an Austrian masterpiece, probably a gift from one of Davidson's European admirers. He fondled its hard plastic stock, then moved softly along its ceramic barrel.

The Glock was constructed without a hint of metal, the contemporary answer to standard detector screens. Alongside it was a silver pen, its girth reminiscent of the old Watermans. Curious, Withers toyed with it, finally pressing down on its gold pocket clip. The top suddenly moved upward, almost imperceptibly, revealing a hidden screw thread. Inside the pen, Sam saw two 9mm bullets, the concealed armament for the weapon.

He took the gun, placed the pen in his breast pocket, and descended into the kitchen, all caution drained from him.

Chapter 31

Sam parked his car at a suburban Westchester railroad station, insurance no one could connect him to the North Carolina plates, then to "Robert Doherty." By commuter train, he returned to New York City, then by cab to the huge center on Eleventh Avenue.

It was Tuesday, the second night of the convention, the session at which Hankins was to speak. The escalator brought him to the Press Office, where Withers resumed an old identity. His CIA-procured press card, made out in a pseudonym, showed him to be a reporter for the Washington Political Information Service, a small news outfit whose main customer was the Agency.

Sam knew he could enter the convention hall with that credential. But how long before the Agency learned that he had surfaced?

The metal detector regimen went smoothly. As he filed through after other newsmen, his house keys and silver "pen" set off the alarm. But once they were laid politely aside, he walked through the screen effortlessly, the undetected Glock 25 tucked into his rear waistband.

Inside, Sam used an empty men's room booth to load the 9mm bullets, then returned to the press section. He stared out, seeking his bearings. To his left was a television news booth with Doug McDowell at the desk. The main podium was to his right and some distance away.

There was no hesitation in Withers' mind, the hatred overwhelming any doubts. The first bullet would be for Hankins. His perfidy had ignited the events that had killed his Mary and now threatened the democracy. Hankins would never see the White House. If he didn't need it tonight, the second bullet would be held in reserve for another day, for Baneyev. Mary's death was the Russian's type of artistry.

He knew he could never fire accurately at Hankins from where he stood. It was imperative no one else be hurt. He moved slowly onto the convention floor, apparently a hazardous place, with broadcast people collaring even stray delegates. Suddenly, his leg almost tripped up a young woman. Attractive, he thought, wearing a green silk dress and a long strand of pearls.

"I'm sorry, miss," Withers said as the woman moved on without responding.

☆   ☆   ☆

Meg Larsen stopped and glanced back at the pale, small man with blackened shadows under his eyes.

"My God, it's Withers. Sam Withers," she muttered, mentally matching the face with the photo Cavanaugh had shown her.

Meg moved away from Withers, torn between following him and reporting his presence. The ploy of flushing him out had worked. Better than she had thought. Fortunately, Rausch was at the convention tonight. She walked briskly toward his guest box.

"Walter," Meg whispered. "Withers is here. He looks enraged. I have no idea what he's up to, but I thought you should know right away."

She leaned her head forward, using her nose as a pointer. Rausch followed her lead and spotted Withers moving determinedly through the crowd toward the podium.

"Meg, interview me briefly about the documentary. Then leave quickly. I have to make a call."

Larsen made the perfunctory motions of an interview, then moved away. Rausch exited immediately in the opposite direction, toward the pay phones at the rear of the auditorium.

The water cooler company. That was the emergency number in New York given him by Baneyev. It was to be used only for a man-power call. It would bring a delivery van with a driver and a helper, two of Colonel Baneyev's men who were living as illegals in New York, he presumed.

Rausch dialed the number, then waited. The phone rang four

times. Then a voice, gruff, speaking in a vague European accent Walter couldn't pinpoint, perhaps Czechoslovakian.

"Yes, this is the water cooler company. Who wants us?"

"This is R. Sam Withers, the Agency man, is here at the convention. Do whatever is needed. Do you understand?"

"Yes. We already have our instructions in case you called." The man hung up.

Rausch walked back toward the convention floor, straining his eyes to locate Withers, but he had been swallowed up by the crowd.

☆ ☆ ☆

Sam moved forward, searching for an inconspicuous spot to wait until the moment. In the Ohio delegation, directly in front of the podium, he found an empty chair. He sat down just as the gavel resounded.

His mind was not fully focused, the thoughts moving through a storm of confusion, repeating the same rage he felt when he first heard his wife's death announced like a commercial on television. But, through it, he could make out the beginnings of an introduction. It was for Hankins' speech.

Withers seethed. A Communist was unknowingly being honored by the Democratic Party. But it would soon be a posthumous honor, he swore, his right hand reaching back to his waistband to stroke the finite message of the gun.

Sam calculated the timing. It was nine fifty-five. Hankins would be introduced for about five minutes, then would appear at 10 P.M., the perfect prime-time audience. He would let Hankins speak for five minutes, then end it. No better way to honor Mary.

The chairman was reciting the historic blessings of Virginia, the home of Presidents Washington, Jefferson, Madison, Monroe—and Senator Hankins. As Withers swayed in impatience, he turned his head, stopping halfway into the arc of his sight.

Against the wall, he could make out two men who knew him. Jim Barber and Davie Hopper, the veteran CIA agent and the kid, apparently teamed by Springs to take him, should he show. Withers' eyes met theirs, and he could see Hopper almost lift off the floor, then gesticulate openly in his direction. They had spotted him.

It was a poker game, bluff on both sides. Withers knew the CIA men wouldn't move against him in the middle of the proceedings. A fuss on national television would disrupt the convention and Springs and the Administration would be assaulted by the media for sabotaging the opposition's finest hour. Sam could wait them out. He had come to kill.

He could see Hopper entering the delegation next to his. Because of the CIA men, he would make his move a few minutes earlier than planned. The gun pressed through his jacket, stimulating the small of his back just as if it were nestled assuringly in his hand.

"Ladies and gentlemen," the chairman addressed the now quieting crowd. "I have the pleasure to introduce one of the party's most energetic and promising young leaders. A candidate for the nomination as President of the United States, our distinguished senator from Virginia, Jedidiah Breckinridge Hankins."

The chairman finished to a whoop from the convention floor. Withers could feel his mind, once spinning in incoherence, now focused on one targeted zone—the tall candidate who grasped the lectern with his bony hands and raised his arms above his head. First directly up, then slowly outward, until they were spread-eagled into the victory symbol. Much of the audience shouted back in acclamation.

As Hankins looked down to arrange his notes, Withers, still standing with a few party enthusiasts, reached under his jacket to the back of his pants and grasped the gun firmly in his fist.

At this range, less than fifty feet, Withers was confident he could pierce either Hankins' heart or his brain. He decided on the head. It was in sharp, clear view from where he stood.

☆ ☆ ☆

Hopper had cautiously moved closer to Withers. Why had Sam come to the convention at all, exposing himself so easily to the Agency? the young CIA officer wondered. Sam must have known Springs had issued orders to bring him in. Whatever, Hopper was grateful for the chance to make up for his amateurishness in losing Withers in the Washington Metro.

But there was no hurry to take him now. Barber was backstopping forty feet behind and all the exits were guarded. Might as well wait until Hankins was finished, Hopper decided.

Before turning toward the podium, Hopper glanced at Withers. A flash interrupted his eye. Something at Sam's back was catching the light. As the flap of Withers' jacket lifted for an instant, Hopper could make it out. Yes, he was sure. It was a gun.

Their movements were simultaneous. Withers extracted the re-

volver from his pants and started its seconds-long journey up to eye
level just as Hopper, exercising the dormant muscles of his high
school halfback days, bulled through the delegation, pushing over
chairs and delegates.

As he raced forward, Hopper could see Sam methodically raise the
automatic and extend his hand, lining the sights at Hankins' exposed
head. Absorbed in his notes, the candidate was oblivious to the threat
only fifteen yards away.

Hopper and Withers crashed at the exact moment of explosion.
The gun in Withers' hand fired as Hopper's body hit him below the
waist in a desperation lunge. The instant of contact forced Withers'
hand upward only an inch, but the trajectory of the bullet was al-
tered. The shot raced through the air, passing less than a foot over
Hankins' head.

Unceremoniously, the candidate hit the podium floor as the convention gasped at the sound of the bullet ricocheting through the hall.

Hopper had taken Withers' small body to the ground, but he
squirmed loose. The gun? As Hopper desperately searched for it on
the floor, he could see the wiry Withers scrambling on his knees
between the folding chairs. Withers snatched at the revolver and,
rabbitlike, rose to his legs and flashed across the floor out of Hopper's
grasp.

☆ ☆ ☆

"Someone has fired a shot at Senator Hankins!" McDowell was
shrieking into the microphone.

Doug McDowell was on camera, feverishly trying to recount the
assassination attempt to a stunned national audience.

"It's an unprecedented attempt to kill a candidate at a national
convention! No one has any idea who the gunman is except that he
was seated in the Ohio delegation. Senator Hankins was saved by
someone—probably a Secret Service agent—who tackled the assassin
just as he fired. Our cameras are panning the floor, trying to pick up
the gunman. I have just been told that the exits are closed. There's no
chance of his getting away. . . . My God, there he is. . . ."

As the last word left McDowell's throat, Withers had arrived at the
door of the television news booth, brandishing the gun in the security
guard's face.

"No one need get hurt. Just stand aside and open the door—now."

The frightened guard responded. Within seconds, Withers had

burst into the news booth. Everyone stood rigid as he strode over to McDowell's desk.

Without a word, Sam pressed the gun against the newscaster's freckled temple. McDowell turned in disbelief and stared insensate at Withers, watching the weapon coming up at him as if it were a routine episode of television violence.

"Wha . . . what the hell's going on?" McDowell exclaimed into the camera.

In the control room, the director froze as the drama unfolded on his monitor—then suddenly disappeared, replaced by a view of Hankins still crouched behind the lectern.

"Are you crazy!" the director screamed. "Who the hell switched cameras on me? Quick. Give me number 2. The gunman at McDowell's head. And keep it there!"

In the newsroom, the men held captive with McDowell exchanged glances. There were seven against one 130-pound man.

"Don't try anything," Withers warned. "Any two of you can take me, but McDowell's going to be dead the second someone advances."

Withers was only vaguely aware that his image, gun to McDowell's head, was being broadcast to a transfixed television audience, coast to coast.

"As for the Secret Service here and police outside, I want you to hear this same message. I intend to leave here in one piece. And those who know me—Sam Withers of the CIA—know I mean it. If I don't leave here, neither does Mr. McDowell, alive."

McDowell watched the bizarre proceedings as if it were a television movie. From the corner of his eye, he peered at himself on the monitor, locating the revolver in the picture, pointed—as it was in life—at his temple. He stared into the camera and spoke to Withers not as if he were only inches away but on the other side of the tube, watching at home, secure in the notion that the whole episode was a TV crime fantasy.

"Mr. Withers. This is Douglas McDowell. You're an honored member of our intelligence agency. You know this can't lead anywhere except to your imprisonment. Why not surrender now?"

McDowell could see Withers staring into the same camera.

"McDowell. Just get up, slowly, and start to walk in front of me. Take a step each time I apply a slight pressure to your head with the gun barrel. To the New York City police: you fellows are great, but don't have a SWAT team waiting outside. I won't wait until you try to take me. I'll shoot McDowell in the head as soon as you make your presence known. It makes little difference whether I'm dead or alive, so do what I say."

McDowell took in every word Withers said, but he was juggling two conversations at the same time. In his earpiece, he could also hear the director, Sal Marco.

"Doug. Do what he says, for God's sake. People only love a dead hero for a week. But we need everything on camera. Tell Withers you'll play ball, but ask him a favor. Could one of our guys with a shoulder minicamera follow the two of you out of the convention hall, right up to the car, and wave you good-bye on national television? Tell him that's the only way you'll cooperate. He may not believe you, but it's worth a shot—you should excuse the expression. And, Doug." Marco paused. "We're with you."

McDowell was afraid to turn his head to speak directly to Withers. Instead, he continued to talk to the tortured CIA man through the camera.

"Mr. Withers. I'll go along with you. But I have only one request. Could my network continue to cover us on television as we exit?"

On the monitor, McDowell could see Withers halt briefly, then nod his head.

"If anyone from the city government is watching, please don't try to apprehend Mr. Withers," McDowell continued. "We're going to walk out of this hall, in full view of the nation, go to my car, and drive wherever he wants to with no interference on the highways. No roadblocks, nothing. Please don't try to stop him. He'll kill me."

As McDowell started out of the booth, Withers alongside, he weighed what he had just said.

Did he really believe Withers would kill him?

The response came back, no. Despite the evidence of a gun ready to explode his brains onto the convention floor.

But if he thought Withers was bluffing, why was he cooperating in his escape?

The self-probing took place in the instant the two men exited the booth before the audience of 13,000, who were standing, watching the real drama as it occurred, then seeing it transposed in giant proportions on the TV screen anchored to the back of the convention floor.

"Hurry up, damn it," the director shouted. "Bring the camera right up to Withers and Doug. Hold it there. Yeh. Gimme a close-up of the gun and Doug's head, then switch to Withers' eyes. Good. Keep going. Follow them."

Sal Marco was barking orders to the mobile camera crew shadowing the two men as they moved toward the exit.

"It's okay, fellows. Withers said you'll be safe. Just be sure to duck if any shooting starts."

But the shooting did not start. As McDowell had requested, the authorities stood down. The crowd hushed, then parted as Withers and McDowell, like two victorious gladiators leaving the Colosseum, moved forward.

First through the ornate center lobby, then out into the air, where McDowell's red Corvette was waiting. It had been brought up by the police, who stood by immobile as Withers motioned the newsman into the driver's seat, then slid in alongside.

"Take it slow. Don't panic," Withers cautioned McDowell as they started out onto the street. "If we go orderly, they'll respect the accord. But if you speed, it'll break the spell and some hothead will pull the trigger."

As they drove through an entourage of unbroken, respectful police cars and out onto Twelfth Avenue, a civilian vehicle was parked a few hundred feet away. It was a van, a new white one, without lettering on its clean surface. Neither man noticed, but as they turned up the avenue the van left the curb and moved in slowly a few hundred feet behind the Corvette.

Glancing behind to check that no police were following, Withers eyed his hostage. "Where are you staying in New York, McDowell?"

"In Westchester, with a friend. In Scarsdale to be exact. Why?"

"Because that's where we're going."

It was at that moment that McDowell realized why he had not called Withers' bluff and brought the law down on him.

The murders of Jack Granick and Mary Withers. He sensed that somehow they were connected.

Chapter 32

Withers couldn't believe how smoothly the exit had gone off. The police and the CIA were surely following, but at a discreet distance. Overhead, he could see an occasional helicopter, a spotter plane making an incursion, then retreating. He hadn't worked out a plan to escape his pursuers—probably in helicopters and unmarked vehicles. Instead, he decided to see what developed.

"McDowell, you did a good job back there. Nobody got hurt, and we're out of the convention."

Withers' gun was pointed at McDowell's side as he drove.

"Do you have any idea what's going on? Why I tried to kill Hankins? Who murdered my wife? And why?"

Within minutes the car had reached the West Side Drive and was headed northward, traveling up the Hudson.

"No. I haven't the slightest. Do you want to tell me?"

"Do you remember Jack Granick?" Withers asked.

"Sure. Before he was killed he came to see me with a story about one of the candidates. Do you mean that you were involved with Granick too?"

"I was the one who created the file that he was killed for. I was there, at Granick's house, when he was murdered."

"Did the same people kill your wife?"

As they drove onto the Hutchinson River Parkway headed toward Scarsdale, Withers told McDowell part of the story, omitting two major points—any mention of Davidson, and the identity of the person in the file.

"If the KGB, this Colonel Baneyev, was responsible for the death of both your wife and Granick, won't he be after you too?" McDowell asked.

"Absolutely. Killing Mary was their way of smoking me out. You can see that it's worked. They're bound to turn up at any moment. Probably be waiting for us at Scarsdale, along with the CIA and the police."

Withers could feel McDowell's hand become unsteady at the wheel.

Playing reporter on the air, separated from the gory tragedy of life by cue cards, was one thing. But being held captive, gun to flesh, was apparently another.

"Anything wrong, McDowell? We're weaving all over the road," Withers said, steadying the wheel with one hand.

"No. I'm okay. What about the file, Withers? Do you still have it? And you don't have to answer this, but is Senator Hankins connected to all this? Is that why you tried to kill him?"

"You're better off not knowing. Let well enough alone, for now."

At that moment Withers swung about and saw an unmarked white van moving alongside the Corvette, pressing against the rear fender. It was too close a maneuver to be accidental. Either the driver was drunk or they had unanticipated visitors.

"Hit the accelerator! Quick!" Withers shouted.

But McDowell was paralyzed in place. Withers pushed the newsman against the door and depressed his own foot on the pedal, simultaneously grasping the wheel. But the white van had beaten them by a second, inching in front of the Corvette, forcing the car to move perilously close to the edge, separated from a six-foot drop by only a short wire fence.

Withers was now driving with one hand and a foot, seeking to pass the white vehicle, which had edged in front, pressing its wheels against the left fender of the red Corvette.

"Withers, look. It's the helicopter!" It was McDowell, jarred out of his paralysis, pointing at a wingless craft flying less than fifty feet above the careening cars.

Withers glanced upward, then pumped once, twice, on the brake, quickly dropping the Corvette ten yards behind the van. He punched the accelerator to the floor, hoping to pass, but the van driver sensed the move and swerved.

The crash was instantaneous. The Corvette hit the van just behind the driver's seat, spinning it into a rotating top. The van came to a stop where it had started—in the front end of the Corvette, its fender assembly caught in the twisted wreckage. As two cars behind them hit their brakes, then crashed into the rear of the Corvette, Withers realized he was pinned in a highway sandwich.

His thinking was suddenly punctuated by a bullet, which pierced the Corvette windshield only inches to his right. In rapid, succeeding movements, Sam pulled his gun forward and pushed McDowell down under the steering wheel.

Through the window he could see that the driver of the van was injured but that his accomplice was unhurt. Clad in a brown leather jacket and cap, he stood in the center of the road, hands clutched on a gun extended at eye level.

"Agent Withers!" The voice was slightly accented, but firm. "Come out slowly. Hands up. Don't make a fuss, or we'll kill everyone on the road."

Withers knew it was only partially a bluff. Within minutes, a Highway Patrol car would arrive. But he, McDowell, and the others could be killed in the interim. Withers slid to the floor and pressed open the handle of the door. As he did, a shot ricocheted off the metal.

Within seconds, while Withers and McDowell were sheltered in the well of the Corvette, the helicopter slammed to a landing on the highway thirty feet ahead of the crashed vehicles. From over the edge of the windshield Withers could see three New York City SWAT police leap out, equipped with rifles, helmets, and vests. The leather-clad KGB man had moved behind a tree off the road shoulder and was shooting at the police.

Withers whispered to McDowell, using his Christian name for the first time.

"Doug, if you want to know more, speak to John Davidson! Good luck."

With that cryptic message, Withers pushed open the door and raced for the grass, somersaulting just as the KGB agent turned away from the police and fired, late, at him. Sam hit the ground, then rolled over into the ditch below the shoulder. He turned in time to see two SWAT men pump shotgun shells into the KGB gunman, who fell into his own blood.

Sam continued to run, hoping his escape had not been noticed in the melee. He crossed a small, wet ditch, then ran up the other side. Within a minute he was on a suburban road paralleling the parkway. No one seemed to be following him, but he covered the next few hundred yards at his top speed.

It seemed predestined. A taxicab, its dome light lit, was coming directly at him. Withers moved into the center of the road and stood stubbornly fixed, waving the cab down.

"What are you, crazy, mister?"

It was a yellow medallion New York City cab, obviously high-tailing it back to the city after a call to Westchester.

"No, Mac. I'm not crazy. Just tired. Here's twenty dollars. Take me to the Mount Vernon railroad station."

Ten silent minutes later, Sam spotted his old Ford, its North Carolina license plates inviting him.

"Pull over here," he instructed the cabby. Withers waited until the taxi had left, then removed the car keys from his pocket.

He had not avenged Mary. Hankins was still alive, but Withers felt some of the frustration drained from him. Perhaps McDowell would become an ally. And Davidson would now be pushed into making his move. Sam sighed, thinking how improbable his life had become, how forcefully he was being tested on his will to fight back.

Chapter 33

"Jed, it proves what I've been saying all along. This country is basically fascist. It's no different than the killings of the Kennedys and King. All CIA-inspired. There's a right-wing conspiracy forming against you. I can feel it."

Fenton and Hankins were in the library of the townhouse on Wednesday morning after the assassination attempt, twelve hours before the nominating ballot, rehashing the narrow escape. The shooting, the first at a national convention, seemed to have shaken up Fenton more than it had the senator.

Hankins smiled at his AA. Fenton was becoming obsessive in his fascist hunting again. But the assassination try was surely no joke. Another second and he would have been dead. Of course, Fenton failed to mention that it was a young CIA man who had saved his life.

"Bill, don't you think it could just be the work of a single nut?" Hankins asked. "After all, the guy's wife was murdered a few days ago. Maybe he just went crazy and decided I was a logical target."

Fenton shook his head.

"No, Jed. This is part of something bigger. They'll never let you get to the White House. My guess is that Withers is a hired gun for Senator Delafield or some of the old-time warmongers like Orvil Hoopes, or Danny Bradshaw, the head of House Judiciary. A staffer on the Senate Intelligence Committee heard that old man Davidson of the CIA—a real Red baiter—was getting active again. It wouldn't surprise me if he was also involved."

The phone ring interrupted Fenton. "Jed. It's for you. The White House."

Hankins lifted the instrument, bemused.

"Thank you, Mr. President. I appreciate your concern. Yes, sir. I think honoring agent Hopper is a fine idea. We could use more good CIA men like him. And, Mr. President? Could you please redouble your efforts to catch Withers? I'd feel much safer if he were behind bars."

"The President?" Fenton asked, surprised. "What did the chief fascist honcho want? Is he sorry Withers missed?"

Hankins didn't respond, turning pensive.

"Bill, it just occurred to me. Could Withers have learned about me —about us? If he knew everything about my politics, he might want me out of the picture enough to kill me. I'd hate to think there's information out there that we can't control."

Fenton's face paled. "No, Jed. I doubt that Withers knows a thing. These paranoid fascists don't trust anyone, so it's possible he suspects. But as far as having any real information—no. I'm sure you're safe there."

The phone rang again.

"Thanks, Mike. That's good of you. Welcome aboard the team. Every vote counts."

Hankins hung up, the satisfaction displayed at the edges of his mouth.

"That was Congressman Mike Manucci from Connecticut. Says he's outraged by what happened last night. Was on the fence, but now he wants to show his anger at the CIA by supporting us. Great, eh?"

"How many is that today?" Fenton asked.

"He's the eighth. By tonight we should be looking at 30 sympathy votes. With Maynard's people, we're still very much alive. By the way, who's speaking tonight?"

Before Fenton could respond, the image of the convention podium, with his own body crouched behind the lectern, entered Hankins' mind. For the first time, he could see Withers aiming in the instant before the shot went off. He was experiencing a near panic after the fact.

"Bill, is there anything you can do to help get this guy Withers off the street?" Hankins' voice was almost plaintive.

"I've been thinking the same thing, Jed. We can't count on the FBI or the CIA. I'll talk to my people and see what more they can do. But please, Jed. Don't worry too much. We've got a nomination to go after."

Hankins was lost inside himself. "I know, Bill. But I keep thinking there's a madman out there determined to kill me."

☆ ☆ ☆

After Hankins left, Fenton sat in the library, exploiting the solitude to weigh their position. He was sorry Jed had asked about Withers but was confident he had allayed his suspicions.

Baneyev had already relayed the news to him through his contact on the Hill, Marge Coulton, a House committee staff member. A file on Hankins' entire political history had been compiled by the CIA man, who was still out there, a potential ravager of Oval Red. If Withers had only stayed within the Agency, Baneyev's people at Langley would have already defused the awkward situation.

The colonel had insisted that Hankins was not to know about the file. It would only unnerve him at this critical juncture.

Ironman was in Washington, Fenton was sure. Baneyev had informed him of the agent's imminent arrival and he had told Jed about it. But the timing for contact was up to Ironman's discretion. They had heard nothing.

Was there anything Baneyev could do so late in the race? The voting was tonight. The media were Hippodroming Jed's new political vitality, but Fenton was worried. The new totals had brought Jed and Daniels within only 150 votes of each other—1350 to 1200, with 1967 needed to win.

Where were the next votes to come from? Jed needed either Rawlins or Meredith, but there had been no movement from either one. Without them, or some unexpected rescue, Oval Red would remain an unfulfilled fantasy of the little man in the Moscow woods.

Perhaps Baneyev could help. Fenton lifted the phone and impatiently dialed the Sheraton Russell Hotel, where Marge Coulton, who had taken a few days off to be available at the convention, was staying.

"Sheraton Russell. Who would you like to speak to?"

As the operator repeated her question, Fenton realized he was yielding to impulse. Baneyev would have reached him if he wanted to. Perhaps Ironman was already moving on their behalf. Fenton replaced the phone in its cradle.

It had been four years since his first liaison with Colonel Baneyev. Critical years whose future now seemed hinged to a vote only twelve hours away. He could recall, as if imbedded on video tape, the drama of that beginning, whose accidental origins were on a Washington reception line.

☆ ☆ ☆

There was still natural light at eight o'clock that summer evening four years before when Hankins and Fenton arrived at the elegant old stone Pan American Union Building on Constitution Avenue. The young senator had been invited to celebrate a cultural exchange program and had brought along his AA.

The hosts, the ambassadors of seven Latin-American nations, were in the ballroom, where Hankins and Fenton took their places at the end of the slow-moving reception line.

"Bill, isn't this a nice old place? I think I'll just stand here and admire the building," Hankins said. "I hope you don't mind if we don't chat."

Before Fenton could respond, the man in front of them turned abruptly around.

"Senator Hankins, perhaps you won't mind talking with me. I hope you'll forgive me, but I recognize your face from the newspaper photos."

The man had surprised them.

"Oh, I'm sorry again. I should have introduced myself. I am Nikolai Baneyev, cultural attaché at the Soviet Embassy. It seems I have the honor of arranging for the Soviet scholars to study in Latin America. So I am here on the same line as you." He extended his hand to Hankins.

"This is my administrative assistant, Bill Fenton," Hankins responded. "He's been to your country and has found much to admire. Am I right, Bill?"

Fenton smiled self-consciously. While Hankins and the Russian chatted, Fenton stared at Baneyev's eccentric features.

I have seen this man before, Fenton thought. Not here in Washington, but elsewhere, some time ago. Fenton continued his gaze, but the man's second identity, if indeed he had one, eluded him.

"Have you ever been in San Francisco?" Fenton asked, grasping at a thin memory.

"Why do you ask?" Baneyev offered Fenton a suspicious, professional look.

"Oh, I was a graduate student at Berkeley for a year. I attended a few Soviet-American friendship functions at your consulate. Wasn't it on Green Street?"

"Yes. Our consulate is there. So?"

"Weren't you on staff? I almost seem to remember you speak. Your English accent is not quite Russian. Maybe more German. Right?"

Baneyev threw back his head, his laugh loud enough for a few people on line to turn their heads.

"By ginger, you are observant. CIA? Yes? I was in San Francisco, during that whole fracas at the University of California. What did you people call it? Oh yes. The Free Speech Movement. My accent? Right again. I studied English for several years, but not in my native Russia. I picked it up at graduate school in East Germany. With a slight German intonation, you say? I didn't know that myself."

The Russian turned toward Hankins. "Senator, you've made no mistake choosing this young man as your AA. In a few minutes, he has my whole c.v. What more is there to know about a cultural attaché, the most prosaic of all diplomats?"

The line started to move. They said their pleasantries to the Latin ambassadors, then walked toward the large buffet table. Fenton located two chairs in the corner and he and Hankins were balancing their food like veteran Washingtonians when Fenton gulped, coughing on a piece of boneless fish.

"It's okay, Jed. I startled myself when I suddenly remembered something. I'm okay now. Would you hold my plate? I'll be right back."

Fenton sped his thin frame across the ballroom, moving toward the back of Baneyev, who was in conversation with a Latin ambassador.

"Penshekov! Penshekov! That was it!" Fenton shouted as he approached, his eyes displaying discovery.

The Russian dropped his teacup and wheeled about to face Fenton, a scowl dominating his unique features.

"You surprised me, young man."

In a moment the scowl was gone, replaced by a labored smile intended to cover his gaffe. As Baneyev bent to pick up the cup, the ambassador waved in a maid.

Baneyev placed his hand warmly on Fenton's shoulder. The AA had become silent, aware that his impulsiveness had upset the room's diplomatic balance.

"Mr. Ambassador, would you excuse me for a moment?" Baneyev asked. "This young man wants to ask me something."

The Russian gracefully led Fenton by the arm into a quiet corner of the room.

"Please keep your voice down, Mr. Fenton. We don't want to embarrass anybody more than we have already. Do we? Now tell me, what is it that you called out before? Penkovsky? Some name like that?"

"Penshekov. Now I remember. That's what you called yourself when you came to visit our group at Berkeley. Do you remember? It was a lecture to our SDS group. Then after that we had an activist cell and you . . ."

Fenton silenced himself. This was no place to discuss his Weathermen activities of almost two decades ago.

He could see Baneyev fidgeting, probably concerned that the conversation had gotten away from him.

"Young man, this is all very interesting. You have obviously confused me with another Russian. But be that as it may, I am pleased that you are an American with progressive persuasions. Is that still the case?"

When Fenton nodded, Baneyev offered a parting comment between half-closed teeth.

"Mr. Fenton, this is not an acquaintance that should end prematurely. Would you do me the honor of meeting again? Let us please be judicious. You are the AA to a prominent American senator and I am a Soviet diplomat. Let us say the National Zoo, tomorrow at noon. In front of the . . ."

Baneyev smiled, exposing a silver tooth. ". . . the grizzly bear area."

☆   ☆   ☆

Within weeks after Fenton had his secret rendezvous with Colonel Baneyev at the zoo, he had several more clandestine meetings with Soviet Embassy personnel and was recruited into the service of the KGB. Every Tuesday and Friday, at noon, Fenton met with Marge Coulton, his courier, who lived in suburban Bethesda, Maryland. Even though she worked at the Rayburn House Office Building, it was safer to communicate with Baneyev through a series of three rural drops.

Fenton and Marge, both single, were to appear sexually interested in each other, encouraged to meet regularly to exchange classified papers, or for lunch in various restaurants. The dining conversation was invariably friendly and romantic, never the true business of their date. Washington restaurants, Baneyev reminded them, are notorious for overheard indiscretions.

The initial meeting place was always the same, beneath the Robert A. Taft Memorial, the carillon tower near the Capitol. Baneyev thought it fitting to honor the conservative Ohio senator's memory with a long-term espionage plot against his country.

Now, four years later, Fenton's relationship with Baneyev had matured into Oval Red. Fenton knew that Senator Jedidiah Hankins, nurtured for thirteen years, represented the best chance he—or the Center—would ever have for political subversion in America.

Chapter 34

Between Moscow's hopes and its execution of Oval Red stood one man, Governor Marc Daniels. And between Daniels and his victory was Senator Angus Delafield, party hawk.

"I don't know why the hell I should see you, Daniels. I've been listening to you for over a year and you don't sound much better than your dovish friends."

Daniels had called Delafield at the Greenwich, Connecticut, estate where he was staying for the convention week as a guest of an Air Force buddy who had married wealth.

"Angus, I need you. And the country needs you. Would you prefer Jed Hankins as President?"

The phone turned silent for a second.

"Marc, God damn it. Now you've aggravated me. Did you see who's coming out of the woodwork for that punk kid? An army of peacenik delegates. All moving in one direction—the Soviet Union. I'm scared."

"Then maybe we should talk, Angus," Daniels offered.

"Look, Marc, I'm not just going to trade a Hankins for a mealymouth like you. Maybe you don't like the Russians but you're deathly afraid of them. You're also petrified by the left wing of our party. And I'm still in this race myself. When the party realizes it can't win without patriotism, they'll come over to me. I don't care if it's on the twenty-fourth ballot. I think it's a waste of time, but if you want to talk, I'll see you tomorrow morning at eight. At your place."

"Could you make it a little later? I'm going to be up late with my staff."

"Hell, Daniels. Half the day'll be gone. Eight o'clock or nothing."

Delafield woke on Wednesday morning at 5:30 A.M. in his friend's Round Hill Road estate. By six-thirty he had washed, jogged, and dressed. By six forty-five, he was on the road to New York to keep the appointment with Daniels.

At the Triplex Suite, Daniels was having breakfast with Les, who had slept in her own bed for the first time in days.

"Are Delafield's 280 votes so important?" asked Les, obviously troubled by Daniels' mood.

"Yes, Les. They're crucial. The voting's tonight and the desertions to Hankins haven't stopped. I just got two phone calls, from Georgia and Massachusetts. People I was counting on for the second ballot are moving to Hankins. Even some of Hawley Briggs's delegates."

"But why, Governor? What's doing it?" Les asked, concern for Daniels' dilemma in her voice.

"They always give the same answer. That Hankins is better equipped to make peace with the Soviet Union. Baloney. So, Delafield's essential now. He'll put us within three hundred of the mark."

Daniels pondered Hankins' quick rise. How had it been orchestrated so thoroughly, so covertly, and across the board nationally?

At 7:55 A.M., Les greeted the ruddy-faced Delafield at the door.

"Senator, Governor Daniels has been looking forward to this. I hope you'll join with us."

"We'll find out, young lady. Whoever's for America, I'm for him," Delafield responded loudly enough for Daniels to overhear.

Les escorted him into the living room, where Daniels was waiting.

"Governor, they tell me you're the front runner. Is that true?"

"I think so, Angus, but please don't tell the press. It'll cost me." The two men laughed at the campaign joke.

"Governor, what can I do for you?" Delafield's question was rhetorical, almost insulting. "You know what I believe in. But I've heard you on every side of the Soviet threat. I promise not to tell the voters. What do you really think?"

What did he believe? God, sometimes he didn't know what was right and wrong when it came to relations with the Soviet Union. But wasn't it more complex than the ex-SAC bomber pilot saw it—as a matter of targets and defense budgets?

"Angus, I want the same thing for America as you do. Only this is not 1941. We lost 440,000 men in that war. The next time more will die in the first second. So we have to look at it differently, don't we? The question, Angus, is how do we keep the peace with Russia and still try to develop more democracies around the world?"

Delafield's expression turned stern. "Maybe I can help you, Governor. Every administration that has had a strong defense and called the Soviet bluff has won out. The Reds are bullies. They only attack when the coast is clear. Truman stopped them in Greece, then in Western Europe with NATO. Eisenhower threatened them in Korea and they made peace. Johnson moved into the Dominican Republic with no problem, as Reagan did in Grenada. Nixon called the Soviets' bluff in the Yom Kippur War when Brezhnev threatened to send Soviet troops to Egypt. It's the cowards who lose to the Russians."

Delafield stared down his fellow candidate. "So where do you stand, Governor?"

Daniels shifted in place, his face paler, aware of the significance of this one answer.

"Angus, I really don't know how I'll handle the Soviet Union except that I have no intention of starting a war against them, anywhere. But I can tell you this. If they push us into a conflict, I'll insist on being ready for it militarily.

"I'm not making any deals, with you or anybody else," he continued, his voice escalating in confidence. "But I'll let you in on a secret. I've already asked a friend of yours, former Air Force Chief Willie Jamieson, to become my Secretary of Defense. He's accepted. I'm not announcing it yet, but I thought you'd like to know."

Daniels could see the disorientation spread across Delafield's face.

"Jamieson? Tough Willie Jamieson? My God, Daniels, I came here to beat you up politically. But you've given me exactly what I want."

Delafield smacked the governor's shoulder affectionately. "Daniels, damn it. That's good news. Good enough for me. You've got my vote and I think at least 270 of my 280 delegates. Yes, by God, that's good news."

The general extended his hand to Daniels, who grasped it in return.

"Mr. President, I'm with you. All the way."

After the two men exchanged good-byes, Les escorted the senator to the door. He was still muttering as he exited the suite.

"My God, that's something. A real surprise."

☆　☆　☆

The activity was hectic at the Triplex Suite. It was 6 P.M., Wednesday evening, less than four hours before the voting.

"Les, could you give me some help with this batch?" Stan Gordon, Daniels' campaign manager, called out. "I've got a bunch of uncommitted delegates who were out of their hotels. Every vote's going to count tonight."

"What do the latest numbers look like, Stan?" Les asked.

"Good, but not so good. With Delafield's people, we're up over 1600. But we're still 350 short. Hankins can't make it on the first ballot, but he's getting a lot of noise on the so-called 'peace delegates.' And that crazed CIA man helped him too. If we're stopped on the first, there could be a lot of drain. Hankins could even take it on the second or third ballot."

Gordon was expressing the concern that had gripped the room. Governor Daniels, Les, and Gordon had been on the phone continuously, but for every vote they recouped, they lost another. The night looked long and indecisive.

Then, just before seven o'clock, Barry Ladd called from the other room.

"Hey, everybody. Look who's on the tube."

The Daniels staff gathered around the television set, the governor the last to arrive.

They could see the camera move in for a close view of Doug McDowell, seated expectantly at his desk. The camera then shifted to the left as Senator Katy Meredith walked onstage and moved toward the newscaster.

☆　☆　☆

Never before had McDowell been so distracted. The events of the past weeks, beginning with Granick's untimely appearance, the col-

umnist's death, then being held captive by a CIA man turned would-
be assassin, were muddling his rules of journalistic involvement. He
was supposed to report and evaluate news, not live it. McDowell felt
like a player in an athletic event for which there were no rules.

He was frustrated. McDowell still didn't know the identity of
Granick's Red candidate, and Withers' advice to see Davidson had
been fruitless. Before the convention, he had made another trip to the
Cosmos, but the old spy had again pleaded ignorance.

Fortunately, things were moving more conventionally tonight. He
had a potential scoop sitting next to him. Senator Katy Meredith, like
Congressman Rawlins, was a stubborn holdout, even resisting the
entreaties of the press. But he had snared her for an interview. Mc-
Dowell believed he knew why. Meredith preferred to do her dealing
in the open, even on television.

"Senator, welcome to showdown time," McDowell began. "How
large is your delegate strength?"

"Doug, it's considerable, about 680. But not enough. So I'm here to
tell you I don't expect to become the first woman President of the
United States. At least not this time."

That wasn't news. But McDowell sensed that Meredith was only
warming up.

"Senator, then what about a deal for the VP slot? Will you consider
it?"

"No, I don't want to be Vice-President. On that I'm willing to go
the Sherman route. Should anything happen to the President, people
will say a woman gained the Oval Office only through accident. No,
on my own, or not at all."

That was not exactly news, either. But McDowell was pleased that
she had added the Sherman pledge.

"Senator, you'll be getting a lot of first-ballot votes. Will you be
throwing them to another candidate on the second ballot?"

"Doug, it may surprise you, but the answer is yes. I expect my
delegates to back me on the opening ballot. On the second one, I'll
release them. To whom? Earlier today, I met with Governor Daniels
for an hour. He repeated that he'd make no deals of any kind. And I
believe him. I respect all the candidates, but I think there's only one
man who can unite the party and the country. That's Marc Daniels."

The convention floor erupted, the cameras panning in every direction, capturing the origins of a mad victory parade for Daniels. Mc-

Dowell knew he had produced the scoop of the convention. The nomination was now Daniels', possibly on the very first ballot.

At the Palace Hotel, the mood shifted in that one precious instant.

"We did it!" screamed Les Fanning, throwing her arms around Tom Ward. "It's only 7 P.M. and we've got it all locked up!"

She raced over and kissed the governor. "We did it!" Les repeated, casting her wineglass against the Triplex wall.

The meeting erupted into a party, the governor circulating, receiving congratulations, which he modestly turned back onto the staff. Everyone's happiness overflowed.

All except Tom Ward's. Yearling's defeat was hardly gratifying for Ironman. Had he trained for years and traveled thousands of miles only to witness the premature end of a potentially brilliant scheme?

Then it struck him. Of course. Within hours, Daniels would be choosing a vice-presidential candidate. Ward now saw that he had a clear assignment. To convince Les, then Daniels, that Jed Hankins, the youthful hero of the under-forties, was the logical running mate on the Democratic ticket.

"Les, it's wonderful news." Ward smiled at her. "Let's go over and congratulate the governor. He's got a busy road ahead before he gets into the White House. I'd like to help as much as I can."

"I think he'll love the idea," Les said as she grasped Ward's hand and guided him toward the nominee.

Chapter 35

"Tom, don't fret. It'll only be a couple of hours. I'd rather stay with you, but Marc expects me at this meeting. We're going to pick the VP."

Ward sensed that Les had misinterpreted his muted mood as loneliness, rather than what it was—one fixed on the upcoming choice of the vice-presidential candidate. He and Les were in his room at the Hilton at 11 A.M. on Thursday, the morning after Daniels' nomination. Tom was in bed, reading. Les had just emerged from the shower, singing in a half-flat contralto. She was toweling herself, primping for the noon meeting at the Triplex Suite.

Ward stared at Les's supple body but realized this was no time to be diverted. He hadn't been invited to the confab, and these precious minutes had to be used to influence Les.

"Don't worry about me," Ward said. "I'll be fine here. By the way, Les, who do you think Daniels will choose?"

Nude, Les positioned herself on the edge of the bed to put on her underclothes.

"Tom, I've been thinking about nothing else. Who do I think? Well, the only one he ever mentions is Hawley Briggs. He's crazy about the old coot. He thinks he's Harry Truman reincarnated, and then some."

Les stopped the motion of her dressing.

"Tom, I know you're a novice at politics. But I think you've got good instincts. Who do you think would be the best choice?"

He had hoped for such an opening.

"I haven't given it much thought, Les. But if I were Daniels, I wouldn't be looking for someone sympatico, like Hawley Briggs. I'd be trying for a strong contrast, someone who could bring in voters who weren't sure about me."

"But aren't Briggs and Daniels a good old-time mix?" Les asked. "You know. Like FDR and Truman and JFK and Johnson?"

"I'm no expert, Les. But I don't think that plays any more. The sun belt is becoming more Republican all the time. They won't vote for a politician just because he's Southern. Someone like Briggs works only with the yellow-dog Democrats—those who vote the star no matter what."

Ward could see that Les had become intrigued by his argument.

"If not Briggs, who do you think would be right for Daniels?" she asked.

He waited. Verisimilitude, he remembered. The appearance of truth. The essence of deception.

"I suppose there's only one of the six who fits my theory," Ward finally answered.

"Who's that?"

"That's . . . well, it's Jed Hankins."

"Hankins?" Les's shock was apparent. "I think Marc really dislikes him. He feels he almost spoiled his candidacy."

"Well, I wasn't talking about soul mates, or even friends. You asked me who would bring in new votes. Hankins would do that. Sometimes he talks like a leftist. Other times, like a Republican. He'd bring Daniels the young professionals who support no ideology except to make a dollar and be politically fashionable."

"But why should they want Hankins?" Les asked.

"Because he's got everything they admire. Youth. Style. Money. And—they're peace-oriented. Scared stiff at the thought of nuclear war taking it all away. Hankins plays pied piper to their fears beautifully. Most important, there's very little overlap in the support for Daniels and Hankins. I think it's a winning team."

Les stared at her lover, who seemed to be reclining phlegmatically on the bed, yet divining so cogently off the top of his head.

"Tom, I think you're right. If Marc looks at this emotionally, he'll lose. Hankins may be a son of a bitch, but look what he's done at thirty-nine. Almost took the nomination away from the party favorite. And you're right about the young professionals. I don't see it, but all my girl friends think he's great."

Les was suddenly thoughtful.

"Darling, I have an idea. Would you like to attend the meeting with me? I think I can arrange it with Gordon."

Ward smiled softly. "Of course, Les. Anything you say."

☆ ☆ ☆

Waiting impatiently for Daniels in the Triplex Suite, the staff asked themselves, "Who will be on the ticket with Daniels?"

In 1956, Adlai Stevenson had defied tradition and thrown the VP choice to an open convention. But who remembered his running mate—Estes Kefauver, the man who beat out John Fitzgerald Kennedy for the number two spot that year? The VP selection was usually the candidate's, who then force-fed it to the delegates, like it or not. That's what they were here to do today.

When the meeting opened, Gordon spoke first. "In spite of her Sherman pledge, I like Katy Meredith. I know it hasn't worked in the past, but I think this is different."

Following Gordon, the campaign's intellectual mentor, Barry Ladd, insisted that Hawley Briggs, the former Arkansas governor, would bring back the middle-of-the-roaders who had become Bible-toting Republicans. As Ladd spoke, Daniels' approving smile filled the room.

Next, Daniels called on Josh Martin, the campaign pollster.

"I prefer to wait until everyone is finished. Okay?"

Daniels nodded.

Sally McIver, the chief "advance man," seconded Gordon's choice of Katy Meredith, while her assistant, Jane Rubinstein, opted for Clarence Rawlins.

Les stood waiting her turn. Tensely, Ward thought.

"I have something to say that will be unpopular in this room," Les began hesitantly. "Maybe it even sounds traitorous. It's simply that I think the governor, and the party—if we are going to win—need Jed Hankins in the number two spot. . . ."

As Les uttered the name, audible noises filled the air. McIver got out of her chair and stood against the wall, controlling rage.

"Now hold on, everybody." It was the governor. "I didn't call this meeting to exorcise any ghosts or condemn anyone. Les is trying to express herself honestly. Please, everybody. Les, now what were you saying about Jed Hankins?"

Les continued, elaborating what she and Ward had discussed at the Hilton, adding the fervor of a recent convert. She sat down to a room of silence, even to a pinch of hostility.

The pollster Josh Martin, who had initially passed, was next.

"I thought Les was looking over my shoulder," Martin said, waving a sheaf of papers, as if to prove they existed.

"The numbers are clear. When Governor Daniels is matched with Briggs, Rawlins, Meredith, Sommerville, even Delafield—the popular vote varies geographically, but it's the same nationally. It's 39 percent for Daniels and 61 percent for either of the two leading Republicans. The only change is when Daniels is matched with Hankins. The Democratic ticket picks up seven points everywhere. I'm only a pollster, but I agree with Les. Jed Hankins as VP is our only chance to move into the White House."

"Oh, shit!" It was Stan Gordon, on his feet, bellowing, "No. No. NO." The decibels peaked. Hostility. Frustration. The handmaidens of politics had confronted an abrupt change of direction.

"Stan. Everyone. Please sit down," the governor called out. "I listened patiently. Now I want to put in my two cents. It's no secret that I came here hoping to have my choice of Hawley Briggs confirmed. But I have to confess something. Hawley Briggs is my sentimental choice, but my instinct has always been that Hankins was the way to win. I resisted it. He's a proven liberal with a good voting record, but I don't particularly like the man. Did Reagan like Bush when he chose him? Did FDR like, or even really know, Harry Truman?

"Hankins comes from another world than I do. I don't even fully understand his appeal. But I guarantee you it's there. I suppose there's something in being rich in a nation that extols money. And he is handsome, and tall, and young, and stylish, and clever, and single. Whatever he's got, it's something I'm missing. I'm afraid Les is right. Separately, we'll lose this race. Together, we have a chance.

"So before I sit down, I want to tell you that I've decided. I will ask Jed Hankins to be my vice-presidential running mate."

Daniels stared at his staff with a conflicted expression, then turned back into his room.

☆　☆　☆

"Jed, I think you're making a big mistake."

Bill Fenton, struggling under an electric typewriter, placed it down on the dining-room table.

"I don't want to be your nagging aunt, Jed, but if we're to have a chance next time, you have to play the party regular. That means grinning all the way to hell on the convention podium tonight."

Hankins shook his head.

"No, Bill. Form be fucked. I won't do it. I'll plead Senate business and send Daniels a telegram he can wave on the stage. I've had it."

It was Thursday afternoon, about one o'clock. Jed Hankins was disconsolate, sitting on the edge of a chair in his New York townhouse. Around him, his aides and chauffeur were packing.

Propriety held that Hankins stay for Daniels' acceptance speech and the voting for Vice-President. But he'd be damned if he'd donate another minute of humiliation to the Democratic Party. He was going home to Homestead. He'd rather be with a horse right now than with his fellow politicians.

All the hope of leading America into the world socialist orbit had evaporated. All the pain and risk of dealing with Baneyev and the Soviet Union had been wasted. He wanted no more of it. Neither the Russians, with their Byzantine intrigue, nor, for that matter, Washington, with its bland, compromising politics.

Hankins stared out the window at the unlit street lamp across the way, distant in thought.

The phone rang. "Would you get it, Bill?" Hankins asked, his eyes still focused elsewhere.

Fenton lifted the phone. His voice dropped, almost to a whisper.

"Jed, it's for you. Governor Daniels on the line."

Daniels? What sadistic ploy had he in mind? Hankins wondered. Would he have the gall to ask him to head the pageantry committee for tonight's coronation? American liberals nauseated him. He could tolerate the conservatives. They were perverted, but they had a sense of duty. But Daniels and his crowd. God, what transparent divinity. The Church of the Liberal Ghost. It was too much for even the deity, should there have been one, he thought.

Hankins indifferently picked up the receiver.

"Yes, Governor?" he asked, as if the hold button was delaying another, more important call. "What can I do for you?"

Daniels spoke. As he did, Hankins' eyes transmitted a new light. The lethargy left his bones, his frame was now upright. His voice rose in register.

"Governor Daniels, it will be a privilege! I accept unconditionally! Thank you. Thank you!"

Hankins paused to listen. "Yes, Governor. I'll keep it absolutely confidential until you announce it. Thanks again!"

Hankins turned to Fenton, his tone at first muted.

"Daniels has just asked me to be his vice-presidential candidate."

Then as it struck him, he yelled out his joy.

"Bill! We've done it! We're going to make it. Only a heartbeat from the White House!"

He moved toward Fenton and for the first time in their thirteen years the two men embraced.

Chapter 36

Lightheaded with success, Tom Ward left the Daniels suite and walked along Madison Avenue, seeking air. Les had decided to stay with the nominee. Daniels might need help.

Ward had to contact Rausch, to convey the good news about Yearling before it was announced. Walter would be the one to relay it to the Soviet Embassy in case they required some immediate action.

Ward also had an unanswered question for Rausch, perhaps to pose to Moscow. It was one of presidential "wet business."

Ward decided to take the next shuttle down to Washington, where Rausch had returned after the documentary showing.

The taxi from National Airport found the Washington traffic heavy, but Ward was at the door of Rausch's colonial home by three-thirty. Only seconds after he rang the large brass bell, Rausch answered.

"What are you doing here?" Rausch asked, somewhat irritated. "I figured you'd be with Les and Daniels. What's up?"

"I just was. Can I come in? I have news."

The two men sat on the couch in Rausch's paneled library.

"What is it, Tom? Now that Daniels has the nomination, I suppose Oval Red is finished? So soon?"

Ward understood the source of Rausch's negative mood.

"Not necessarily, Walter. I've just come from a meeting at Daniels' place. Hankins has been given the number two spot on the Democratic ticket. It won't be announced until tonight, but I knew you'd want to know right away."

Ward sensed that Rausch was straining not to react excessively. Perhaps it was unbecoming in front of an agent. But the exhilaration finally covered his features.

"That's wonderful!" Rausch exclaimed, rising buoyantly to shake Ward's hand. "I'm sure you had something to do with it, Tom. But in any case, I must get the news to Baneyev right away. We have no time for a drop. Withers is still out there."

"Can you reach the embassy quickly?" Ward asked.

"I have a way. Please, Tom, come with me."

Rausch led Ward down the hall, then to the basement, where they moved through Rausch's plush projection room, large enough to seat eighteen. Then down a smaller hallway, presumably to a storeroom, where Rausch withdrew a key and opened the door.

Ward was stunned by the electronic paraphernalia. Two walls of the room were crowded with a large short-wave radio transmitter and receiver and peripheral recording equipment. Over a desk were framed certificates, testimony to Rausch's technical legitimacy.

"Yes, I've even got a ham radio license from the FCC—at the top level of EXTRA. The equipment is the finest made, a Mil Spec 1030 transceiver. Just the basics cost me $12,000. I show people how it works. They think it's a harmless hobby. Watch."

Rausch withdrew his logbook, then dialed a transmitter frequency in the 40-meter band, 7 megahertz.

"Hello, Brussels. Brussels. This is for Monsieur Blanchette. Blanchette. Please return my call. This is John. John calling."

"We'll have to wait," Rausch explained to Ward, now observing curiously. "Blanchette—his code name—has several frequencies in an open receiving position, including mine. My signal is being taped. When he sees the light on his recorder, he'll listen to the message, then call me back."

Ward was confused. "But why Brussels? I thought you were trying to reach the embassy in Washington?"

"Yes, but it's too dangerous to do it directly. I have to go through Moscow. Even that's not totally safe," Rausch explained. "The National Security Agency monitors the radio messages from the United States to the Soviet Union. But they can't be everywhere, so I relay mine through special agents in other countries—this time Belgium. Blanchette will take the message and send it on to the Center in Moscow in Morse. Then they'll radio Baneyev in Washington in diplomatic cipher."

Rausch halted as static came out of the wall speaker.

"Listen. Blanchette is coming in."

Ward could hear crackling, then the uneven sounds of a radio being adjusted for clarity. Finally, a sharp voice from overseas.

"John. This is Blanchette. Are you there, John?"

"Yes. This is John. Blanchette, I have some good news for your daughter Nicole. Her horse, Yearling, has come in second in the big race. He paid off beautifully. I know she'll want to know right away. Repeat. Yearling has come in second in the big race. Confirm."

The radio was silent, then it stuttered. Soon a clear sound came from the speaker.

"This is Blanchette again. Thanks for the message. I'll tell Nicole immediately. Everyone here is fine. Au revoir, John."

"Au revoir," Rausch responded, turning off the set.

The two men returned to the library, to wait. For what, they didn't know. Except that in the next minutes, or hours, the other end of the Moscow connection should fall into place. Meanwhile, they could not afford to be elsewhere.

Walter turned on the television. He and Ward sat for twenty minutes watching a convention commentary, until the phone rang.

"Yes. This is Walter Rausch. Can I help you?"

"Mr. Rausch, you don't know me. I have a plane to catch, but I thought I would try you before I left. My name is Billings, Robert Billings. I'm executive director of the Federal Organization. We're a think tank here in Washington. I wonder if you could meet a member of my staff later this afternoon. We'd like to discuss a documentary film, and . . ."

Rausch broke into his mid-sentence.

"Mr. Billings, I'm sure I can help you, but couldn't this wait until you get back? I'm expecting an important call."

"Oh, I forgot to tell you, Mr. Rausch. We were recommended by a mutual friend, Mr. John Yearling. Yes, that's right, Yearling."

The message had gotten through. With his fingers, Rausch signaled a V to Ward, then pointed for him to pick up the phone extension.

"Oh yes, Mr. Billings. In that case, I can meet as soon as possible. What about the old Chesapeake & Ohio Canal? I sometimes jog there."

"Where? Yes. Why not?" Billings replied. "I don't jog, but my colleague, Miss Carole Slater, is training for the Washington Marathon. Yes, surely, in an hour. Outside Fletcher's Boathouse alongside the canal. You'll recognize her. She's quite tall. I hope we can make a deal on that documentary for the Federal Organization. And thank you."

Ward could see Rausch's face, moments before drained by anticipation, relax. It had been correct to reach Moscow after all. Otherwise they wouldn't be risking a new avenue to reach them. Like Rausch, he now knew the Federal Organization, an ultra-left think tank, was KGB. Of course, the secret was safe with them.

"Well, it's done," an exhilarated Rausch told Ward. "I'll be meeting my contact soon. I'd invite you, but you should get back to the convention."

"Yes. I will. But first, Walter, I have to ask you something. That's one reason I came down personally."

"What is it, Tom?"

"Now that Hankins is the VP nominee, shouldn't we consider eliminating Daniels? With the candidate dead, the Democrats will surely choose Hankins to replace him. Yearling will be a step closer to the White House. What do you think, Walter? Should we query Orlov?"

Rausch was clearly surprised by the boldness of the assassination idea.

"Tom, good point. But let me turn it around. What do you think of taking Daniels out now?"

Ward smiled at Rausch's tactic.

"I've been mulling it over all afternoon. What do I think? Well, with Daniels dead, I'm pretty sure Hankins would get the nomination. But I don't think he'd win the election. There's something too smug about him. Too youthful, too handsome. Too rich. He'd make a nice showing but lose to the Republicans. Then we'd have nothing. But Daniels has a mature warmth the voters like. I think he has a chance at the White House. Then with Hankins as VP . . . Well, we can see then."

"You've answered your own question. Do you still want me to query Moscow?"

"No, Walter. Let's keep it between us. I'm afraid they'd make the wrong decision."

Rausch touched Ward's shoulder. "I agree. I've already told Baneyev to let Orlov know he chose well in you."

He glanced at his watch. "Well, it's time for my jog. See you."

☆ ☆ ☆

For Rausch, the Chesapeake & Ohio Canal, which wends through Georgetown alongside the Potomac, was one of the more pleasant features of the capital. At least twice a week he ran on its well-kept dirt towpath.

The canal, which stretches from Georgetown 185 miles upstream, was George Washington's dream—a waterway that would open the new Federal City, as the capital was then called, to the West. But when the canal was finished, in the 1850s, the railroads had already become insuperable competition. Reconstructed as a national park, the canal added another historic touch to Georgetown.

Fletcher's Boathouse was less than two miles from Rausch's home. Rausch picked up the canal in Georgetown and joined the other joggers moving up and down the soft roadway. As he approached the boathouse he could see her. He was surprised by her size—at least six feet tall, he guessed. Even in her jogging suit, she was a striking, shapely woman with large eyes and long, almost jet-black hair reaching below her shoulder blades.

Rausch crossed the small wooden bridge to the boathouse side and chugged up to her.

"Miss Slater, I presume." She nodded. "I'm Walter Rausch. I've come to discuss the documentary film with you."

"Pleasure, Mr. Rausch. Why don't we jog together and talk? I'm in training for the marathon. I suppose Mr. Billings told you."

It was pleasant conversation, but she meant it as her end of the identification. The two jogged side by side, Rausch moving more briskly than usual to keep up with her long strides. She was silent for three minutes as they moved in harmony. Finally, Slater spoke.

"The message is simple, but urgent." She was speaking effortlessly, running without missing a beat. "First, I'm to make it clear that I don't know its meaning, so I can't help you with any clarification.

"The message is: 'Congratulations on Yearling. We believe the missing file is on the farm of CIA man Davidson in Leesburg. Active measure by the embassy is too dangerous. Use your own people and secure it without delay. Yearling's success depends upon it. The Center.' "

For a moment Slater slowed her running pace and turned toward Rausch, offering him a warm smile.

"That's it. There is no more. Happy jogging."

With that, she stretched her long legs and moved down the canal path, leaving Rausch behind to view the back of her large, disappearing frame.

Rausch slowed to a walk. Davidson? That meant dealing with the thirty-five-year CIA veteran. Baneyev had thrown him a difficult one, but he had no option. Without the file in safe Soviet hands, Hankins had no chance to become VP, or even to continue in American politics.

Despite warnings to himself that he was too old for direct action, Rausch knew he had just been pushed to the apex of a short list of selection. This was one job he would have to do himself. Even if he didn't enjoy the prospect of taking on John the Baptist.

Chapter 37

The presidential election campaign began a week before Labor Day, the politicians sneaking up on the still vacationing public.

It looked unexpectedly good for the Democrats. The first polls showed a tight race, with Republican Amos Lincoln McCauley of Vermont ahead of Daniels by only six points, 53 to 47.

McCauley was not an ideal candidate, but frustrated Republican Party leaders were offering him as the best they had—considering. The consideration was the sweet memory of Ronald Reagan. The Republican candidate was doubly frustrating because he was experienced—chairman of the Senate Foreign Relations Committee—tall, spare, with a reasonable amount of hair, and all the Reaganesque friendly reassurances.

But he was not Ronald Reagan. The fault lay in his smile. At first convincingly hearty and familial, it transformed in minutes, cracking at the edges, an epidermal hint to the testiness within, especially a hostile intolerance of his detractors on the Hill and in the press. Some people were fooled, but increasingly the television icon tube was unmasking the Reagan act-alike.

Daniels was proving more believable as a father figure. And buoyed by the boyish image of running mate Jed Hankins, Daniels was pulling up slowly, and cumulatively. It looked like a long, tight horse race.

But every American presidential campaign comes equipped with a surprise. This one erupted on September 15, just prior to a rally in Chicago, when reporters huddled around Daniels in his Ritz-Carlton suite, hoping for something to enliven a contest that was generous in rhetoric but miserly on news.

The press conference was about to conclude when a tall woman in her forties rose, her hand shyly seeking recognition.

"Yes." Stan Gordon pointed. "Please identify yourself, then ask your question."

The woman peered at Daniels, then down at the ground, without uttering a word.

"Please speak up," Gordon said impatiently. "We have only a few minutes."

Her eyes lifted. "Governor Daniels, my name is Molly Lyons." She spoke haltingly, almost embarrassed, in a high, ethereal voice. "I'm with a string of small weeklies in Tennessee. I don't mean to trouble you, but when you were greeting people at the Evanston train station early this morning . . . I saw you put a pill in your mouth. My question, Governor, is—was it only an aspirin? Or are you taking medication for something serious?"

Gordon bristled. "We've already issued a definitive medical statement on Governor Daniels. Is there another, closing, question?"

Daniels' hand swiftly cut the air.

"No, Stan. Don't move on. Madam, I compliment you. No, it wasn't an aspirin. My physician examined me just yesterday. He thinks I have a heart condition. The pill is nitroglycerine and I started using it only this morning. Does that answer your question?"

The uproar was deafening. So many microphones were thrust into Daniels' face that Gordon moved in.

"Okay! Ease off! Please! The press conference is over!" he shouted into the din. "We'll issue a press statement this evening."

For the next days the nation argued nothing except the merits of a man with a "heart condition" running for the presidency. The networks ran "specials," while the news magazines anatomically dissected the human heart.

"Angina pectoris" presented a complex set of symptoms. Daniels felt pain in the upper quadrant of his chest, to the left of the sternum, the breastbone, and throughout the left arm. The illness, the nation was told, was a precursor of a myocardial infarction, an often fatal heart attack in which the coronary artery cannot supply sufficient oxygen-laden blood to the myocardium, the striped muscle that is the principal component of the heart wall. Nitroglycerine helps alleviate the pain by dilating the vessels and increasing the flow of blood.

In the days following, Gordon and Les issued position papers on defense, Social Security, crime, but the news media were listening to another drummer. They asked only one question:

Can a man with a heart condition serve in the White House?

☆ ☆ ☆

In the living room of the old Leesburg farmhouse, John Davidson stroked Dulles, his aging Labrador. Outside, the autumn countryside was painted gold as the passionate part of the presidential election drew near.

He was content. Sam's incriminating file on Senator Hankins was safely hidden in the smokehouse, and Withers had sent him the missing cassette the way jewelers shipped their million-dollar diamonds— by registered U.S. mail.

Luckily, all the evidence now seemed useless. The heart question had so injured Daniels that the Democratic ticket had dropped to below 38 percent in the polls, a replay of the old Reagan days. No need to expose the senator and drag the country through another wrenching Watergate, and probably worse. Jed Hankins, Davidson was certain, was about to join the ranks of former Congressman William Miller, Goldwater's vice-presidential candidate, who came no closer to the White House than a free lunch.

After the election, he would place the Hankins file in the hands of his young attorney, an ex-CIA agent, should the senator try to rekindle his quest for the White House after he was gone.

For now, Davidson would wait out the three weeks left until election, then take the longest drink of bourbon in his life.

☆ ☆ ☆

"Everybody, listen carefully," Daniels said exuberantly to the staffers assembled in his office at the K Street headquarters. "This is the beginning of a new campaign."

"What's the miracle, Governor? Are you cured?"

Daniels smiled through Barry Ladd's crude jest.

"I just came back from my doctor. I told him that the angina pain has been gone for a week. He was surprised, but it seems that a spasm of the esophagus sometimes mimics angina, then just goes away. He thinks it may have happened in my case. I'm off the medication and I never felt better."

"My God, that is a miracle!" Les exclaimed.

"Les, you haven't heard it all. Stan, I want you to arrange a press affair. Tomorrow morning at 8 A.M., right in Rock Creek Park. Everyone is invited. I'm going to run five miles through the park. We'll show the world there's life left in the old pol."

More than a thousand people showed that cloudless, warm October day as Daniels, clad in a University of Chicago sweatsuit, crossed the finish line forty-five minutes later to cheers. It was not the image of a man facing imminent death.

In Boston, the next morning, a reporter from the *Globe* goaded the candidate.

"Let's see what you can do," he yelled.

"Do what?" Daniels asked.

"Run, of course. What else?"

Daniels opened his collar button, handed his jacket to a surprised Gordon, and to the great glee of the press, started to run across City Hall Square, reporters jogging alongside.

It became his trademark. Sometimes it was only a block. Other times, Daniels became extravagant about his new-found health and ran a mile through the streets of a campaign city, always dressed in his brown dress clothes and heavy black "Herbert Hoover" brogues. Often, he was accompanied by Jed Hankins, loping gracefully at his side, discreetly holding back his youthful speed. The press, impressed by the performance, punned that Daniels was "truly running for office."

The theatrics focused attention not just on the man but on what he had accomplished in Illinois, and on his basic traditionalism. Delafield's support was also gaining him middle-of-the-road voters. Unlike some of his colleagues, the senator assured everyone, Daniels was a true patriot.

A week before election, Daniels and Les arrived at the Bel Air Hotel, where the scent of victory was mixed with that of hibiscus. The increased support had turned Daniels' desire to win into an obsession. His day began at 6 A.M. in San Francisco, after which Daniels made appearances in Marin County, Silicon Valley, and Santa Barbara, then flew down to Los Angeles for a dinner rally and a television talk show.

At 11 P.M., Daniels fell back on the bed in his hotel suite, drained. Les reached over to take off his shoes, but the governor waved her away.

"Les, you're wonderful, but I'm just a little pooped now."

The candidate's hand darted to a soothing position near his heart, then he abruptly pulled it back, as if to cover. The angina had returned.

"Les. I ate too much rubber chicken. Would you get me a Di-Gel?"

She was on her way back with the antacid when she heard Daniels call.

"Les, come quick! It's a new poll on television."

They sat together on the edge of the bed, intent. "The latest Gallup

poll shows a dramatic rise in support for Governor Daniels," the
announcer read. "The last national survey, taken two weeks ago,
showed the Democratic candidate with only 38 percent. Today, that
number has risen to 48, and the spread has narrowed to only four
points. Anything can happen on Election Day."

"My God, that's good news. I've got to call Sally and tell her."

As Daniels' fingers touched the instrument, it rang.

"Yes. This is Governor Daniels. Who is this? John Davidson? The
CIA? Yes, surely. I know who you are. What can I do for you?"

Chapter 38

Davidson was fixed to the same news program.

A week after Daniels' five-mile run, The Baptist had begun to itch
philosophically. His plan was backfiring. At first, he was convinced
Daniels was experiencing only a momentary rise, not unlike Mondale
after the first Reagan debate.

But as he watched the Ladbroke of London odds on a Republican
victory slip precipitously to 5 to 4, Davidson recognized that he had
to reach Daniels immediately and divulge everything. He had to convince the candidate to force the resignation of Hankins as his running
mate. If Daniels balked, he would have to go public. It was getting too
close.

From a newsman, Davidson learned that Daniels was at the Bel Air
Hotel, on his way to Phoenix. He phoned the hotel, identifying himself to the Secret Service operator. It was a matter of extreme national
urgency, he told the agent, who ordered a phone trace. Within three
minutes Davidson was put through.

"Yes. John. What can I do for you?" Daniels asked, curious about
this late-night intrusion from the ex-CIA man.

"Governor, I can't discuss it over the phone, but I assure you it's
vital to national security. I must meet with you in person, and alone.
What about tomorrow? I'll catch an early plane to Phoenix and be at
your hotel at noon."

Daniels held his hand over the phone, searching out Les's eyes.

"Les, I'm so damn rushed. It's John Davidson, an important former

CIA man. He says it's urgent to see me tomorrow. A matter of national security. What do you think?"

Les hesitated a moment, then nodded.

"Okay, John. Meet me at the Hyatt Regency in Phoenix. It's downtown opposite the Civic Plaza. See you then."

Chapter 39

In his Phoenix hotel suite, Governor Daniels waited. A matter of national security, Davidson had said. What could that possibly mean?

Daniels had not been idle. After the call, he had checked Davidson out with Al Springs. In the gray-shadowed universe of counterespionage, the CIA director informed Daniels, Davidson had been under attack by both bureaucratic simpletons and KGB infiltrators into the Agency. But Springs would personally vouch for him as a loyal, very loyal, American. The director was concerned about the meeting. Could Daniels phone him the second it was over?

The ex-CIA man arrived at noon, and the two protagonists were soon seated in the Hyatt suite. One a tall ascetic with the dark eyes of a seventeenth-century Jesuit and the demeanor of a lifelong Washingtonian. The other, a ruddy-faced, optimistic American farmer, lacking only the peaked cap to complete the Midwest image.

"Governor, what I have to say is painful," Davidson began.

They were alone after a waiter had poured them coffee and left.

"In this briefcase I have proof, accumulated over a four-year period, that your vice-presidential running mate, Jed Hankins, is a Communist."

Daniels' chest muscles contracted.

"Not just a sympathizer but a dedicated Marxist-Leninist who has infiltrated the Democratic Party. His goal is to reach the White House and subvert the nation to the interests of the Soviet Union and world Communist revolution."

Was this man mad or had his universe just collapsed?

"Involved with him is his AA, Bill Fenton, who originally turned him," Davidson continued. "Hankins is not KGB in the formal sense, but he is working along identical channels."

"How long have you known this?" Daniels asked.

"Governor, I must confess that I've had this information for months. I was holding back in the hope I could avoid a national furor. Frankly, it looked like you and Hankins were losing badly. But now, your good prospects make it essential that I reveal everything."

His better prospects were why Davidson was now telling him that his running mate was a Communist? What could he do with that? Ike had faced Nixon's campaign contribution irregularities, which miraculously evaporated after the Checkers speech. Eagleton had resigned from the McGovern campaign when news of his nervous breakdown surfaced. Nixon had suffered Spiro Agnew's *nolo contendere* and resignation, and would have survived as President except for Watergate, Daniels believed.

Could he influence Hankins to go on national television and plead innocent? That he had been duped into becoming a Communist? Daniels laughed at his own fantasy.

No, the charge couldn't be true. Surely it was the concoction of paranoid spooks isolated from the real, multi-shaded world. Despite what Davidson was saying, only irrefutable evidence would sway him.

Davidson continued. From Granick's case, he removed the four-page written summary, the photos, and the cassette, then laid them out on the table.

"Governor, please read this first."

Daniels absorbed the summary slowly, without comment. Davidson then moved to the photographic evidence.

"Here's the first picture that started the investigation by Sam Withers."

"Withers? The crazy CIA man who tried to kill Hankins at the convention?"

"Yes, the same. He compiled this file over a period of years. The murder of his wife—by the KGB, we're sure—was the first result. Withers tried to take revenge. In any case, this picture of Hankins in Fredericksburg at lunch with a known KGB agent started the case. With the help of friends in the FBI and the CIA, Withers accumulated the evidence I have here."

Davidson turned to the photographs, one at a time.

"Here's Hankins in Sri Lanka, supposedly on vacation with a Washington society girl. But here's another photograph of Hankins in a local Colombo pub with a Czechoslovakian named Anatole

Murchak. The CIA knows him as the leader of KGB active measures in Sri Lanka, everything from spying to assassination."

Daniels stared intensely at the photo, the pain now pressing viciously against his sternum.

"Couldn't that be an isolated incident?" Daniels asked. "Perhaps he was innocently introduced to Murchak?"

"That's always possible," Davidson conceded. "But it's only one of a sequence of contacts—far beyond any possibility of chance. Look at this."

Davidson selected another photograph.

"Here's Hankins on vacation again, this time in Marrakesh with a blond starlet. But this photo, taken with an infrared camera, shows him at two in the morning being passed a note by that tall Arab. A magnification of the picture has identified him as Assad Mafstullah, a key in the Libyan terrorist network."

As Davidson proffered more photos of Hankins—in Mexico City, Surinam, Tokyo, Vienna—each depicting him in secret contact with another Soviet-bloc emissary, Daniels tried to fight off the unwholesome reality.

"Governor, I've saved this one—the best, or the worst—for the last. We have forty minutes of an intimate conversation between Fenton and Hankins on tape. It was recorded by a bug planted by Withers' FBI friend in an overhead light fixture in Hankins' office."

Daniels cast a disapproving look at Davidson.

"I know, Governor. I don't normally approve of bugging U.S. senators either. But Withers felt he had sufficient prior evidence to justify it—morally, if not legally. I'll play it now. Tell me when to stop."

The tape unwound, and with it any doubt of Hankins' innocence vaporized. The conversations were candid, taking both men through the need to use Hankins' Senate power to delay American rearmament, then the decision to enter the presidential primaries to gain the White House for the future of world revolution. Although authentic, the dialogue seemed almost staged in its absolute, classic political exposition.

"Enough."

Daniels moved his hand to shut off the cassette player.

"God, I do believe it. But I wish I didn't. What can we do now?" he asked the CIA veteran.

"I think you have little choice, Governor. You have to confront Hankins and demand his resignation from the ticket. The Democratic

National Committee can choose another vice-presidential candidate, just as they replaced Eagleton with Sargent Shriver under different circumstances in the '72 McGovern campaign. Is there any other course of action?"

The pain was a sharp reminder that his angina had returned. Daniels could no longer fool himself that he had been the beneficiary of a false positive. It had been only a temporary remission of his heart condition, probably a placebo of hope. Daniels rubbed his chest, massaging the point of dagger penetration.

His thoughts were rapid. What was the morally permissible course?

"Who else knows about this?" Daniels asked.

"Almost no one. Withers never told his friends why it was being done. Only he saw more than one piece of the evidence. He showed the entire file to Jack Granick, but he was killed right after, by the KGB. Now that you know, there are three of us."

The dagger lifted a millimeter out of Daniels' heart.

"Good. What I'm going to propose will require absolute secrecy until after Election Day. First, I want you to know where I stand. John, I think dealing with the Russians is like dealing with a juvenile delinquent—only strength and understanding work. I know that some politicians are for weakness and understanding, but I'm not one of them. As I've announced, I'll have a former Air Force Joint Chief as my Defense Secretary.

"But I also intend to turn détente around on the Russians. For twenty years it made them strong because we foolishly accompanied it with a unilateral disarmament. For only God knows what reason. Reagan worked hard to build up our depleted defenses, but we still have a long way to go. We can have a real friendship with the Soviets, but only if we arm to the teeth and behave like gentlemen. Then force them to do the same. You know I can't talk this way publicly. It would kill my role in unifying my party. But I have plans to make America stronger than ever as a peacemaker."

Davidson was about to interrupt, but Daniels spoke through.

"John, this is going to sound like a deal, but it's not. Whether you accept what I'm going to tell you, or not, I want you to head the CIA if I'm elected. That should scare the Russians a little."

Davidson again tried to respond, but Daniels waved him silent.

"Please, John. Before you answer, let me tell you what I have in mind. I'm convinced that my VP is a traitor. I swear that my first act as President-elect will be to demand Hankins' resignation. If he re-

fuses, I'll go on coast-to-coast television and expose him. Your file will
be my ammunition. In either case, Hankins will be finished.

"But it's too late to change the ticket now. Any ruffle would mean
the end of my chances. What I am asking is just one week of silence.
Time to win, then drop Hankins. For my part, I'll say nothing. Not
to Springs, nor anyone. John, history rests in your lap. What do you
say?"

☆ ☆ ☆

Davidson had faced crisis with stoicism many times. What separated this from other experiences was that no one could help him
make the decision.

He pushed the question out of his crowded cortex and reacted with
instinct. In Daniels' eyes he saw what he had seldom viewed in the
political universe: total sincerity.

"God forgive me, but, Governor, the answer is yes. As for the CIA
director's job, I'll have to mull that over. There's great freedom in
being unemployed. Now I'll go home to Leesburg and you do whatever you need to do to get to the White House. Then drop Hankins.
Good luck."

The men parted with a warm handclasp.

As John Davidson descended in the elevator to the hotel lobby, he
asked himself only one question.

Did Daniels' offer to make me CIA director influence my decision?

In the bright sun, he walked toward the taxi, confident he would
never know the answer to that one.

Chapter 40

The days leading up to the election were tortured ones for Governor
Daniels. He now husbanded two secrets, each of which tore at him.

His angina had returned, but he kept away from his cardiologist for
fear of a news leak. Daniels became a secretive patient, ingesting his
small nitroglycerine pills in men's rooms, airplane latrines, in securely locked hotel bedrooms. When the angina struck in public he

kept his hand away from its soothing place on his chest, grasping it with the other hand and holding it tight like a lover.

The secret of Hankins' politics he handled with equal unease. The almost daily presence of the young man, a traitor posing as a Democrat, sickened him. But none of this was apparent to the public. Daniels' political demeanor was unruffled. If anything, he was pressing his schedule harder, making up to a dozen stops a day, talking, cajoling, laughing, casting away fears of his bad heart and Hankins' perfidy.

Election Day came at the tail end of an Indian summer, the temperature touching sixties in much of the nation. Daniels woke at 5 A.M. at his farm in southern Illinois. Marc wanted to confess his heart pain to Sally but she would only try to halt the campaign. Life, he mused, was a series of petty deceptions, each designed to hold in place what we believe to be the truth.

By 6 A.M., Daniels had voted at the courthouse near his home and by seven-thirty had arrived, via helicopter, at the Ritz-Carlton Hotel in Chicago to begin a last-minute, tradition-defying burst of campaigning on Election Day. He and his advisers could sense the closeness of the race and the absolute necessity of this extra push.

Despite some criticism from his opponent, Amos McCauley, the day went smoothly, at least externally, the media brushing aside his wan look as the result of too much campaigning. After Chicago, his first stop, by campaign plane, was Gary, Indiana, then Cleveland, then Buffalo, then New York City, and Philadelphia. Daniels ended his day in Washington, D.C., where after dinner with Les and Tom Ward, he returned to his Mayflower Hotel suite at eight-twenty, greeted excitedly by Stan Gordon.

"Governor, things look great in Connecticut. The polls have closed there and, with 20 percent counted, you've pulled ahead of McCauley!" Gordon was reflecting the surge of optimism in the room.

Les glanced at Daniels' face, then moved quickly to the largest wing chair, which Gordon pushed into TV-viewing position for the governor. As usual, Les had read him well, Daniels thought. The exhaustion was overwhelming his body.

Jed Hankins, who had voted near Hankins Farms in Virginia, drove the seventy miles to Washington to pay his respects and spend this crucial evening with the presidential candidate. As he entered the suite, Daniels strained for politeness. This was no time to demonstrate anything but harmony.

Daniels' opinion of pollsters rose as the first results started to come in at 9 P.M. Their prediction of a close race was prophetic. Missouri went for the Democratic ticket, Kansas to Amos McCauley. Texas was still up for grabs. The Dakotas were Republican, but Minnesota and Wisconsin both went for Daniels.

At ten, the room turned silent, then erupted into cheers. The electoral vote, estimated from actual results and exit polling, was almost even—146–144, McCauley over Daniels. To win, either candidate needed 270 electoral votes out of a total of 538. The polls in the Western states would soon be closing, with the major prize of California beginning its vote count at 8 P.M. local time, eleven o'clock in Washington.

At ten after ten, when Daniels had been watching the contest on television for almost two hours, the pain returned, the agony fusing with the fatigue of this abnormal day.

"I'm sorry, folks, but I need a little shuteye," Daniels said, rising tentatively to his feet. "I'll just take a little nap. Don't wake me unless you have some word, one way or the other."

Daniels extended his hand to Les, who took it as a signal to escort the worn candidate into the bedroom.

☆ ☆ ☆

Inside, Les prepared the bed for the governor. This time, she took off his shoes, jacket, and tie, then covered him with a thin blanket. Daniels turned restlessly for a few moments, then settled into sleep. Les waited at the bedside for ten minutes, listening to his heavy breathing, thinking that this man, whom she realized she adored, might be President in a few hours.

She tiptoed out of the room.

"The governor's asleep. He's absolutely pooped. I'll stay here with him," Les announced to the staff with soft authority. "Why don't you all go back to your rooms? We have an hour or so until the results come in from California. I'll wake him when that happens—if the news is good. If he wants to see anyone, I'll call. Okay?"

The campaign workers were reluctant to miss this piece of history, but they moved disappointedly out of the suite. As they left, Les touched Ward's hand.

"Could you keep me company on the President watch, Tom?"

Les then approached Jed Hankins.

"Senator, I think it's best that you stay too. If Marc wins, I know
he'll want to greet the press with you alongside him."

Hankins smiled broadly.

Chapter 41

In the Presidential Suite of the Mayflower, Les, Ward, and Hankins
watched television, their conversation at a minimum. They worried
about waking the protagonist of the drama, asleep in the next room.

At ten-thirty the networks announced the early results in Nevada,
giving the state to Daniels. Nationwide, out of over 400 electoral
votes counted, the governor was now ahead of McCauley by one vote.

Hankins closed his eyes, hardly able to contain his fantasies. In
moments, he could become the next Vice-President of the United
States. A new tradition, he knew, had made that passive office a step-
pingstone to the White House. And there, the great opportunity for
change.

He could see that it made no difference who took the remainder of
the Pacific States. Whoever won in California would be President.

A moment later, Les Fanning rose from her chair as if moved by
instinct.

"Excuse me. I think I'll just peek in on the governor. I won't wake
him. I just want to make sure he's sleeping okay."

As Les opened the bedroom door, Hankins thought he heard the
young man alongside him say something.

"Senator?" Tom Ward spoke up, clearing his throat. "I have something to tell you. I know we've only met a few times, but we have
something important in common."

Hankins stared across at Ward. He had always found him a polite,
even urbane person. But he played such a small part in the political
scenario. A writer, wasn't he, on the Democratic Party documentary?
Obviously, his entrée into this inner circle was social, through Les.
What could the man have to say that was so important?

"Yes? Is that so?" Hankins asked somewhat patronizingly. "In what
way?"

"Senator. I've come a long way to meet you. You know me by the name Ironman. And yours, of course, is Yearling. I am your contact for Oval Red."

As Hankins heard his code name spoken aloud, his gaunt cheeks lost even their small sense of fullness. The senator looked at Ward. He had prepared for this moment for years, yet feared the irrevocable commitment.

Hankins' rush to acceptance suddenly slowed. He wondered. Could Ward be a plant? Part of a CIA entrapment?

"That is a surprise, Mr. Ward. But who in the forest sent you to see me?" Hankins asked.

"He's the small man. Nikolai Orlov."

"And where is Orlov?"

"In Teplyy Stan. Room 409."

"Did he give you a message for me?"

"Yes. He said, 'Felicitations on Studs Lonigan. With best wishes for the long race.' "

Hankins coughed nervously, then extended his hand. Ward took it, offering the solidarity of a double handshake. The two men smiled, self-consciously. Then Hankins spoke.

"We do have a lot in common, Mr. Ward. Let's hope we can work together for a better America, and a better world."

"I'm sure of it, Mr. Vice-President. I'm sure we will."

"I hope you're not premature on that title," Hankins said, smiling.

☆ ☆ ☆

In the bedroom, Les trod softly as she moved toward the chair alongside Daniels. The governor was still lying on his back, his eyes shut, a peaceful expression ruling his face. Les sat silently, examining her feelings for the man. They were absolutely loving. Not sexual, she hoped, but daughterly. Marc was the father she never remembered.

Les noticed his breathing. Rather, she noticed that his chest was no longer heaving with exhaustion. In fact, it was not heaving at all. Les rose from her chair and moved closer to Daniels, placing her face in front of his mouth. She could not see, or feel, the exhaled breath.

She placed her head down on his chest, but the heartbeat eluded her.

Les was feeling the first stirrings of panic. Yes. It was time to wake him anyway. He should know that California could make him President.

Les pushed softly on Daniels' shoulder.

"Governor, it's time to wake up," she whispered. Then she pushed harder, with the frustration of fear.

"Governor. Wake up! Wake up!"

Daniels refused to move, immune to her blandishments.

Les stifled a scream. Instead, as if not to disturb Daniels, she walked gingerly into the living room.

"Tom, Senator. Hurry. Please follow me into the bedroom."

The two men went with her, unquestioning. Once in the bedroom, Les closed the door and turned to them, tears forming on her makeup.

"I don't know what to say. I sat with him a few minutes and got worried that I couldn't see his breath or feel his heartbeat. I tried to wake him. I even pushed him hard, but he didn't move. Could you help me?" Her voice was plaintive.

The men moved rapidly to the governor's bedside. Ward pulled open the eyelids and examined the pupils, while Hankins placed his fingers on the governor's pulse. In turn, they placed their faces at his face, then their ears to his heart.

Hankins was the first to speak.

"The governor's dead, Les. He went in his sleep. Could have been only minutes after he came in here. Probably a heart attack, or maybe a cerebral hemorrhage."

Les's face was contorted, as if punched.

"Sit here, honey," Tom said, pulling over a bedroom chair. Her eyes searched out his, seeking confirmation.

"Yes, Les. The senator is right. If it's any consolation, the governor died without pain. You can see that on his face."

Les sat quietly for a second, then suddenly bolted out of her chair.

"Quick! We have to get somebody! A doctor. Anyone! We have to call the Secret Service," Les cried, nearly hysterical. As she reached the door, Hankins blocked the way, manipulating her gently back into the chair.

"Les. Easy. Easy. We feel the same way you do. But we have to think for a minute. A doctor won't do us any good. Marc is gone. Even if he could be revived, which he can't, he would be brain-dead. He wouldn't want that. Listen to me. The future of the country is at stake in this room."

Hankins' voice strengthened in resonance as he spoke.

"Les, in twenty-five minutes the California polls will close. It's a tight race there. If anyone learns that Governor Daniels is dead, thousands of Californians going to vote and those waiting in polling places will never pull the lever for him. They'll abstain or vote Mc-Cauley instead. Everything he worked for will be gone."

Les listened, not sure what Hankins was trying to ask. She grasped at innuendos.

"What are you trying to tell me, Senator? That we should say nothing about his death until the polls close in California? That would be a fraud on the people. I can't believe you mean it!"

She could feel Hankins take her hands, his stare imploring.

"Les, it's the only way we can carry out the governor's plans for the country. If we wait just twenty-five minutes before revealing his death, I know we'll take California and he'll be elected President. Then we can announce the truth.

"As Vice-President-elect, I will become President-elect, then President in January. I'll serve in Marc's place. And I swear to you, I'll be him in the Oval Office. I'll do whatever I believe he would have felt was best for the nation. Through me, he'll survive for history."

Her mind was spinning, unsure of what was actually being said. Les was trying to encompass this last reality into a still unabsorbed sense that Daniels was dead. She sat in the chair, sobbing, then looked up at Tom Ward, her only contact with a former reality.

"Tom, what should I do?"

☆ ☆ ☆

Ward stood over Les's crumpled frame, aware that everything he had done in his life could be summed up by this moment. He loved Les, but their affair would be only a footnote in the history being shaped in this suite. Judging by Les's consideration of the bold scheme, Hankins' lies were apparently convincing. All it needed was his own assurances to Les.

Then it would be done. Oval Red, once a Kremlin theoretician's fantasy, would become an extraordinary reality.

"Les, the only way I can look at it is to try to understand what Marc would want us to do. I think Senator Hankins is right. It's our only chance to put Marc's program into effect. Why don't you take a couple of aspirins and rest on the couch inside for a while? Then, after eleven, the senator will call the Secret Service and the press and tell them that the governor has passed away. Everything will continue just as we had hoped it would."

Ward watched Les expectantly. Beaten by death, persuaded by the man she trusted, she nodded faintly.

Les, Hankins, and Ward then left the bedroom together, closing the door softly on the corpse of the President-elect.

Chapter 42

At five past eleven a network newsman appeared on television, an announcement in hand.

"The polls have now closed in California. From exit sampling and early returns, this network is projecting that the Democratic candidate, Governor Marc Daniels, has narrowly taken the state of California and has been elected President of the United States."

At eleven-six, Senator Hankins opened the door to the suite and tugged at the arm of the Secret Service man stationed outside.

"Come in," he said calmly. "Something has happened."

Five minutes later, four newsmen, a pool quickly chosen by Bill Fenton, whom Hankins had called immediately, walked solemnly into the living room of the suite. The closed door to the bedroom, where physicians were examining the presidential corpse, was guarded by two armed Secret Service men. Les and Ward had already left, disappearing into the crowd.

The television director seated Hankins on the couch and moved the cameras into place as the announcer began the interview.

"According to the Twentieth Amendment to the Constitution, adopted in 1933, the death of the President-elect prior to taking office automatically elevates the Vice-President-elect to the status of President-elect," the television announcer explained. "This is the first time in the nation's history that this has happened."

The newsman turned to face Hankins.

"Mr. President-elect. Please tell the national audience what has happened and what it will mean to our country."

As Hankins heard himself addressed for the first time as the future Chief Executive, he squared his shoulders. Just as if death had never inhabited the room, he began to speak.

"As your next President . . ."

☆ ☆ ☆

In Leesburg, Virginia, the two announcements came a few minutes after one another on television. John Davidson watched the first, the news of the election of Marc Daniels, with interest.

Now, Davidson thought, it's only a matter of hours before Daniels fulfills his pledge and forces Hankins' resignation. Finally, the close of a chapter that had muddied his life since Sam's early morning visit four months before. It also meant that he could head the CIA, if he wanted. But Leesburg had begun to work its gentle magic. He would have to sleep calmly on that.

Davidson rose from his chair, patting Dulles' mane confidently, then started across the room to refill his glass of madeira.

As he did, he could hear raucous, uncoordinated noises coming from the television, as if people were shouting at one another. He turned to look at the screen. It was the same announcer, but his demeanor had changed.

"I cannot believe it, ladies and gentlemen, but I have just received official word from the Secret Service. The President-elect is dead! Yes, dead!

"Governor Daniels died in his sleep of a massive heart attack while taking a nap during the vote counting—the doctors say at about ten-thirty. He was not found until a few minutes ago when the new Vice-President-elect, Senator Hankins, and the President-elect's assistant, Les Fanning, went into his room to wake him with the news of his election.

"According to the Twentieth Amendment to the Constitution, the Vice-President-elect, Jedidiah B. Hankins, will become the President-elect and be sworn in as our new President on January 20. Now we move to the presidential suite for an interview with our next President, thirty-nine-year-old Jed Hankins, the youngest man ever to occupy that office."

The wineglass dropped from Davidson's hands, now trembling without control. Life was conspiring. Everything malevolent was coming to pass. Hankins in the Oval Office.

Then he remembered, as if in an old memory. He still had Withers' file. It was his insurance. President-elect Hankins was not yet President, not for over two months. During that time all authority rested with the man, lame duck that he was, who still occupied the White House. And his friend, Al Springs, still controlled the CIA. He had only to mount a new attack on Hankins, a more frontal, more brutal one.

Faster than he had in years, Davidson ran down the stairs of his farmhouse, out the door, and into the moonless night. Without a flashlight, he ran by instinct the hundred yards to his smokehouse behind the barn. He felt for the lock, then for the key on his chain, missing the hole twice, cursing in the dark.

Then he found it and turned the lock. He raced into the small room and over toward a large wooden pantry against the wall. Again he used a key, this time lit by the small bulb dangling from the ceiling. He opened the lower door of the pantry and felt for Granick's briefcase. His hands thrashed about, touching only air. Davidson moved down to the floor on his hands and knees and peered inside.

There was nothing there. The briefcase and its file, the only proof of the treachery of Jed Hankins, the President-elect, was gone.

For the first time in his sixty-eight years, John the Baptist Davidson felt old, truly old.

Book Two

Chapter 43

The fit of the high-backed presidential chair, lined in buttery leather, was snug, as if designed for him. Fourteen years of painful subterfuge had fed this dream, and now, on January 21, the morning after the inauguration, President Jedidiah Breckinridge Hankins knew the office was truly his.

He had completed his phone conversation with the General Secretary. The Russian seemed hearty, eager to establish only the warmest relations with America, a partnership that could change the world's vision of itself for a thousand years, the Secretary had said.

The President's eyes kept returning—Hankins thought involuntarily—to the portrait of Jefferson on the far wall. Would historians someday compare him to the sage of Monticello? Or was he deceiving himself? He had come to this august room to move America into the Marxist orbit, alongside Moscow. There was no glory in excuses.

The Peale portrait of Jefferson was part of Hankins' plan to enrich the Oval Office with the aura of Virginia, perhaps the only land he truly loved, socialist or otherwise. Redecorated before inauguration, the room bloomed with Virginia life, including Federal wing chairs borrowed from Homestead, old prints of Jamestown, Georgetown, and Alexandria, even recent views of Hankins Farms champions raced under his colors of chocolate and pink.

"Good morning, Mr. President."

It was Bill Fenton, now Hankins' chief of staff. Hankins had long been simply "Jed" to him, but even Fenton had to follow presidential tradition.

"The folder on your desk has the names of the cabinet nominees," Fenton said, a lifetime of satisfaction etched in his face. "I've scheduled a press conference for later today. A lot of people are waiting for your choices."

Most administrations announced their nominees between Election Day in November and Inauguration Day, January 20, the most awkward period in American political life. But Hankins and Fenton hoped to avoid rancorous preappointment controversy by declaring their cabinet choices on this first business day.

"It burns me that you have to wait on the damn Senate to confirm that your people are actually accepted," Fenton commented. "It's an archaic concept."

The President laughed, sometimes finding Fenton's stern philosophy humorous.

"Bill. You'll have to practice a little patience. This isn't Moscow, you know. Meanwhile, remind me to check the bios of the nominees before the press conference. I don't want to flub anything the first time out."

A look of sudden remembrance crossed Hankins' face.

"Don't we have a meeting with Tom Ward this morning?"

Fenton nodded. "Yes. He should be here any minute."

☆ ☆ ☆

"Mr. Ward, may I see your identification?" the White House gatekeeper asked, checking off WARD, T.S. for a 10 A.M. appointment with the President.

Heading toward the executive offices in the West Wing, Ward searched out the awesome white presence before him, reflecting how far he had come from Orlov's place in the Moscow woods in just six months. The small man must be dancing in his dreams.

At the entrance to the Oval Office, the Secret Service escort handed Ward over to Fenton.

"Welcome to the White House, Mr. Ward."

The warmth of the greeting was revealing. Fenton obviously knew all about this unconventional contact between the two superpower leaders. No secrets between the President and his longtime aide, Ward was sure. Thicker than brothers.

He approved of the system Orlov had established for Ironman and Yearling. It avoided the slipshod security of diplomatic channels by funneling everything through the protected KGB communications network—from Orlov in Teplyy Stan to Baneyev in Washington, to Rausch, then to Ward—and return by the same route. And, he liked to think, Orlov trusted him to be persuasive with Hankins, even to use his own initiative when called for.

Ward found four men waiting for him in the Oval Office. The President, Fenton, and two others. One, a thin patrician with a balding head, was dressed impeccably in an English-cut suit. Seated next to him was a rougher-hewn bureaucrat, a tweedy, burly man of average height with curly, gray-flecked hair, smoking a pipe. A less sophisticated Midwestern tintype of Allen Dulles, Ward surmised.

The President opened the meeting.

"Mr. Ward, I believe you know Mr. Fenton."

Hankins then nodded toward the patrician. "And this is Mr. Robert Billings, former head of the Federal Organization and my nominee for Secretary of Defense. We'll be announcing his appointment later today."

Billings? The name echoed. Where had he heard it? Yes, Billings was the one who had arranged delivery of Baneyev's message on the C and O Canal. Hankins was leaving little to political chance.

As Billings muttered a few words, Ward recognized traces of a British accent. Rausch had mentioned that Billings had spent three years at Oxford. The cherished mannerisms had apparently stayed with him this quarter of a century.

"And this is Matthew Miles, acting head of the CIA," Hankins was saying, indicating the tweedy man. "Matt has done an enormous job for peace over the years keeping détente on course in the Agency, despite formidable opposition."

Even in Warsaw, Ward had heard that a Soviet mole had infiltrated the CIA twenty years earlier and had risen to a top position in the hierarchy. He was obviously sitting with him now, face to face.

"I've jumped Matt over less trustworthy men. He'll fill the director's spot until Bill is confirmed," Hankins continued. "Oh. I forgot. Mr. Fenton is my nominee to head the CIA."

Hankins gestured toward Ward.

"And, gentlemen, our guest this morning is Tom Ward, an unusual young man with diplomatic experience in both the United States and the Soviet Union. Tom's here to advise us on some delicate matters— outside of normal channels."

As Ward listened to the President, he felt an uncommon twinge of self-doubt, even a touch of awe at his role in the White House. But just as quickly, he dismissed the thought as debilitating.

"Since it's the President's first day, I'll hold my suggestions down to two joint projects for the U.S. and the U.S.S.R.," Ward began, all eyes on him.

"The first involves peace in space. I can vouch for Moscow on this. They'll agree to a treaty to keep all weapons out of space. But, as evidence of good will, they'd like to see the operational Star Wars unit dismantled and brought back down to earth."

Hankins was now standing. "Good. Good," the President said, motioning toward Fenton.

"Bill, the shuttle flight is scheduled for next Thursday. Let's make it a political event. It was supposed to deliver the second Star Wars unit. Instead I want a grand showing as we take down the first one. Arrange a three-way television show—myself, our shuttle in space, and the Soviet Chairman. But, Bill, make sure I'm not sandbagged. Get on the teletype hot line and tell the Chairman that I expect a pledge, on worldwide television, that he'll maintain the peace in space."

Ward was enjoying the rapid interplay, orchestrated in response to his suggestions. When the talk about Star Wars subsided, Ward continued.

"Gentlemen. I have another opportunity. It's for a joint covert action by the Soviets and America—to show the American people that partnership with Moscow doesn't have to be threatening. It involves Tomasi Kambula, the new ruler of the East African Republic."

"Kambula? Isn't he that crazy Idi Amin character?" Hankins asked.

"Yes, Mr. President. Moscow is convinced he's mad. Since he took over, he's been evenhandedly killing Marxists and pro-Western businessmen. They would like to work with you to overthrow the Kambula dictatorship."

"Really?" Hankins was surprised by the invitation. "And replace it with what?"

"A pluralistic junta, democratic and nonaligned with either superpower. It would be a great step, Moscow and Washington working together—I suppose for the first time."

Ward could see Miles studying him, trying to visualize his place in the scheme. The CIA official was surely asking himself how such a young man had gotten here to tell the President of the United States what Moscow did and did not want.

Ward glanced up at Hankins, in thought. Would the President concur on Kambula? Moscow had great hopes for the project.

"Yes. We'll go ahead. Just as Tom has outlined," the President was saying. "It's a perfect model for what I want to do. It'll accomplish a lot for peace and still keep the good will of the American people. Matt, use any surplus arms for the coup. Tell your field people that they are to cooperate—covertly—with the KGB. But confidentiality is the key. No leaks to the press."

Hankins' gaze moved toward Ward.

"Tom. One caveat. I want to stay in the White House. Tell your people this—with no maybes. The new East African government is not to be an outright Moscow takeover. It must be nonaligned with a pluralistic economy. I want to hold this up as an example that the Soviets and Americans can really pull together. Understood?"

Ward's nod was sharp. "I'll report it exactly as you have stated it, with emphasis on the warning."

"And another warning, this time for our own people." Hankins was suddenly addressing Fenton.

"Bill, I don't want Brock Sommerville at State to know about this until it's all done. He's a good liberal, but he's an old lady. He probably won't like the idea of a coup."

Hankins rose, a sign that the meeting was over, and approached Ward, his grin friendly.

"By the way, Tom. I saw Les after the inauguration. She thinks she's going to like her new job in White House communications. I'm sure the press people will love her."

"I hope not too much," Ward smiled. "She's a mighty popular girl."

"Little worry over that. She seems mad about you. And, Tom, thanks for a good briefing. Just call Bill when you have something new."

As the men started out of the room, they chatted softly, seemingly at ease with the way they had begun to reorder the world.

Chapter 44

Less than a week after Hankins' inauguration, John Davidson left the Leesburg farm in his Volvo wagon and drove through the blackened snow into Rosslyn, Virginia, across the Potomac from Georgetown. He parked the car and took the Metro to the center of Washington. In the lobby of an office building on K Street, Davidson verified his watch against the wall clock. It was 10 A.M.

From a pay phone, Davidson dialed a number at Langley, 703-355-9433. It rang three times before a tinny recorded voice answered.

"This number at the Central Intelligence Agency is no longer in use. Please call the main number for information. 703-482-1100."

Davidson listened but, instead of hanging up, he spoke animatedly to the lifeless line.

"Oh. I'm so sorry. I must have dialed the wrong number."

He softly replaced the receiver. It was six months since he had called on the system. Was it still in place?

Davidson hoped so. He was at the climax of his political nightmare. Everything he dreaded was coming true. The Oval Office was in the grip of a Communist. At the President's first press conference, Hankins had shown his hand, if only to those able to read Washington palms.

The head of an ultra-left-wing "think tank"—the Agency had always considered it a KGB front—nominated as Secretary of Defense. Fenton, the Svengali, was to be the new CIA director. Senator Sommerville, author of the "nuclear-free Europe" concept, named as Secretary of State. Where would it end?

Davidson smiled at Hankins' political acumen. He had chosen Everett Chase, the conservative Federal Reserve Board chief, as Secretary of the Treasury. In the beginning, at least, Hankins had no intention of hitting the American people where they lived—in their pocketbooks.

The President's appointment of Marine Colonel John Marshall Abbott as Chairman of the Joint Chiefs of the armed forces—the first Marine to hold that job—was his cleverest move, Davidson decided. The nomination had shocked the military bureaucracy, but no one doubted Abbott's patriotism. The decorated Vietnam hero had been catapulted over eleven hundred senior military men, Davidson was sure, because of his love of conventional mud-and-march warfare and his disdain for "the high-tech boys" with their missiles and space gadgetry. Hankins would let Abbott refight Iwo Jima while he gave the world away to the Russians. A touch of adolescent macho in defeat.

Attack. Blocking the President from exercising the enormous powers penned into the Constitution by the trusting fathers was his only avenue, Davidson concluded. For that he would need to call in old favors from old friends. Only a cabal of the loyal, in the CIA and the Congress, could resist Hankins. But with what chance of success?

After Daniels' death, Davidson had approached Springs and the outgoing President, who listened sympathetically. But they couldn't act against Hankins without proof, they insisted. Davidson was sure that commodity was securely locked away in Baneyev's safe on Wisconsin Avenue.

The colonel had obviously learned, or deduced, that he had the Hankins file, then used some extravagant high-tech device to pierce the sonar barrier while he was away from the farm. Davidson had long ago vowed never to rely solely on technology. But as he aged he realized how mortal he had become. Mainly in not following his own counsel.

Reconnect. Davidson knew that was his next step. There were still good counterintelligence men in the Agency. Hankins would cashier some, but others were expert at protective coloration.

He could entrust his soul to Clinton Low. A senior officer who had come of age under Davidson's tutelage, Low was an Ivy Leaguer, but with redeeming qualities. Less false panache and more guts than most. If the "disconnected" number was still in place, he would be seeing Low shortly.

Davidson returned to Leesburg, then left his home again at 9 P.M. that evening, heading northeast to the District. He drove up Connecticut Avenue to a shopping center just within the city limits. The decidedly middle-class section should be free of embarrassing acquaintances.

A barber pole was the rendezvous point. He parked the car in front of the shop and waited. It was 9:45 P.M., the standard meeting time.

Originally designed by Davidson to prevent the Agency from interferring in his special contacts, especially MOSSAD, the Israeli Secret Service, the "disconnected" number had since been turned over to Low. It now served as in-house contact for men purged by various administrations, who maintained an informal network—The Baptists —with the "dead line" as their electronic locus.

The first words—"I'm so sorry"—activated the system, after which a voice scanner verified the caller's identity. The follow-up included three rendezvous points, to be used on subsequent days—the Connecticut Avenue shopping center, the parking lot of an all-night diner outside Falls Church, Virginia, and a small movie house in Bethesda. After an ID in the back row, rendezvous was to be made outside.

Time for the meeting was always the same, 9:45 P.M., on the evening of the call.

It was a disappointing first hour. Sitting in the car, listening to classical music on WGMS, not truly expecting anyone. At ten forty-five, Davidson turned on his ignition, prepared to try again the next evening, when a casually battered 1979 Buick with a Virginia license plate pulled in alongside. The window rolled down.

"Shut off the engine, John. I'm sorry I'm late. I went to Bethesda before I realized it had been our last rendezvous. Good to see you again."

Neither man left his car. They spoke quietly through the open windows.

"John. I know why you called," Low began. "Things are bad. Hankins has fired four of our best men and he's putting the clamp on any anti-Soviet work. Our experienced agents are being called out of the field and given crummy desk jobs clipping newspapers. One of our guys in Paris says he's afraid an Agency man just sent there has tipped the KGB to our people—names and locations. Two guys have disappeared. We don't know what the hell is going on."

Davidson could taste the acidosis. The agonies of the last weeks were multiplying as he heard evidence of the decimation of a lifetime's work.

"Who's actually in charge?" Davidson asked, trying to visualize the chaos at its center.

"Miles. He's acting director until Fenton is confirmed by the Senate. John, I never trusted the guy. He's been friendly with both the conservative and liberal regimes. Now he's kissing ass for Hankins. A real power grabber. God, could Miles be the mole we spent twenty years looking for?"

"And what about Fenton?" Davidson asked, seeming to ignore Low's question. "Has he interfered yet?"

"I'm not directly involved, but I heard he's ordered our people in East Africa to work with the KGB. They're going to pull off a joint coup. Can you imagine? That Fenton will be a disaster for the Agency."

Low hesitated. "John, if you know what's happening, let me in on it. No matter what people say, I know Sam's no nut. He must have known something when he went after Hankins."

"Clint, something is happening. But I can't tell you yet. For everyone's sake, don't crack under the pressure. Do what they tell you and report anything important to me. I'll call the disconnect number when I need you. If something can't wait, use Leesburg Pike. Park your car on the shoulder. Shine your brights toward my place for thirty seconds, then meet me in the shopping center."

"Fine, John. But please put me in the picture soon. I want to help."

"Clint. You're helping, more than anybody."

Davidson's hand tensed to turn the ignition, then backed off.

"Just one more thing, Clint. Have you noticed anything that surprised you in the last couple of days? A new project, or anything?"

Low was pensive, but nothing seemed to come forward.

"No, John, nothing important."

Then the intrusion of a small remembrance, perhaps worthless.

"You know, John, there is one thing. A Soviet source in Vienna called our people with just two words. 'STAND DOWN.' He didn't know its meaning, but he had heard it mentioned at the Lubyanka. Our Operations Desk guy opened a file on it. But nobody has any idea what it's all about. Do you?"

"No, I don't, Clint. But thanks for telling me. Keep your ears open."

Davidson flashed his brights off and on as a parting gesture, then wheeled the station wagon around and headed back to Leesburg.

STAND DOWN? It meant nothing to him, but it was all he had.

McDowell? Had the young newscaster become sufficiently skeptical about Soviet intentions to be of value? The KGB had used him to get to Withers. Could he turn the strategy around?

Chapter 45

At 7 A.M. that same morning, the telephone woke a groggy Colonel Orlov in the neat pine-paneled bedroom of his prefab Finnish dacha in Teplyy Stan, the gift of a grateful government. The steam heating had never functioned properly, and making his morning ablutions in the chilled room unnerved him more than any foreign crisis.

Comfort had always been his handmaiden, and Orlov had never married for fear that a woman would come between him and that lifelong affection.

"Lev Andreievich," KGB chief Grigori Vassilin was saying on the phone, employing the friendly patronymic. "Sorry to wake you, but I have to see you immediately. This is as important as the day Oval Red became real."

Orlov couldn't interrupt Vassilin's flow. "Now that Yearling is in the White House, I must show you something I've been holding back. In my office in one hour." He hung up.

This was not the first time Vassilin had woken him. Orlov recalled the morning of Hankins' election two months before, at 7:30 A.M. Wednesday, Moscow time. He could still hear Vassilin's strident, untutored Siberian voice telling him of the success of Oval Red, of Yearling's elevation to the White House.

Yearling in the White House? Vassilin had surely muddled his Americanisms. He meant that Daniels and Hankins had won the election. Yearling in the Vice-President's Naval Observatory house on Massachusetts Avenue was more like it, Orlov had thought, reminding the general of his error.

Orlov had spoken gingerly, fearful of wounding Vassilin's vanity. The old soldier had come up through Red Army and KGB ranks and bore the defensive marks of the unschooled in positions of power.

But Vassilin had only laughed. "Orlov, Orlov. You're paying the price for loving your sleep too much. You really haven't heard? Daniels has died of a heart attack. Yearling is President-elect of the United States!"

"My God!" Orlov had said out loud, waving the air to erase the pious expletive. What a turn of history. Daniels dead? Nature, he was learning, sometimes fortuitously accomplishes what man, with all his exaggerated reason, can, or will, not do. Hankins actually in the White House! If only his sainted mother were alive.

Now, over two months later, a day after a January blizzard, Vassilin had woken him again. Orlov had come to believe that Vassilin, a compulsive early riser, disturbed his sleep only to dramatize the immorality of lingering in bed after 6 A.M. But Orlov refused to mimic the homey virtue. The small colonel credited his ritual of late to rise and late to bed not only for his unlined face but for his entry into the magical world of the Soviet successful—as the chief of Active Measures, American Section, KGB.

The hours after 10 P.M., when the outer Moscow suburbs were subdued and television even more boring, was his time to read everything American. A supply of American books and magazines was dispatched to him each month by the UN Mission in New York, and Orlov had built a library of several hundred inadmissible volumes and magazines.

Junior KGB officers in the American Section had access to such periodicals as *Time*, *Newsweek*, and the *Wall Street Journal*. But they buzzed expectantly about Orlov's bookshelves, hoping he would reward them with an American girlie magazine or an occasional fiction best-seller.

Personally, Orlov favored the densest espionage novels with their convoluted plots. They provided him with ideas, which he experimented with on long, lined yellow pads. The cursive Cyrillic script contained the embryos of scenarios for American subversions that his juniors would later fill in.

This morning Orlov called the Center for his car and was dressed, fully uniformed, in twenty minutes. Breakfast would have to wait. Moments later his driver, Sergeant Vershonev, arrived in front of the dacha with the Chaika, precisely on time.

"Where to, Comrade Colonel?" the graying soldier asked. Orlov guessed the man was in his fifties, and that he rose regularly at five o'clock, convinced that a spartan regimen was the route to socialist reward. The crude, obedient sensibilities of czarist peasant Russia, Orlov had observed, had merely been transferred to the Leninist state.

In the Chaika, Orlov raised his legs onto the custom-built stool.

"Lubyanka," he ordered.

"What do you think of the new American President, Colonel?" Vershonev asked as they moved northward toward Moscow. The blizzard had dropped seven inches of snow, but this vital highway had been swiftly cleared. "Do you think he's good for the Soviet Union?"

"Yes, Sergeant. I'm sure of it. The new American President is a man of peace. I expect a détente, perhaps even stronger than the one we had in the 1970s."

"Good, good," Vershonev muttered. "With peace, I expect we will become richer. No?"

"Oh yes, Vershonev. Rich, indeed."

Within a half hour they had crossed the Moskva and were at the KGB headquarters on Dzerzhinsky Square, the baroque building a few blocks northeast of the Kremlin. The onetime czarist insurance company had been transformed into the last home for Stalin's most illustrious victims before becoming the secret police center. A disciplined guard clicked his heels as Orlov left the vehicle.

"Lev. I know it's early for you, but I couldn't contain myself," Vassilin greeted his protégé as Orlov entered the office, elaborately decorated in cumbersome, dark pre-Revolutionary furniture.

The KGB chief came from behind his desk, grinning, a gold front tooth his mark of membership in an older Soviet hierarchy. A foot taller than his American section chief, Vassilin wore his lined face and white crew cut like badges of honor. Unlike Andropov, Vassilin was no intellectual, Orlov knew. More the stolid peasant who had helped forge modern Russia with iron will.

"Colonel, Oval Red was masterful," Vassilin was saying. "Now we have an exciting follow-up. Come."

Orlov watched the KGB chief cross the room with the rigid posture of an old revolutionary. Although too young to have fought in the Red-White confrontation that ended in 1921, Vassilin was in his late seventies and one of the few remaining survivors of the great Stalin purge of 1936, when he was a novice agent in the NKVD.

"I have it here for you, Lev," Vassilin said, "all laid out in one summary volume."

As Vassilin placed a scarlet folder on the table, Orlov's eyes glanced at the binder. On its cover was a pasted label marked in large black letters: STAND DOWN.

"It has been long in the waiting, Lev." Vassilin's fingers were emphatically tapping the file. "We developed this contingency right after Yearling joined our Washington apparatus. It sat for years. But now that he's in the White House, the Politburo has approved it for action. I want you to read it. But first I must ask you something."

Vassilin studied Orlov's deceptively simple round face.

"How do you gauge Hankins? Can he get his program through without much public opposition?"

"He's a superior politician, Comrade Minister," Orlov answered effortlessly. "He plays superbly to the naive American voter—a master at clouding the real issues. Yes, he should be able to carry out a serious disarmament in the name of peace. Americans are used to being unprepared. During détente, then when Carter killed the B-1 and the MX. I've even come to believe they're governed by a secret Pearl Harbor syndrome. But . . ."

"But what, Colonel?"

"Americans are strange," Orlov continued, now employing the

confidential tone of experts. "They don't like to be bothered by complex ideas, particularly the educated classes. Thinking about money takes most of their energies. What's left over goes into golf and spectator sports. They prefer to leave public matters, especially matters of defense, to their politicians."

"So? This has been good for us. Has it not?"

"Yes, Comrade Vassilin. The easiest people for us to reach are members of the Congress—through the media and our disguised front organizations and foundations. Overall, Americans are childlike and uninformed, especially about matters of defense and their own survival. But . . ." Orlov halted again.

"Yes, Comrade Colonel?"

"But they can be very dangerous when united—and aroused. We can't let that happen. New Presidents are given a political 'honeymoon,' several months in which they can do virtually anything. But I can't vouch for anything farther down the line. Unless"—Orlov waited—"unless we tell Yearling to go slowly."

"Good thinking, Colonel." Vassilin's hard blue eyes reflected his confidence. "Exactly my thoughts. But I don't want Hankins to go slowly. He must continue as is, even accelerate, before the opposition sets in. We have to assume that Yearling's time in the White House is limited to six months. Either because of assassination or impeachment. We must make our move before then."

"What move, General Vassilin?" Orlov asked.

Vassilin continued as if there had been no question.

"Colonel, there is still no Vice-President and who knows who'll take over after Hankins? STAND DOWN must go forward while he is in the Oval Office. Take the folder with you. Let me know what you think."

His rimless glasses in place, Orlov opened the crimson document. As he moved forward into its early pages, he looked up at Vassilin, his delicate eyes registering surprise.

Chapter 46

At his desk in the L Street office early that morning, Doug McDowell was sipping a bitter wake-up espresso, preparing for his evening news commentary, when the phone rang.

"Doug. I know it's early. But could you come to the Cosmos Club right away? I'd consider it a special favor."

It was John Davidson, his tone more brusque than usual.

"I'll be there in half an hour," McDowell answered.

He was surprised that his response had been so quick. Ever since his first meeting with Davidson he had felt increasingly drawn to the old spy, and to his anxieties about the country. He seemed to be following the complex track of Davidson's mind as would an insect exploring the geometric patterns of a spiderweb. But, he hoped, with less tragic result.

Davidson's phone call was opportune. He had been thinking about politics, specifically the news created by just one man, President Jed Hankins.

The newscaster had never been a hawk, not even an eagle. But he was becoming confused, even somewhat depressed, by these first weeks of the new administration. In a televised address the night before, President Hankins had announced a massive cutback in defense, in the name of peace. A moral example for the Soviet Union to follow, he had said.

Fifty MXs already in the ground at Warren Air Force Base in Wyoming were enough to protect the nation, Hankins assured the country. He was withdrawing the previous administration's request for 150 additional MXs.

The public was also wisely showing its disinterest in mobile missiles. This was not the Soviet Union, Hankins reminded everyone, where SS-24s and SS-25s on trucks and trains could freely move nuclear warheads around, jeopardizing the environment and everyone's safety. What if there were a nuclear accident? He would spare the nation that. There would be no Midgetman mobile missiles in his administration.

Was Hankins the Communist of Withers' file? Damn it. McDowell was angered with himself for asking that same question over and over. He confessed that he was troubled by the new President. But not only didn't he know the answer, he didn't even know his own mind on the subject. Maybe Hankins was truly sincere in offering a peace gesture to the Soviet Union. Who knew? Like many Americans, he was sure the Russians had *some* good intentions.

Whatever Hankins' politics, it was clear that the President was the consummate politician. His defense cuts, Hankins had told the nation, would save $100 billion a year and spell the end of the crippling budget deficits. On that news, Wall Street first sank as high-tech stocks staggered. Then, within hours, it turned. By the end of the day the DJ average had zoomed 51 points—a record gain.

They're laughing at their own funeral, McDowell thought, recalling Lenin's aphorism that the capitalists would sell Russia the rope with which to hang the West.

He was surprised at his own anger. Hadn't he, just months before, advocated steep cuts in the defense budget, including elimination of the new Stealth bomber? Right on the air?

McDowell started opening his mail, combing through a handful of newspapers and magazines on his desk. He was drawn to the cover of the *American Spectator*, a conservative tabloid-sized journal which had followed the path of William F. Buckley's *National Review*.

He picked up the *Spectator*, staring at the large cartoon on its cover.

RED STAR OVER WASHINGTON? the headline read. The cartoon showed Hankins addressing the nation. But where the eagle should have been perched on the presidential seal there was another symbol: a hammer and sickle.

McDowell first laughed, then looked sadly at the cover. Was he catching Davidson's paranoia? Even the old spy had warned that it was an inevitable result of hanging around with intelligence people.

McDowell reminded himself that he was a liberal. His politics hadn't changed, but it now occurred to him that he was becoming a worried liberal, troubled about national survival.

A few minutes later the newsman was in a cab on his way to the Cosmos Club. He met Davidson in the library, where the old spy seemed more subdued than usual.

"I suppose Hankins is getting you down," McDowell said in greeting.

"Well, things are not good, Doug. His disarmament moves could give the Soviets a message that we're vulnerable. I'm especially worried that he's canceled the Stealth bomber and the new TAV, or 'Buck Rogers,' as the press calls it. That Trans-Atmospheric Vehicle is both airplane and space ship. It could make our Star Wars defense and our satellites invulnerable. But Hankins has killed that too. I'm afraid it's only the beginning."

McDowell thought it was the ideal time to probe Davidson.

"Mr. Davidson. Was Granick right? Is Hankins his man? With what's happening, and with some of his cabinet appointments, I wouldn't be surprised."

"Doug, I don't have that information. And even if I did, I couldn't share it with you. But I do need a favor."

The rest of the conversation was so short and mysterious that McDowell didn't know what to make of it. All the old spy said was that if two words, STAND DOWN, were broadcast on network television, it might accomplish a miracle.

"Can you at least tell me what that's all about?" McDowell asked.

"I would, Doug. But I swear I don't know. I just have a hunch that it could smoke out something important."

As he left the Cosmos, McDowell asked himself, should he do it?

He had never borrowed the air waves for personal reasons. But, of course, this was not for personal gain. Davidson had refused to say, or he really didn't know, but McDowell assumed it somehow involved the enigma of President Hankins.

☆ ☆ ☆

At six-thirty that night, standing in front of a colorful studio backdrop, McDowell was ready to go on the air. The wall behind him was decorated with a series of large question marks, on which were superimposed the words STAND DOWN, in foot-high luminescent letters competing with his red hair.

The item itself took less than thirty seconds for McDowell to read, straight-faced, into the camera.

"An anonymous source in the Defense Department has informed this reporter that the Pentagon is involved in a new program so hush-hush that only a handful of people in the White House and the Pentagon are privy to it," McDowell said, urgency laced into his polished tones. "We have learned that the code name is STAND DOWN, and that it is of monumental importance to national security. But when contacted, the Defense Department refused to comment. We will report any additional information as we receive it."

If Davidson was right, the gambit should smoke out something or someone. McDowell hoped it wasn't his hide with the network.

At six-forty, he was back in his office when the intercom buzzed, insistently.

"Doug. It's Milt Samuels on the phone," Meg said. "And he seems angry."

The response from the news chief in New York was quicker than he had expected.

"Doug. Milt here. Jesus, kid. What are you doing with those precious minutes of yours? Playing guessing games with national defense?"

Before he could answer, the tension rose in Samuels' voice.

"The second you were off the air, I got a call. From guess where? The White House. The President's aide, Bill Fenton, got on personally, screaming the damn phone off the hook. How the hell can they run a country, he says, when a network broadcasts the code name of a top secret defense project? 'Don't you have any patriotic sense?' he says. Doug, I'm going to have to apologize. But do me a favor, stick to commentary. Forget about espionage. Okay? They put you in jail for that."

McDowell was surprised that the response had come from the White House itself. He'd have to tell Davidson.

"Okay, Milt. I understand. But I thought, with all the cuts Hankins announced in national defense, it might make a good controversial piece. I'm sorry if it aggravated the powers that be."

He was straining to hang up, but Samuels wasn't finished.

"Doug. That's not all. The Old Man was the one who first got the call from Fenton. You know, he was a big backer of Hankins. Well, he wants to see you in New York. Yes, you guessed it. Tonight. I want you on the eight o'clock shuttle and here by nine-thirty. He's going to wait. I'm afraid if you don't show he'll have apoplexy. And that won't help your career. Okay?"

With that, Samuels hung up.

As McDowell put down the receiver, he could hear a second click, as if someone had been listening in. Could it be Meg? Was she spying on him?

Then he berated himself. You're catching a case of paranoiac nerves. Settle down, boy.

"Meg," McDowell called into the intercom, "I'm going up to New York in about an hour. Could you pack me a little bag? A suit and some toilet stuff. They're in my closet. And, Meg, get me a limousine to the airport."

Fifty minutes later, McDowell was on L Street in front of the network building walking toward a large black stretch limousine, its windows mirrored over for privacy. As McDowell placed his hand on the door handle, the driver came out of the car.

"Mr. McDowell?"

"The very same. Please get me to National Airport in time for the eight o'clock Eastern shuttle to New York. All right?"

From L Street, the car turned left onto Pennsylvania Avenue, passed the White House, then moved toward the 14th Street Bridge. Soon they were in suburban Virginia, on their way to National Airport on the George Washington Memorial Parkway.

McDowell had memorized the airport route, the milk run of the network news television world. Washington to New York. New York to Washington. National to La Guardia and return. Was there anyplace else?

His head nodded forward into momentary sleep. As he woke, he was jarred by the sign NATIONAL AIRPORT. But as he bent over to retrieve his bag the limo picked up speed and moved past the sign, heading south beyond the airport.

"Hold on!" McDowell screamed into the intercom. "You just passed the airport. God damn it!"

McDowell waited, but there was no response. He leaned forward and hammered on the glass.

"Driver! You just passed the airport! Get off at the next exit and double back. Quick! I can still make the eight o'clock shuttle."

Again, no answer. Only the ominous click of the door locks and the whirring sound of a metal shield moving down, cutting off the rear of the sedan from the driver's compartment.

McDowell reached out to twist open the door handles, but they were firmly locked. Where was he? He peered out at the passing highway, but as he did dark gray curtains—actually metal simulating pleated cloth—dropped down on each of the four windows at the side, and one at the rear, sealing Doug's vision. As they closed, a light went on overhead.

He was incarcerated in a limousine on its way southward. But to where, he had no idea.

Chapter 47

McDowell opened his eyes and searched the room for any signs he could recognize. He had been asleep on a four-poster bed, his head reeling.

He looked at the bureau mirror directly across from him, searching for his reflection. No. He had not been beaten. His clothes were disheveled, as if he had been sleeping in them for hours. What time was it? There was a clock on the dresser. A digital, incongruous with the dated decor. It read 3:05 P.M. He had been asleep all night and morning.

Where was he? His last memory was that of the limousine turning, probably leaving the George Washington Parkway only six or seven minutes after they had passed National Airport. He had been unconscious since then, possibly from a sleeping drug.

At that moment, the door to his room opened. A young man, about twenty-five, ruddy, collegiate-looking with an open face, walked in, almost haltingly.

"Mr. McDowell. I hope you're feeling better. I'm sorry for what we had to do, but it was orders. And they were clear."

The young man was apologizing for having kidnapped him. What kind of thug was this?

McDowell strained to examine his face.

"Haven't I seen you somewhere before?" the newscaster asked.

"Maybe. But I know you, Mr. McDowell. I saw you at the convention when Withers took you prisoner. It seems everybody wants you. What's it all about?"

McDowell weighed the young man's expression. Was he being frank or just faking naiveté?

As the man spoke, his features were being called out of McDowell's memory. The convention. Of course. He was one of the two CIA men who were chasing Withers on the floor.

"My God, you're CIA. You're that fellow—Hopper, isn't it? What the hell do you want with me?"

"I swear I don't know," Hopper answered, obviously embarrassed by his role as abductor. "And I don't like the idea of picking up Americans like they were criminals. All I know is that Barber and me got orders to grab you and hold you here. Then we're supposed to turn you over to someone else with the password."

"To whom?" McDowell couldn't believe he had fallen into the CIA's bad graces. "And why, Hopper? Damn it. Don't you know the CIA has no jurisdiction over civilians?"

"I know that, Mr. McDowell. Like you, I think whatever's going on is creepy. You're a network television guy. I don't think it's smart to play around this way."

Hopper paused. "I've got to go downstairs and touch base with my partner," he said, exiting the room.

As soon as Hopper left the room, McDowell considered his predicament. He had been captured by his own countrymen in an unprecedented civil rights rape. The whole thing was unsavory. Someone at the White House had to be involved in this misadventure. No one else had the power to order such an abduction.

Could just two words on national television—STAND DOWN—whatever they meant, have triggered Hankins into ordering such a mad mission?

No. Hankins was too smart to use the CIA this way. Wasn't he? Even if he was the Red candidate, now the Red President, of the Withers file.

"Where are we, Hopper?" McDowell asked when the young CIA man returned.

Hopper's expression was troubled. "Jesus, they'll hand me my head for telling you anything. But this whole fucking thing bothers me. We're in a safe house in Old Town Alexandria, near the waterfront. Don't worry. Nothing's going to happen to you. I'm just waiting to find out what comes next."

"Hopper! There's a car coming up in front of the house. Looks like a van."

It was a loud voice from down the stairs. The other CIA officer, Jim Barber.

"Right," Hopper responded as he moved toward the door, his revolver now out of his shoulder holster and loose in his hands. "Find out who it is and what they want. Be sure to check the password."

The noises coming up the stairs now became mixed and agitated—what sounded like two men in conversation with Barber in the entrance hall downstairs.

"Hold them there," Hopper called down loudly. "I'm coming right down."

He turned to McDowell. "You better wait here until I find out what's going on."

McDowell edged to the upstairs rail. He could hear four men zealously arguing over something. Then he could make it out. He was the prize.

"We have come for McDowell."

It was the huskier of the two men, dressed in a brown leather jacket with no tie. He spoke in a slightly accented, coarse voice, while staring unconcernedly into Hopper's gun barrel.

"Put that toy away," he warned Hopper. "This is official business, at the highest level. Like I told your friend, the password is 'Glassboro.' Give me the prisoner. We're taking him with us."

"Who is 'us'?" Hopper asked, his gun moving closer to eye level.

"Easy, little cowboy." The burly leather-clad man jabbed his index finger into Hopper's chest as if to goad him, laughing as he did.

"Now be a nice boy and hand over McDowell. That's why we were sent here. You have your orders from Langley. Now do it."

Hopper looked dumbfounded at the whole scene, but Barber's temper had surfaced.

"You know what? I think you're a bunch of KGB bastards!" Barber shouted. "Where do you come off, walking into our safe house with your shitty password, and expect us to hand over an American television announcer to you? This is Washington, not Moscow, you cocksuckers."

Barber stopped for an instant, then, forming his mouth, spat directly in the leather-clad man's eye.

"Fuck you!" Barber released the epithet with passion, then wheeled, reaching for his shoulder holster.

As he did, the other Russian pulled a small pistol from his pocket. His first shot nicked Hopper in his firing arm. His gun dropped abruptly. The second shot hit Hopper in the side and he fell to the floor into a gush of blood.

At the same instant the burly man kicked Barber in the groin before the CIA officer could extract his gun. As Barber fell, the other Russian pistol-whipped the prone agent on the head. He groaned, then moved into unconsciousness.

The KGB men stepped over the two fallen Americans and rushed up the stairs.

"McDowell. Come peaceful. Otherwise you'll get the same treatment."

The commentator nervously raised his hands.

"Lower your hands. Look natural as we leave the back door of the house. If you see anyone on the street, just smile. Enter the van and sit between us, and say nothing. We are going for a ride into the countryside. You like the Chesapeake. No?"

Chapter 48

President Jed Hankins was exultant.

"Bill, in just a few minutes we're going to make a television first."

Hankins, Fenton, Maude Holly, the President's secretary, and Defense Secretary Billings were gathered in the Oval Office, where television cameras had been set up.

"Stand by, Mr. President."

The director waved Hankins into his favorite wing chair. He had already been made up and, despite the director's suggestion, was dressed casually in a tweed sport jacket and slacks.

"We're leading the next generation into a real revolution. No suits," Hankins quipped.

In a moment, he was on the air.

"People of good will have always warned of the militarization of space," Hankins began. "Today, I am going to end it, once and for all. The last administration had planned this voyage of the shuttle *California* as a deadly mission—to deploy the second part of the Star Wars antimissile system."

Hankins grinned ingenuously into the camera.

"Well, I've changed the ship's name to *Friendship* and reversed its mission. Instead, it will rendezvous with the Soviet shuttle team, who will observe as the *Friendship* plucks the first Star Wars unit out of the heavens and returns it to earth. That's all I have to say before we watch history being made."

The networks switched to space, where television cameras showed four American astronauts flying free toward the X-ray laser Star Wars framework, some three hundred feet in front of them. In the background, the camera picked up the hovering Soviet shuttle, *Brezhnev*.

As the astronauts began dismantling the system, the cameras switched to Moscow, first with an exterior scan of the Kremlin onion domes, then to the Party General Secretary.

"We honor the United States for its bold move toward peace," the Secretary began. "Just this morning, President Hankins and I have signed, informally by computer hot line, a joint resolution to demilitarize space. Since the Soviet Union has never taken such a step, we have nothing to give up. Our work on a killer satellite is well advanced, but it will remain with our scientists in the Urals. President Jed Hankins has shown his elders that peace is the product of the young."

The cameras flashed briefly to the American astronauts efficiently dismantling the $12-billion antimissile unit, then moved in for a closing shot of President Jed Hankins' satisfied face.

☆ ☆ ☆

"That no-good son of a bitch! He's going to kill this country."

In the Democratic cloakroom of the United States Senate, Angus Delafield and two colleagues stared incredulously at the television set.

"I can't believe my eyes," Delafield said. "Years of work and billions of dollars and that punk kid sends up our shuttle to bring it back down."

Delafield was talking to his guests, a Republican senator and a Democratic congressman, both adamant supporters of a strong defense.

"And what do the Russians give in exchange? A promise not to militarize space. Why? Because that's the only area where we're ahead. He's giving them exactly what they want—but for what reason? God, Daniels' death has proven more horrible than I ever believed. What the hell are we going to do with this President?"

The face of Congressman Danny Bradshaw, Kentucky Democrat and chairman of the House Judiciary Committee, displayed equal despair.

"I don't know what we can do, Angus," echoed the blond former country western singer. "That young man has us by the short hairs. He has more support in the Congress than I'd like to admit. A few more peaceniks get elected to the Hill every two years. I don't know what the hell the people are thinking about."

Bradshaw kicked the side of the television set in disgust.

"We can refuse to ratify the space treaty with the Russians," Bradshaw added. "But we can't force him to send Star Wars back up. He is the Commander-in-Chief, God help us. Tell me, Angus. You're a smart Northern SOB. Is he really trying to make peace or fuck the U. S. of A.? I'd love to impeach the bastard just on general principles. But on what charge?"

Delafield stared at his demoralized colleague, then turned toward his other guest, Republican Senator Maury Feldman, chairman of the Rules Committee, a short, shaggy-maned former criminal defense attorney whose eloquence had brought him millions before he made his successful Senate bid from Michigan.

"Maury, what say we go see Hankins?" the North Dakotan asked. "Find out what makes him tick. Maybe we can talk business."

Feldman shook his grayed head approvingly.

"My Rules Committee and Danny's House Judiciary are going to start hearings soon on Hankins' VP nominee—that Congressman Terry Maynard," he responded. "Maynard's no better than Hankins, but the Twenty-fifth Amendment says we have to fill the slot. Maybe that's our weapon. To block Hankins' VP and make a deal to curb his mad program. I can't think of anything else. What do you say?"

"Okay. We'll be a committee of five," Delafield said, assuming the leadership role. "I'll ask Senator Masoni and General Willie Jamieson to join us. He would have been Chairman of the Joint Chiefs if Daniels had lived."

Delafield paused momentarily. "I'll call the White House and see if His Highness will see us. I'm sure Hankins won't like the idea. But he doesn't have the balls to lock us out."

Chapter 49

Clint Low had come through.

The evening after McDowell's STAND DOWN broadcast, he had driven to Leesburg, parking on the shoulder of the Pike, flashing his brights off and on in the direction of Davidson's house. The reflectors in the bedroom and library trapped the light, and Davidson and Low were soon parked, head to tail, in the shopping center. Their car windows were open, facing each other.

"John, I had to come quickly. I think the whole Agency's gone bananas."

Low's voice was absent his usual well-bred restraint.

"What's going on, Clint?" Davidson asked.

"I still can't believe it. One of the fellows in Miles's office says Fenton called Langley from the White House last night around seven. Told the duty officer that he had to speak to Miles. But Miles had left and wasn't home, so Fenton talked to the deputy. You won't believe this. Fenton gave him orders—said they came directly from the President—to pick up that newscaster, Doug McDowell."

Davidson felt the stirrings of hope. The smoke-out of STAND DOWN, whatever that meant, had prompted Fenton to move.

"Have any idea where they took him?"

"No. My informant didn't know and I was afraid to ask anybody else. But I can give you my hunch. Remember that safe house in Old Town Alexandria? It's the closest one to the airport."

When Davidson reached Old Town Alexandria after midnight, the streets of the fashionably rebuilt colonial city were deserted. He drove down toward the waterfront, turning one block before the old dock area. The safe house ahead of him, a small, two-story renovated brick colonial with green shutters, was dark.

He moved past the house, turned the corner, and parked on the next block. From the glove compartment he removed a .45 pistol and a flashlight, placing one in each jacket pocket. Davidson walked the hundred feet to the front door and was about to ring the bell when his instinct warned him to employ a warier approach. Pulling out the .45, he turned the brass knob of the heavy paneled wooden door and kicked it.

The door opened. There was no light within, not a candlespot. Davidson was flashing his torch across the front foyer, the beam bouncing off the old marble tiles, when he heard a violent voice coming from a dark corner.

"Whoever you are. Don't move an inch, or I'll kill you! Walk in here with your hands up and identify yourself."

Davidson doused the flashlight and retreated into the street. Darkness again settled on the house.

"Who's in there?" Davidson called through the open door. "I'm John Davidson. Do you know me? If so, speak up."

He could hear an indistinct, painful groan, then a voice, less angry.
"The Baptist? God, I almost shot you. Come on in."

The searchlight now panned the floor until it stopped at the bodies
of two men, sprawled out next to each other, lying in a pool of blood.

"God almighty, what happened here? What's your name, son? And
who's this?"

Before he could get a response, Davidson turned over the unconscious body of the other CIA man and put the light in his face.

"It's Barber. What's he doing here? And what about you? What the
hell's going on?"

Davidson turned the searchlight on the young man, sitting on the
floor, his feet outstretched, a bloody handkerchief stuffed into a hole
in his side.

"I'm Hopper, sir. We were ordered to pick up Mr. McDowell, then
turn him over to men with the password 'Glassboro.' But when the
goons showed they sounded like KGB. When we wouldn't hand over
McDowell, they shot me and pistol-whipped Barber but forgot to
pick up my gun. I tried screaming, but nobody heard me."

"Hopper. I don't want the police in on this. I'll bring my station
wagon around and get you both to a doctor," Davidson said. He
looked inquiringly at the young counterintelligence man. "Do you
know where they took McDowell?"

"I can't swear, Mr. Davidson, but I heard one of them say 'Chesapeake.' You know that estate of theirs on the bay, about fifty miles
from here? He could be there."

Hopper paused. "What's going on, Mr. Davidson? Why would the
CIA want to give an American over to the KGB? Has the Agency
gone crazy?"

Davidson could only afford an enigmatic smile. "Don't worry, son.
We'll figure it out."

An hour later, Davidson drove up to the front gate at Langley, his
car heavy with two men, one bleeding, the other now groggily awake,
probably suffering a concussion.

"I'm John Davidson," he told a CIA guard wearing the patch of the
U. S. Protective Service. He recognized Davidson, then inspected the
two men on the back platform of the car.

"Please call the doctor and get them to the dispensary," Davidson
said. "Tell the duty officer I said to keep it out of the papers. Okay?"

After a polite salute, Davidson was on his way back to Leesburg,
one thought dominating his mind. Sam Withers would like the job of

finding McDowell. If the newsman was being held captive at the
Soviet estate, it could be the opening chip in the war against Jed
Hankins.

☆   ☆   ☆

Sam Withers was listening to old Glenn Miller records at the beach
house, the waves playing background to "Sentimental Journey." First
a tear watered his face, then he pushed it aside angrily, cursing the
world.

As he moved toward the record changer, the phone rang.

"John. Is that you? Thank God."

Sam brightened at the sound of Davidson's liquid accent.

"John. I'm going nuts here, listening to that son of a bitch Hankins
on television. Killing our defenses, giving away the damn world to
Moscow."

"I know what you're going through, Sam. But we've gotten our
first break. Someone in Hankins' administration went too far, too
fast."

Davidson quickly related the story of McDowell's abduction.

"Sam, I want you to meet me. We're going to the Russian summer
place on Chesapeake Bay. I think they're holding McDowell there.
We won't try to free him. It's too dangerous. We'll just make sure he's
there. I'll take the information to the President and see what he has to
say. It'll make good copy for the papers or great blackmail for us. If
we can find McDowell, we'll win either way. Can you do it?"

As Davidson was talking, Withers could sense his spirits revive.
With his free hand, he was pushing the .38 special into his waistband.

"John. I'll be in that crappy car in minutes. Give me five hours and
I'll be in Leesburg," Withers said, his voice animated for the first time
in months.

Chapter 50

Colonel Lev Orlov sat in his fourth-floor office at Teplyy Stan, alter-
nately placing his glass of hot tea precariously down on the blond
wood, then lifting the 90-page STAND DOWN document, leafing
through the dense documentation for a flaw in its theory.

He had to compliment Vassilin and the War Plans Bureau of the
Central Committee. STAND DOWN was ambitious, the most aggressive project he had seen in his twenty years with the Center. It was
the ultimate operation. A plan to bring the United States to its knees
by nuclear blackmail during these first six months of Jed Hankins'
administration.

From the text, Orlov could decipher that nuclear blackmail was
played by its own eccentric rules. In that global chess match, just the
threat of a Soviet first strike, played out mathematically by the under-
prepared Americans, would substitute for a lost, bloody war. Dictated to in a weakened position, America would be forced to accept
Soviet domination without a fight.

The strategically defeated Americans would then be "invited" to
become a fellow socialist state, a junior partner in the world Communist order. The East Germany of the West. Or suffer the indignity of
Finlandization, a country without external power.

The alternative? A Soviet first strike and mass murder.

The colonel blushed immodestly when he realized that Oval Red,
and now President Hankins, was the key. Before STAND DOWN
could be implemented, Yearling would have to disarm America even
further, to enlarge the Soviet's enormous nuclear superiority.

Orlov recalled warmly that he had helped America disarm once
before. It was an elegant piece of disinformation orchestrated for him
by the United States' own CIA. At the outset of détente in the early
1970s, the CIA had prepared an assessment of Soviet military buildup
which falsely claimed that the Russians were proceeding slowly.
Pushed by Orlov's doubles in the Agency, and stimulated by American wish fulfillment, the report had spuriously stated that the Soviet

Union was not arming because of détente. It was, of course, their period of greatest buildup.

The CIA document had even fooled the American presidents, who had reduced their defense budgets, even canceled vital weapons systems. America had frantically tried to rebuild their defenses in the 1980s, but Orlov knew that they had not overtaken the Russians, or even matched their output. Only 50 MXs, for example, compared to the Soviet's 600 powerful SS-18s, 19s, and 24s, including mobile versions of the latter. The SS-25 single-head mobile missile was already deployed in the hundreds, while the Americans were still discussing their version, the Midgetman, after a decade of indecision. And now Hankins had canceled that.

Orlov pondered his KGB charge—America. She was an easy client, he decided. When it came to its own survival, America was a childlike giant. Its people would be lulled once again by Hankins, just as they had been by others.

But disarmament wasn't enough, Orlov could see as he read on. For nuclear blackmail to succeed, without mass murder, it required the intimate cooperation of Yearling.

Orlov closed the red folder, feeling a surge of mastery. The Americans would be presiding over their own demise.

General Vassilin had been most accommodating today. He had called earlier, offering to meet Orlov at the Center, rather than in Moscow. He was anxious, he confessed, to hear the colonel's opinion.

The KGB chief arrived moments later, shaking out his beaver-collared greatcoat, a souvenir of his Red Army service as a young major in the Great Patriotic War.

"So, Orlov. What is your professional conclusion? What do you think of STAND DOWN?" Vassilin asked, now seated, sipping hot tea from a glass.

Orlov nodded confidently.

"It is excellent, Comrade Minister. I could not have done better myself."

As the words left his throat, the small colonel's face flushed with embarrassment.

"It's all right, Orlov." Vassilin offered a gilded smile. "You deserve that small touch of immodesty. But I'm pleased you like it."

"Yes, I do. But I have one question. What will happen if Hankins agrees to our nuclear threat, but someone else—maybe an American general, or a group of them—try to resist?" Orlov's head was clearly immersed in the strategic game.

"If the American military interfere, we'll carry out our threat of a first strike," Vassilin replied without hesitation. "Yearling will have paved the way by disarming. With their Star Wars deactivated, and our ground-based laser ABMs protecting our cities, we'll win easily. Their Minutemen are useless against our hardened command posts and silos and the Americans don't have enough accurate MX missiles to do the job. But we can eliminate every one of their silos and cities on a first strike. We may take some losses, but America will be totally annihilated. Removed from the earth as a people."

The hostility that had been leaking from the old Bolshevik's eyes now subsided.

"Of course, Orlov, I much prefer STAND DOWN. If Hankins comes along, we needn't sacrifice a single Soviet life. I have no desire for bloodshed. Only for victory."

Vassilin paused. "Orlov, who in America can we trust? Should Yearling be told about STAND DOWN right away?"

His answer was more than a formality. Orlov knew Vassilin would abide by it.

"No, wait on that. We need bring in only three people at first. Baneyev at our embassy. The second is William Fenton—a stalwart Marxist-Leninist, the one who recruited Hankins in the first place. Fenton has already chosen a trusted Washington professional, Robert Billings, to head the Pentagon. He would also have to know. But only those. At least for now."

"Are you sure? Can we really keep it from Hankins?" Vassilin asked again.

"Yes, absolutely. Hankins should be left to do his political work. Maintain the illusion of altruism. Fenton can bring him in later, as needed. I have complete confidence in his ability to manipulate the President."

"And our man in place, Captain Semanski—Tom Ward?"

"No, he needn't know either. He performs best as an apparent American, relaying our private wishes to Hankins. Let's hold him in reserve."

Vassilin, whose burly peasant stature overshadowed the diminutive Orlov, bent to grasp the colonel's hand.

"Lev Andreievich, today we have set history in motion. There's no looking back."

Chapter 51

From the wooden veranda of the American Embassy, a gracious white Victorian home built for the mistress of a former British governor-general, Harry Decker surveyed the tranquil setting.

The temperature in this highland town, capital of the East African Republic, was only 75° Fahrenheit, balmy for a nation that straddled the equator. Cooling mountain air wafted across the lawn most of the year, bringing the scents of African lushness. Orange trees and bougainvillea outlined the choice property. The embassy compound was situated off the main road, about a mile from the town of Victoriaville, a nineteenth-century vestige of British colonial rule, replete with architectural gingerbread.

Life was good for Decker. He was single and the female members of the foreign colony adored his humor and his apparent power at the embassy. Decker was nominally chargé d'affaires, but his true responsibility as CIA chief of station was a common secret in the isolated little republic.

But the local air of contentment was deceptive. Beneath it, a contagious fear had captured the city ever since the Tomasi Kambula coup three months before. The fiery six-foot-three Army captain had murdered his opposition, toppled his pro-Western uncle, King Banusa, and was operating as an international loner. Even the capital had been renamed. Victoriaville was now Kambula City.

Little consolation to Decker that Kambula hated the Communists. He had killed the Marxist chief of the NIKIDI rebels, but was as ruthless with the pro-Western opposition led by his own cousin, Moise Utana. Hanged by his thumbs in the public square until he was dead, Utana's corpse soon soiled the air.

Decker had leaned back into the rattan rocker on the embassy's veranda that morning when his assistant, John Manning, approached.

"Harry, a cable just came in. I decrypted it personally. You won't believe it."

Manning handed it to Decker, who ripped open the secure envelope.

The more he studied it, the less sense it made.

CONTACT MAJOR CHOLKIN, KGB CHIEF AT LOCAL SOVIET EMBASSY.
DEVISE JOINT STRATEGY FOR COUP AGAINST KAMBULA TO BE LED BY
REMAINING LEADERS OF MARXIST AND PRO-WESTERN OPPOSITION. NEW
GOVERNMENT IS TO BE NEUTRAL AND DEMOCRATIC. ARMS BEING
SHIPPED AS DISGUISED AIRLINE CARGO. GIVE NO INFORMATION TO U. S.
STATE DEPARTMENT PEOPLE IN KAMBULA. COORDINATE EVERYTHING
WITH CHOLKIN OF KGB. THIS IS HIGHEST PRIORITY ORDER OF PRESIDENT
HANKINS. PLEASE SHRED AND REPORT PROGRESS REGULARLY. MILES.

Work with Cholkin? Who was the author of this madness? Langley
or the White House? The KGB had almost engineered a coup that
would have added the East African Republic to Angola and Ethiopia
as Communist satellites. Another coup to bring in Utana's men?
Good enough. They would offer a friendly face to the West.

But a joint coup with Cholkin to create a supposedly neutral and
democratic regime? Was Washington suffering political amnesia? Had
they already forgotten what happened in Nicaragua? It was lunacy.
Langley surely didn't understand what was going on. He would have
to wire his protest.

Decker cabled Washington with an immediate request for clarification. Manning brought the answer to Decker shortly after lunch.

PROJECT KAMBULA IS CORRECT AS RECEIVED BY YOU. MAJOR CHOLKIN
HAS RECEIVED IDENTICAL ORDERS FROM THE SOVIET GOVERNMENT.
PLEASE EFFECTUATE WITHOUT DOUBT OR DELAY. MILES.

Decker was still shocked, but in some ways it fit in with his personal misgivings about Hankins. The President's aggressive peace initiative with Moscow was troubling. Since when could anyone expect
honesty from Cholkin and his crowd? But Decker had no choice, at
least if he expected to stay in the Agency.

He lifted the phone, then thoughtfully placed it back down. He
could hardly call Cholkin. The operators in this town listened in on
all conversations. Instead, he buzzed for Manning.

"John, what's the name of that girl friend of yours who works at
the Russian Embassy? Don't use the phone. Go see her tonight and
tell her to tell Major Cholkin—and nobody else—that I want to meet
him. We'll use that house in the hills, the place of the old British

planter, Jenkins. He's reliable. I'll call Jenkins and make it for tomorrow night at 9 P.M. Just Cholkin and me. Nobody else."

"You and Cholkin?" Manning asked, his face distorted in surprise.
"Have you gone mad?"

Decker looked sympathetically at his aide.

"I think so, Manning. I really think so."

Chapter 52

Bill Fenton's attempt to avoid John Davidson's stare was futile.

Fenton was in the lobby of the Cosmos Club, awaiting his lunch
date, Secretary of Defense Billings, when the Baptist walked through
the grillwork front door and stared intently at the young man.

"Oh, Mr. Davidson. Good to see you," Fenton said, resigned to the
confrontation. "How's the spying business? I understand you've retired to your farm. Where is it? Leesburg?"

"Yes, Mr. Fenton. Perhaps you've driven by. When was it? Oh yes,
just after the convention? Am I retired? Forbid. Protecting the Union
becomes an obsession—one never gets out of the habit. But you
wouldn't know about that. Would you?"

Davidson touched the wilting brim of his tweed rain hat and
moved toward the cloakroom.

Damn fascist, Fenton thought, then dismissed the Baptist from his
mind. The old spy was immobilized now, while, as White House
chief of staff, he had a nation, perhaps more, to run.

As Fenton waited for Billings, he looked about the club, concluding
that he approved. The Cosmos was a haven for Washingtonians weary
of being recognized. The members were not noticeably awed by the
presence of the President's chief of staff, or even the head of the
Pentagon. Only the appearance of the President himself would move
these status-sated people, Fenton was sure.

Fenton had found that he could be there, silent and solitary, or
quietly with a guest. Or, when it served his purposes, he could dip
into the gossipy swamps of Washington life. Everyone was only too
eager to supply useful morsels of news to this new fountainhead of

American power. But today Fenton wanted to avoid casual acquaintances.

A moment later the Secretary arrived and they moved toward
Fenton's special table in the far corner of the dining room. It was one
forty-five, and most of the members had already eaten. No one was
close enough to overhear their conversation, but they still conducted
it sotto voce.

Fenton was learning the presidential security game. What appeared
to be clear, debugged territory in the White House and the Pentagon
was not necessarily so. Nixon and others had proven that. The Cosmos Club was far safer turf.

"Bob, how are we doing on STAND DOWN?" Fenton began after
he had scribbled their lunch orders. "How's the disarmament progressing?"

"Actually better than I thought." The Defense Secretary's manner
was openly bright. "There's a little grumbling in the military, but
they're good constitutional citizens. The Air Force is the most annoyed, but the Army and the Marines are almost happy—bustling
around with the new helicopters and field artillery Abbott has bought
them. Meanwhile, we're dismantling the strategic forces."

Fenton could feel Billings' inquiring stare.

"And, Bill, what about you. Anything new from Orlov?"

"Yes, as a matter of fact," Fenton responded. "He wants all our
missile launch codes. We won't need them if Jed cooperates, but
Orlov insists on a backup in case Jed balks. Who knows? We might
have to block a missile retaliation against a Soviet first strike, or even
the threat of one."

"Do you think the President will come along on STAND
DOWN?" Billings asked, exhibiting his first sign of anxiety.

As Fenton measured his answer, he surveyed the former foundation executive. Balding and distinguished-looking, Billings seemed
the model of American governmental propriety. Yet he was at the
center of the extreme left establishment. Everything Fenton knew
about him, from his service going back to Eisenhower, up to his years
as director of the Federal Organization, confirmed that, of all
Fenton's allies in Washington, Billings deserved the most trust.

Yet Fenton could never understand Billings' class of Marxist. Gen-
tlemanly, apparently concerned with individual rights, yet willing to
sacrifice all that—and the future of their fortunes—for the Utopia of
socialism. Mainly Easterners, they came from what are commonly

called "good families." Anglo-Saxons who could trace their origins back hundreds of years, with ties to the most restricted clubs, the well-endowed universities, the prestigious law firms.

Fenton thought it strange that Billings, scion of a Boston textile fortune and graduate of Harvard, should be of like mind with him. But it was far from uncommon, he had learned. It was somehow related to religious sacrifice, of guilt sublimated into politics. As a seminary graduate, he knew something of that himself.

Perhaps it was part of their racial unconscious, the last step in the liberalization of the old American church. From fierce Puritanism dating back to the 1600s, through more liberal Congregationalism, to free Unitarianism, then to Marxism. With a touch of Freud along the way.

"Yes, I really believe the President will come along, Bob," Fenton finally replied. "In which case, Jed will order a nuclear surrender to the Soviet Union. But we have to be prepared for two contingencies. One is that he'll refuse. And two, if he does cooperate, that the military will try to override the President. That's why the missile codes are so important."

"Which codes, exactly, do you need?" Billings asked.

"All the missile launch codes. That includes the GO codes for the President and his Cabinet—the only ones that can authorize a nuclear strike—down to the numbers that activate the computers in the missile silos. Once we get them, we'll have to make them all inactive at the exact time of STAND DOWN. The Pentagon's Command and Control will be paralyzed for hours."

Fenton's eyes were displaying uncertainty. "Can you do it, Bob?"

"I think so, Bill. But it's a tall order. We're dealing with five major centers—the White House, the National Military Command Center at the Pentagon, the underground Alternate Command Center in southern Pennsylvania, near the Maryland border, the SAC HQ at Offutt Air Force Base outside Omaha, and the NORAD Command Center in the Cheyenne Mountain complex in Colorado.

"I've got to make sure that, when the two Air Force officers in each of the hundred underground bunkers that control the Minutemen and MXs open their safes and take out the six-digit Emergency Action Message, nothing happens. That the numbers are rejected by the computer."

"Can you do it?" Fenton asked again, his hand still toying with the arms of his spectacles.

Billings allowed himself a few seconds.

"There's a lot to cover, Bill. I've also got to work on the codes for the Poseidon and Trident subs. And there's another SAC command center—a flying one called Looking Glass. One of two converted 707s is always in the air over the Midwest in case the ground headquarters are knocked out. A SAC general is aboard with his nuclear war codes locked in the clacker box, a red steel safe right on the plane."

"What about Jed's 'Football,' that little black case Commander Janet Kelly, his military aide, always carries around?" Fenton asked. "Doesn't that activate the whole system?"

"In a way. She has the combination to the Football. Inside is a laminated 75-page Black Book with all the war plans for the President, along with the GO codes on little 3×5 index cards. The military want to make sure they're talking to the President, not an impostor who wants to blow up the world. The VP, if we had one, and the fifteen people in succession to the President—the Speaker of the House, the president pro tem of the Senate, and the whole Cabinet—have their GO codes in there too. Just in case one of them has to take over if the President is killed."

Billings smiled. "You know, Bill, I'm number five on that list myself."

Fenton could feel impatience pressing in. He could handle hours of philosophical or political argument, but the jargon of modern warfare bored him. He knew nothing about missiles or computers, but he appreciated that he needed people who did.

"Do you know how you're going to do it?" Fenton asked.

"There are two ways, Bill. First, I'll try the chain of command. I am the boss at the Pentagon, you know. I'll see how that goes. If not, I suppose I'll just have to steal my own secrets."

The two men continued their meal, pursuing Washington small talk without mentioning STAND DOWN again. As they prepared to leave the Cosmos, Fenton looked pridefully at his luncheon partner.

He was sometimes surprised, and always pleased, that so many talented Americans were willing to sacrifice so much for the Soviet Union.

Chapter 53

The motor launch moved out from the marina in Annapolis, its bow pointed accusingly across Chesapeake Bay toward the eastern shore.

"Sam, it's time to inflate the rubber boat. We'll be reaching the drop point in five minutes."

John Davidson stood at the wheel of the twenty-eight-foot high-speed power boat, a navigation map alongside him, lit by a small portable light. It was 3 A.M. and bleakly dark. He hoped that Russian alertness against an intruder from sea would be lower at this time of night, that McDowell could be located at the Soviet retreat without a confrontation.

The Russians had chosen well for their summer estate. Purchased over a decade earlier from a prominent automaker family, the imposing structure was on the Point, a tip of land jutting into the bay. Because it was fifty miles from the capital, the Russians had received a special exemption from their twenty-five-mile travel restriction.

As time for the drop approached, Withers stood farther back on the deck, preparing the small motorless rubber boat in which he would make his landing. Russian radar charted the waters, but the rubber raft, with only wooden oars, would evade detection. The power boat would leave the area as soon as Withers was dropped into the water.

The rendezvous had been set for 4:15 A.M., the time Davidson was to return to pick up Withers. If Sam was not there, the boat would come back every half hour for three hours before yielding to the obvious.

As Davidson brought the engine to a stop a quarter of a mile off the Point, Withers dropped the raft into the calm bay. The night air was chilled, about 40° Fahrenheit. The water was only a little warmer, and Withers worried about falling in. He lowered himself by rope ladder, then eased his body downward, balancing to keep the raft from tilting. After he was seated, Sam retrieved the rope ladder and dipped his hand tentatively into the water. He pulled it back. No one could long survive in that frigid bay.

Davidson called down his partings.

"Good luck, Sam. Remember. If you have any trouble, use the walkie-talkie. Even if the Russkies listen in, it'll take a little while to triangulate you. And keep the flashlight in your pocket as a last-resort signal. Please, Sam, if you see McDowell, don't try heroics. Let's settle for proof that they've taken him prisoner."

The trip in was quiet. Withers used only one oar, dipping it softly as he glided toward the shore. He steered the raft toward the other side of the Point, as far as possible from the house and the dock.

Withers landed the raft on a small, pebbly beach and dragged the boat ashore. From the metal ring at the bow he tied the thin chain to a scrub tree, pulling it taut as a test. It seemed secure.

He had three hundred feet to cover before he reached the first obstacle, a chain link fence on the other side of the Point. Undoubtedly wired for both sound and touch.

Sam stood about a hundred feet from the perimeter and tossed a small rock at the fence. His aim was good, but it failed to set off the alarm. He chose a larger rock. This time its impact with the fence triggered the expected response. Blazing floodlights around the main house went on instantly, illuminating the compound. As a wail-like noise penetrated the night, Sam turned and ran in the opposite direction.

Moving into a clump of trees a little inland, Withers could see several armed men in the compound darting frenetically about, searching for the source of the intrusion. But he was outside the fence, away from their reach.

He sat on the damp ground, pulled his jacket hood over his head, and waited. After five minutes he returned to the pebbly beach area. Again he picked up a rock and threw it at the sensitized fence. As the alarm roared, he retreated to the same spot, away from the cyclone barrier.

Davidson and he had decided that the easiest entry to the Point was to employ the alarm game. Three more times, every five minutes, Withers set the system into action with a rock. By the last time, even though the lights went on automatically, he noticed less alertness by the armed men inside. They had already scoured every inch of ground within the fenced perimeter, then the house itself, and found nothing. They assumed there had been no penetration. And they were right.

It was now time for Withers to enter the compound. Instead of a hurled rock, his own body set off the alarm as he threw a rope ladder over the seven-foot fence and scaled quickly down the other side. As the floodlights went on, he moved away from the house into a small patch of darkness at the far end and waited.

After ten minutes the compound returned to normal. The Russians were convinced that some malfunction, or a small animal, had been setting off the repeated false alarms.

Sam waited a few minutes, then cautiously moved, almost at a crawl, toward the large residence. One by one, the house lights put on during the alerts were being extinguished. All except one, on the second floor at the back. Logically, that should be McDowell's room. They would be checking to see if the alarms were related to him. He had to move toward that singular point of light.

He approached the back of the house, seeking the correct angle of sight. As he reached it, he crouched and looked up. The faces in the bedroom were indistinct, but an armed man in a pea jacket was gesticulating. He seemed to be talking loudly to another man seated on the bed, with only his back facing the window. He could make out a patch of red hair. It was McDowell.

Withers kept his body profile low. Lying almost prone in the wet grass, he continued to focus on that one window. After three minutes the armed man moved out of the room and closed the door. Seconds later the light went out. Now only the moonlight reflecting off the bay lit the house in a weak glow.

The man in the pea jacket appeared outside the house. He had come down the stairs, out a back entrance, and had taken up a guard position directly under McDowell's window. Doug was probably alone.

Withers could no longer see into the room, but its position on the house's exterior was filed in his mind. Davidson wanted only to verify that McDowell was there, but Sam couldn't purge the possibility. Could he bring McDowell out, back to the beach, and into the boat with him?

Darkness was Sam's ally. The Russian guard stood immobile for a few minutes at a time, then paced up and down to break the monotony. At intervals, he stood rigid again. Sam waited until the guard was still, then moved through the shadows against the house. A step at a time, he brushed the wall, reaching to within a few feet of the Russian. From his parka, Withers removed a long-bladed knife.

His lunge was instantaneous. One hand muffled the guard's mouth while the blade went deep into the small of his back, pushing through the leather jacket like cellophane. The body fell, huddled into a dark pocket, invisible to anyone a dozen feet away.

Scaling the wall to the second floor was a minor challenge for Withers. With his small frame and developed arms, he took to it like an agile primate. Sam soon stood on the sill, his hand clutching the drainpipe for security. He tapped lightly on the window. First once, then twice, with a soft tattoo that could be mistaken for the wind, or even a bird. He repeated the pattern in the same rhythm, then waited.

"Who's there?" A voice from inside the room was speaking in English. Withers recognized it immediately.

"Keep it low, McDowell. This is Withers. Your old convention buddy. John Davidson sent me to get you back. Don't say anything. Just come to the window and lift it."

McDowell moved quietly toward the window, then carefully lifted the frame, stopping abruptly as the weathered wood emitted a thin screech. Both men froze. McDowell continued more cautiously, an inch at a time, while Withers grasped the drainpipe, one foot on the sill as a stabilizer. But he could feel his strength ebbing.

"Try to speed it a little," Withers whispered.

"It's done," McDowell said as he started to climb through.

"Hold it just a minute." Withers was insistent. "I'll go down first. Use the drainpipe. If you fall, I'll try to break the impact."

Withers was soon on the ground, only a few feet from the fresh corpse. As McDowell started to shinny down, Sam glanced around. So far, the compound was quiet. In a minute, McDowell had joined him.

"Oh, my God!" The sound from McDowell was involuntary. The newsman had just seen the dead Russian. He bent over and examined the face.

"That's one of the guys who took me from the CIA safe house," McDowell whispered.

"Later. Later." Withers was anxious to move on. "Look ahead. See the tall chain link fence over there. I left a rope ladder over its edge. It's too light to trigger the alarm by itself. But as soon as you use it and hit the fence, the lights will come on like a damn circus. Go over, then keep running in a straight line. Don't stop no matter what. When you get to the Point, run to the right. The boat is beached there near a little inlet, tied to a scrub tree. Take the chain off and get it into the water. I'll be right behind you."

"What happens if you don't show right away?"

"Don't wait. Just keep going. Davidson is offshore in a power boat. Use this flashlight to signal him. Okay?"

When McDowell nodded, Withers restrained him for a second, then released his hold.

"Now. Go!"

McDowell raced ahead of Withers to the fence, then lifted himself onto the rope ladder. The instant his body pressure registered, lights and a high screech flooded the air.

He moved quickly over the fence. Withers followed closely behind and was about to climb upward himself when he saw a figure in the open second-floor window. It was lifting a rifle into position. Withers could make it out. It was Baneyev.

In an instant, Sam had thrown himself onto the ground and extracted the police special. In a duel of split seconds, the two men aimed and fired. As the gun shattered in Baneyev's hand, the wail could be heard above the alarm, his pain filling the bay. Withers could see that he hadn't killed the colonel, but he clearly had hit his hand.

Withers mounted the rope ladder just as three Russians raced across the grounds toward him, their bullets ricocheting off the cyclone fence. He was over and running toward the Point.

McDowell had done his job well. The boat was already in the water, expectant.

"Jump in!" McDowell cried out. Sam hurled his body into the boat as McDowell started paddling. In a moment, Sam had regained his balance and was also pumping his oar madly on the other side of the raft, pulling it out to sea.

"Look!"

McDowell, facing the beach, had seen the three Russians turning the corner of the Point.

Their first shot was slightly wide, piercing the water a foot from the leeward side of the boat. The second one fell only inches short. Both men pulled more heavily on the oars, stretching the distance between them and the Point with each stroke.

The bullets now were falling shorter. None of the three Russians had a rifle and the pistol range was quickly exhausting itself.

As soon as it looked safe, Withers dropped his oar and extracted the walkie-talkie from its waterproof case.

"Baptist. Calling Baptist. Carolina here. Come in."

First a crackle, then Davidson's unmistakable voice.

"Carolina. I am offshore waiting. Use your flashlight. I'll signal back and you come to me."

"Baptist. I can't make it all the way. We'll head out but you must come to us, quick. I'm sure they're launching a boat to intercept."

"Us?" Davidson shouted into the radio.

"Please, Baptist. Come quick," Withers said, bypassing the question and swinging the flashlight into the darkness in a wide arc, first once, then twice.

"Do you see us, Baptist? Do you see us?"

"I do. Am coming ahead full power."

Withers was putting away the walkie-talkie, poised to lift his oar, when he saw it. A speedboat was leaving the Russians' lighted dock and heading in their direction. They too had seen the flashlight signal.

It was a triangle of danger. The raft was lobbing along at its dinosaur speed toward Davidson's power craft, now visible on the horizon in a splinter of moonlight. The Soviet speedboat was approaching rapidly in the opposite direction, trying to head off the raft before it made contact. The two men leaned into their oars, knowing that every foot could mean salvation.

From where Sam sat, it looked like a dead heat. He hoped the word was not appropriate. Within two minutes, Withers was close enough to the power boat to see Davidson at the wheel, one hand on his work, the other cradling a shotgun.

"Hurry, Sam!" Davidson called down.

His fear was justified. The speedboat was now only a little farther from the raft than was Davidson—and bearing in.

Suddenly, Davidson's power boat stopped dead in the water. It could come no closer to the raft for fear of swamping it.

"Row to the ladder! Quick," Davidson shouted into the night.

In seconds, McDowell's foot was stretching for the first rung of the Jacob's ladder. Withers was still in the raft, but not waiting his turn. He had his pistol out, raised to firing height. Davidson couldn't help the struggling McDowell, for both his arms were now occupied with his shotgun, aimed in the same direction as Withers' police pistol.

The Soviet speedboat had arrived, its floodlight illuminating the scene. Four men were facing one another, guns drawn, as McDowell successfully pulled himself up onto the deck, watching the drama.

"It's not necessary for you to lower your guns, gentlemen," Davidson called down from the high bow. "Just put your little boat into reverse. Otherwise I will exercise my two options. One is that Mr. Withers and I will blow your brains out the second you decide to fire. And afterward I'll chase you down and cut your boat in two, engines full. Why don't we call it a night? I'm sure our respective governments can work this out later on."

The Russians spoke rapidly in their native language, then shouted to the driver of the speedboat. With their guns still poised at eye height, aimed at Davidson and Withers, the Soviet boat started in reverse for a few seconds, then began a wide arc, turning back to its retreat at the Point.

Chapter 54

His long legs perched unceremoniously atop the massive desk, Hankins stared through his aviator glasses at a report from Joint Chiefs Chairman Abbott on the "conventionalization" of the armed services.

Abbott was like a child in a toy soldier shop, ecstatic that the mud-slogging Marines and other conventional forces were finally being favored over the high-tech boys with their trillion-dollar projects.

The intercom rang. "Yes, Maude. Put him on."

Hankins smiled at the coincidence. It was Abbott.

"Yes, General. How is the Marine Corps, and all our other defense forces, today?"

"Mr. President, I'm calling just to tell you how much I appreciate your support of our troops. The pay scale is up, and so is the morale, and the supply of ammunition and spare parts. The foot soldier is finally coming into his own. Just wanted to thank you."

Hankins hung up, pleased. Abbott had been his choice of choices. A patriot doing the job he needed—switching money and emphasis away from strategic arms without arousing public ire. Abbott was also helping to defuse the charge that the new administration was "soft" on defense.

Abbott was a puzzlement to the Senate Armed Services Committee, being so far down the military promotion list. But the only information they could muster was that he was stalwart, brave, and loyal. Smart? Probably not. But no combat colonel with seventeen decorations could be termed unsuitable. Not if the senators wanted to be reelected.

These first weeks in office had been exhilarating for Hankins. His cabinet appointments were making relatively smooth progress. The Senate Foreign Relations Committee had received some static on Secretary of State Sommerville's isolationist theories, but his scholarly reputation had won him approval.

Billings was much the same. A scholar, probably left-wing, the committee members thought. But he had an understanding of the defense establishment, even if he sought to deemphasize it. If the President wanted him in that post, there was little they could do.

Not that Senator Delafield hadn't tried, Hankins had heard. The North Dakotan had turned the Senate Armed Services Committee hearings for Billings into a bit of an opera.

"Gentlemen," Delafield had said, his voice rising. "You're voting for the demise of this Republic. I warn you."

But as the other senators had reminded him, Daniels was dead and Hankins was his legal heir. They would have to live with the young President and most of his appointments.

Only one nomination—Fenton as head of the CIA—was not emerging as planned. Hankins was mulling this when his chief aide walked in.

"How are you this morning, Mr. President?" Fenton asked, his voice cheery. "I've just heard the good news about Billings and Sommerville. Anything on Maynard's VP nomination? I understand Feldman's angry because they can't find any dirt on him. That Feldman's a pain—with that shock of unruly hair and his fake naive manner. Who does he think he's fooling?"

"Don't worry, Bill. Feldman will have to approve Maynard in the end," Hankins assured him. "Terry's clean. All he needs is a majority in both houses to become VP, the way Rockefeller did under Ford. That should be easy. Don't you think?"

"No trouble at all, Mr. President. Terry's got a lot of friends on the Hill. So far, so good."

Yes, so far, so good, Hankins agreed. Except for Fenton's nomination to head the CIA, which he hoped he wouldn't have to mention this morning. All his calls to the Senate Select Committee on Intelligence had been fruitless. Just that it was under advisement. No one knew Fenton's true politics, but could they have learned that he had been with the Weathermen at Berkeley? That itself could hold things up.

"Any news on my nomination?" Fenton finally asked, straining not to appear self-serving.

"No, Bill. Not a word. But I'll keep after it."

Fenton's nomination aside, the tone of the Administration had been good. Criticism of his massive defense cuts had been strong, but so had his support. The cost savings had impressed Wall Street, which was caterwauling for a balanced budget and lower interest rates. Their need was his, even if the motives were poles apart. That's what made politics in America, Hankins mused. Republican, Democrat, or Communist.

"Have you seen the editorials on 'Peace in Space'?" Fenton suddenly asked, handing Hankins copies from the morning newspapers. "Most support your new treaty with the Russians. But one sleazy sheet in Chicago attacked us badly—they called you 'a killer of children.' "

Hankins' pupils dilated as he studied the editorial cartoon, a caricature of him removing an ash can shield labeled "Star Wars" from a young girl being pummeled by stones thrown by a bully.

The President fumed, finally discarding the cartoon in the wastebasket. Then he laughed.

"You can't win them all, Bill. But, on average, I think we're not doing badly."

He might be Marxist, but Hankins could feel himself yielding to the predilection of all American politicians. No matter what their ideology, they enjoyed public approval. It was a weakness of the species.

"I think better than not bad, Jed," Fenton assured the President. "The insurrection in the Philippines is going well and the Marxist forces will be moving into Manila in a month or two. You did the right thing pulling out the 450 military advisers."

Fenton stopped, reminded of something.

"Mr. President, please excuse me. I have to make a few calls. I'll be right back."

Hankins was pleased by the break. Only one piece of criticism from the liberal media troubled him. This was a chance to rectify it, without Fenton in earshot.

When he thought "liberal press," Hankins visualized only one man, Jason Cartwright, the author of the syndicated column "Washington

I." Appearing daily in 437 newspapers, the column was as essential to the morning tranquillity of Washingtonians and New Yorkers as eggs-over.

Hankins picked the Cartwright column off his desk. As he read it again, he blanched. His trial balloon of a nuclear-free Europe, an idea proposed by Sommerville, was being shot down.

"Many pronouncements of our new Chief Executive have cheered me," Cartwright wrote. "It's good news, for example, that President Hankins has curbed the asinine Pentagon policy of spend and flex. But his trial balloon of a nuclear-free Europe must be viewed skeptically as a policy that could lead to the abandonment of the Western world."

Hankins reread the column three times. Not only was it negative, he decided, but it expressed the exact limit he could take the nation leftward in foreign affairs at this moment. Cartwright was a litmus test of what was politically permissible and what bordered on treason to Western democratic traditions.

He was learning another potent lesson. It was that he could do pretty much what he wanted in the world without disturbing the American public, as long as he didn't tamper with Western Europe. Giving the Soviets a free hand in Asia, Africa—even Central and Latin America—was generally allowable, if he was clever.

But Europe was where Americans traveled in the summer, where they did business, where most of them had come from originally. It was sacrosanct and Hankins had learned his catechism.

"Maude," Hankins said, depressing the intercom. "Please get me Jason Cartwright. Try his office on I Street."

The speed of White House operators was not idle rumor, Hankins was learning. Within minutes, the intercom rang.

"Mr. President. This is Maude. Mr. Cartwright wasn't in his office, but we found him at a function at the Alibi Club. I have him for you."

"Mr. Cartwright. This is the President."

Hankins didn't expect to awe the columnist. Imperial tones from the Oval Office were routine for Cartwright, who had pushed a few Chief Executives to the brink of antacid addiction.

"Mr. President, pleasure to hear from you. What can I do for the commonweal today?"

Hankins had never met Cartwright, but he already knew he didn't like him. He could hear an insipid, superior voice, some strange cross of Iowan Midwestern flatness and Yale patrician. It implied that politicians were transient, while only Washington fixtures like Cartwright mattered.

The President was nauseated by Cartwright's brand of liberalism anyway, with its vacillations tied to Georgetown fashion of how much, or how little, anti-Communism was in "good taste." But, right now, Hankins knew that he couldn't afford to alienate Cartwright, or the millions of his readers. He was ready, as Machiavelli had counseled, to lie down with the Devil.

"Jason. I hope I can call you that," Hankins began. "I just phoned to congratulate you on this morning's column. It was world class."

"Well, thank you, Mr. President."

"I'm afraid Sommerville went too far in his trust of Soviet intentions," Hankins continued. "And I foolishly took his counsel. I wanted you to know that I've changed my mind, and that you deserve the credit."

Hankins could sense that the arrogant newsman was impressed.

"Why, Mr. President, how gallant of you. Most Presidents would do an about-face and never recognize their critics." Cartwright hesitated. "I hope this will be the beginning of a long, fruitful relationship."

"I'm sure it will, Jason. And you have my permission to handle this as an exclusive. Just don't mention me as the source. You know—some unimpeachable White House spokesman."

"Yes, Mr. President."

Fenton had reentered the doorway of the Oval Office, waiting until Hankins, hand over the speaker, waved him in. He listened as Hankins wrapped up his conquest.

"Jason, I look forward to your exclusive column. When will it be? Day after tomorrow? Good. Glad we could speak. Bye."

"Was that Jason Cartwright?" Fenton asked petulantly. "What did that SOB want? I think his column this morning was pure sabotage."

"No, I called him, Bill. I'm afraid he's killed our nuclear-free Europe. At least for now."

On Fenton's face, Hankins could see the emergence of the disapproving look that always frightened, even devastated him.

"But, Jed. I don't think that was smart. By backtracking on a nuclear-free Europe, we're going to look unreliable to the Russians. They were banking on it."

Hankins could feel Fenton's sting, a combination of sulking and emotional blackmail that had controlled him all these years. Hankins nodded, somewhat sheepish. He couldn't afford to alienate Fenton, the man who had made it all possible. But in the final analysis he, not Fenton, was responsible for moving America closer to world Communism—at the right speed.

"Bill, I know you're disappointed. But it was necessary, at least for now. Wasn't it you who taught me 'two steps forward, one step back'? Jesus, we've taken ten giant steps forward already, and now only one or two back. Let me do it my way. I promise it'll work out."

Fenton was still vigorously shaking his head. "I really don't think you're doing the right thing. But you're the President."

As Fenton started out of the Oval Office toward his own space in the former President's study, he was troubled, for the first time, by Jed Hankins' performance as President. Backtracking on the nuclear-free Europe showed a lack of boldness. Just what they couldn't afford at this point.

He was groping, trying to slice through a maze of contradictions. Was Hankins forgetting his Marxist obligations? Anxious to set his own course, without Fenton? Or was he just burdened by the job?

"See you later, Mr. President," Fenton called as he exited, but Hankins had already disappeared into his work.

Chapter 55

It had been months in coming, but that morning, twenty-five hundred miles away, San Bernardino Detective Sergeant Pete Fuller finally received the call.

FBI Special Agent Rourke had twice been turned down by the brass because of the high cost of screening the enormous film footage of the Beverly Hills Hotel that weekend in July when Stanislaw Wynoski, Polish geneticist, had disappeared. Only the intercession of the governor of California had finally provided Rourke with the go-ahead from the FBI's SAC (Special Agent in Charge) in Los Angeles.

Manpower would be assigned to screen all the footage, Fuller was told. They would call him when they had an outtake of a man who had magically appeared on film leaving the hotel but had never been seen entering it.

Fortunately they were able to narrow their options. Wynoski had last been seen in the lobby at 3 P.M. on Monday, while the charred body had been found in the desert foothills at 7 P.M. Allowing two hours' driving time from Beverly Hills to the murder site, Wynoski—or whoever—had probably left the hotel sometime between three and five on Monday afternoon.

The screening work, assigned to six agents, was done in segments. Each man first viewed the film of that two-hour window of possibility, noting any male leaving the hotel who could, with wide latitude, be Wynoski. The remaining forty-four hours of 16mm film, a total of 95,040 feet of exposed, emulsified celluloid—going back to Saturday night at 6 P.M. when the first convention guest arrived—was divided among the same six agents. They consulted prints of their exiting suspects, then strained to find them entering the pink stucco palace.

The call finally came that morning at 9 A.M. In two hours, Rourke told Fuller, he was to appear at the FBI office on Wilshire Boulevard.

"Bring your eyeglasses," Rourke chided. "The pictures are not large."

Rourke and two other FBI men met the San Bernardino detective and led him into the screening room.

"Hey, Fuller, I have a bill for you."

It was Mike Sarante, one of the agents assigned to the case. "It's for a shepherd seeing eye dog. Did you ever sit in a dark room and look at clean movies for five straight days? Blindsville!"

Fuller smiled as benignly as possible.

"Okay. Hold it down. The show is beginning," Rourke called out.

In a moment the familiar portico of the Beverly Hills Hotel was projected on the screen in 16mm color.

"This is the front entrance to the hotel taken at three-twenty on Monday afternoon," Rourke explained. "Try not to look at the broads and the Rolls-Royces. Concentrate on the spot where the cabs are picking up the people who are leaving."

All eyes were on the screen as people exited the hotel and moved into either taxicabs or cars brought up by parking attendants.

"Stop the roll!" Rourke called out.

The frame froze on the image of a man, handsomely attired in a gray pin-stripe suit, bending over to enter a Peugeot taxi. In his hand was a small airline travel bag.

"We've searched every inch of the damn movies and this is the only male shown coming out of the hotel but never filmed going in. It was a lot of work, Fuller. I hope you appreciate it."

Fuller only nodded. He was too excited for courtesies.

"Can you zoom in on the man and the bag?" Fuller asked. Finally, a chance that he might be looking at the desert killer—Wynoski, the Pole, or whoever he actually was.

Rourke motioned, and the image of a man, grainy yet clear enough to distinguish his features, came up fourfold on the color screen.

"Hold it there. Good," said Fuller, his enthusiasm soaring.

He could make out a light-complected male, about thirty-five, slim but not thin, black-haired, with pleasant but indistinct features. Except for one. A sharp, pointed nose. Irish, he thought. Or maybe Polish. Like his name. Wynoski.

Fuller stared at the airline bag. It matched the one Greenway had shown him, given leeway for the ravages of the Potomac. Like the one fished out of the river, the blown-up view displayed an airline valise lacking a decal.

The California detective leaned back into the chair.

"Rourke. You and your men did a swell job. I think I may have my desert murderer. Could you make up a couple of enlargements of this zoom shot?"

"We're way ahead of you, Fuller," Rourke said, handing the surprised detective two 11 × 14 color prints.

"I want you to understand that the case is still officially closed as far as the FBI is concerned," Rourke added. "But unofficially we'll give you a hand if we can. I don't like the idea of some foreigner coming over here and murdering people on our roads."

"Thanks, Rourke," Fuller said as he placed the photos in his briefcase. "Now all I need is a name to go with the face."

Chapter 56

"Where have you been?" Meg shouted as McDowell entered the network office, unshaven, his eyes ringed with fatigue, a stale odor surrounding his wrinkled clothes. "What happened to you? Milt Samuels called from New York. He's burning because you never showed up."

McDowell realized how ragged he looked. He had come to the office directly from his rescue at the Point, but as far as the inquisitive world was concerned, the kidnapping had never taken place. He had promised Davidson silence.

"Oh, I'm really sorry, Meg. I called my mother from the airport. She suddenly got very sick and I had to go to Oregon for a couple of days. Never even had a chance to change clothes. Remind me to call Milt and apologize."

"Really?"

It was evident Meg didn't buy a word of it. Nor, he recognized, did he fully believe her innocence. The sound of the phone click had never left him. She knew he was on his way to New York when the Agency limousine abducted him. Could sweet Meg be somehow involved in his kidnapping?

McDowell knew that too much had happened for him to let it pass. His kidnapping by a combined CIA-KGB team was proof that the White House was involved. He had never seen Withers' file, but it was no longer necessary. The violation of his civil rights was obviously only the extreme tip of an antidemocratic revolution, a sellout to the Soviet Union, he was certain. McDowell was finally convinced that President Jed Hankins was a Red, masquerading as a Democrat.

Too many Americans were giving Hankins leeway to see where his policies would lead. They had to be alerted. But how?

Why not do something himself, rather than rely solely on Davidson? He couldn't go on the air half cocked with such an accusation. He'd be fired on the spot. But could he develop a probing documentary on the new President? Do some tough investigating and force everyone to look more closely at the Chief Executive?

Milt Samuels was his best bet. This time, McDowell left the office without a word to Meg and took a cab to National Airport. Less than two hours later he was in Samuels' office at the Tower in New York.

"My God, kid. You look horrible," Samuels greeted McDowell, laughing. "You even smell a little. I swear I won't tell anyone. Where'd you disappear to for three whole days? Got a thirteen-year-old mistress stashed away somewhere? I don't buy your sick-mother routine for a minute. And you wouldn't either. I've trained you too well."

The contrast between the two men, seated on opposing couches in Samuels' spacious fifty-third-floor office, was extreme. McDowell was tall, sparer than most, with a sunburst of hair. The news chief was short, almost fully bald, out of shape physically, and vocally proud of it. He wore fashionably red galluses across his chest, which only exaggerated his middle-year protuberance. But for all his lack of a youthful image, Samuels' intuitive news sense and his skillful handling of the Old Man, a painful lifetime endeavor, had brought him to the top of the Tower.

McDowell looked at his boss, hopeful.

"Milt. You're right. I'm covering up what really happened during the three days. The reason is that I'm into something explosive. The biggest story of my career. And you're the only one who can help me develop it. I can't tell you where I've been, but my disappearance is tied into it. Milt, in a nutshell, I'm afraid for the country."

Samuels face took on a mischievous look.

"Doug, unlike those pretty-boy newscasters, you've always written your own stuff. And it's good. That last line, for example, is a beauty. Now you've gotten me curious. What's it all about?"

"Milt. About six months ago, when I was doing the presidential debate, Jack Granick—you remember that conservative columnist— came to see me with a crazy story. At least, I thought it was crazy. He was carrying an old briefcase with a file he wanted me to read before I went on the air. He swore that it contained proof that one of the seven Democrats was a Communist. I kicked him out. In fact, I called him a fascist bastard.

"That same night, Granick was murdered and the CIA man who developed the file, Sam Withers, was missing. Then Withers' wife was killed, and he tried to assassinate one of the candidates, namely Jed Hankins. Then he kidnapped me at gunpoint and told me the whole story, except the name of the subject of the file. Now Jed Hankins is President."

"What the hell has that got to do with your standing up the Old Man?" Samuels asked impatiently. "He's furious, you know. I told him you probably got sick or were taken hostage by terrorists. Otherwise, you wouldn't ever do that. I lied. I told him you weren't that kind of irresponsible bastard."

"Thanks, Sam," McDowell muttered, half sarcastically. "Anyway, Hankins is now in the Oval Office, and I'm convinced his policies are purposefully destructive. Look at the deep defense cuts, the abandonment of Central America, the cabinet appointments, the Star Wars kibosh, even the trial balloon about axing NATO."

"All right. I follow your logic so far," Samuels said. "So what's your grand conclusion?"

"There is only one, Milt. It's that Hankins is the man in Withers' file. The President is a Communist."

In that instant, McDowell's mind flashed back to Granick's visit to his own office months before. Now, with his clothes in disarray, his bloodshot eyes betraying his sleeplessness, his desperation at a peak, he saw himself in the same position as the dead columnist. An obsessed reporter with a wild story, pleading for someone in authority to believe him. It was *déjà vu* with one exception. He, not fat Jack Granick, was the madman.

Samuels rose from the couch, straining his fingers through the remaining strands of gossamer hair. He paced slowly from one side of the room to the other, then stopped and faced McDowell, his expression turned to scorn.

"God damn, Doug. I won't call you a fascist because I know you're not. You're just a fucking crazy nut! That's all! You pile up a lot of horseshit circumstantial evidence about some CIA schmuck and who the hell knows what lousy intrigue. Then you put it all together, and suddenly the President of the United States is a Commie. Meshuga! That's what you are. Plain nuts!"

Samuels slowed his pace, then continued. "All right, I don't like some of the things Hankins is doing either. But I didn't call him a Commie. Did I? And by the way, have you ever seen, heard, or read the so-called Withers file? How the hell do you know it even exists? Doug, I'm surprised at you."

Samuels had exhausted himself. He sat on the couch, his body lazily back into the pillows, staring out the large corner window at the unknowing city below. After the best part of a minute, he swiveled his attention back to McDowell.

"All right, kid. Let's say I buy even ten percent of what you're saying. Which I don't. What would you want me to do about it?"

McDowell felt lifted, sure that the journalist in Samuels was being aroused.

"Milt, all I need is your go-ahead for a documentary on the President. No point of view. No Communist business. Just a chance to look carefully into his past, and the present, and see what we come up with. Then tell it straight. Let the chips fall. What do you think?"

McDowell could see that Samuels felt boxed in, his professional curiosity piqued.

"That Commie stuff is mad, Doug. But I can't say it's crazy to do a probing piece on Hankins. He's not immune to criticism. Just maybe you're not the one to do it. Maybe you've lost your professional detachment. And also, don't sneer. The Old Man likes Hankins. Likes him a lot. I don't want us both to lose our jobs. I'm not ready to retire."

Samuels stopped, drifting into anguished thought. "I just don't know, Doug . . ."

McDowell had a sudden compulsion to convince Samuels, once and for all. He had promised Davidson silence, but the need to enlist Samuels was overwhelming. There could be no more powerful ally against the Red President.

"Milt. I wasn't going to say anything about it. Because I promised someone, and because it sounds bizarre. But . . . I'm going to break a confidence and tell you where I was for those three days."

"Where, kid? Where?"

"You remember I put those two words, STAND DOWN, on the air and ruffled the White House and the Old Man."

"Yeh. So?"

"Well, on my way up here, I was kidnapped."

"My God, kid. Kidnapped? By whom?"

"The limousine took me to a safe house in Alexandria. I was kidnapped by the CIA."

"The CIA? Are you crazy?" Samuels was displaying agitation.

"That's not all, Milt. After a few hours, the CIA men gave me over to someone else." McDowell breathed hard for courage.

"Who the hell was that?" Samuels asked, now caught up in the story.

"They turned me over to the KGB."

Before Samuels, his skin now grayed, could interrupt him, Mc-

Dowell told the whole story. From the capture in the limousine to his imprisonment at the Soviet retreat. He omitted only his rescue by Davidson and Withers, telling Samuels that he had escaped on his own.

When McDowell finished, he could see that the news chief's face was saddened, even a little distorted in dismay.

"Kid, I want to be fair with you," Samuels said, his voice first softly patronizing, then strengthening in intensity. "But I don't want you driving me loony. Let's just say that now I accept your story about going to your mother. For a minute, I almost believed you about Hankins. But this is the screwiest thing I've ever heard. I don't want to hear any more from you on it. Now or ever.

"If you open your mouth about the President being a Communist, or your being kidnapped by the CIA and the KGB—or any other fucking cockamamie fairy tale—on the air, off the air, or even in the men's room, you're finished with this network. Forever. And I think you'll find it hard to work anywhere else. Do I make myself clear? Crystal. Absolutely. Clear?"

McDowell realized he had said too much. As a reporter, he had learned that too much truth is often indigestible, perhaps even the worst method of influencing people. He should have known that Samuels would react that way. The news director was in no position to believe him, whatever the reality.

McDowell walked out of Samuels' office, forgetting to say good-bye. As he moved down the hall, he knew the subject was not resolved. Either he had to soberly follow Milt's warning, or he had to strike out on his own.

☆   ☆   ☆

From his corner office, Samuels watched McDowell's bent back recede down the corridor.

Could the crazy kid be telling the truth? he thought. God, what if Hankins really is a Communist?

Samuels slammed his palm down on the burnished leather desk top, angry with himself. That kind of truth was too awful to even consider.

Chapter 57

After several fruitless days Fuller was becoming depressed about the photo, secured like a miniature hope chest in his inside pocket.

It was a smaller version of the gift from Rourke, the picture of "Stanislaw Wynoski" entering the cab at the Beverly Hills Hotel. As soon as his man was spotted in the FBI movie, Fuller entertained a dream of a rapid arrest, a positive ID from wanted pictures, and finis to the case. Maybe with a promotion to lieutenant.

The thought had sustained him as he circulated the photo to police around the country, even to scores of people in and around the Beverly Hills Hotel, at the Los Angeles airport, at gas stations near the airport and in the interminable desert.

But no one had any solid recollection of the man. Despite a few hopeful false alarms, nothing meshed. At a car rental place, one girl recognized the face—particularly the nose—but couldn't remember the name, or where he was going. Another clerk thought the man was headed for San Diego, then San Francisco, but couldn't connect the face with a name or a particular rental car.

Washington, D.C., the site of the deep-sixed clothes, was Fuller's next best hope. Inspector Greenway had placed the FBI shot on the bulletin board for his patrolmen. But how did one find such a face among millions of white-collar men in the largest pin-stripe community in America? Unless, of course, the Pole, or whoever he was, broke a law or two.

But no such luck. The face might belong to a murderer, but he was no scofflaw, or pickpocket, or even drunk driver. Fuller was getting nowhere with the case, and not so fast.

Then one day a small man with a Russian accent, Vladimir Radofsky by name, walked into the J. Edgar Hoover FBI Building on Pennsylvania Avenue at 9th Street and demanded to see the director. He was shepherded instead to a sympathetic special agent who spoke Russian. The two conversed in a happy combination of English and Radofsky's native tongue.

"I tell you he's a spy," Radofsky insisted to FBI specialist John

Astinof, son of a Russian émigré. "He acts strange like one. Pretends
to be American and fools everybody just because he speaks perfect
English. I'm an American and I speak lousy English. He speaks perfect, but he's no American."

Astinof listened politely, inured to amateur spy hunters stimulated
by the newspaper headlines.

"Why don't you think he's an American, Mr. Radofsky? Why
should you suspect the man of being a spy?"

"I'll tell you why. I'm the super of his building, on Massachusetts
Avenue. A fancy place for rich people. He's in apartment 11A. He
always pretends to be ignorant of Russian. But there is something
about his face when I talk the language to myself—out loud—that just
makes me feel he understands. What? I don't know, but I feel it anyway. If I speak in Russian when I forget myself, he looks dumb, like a
blank face. That's okay if you're American. But what if you're really
Russian? Then sometimes, maybe you forget yourself and you answer
in Russian. No?

"Well, the other day, he was taking his girl friend—a lovely lady—
up to his apartment. I was in the elevator with them. I kept looking at
her face. She's a sweet thing. Always has a nice word to say to me.
You know, 'How are you today, Mr. Radofsky?' And 'Don't work too
hard. It's not good at your age.' Well, that day she just smiled, the
nicest smile you ever saw on a lady. I couldn't help myself. I thought
of my own life in Russia and the nice ladies I once knew. And in
Russian I said, '*Prekrasnaya zhenshchina!*—Such a wonderful woman.' It
had just come out of my mouth. I was embarrassed by talking Russian
in front of them, but then he said it. I heard it clear. No mistake. He
listened and understood every word. He just said, '*Deistvitel'no!*—
Truly!' I almost dropped my keys.

"But when I said, 'What did you say, Mr. Ward?' he answered me
with a lie. He said, 'Nothing, I just coughed, Mr. Radofsky. Excuse
me.' I tell you he's a spy. And a real smart man. I'll bet a big spy."

The agent believed Radofsky. Not that the tenant, Thomas R.
Ward, was a spy, but that he had perhaps understood Radofsky's Russian. It was not a crime, particularly in cosmopolitan Washington.
But was it worth a follow-up? Perhaps a routine check. He would
look at the wanted material and see if there was anything to connect
with a Thomas Ward. He wouldn't give it more than a few minutes,
but he enjoyed Radofsky and his Russian paranoia. Radofsky reminded him of his own father.

Astinof spent an hour going through the files but nothing surfaced. Then he remembered that Rourke in Los Angeles had forwarded the photo of a possible Polish national, believed to be a KGB agent, who might have entered the country illegally. Also, something about a murder in the desert. The Washington agent looked for the picture but couldn't find it.

He placed a call to Rourke in the L.A. office.

"Rourke? This is Astinof in Washington. Remember you sent me a photo of that suspect in the murder case, maybe a KGB illegal, coming out of the Beverly Hills Hotel? Well, I can't find the damn thing. Could you Fax a copy over the wire soonest? Good. I got a screwy lead. It may be worth a shot. Thanks."

The super, Radofsky, had left his phone number, just in case. When the picture arrived, Astinof called.

"Mr. Radofsky. It's a long shot, but we have a picture of a man that we'd like you to see. Could you come in? What's he wanted for? Well, we're not in a position to say. But I assure you, if your tenant and this man are the same person, we will do some investigating. Okay?"

Vladimir Abramovich Radofsky had never been so excited in his years on American soil. This was a chance to work with the FBI against his oppressors. The Communists, the Czars, the Cossacks, the KGB, the anti-Semites, the whole Russian and Soviet systems that had oppressed his people as far back as the Duchy of Moscow in the twelfth century. Would he come down to the FBI headquarters? He would run. The Metro was not good enough for such a mission. He would take a taxi, door to door.

At the FBI headquarters Radofsky was quickly taken in to see Astinof.

"It's not the greatest picture in the world, Mr. Radofsky. It was taken with a movie camera, then blown up. But can you tell? Is that your tenant, Mr. Ward?"

Radofsky handled the occasion solemnly. He extracted his reading glasses from his jacket pocket, placed them securely on the bridge of his nose, then peered down at the photo, turning it in various lights, holding it close, then distant.

"That's him! Absolute! The man in 11A is the man in your picture. We have him! The lousy Russian spy making believe he's an American. Maybe he could fool other Americans, but not Radofsky!"

Astinof was surprised, but this was not the first time so-called cranks had proven invaluable. More so than the sober middle class, who often preferred to look the other way.

"Why, that's wonderful, Mr. Radofsky. Are you absolutely sure about the identification?"

"Absolute! You see that black hair and the pointed nose? It is the same man. I swear on it."

"Good, Mr. Radofsky. Now, we have to develop the case in secrecy. That means you can't say a word to anyone. Not to friends, or family, or to anyone in the building. Surely not to Mr. Ward. Don't change the way you act toward him. Be friendly and in no way suspicious. Okay?"

"I understand exactly. And, Mr. Astinof. It is a pleasure to be working for the FBI."

Chapter 58

"Would you take a look at this? I'll be damned."

Lieutenant Colonel Jake King was seeking to attract the attention of his partner, Major Andrew Tomlinson, a fellow field-grade officer in the Command and Control communications chain that ran from the President to the National Military Command Center on the third floor of the Pentagon to the Strategic Air Command headquarters eight miles outside Omaha.

"Andy, the boss wants the files on all the six-digit firing codes for our missiles, worldwide. The sequences now in use everywhere, including the GO codes for the presidential Football, with the method of daily change. That's a tall order. Why in the hell do you think he wants it?"

"General Abbott looking at missile codes?" Tomlinson asked, looking up from his papers. "I thought he was strictly a footslogger Marine."

"Not that boss, Andy. This comes from the *capo di capi*, Mr. Robert Billings, Secretary of Defense of the U. S. of A."

Major Tomlinson tore the paper from King's hand.

"You're right, Jake. That's the strangest request I've seen in my twelve years in this military Disneyland. I think General Abbott should handle this one personally. Don't you?"

King nodded, a peculiarly sad look engulfing him.

"What in the hell is a guy like Billings, a dyed-in-the-wool disarmer, doing in Defense anyway?" King asked his partner. "I think we're giving away the store."

☆ ☆ ☆

Robert Billings sat in his Pentagon office, the great shield of the Defense Department shadowing him, his work pyramided atop his oversized partners' desk. Across the river from Arlington was Washington, now calm on a late afternoon.

On the desk were two leather-bound folders, one of which he kept opening, then tapping closed with emphasis. The legend—EXTREMELY SENSITIVE—PRESIDENTIAL AND CABINET LEVEL—was marked across it in bold red letters.

The folder held the new disarmament plans beyond those already announced by Hankins, to be issued in slow, publicity-sandwiched stages. Billings checked off the first. The Navy's accurate D-5 Trident nuclear sub missiles would be scrapped. Without them, the submarines were useless against Soviet missile silos. Meanwhile, the Soviet Navy's new SS-N-23 could destroy American silos, in some cases without ever leaving home port.

No more Trident subs would be built, but Billings was handling that announcement with flair. Ceremonies would be held at the New London, Connecticut, yards, honoring the late Admiral Rickover.

No more Tridents could be built under the 1972 treaty with the Russians, anyway. There was a limit on the number of seagoing warheads and the Navy had been deactivating Poseidon subs to make room. The result was a small nuclear fleet, only half the size of the Soviets', one of the many Salt I détente concessions granted the Russians.

One disarmament move would have to be kept secret. Fenton had convinced Hankins to replace the nuclear weapons on the B-1s with conventional bombs. Billings hoped to keep it out of the press, but should it leak, he was preparing a counterbalancing statement.

Old friends in the League of Interested Scientists, an organization of peace-oriented academicians, would publicly swear the B-1 nuclear weapons were not necessary. They would confirm that the "throw weight" of America's land-based missiles—even though only one sixth that of the Soviet Union—now exceeded the blast megatons needed to wipe out the entire Communist world. There was surely no need for B-1 nukes.

Billings closed the folder and contemplated all he had to do. Fortunately, the American people would be an unwitting but willing ally. Born and raised in Boston, Billings continued to be amazed by his compatriots. There had to be some arcane, perhaps Freudian, reason why they paid so little attention to survival, as if there were no real enemy in the world.

As he toyed with the folders, he hazarded a guess that American naiveté was not an accident. Instead, it was the desperate desire of a people to remain childlike, as if ignorance of harsh realities made them special. A protected, youthful people ultimately different from the cynical, selfish Old World. Sometimes, Billings thought, Americans actually believed the peculiar myth that "the just" eventually triumph.

The second leather-bound folder on his desk, unlabeled, contained the plans for STAND DOWN. Billings was working on procuring the missile codes for Moscow. It had taken several days, but Abbott's office had finally produced a document—of sorts. Billings had studied Pentagon capabilities at the Federal Organization, and as he looked at the missile codes, he guessed he was being given truncated information. Not false, just incomplete. The codes in the folder stopped abruptly at a point three weeks back.

He would talk to Abbott about it. Meanwhile, a copy of what he had would go to Fenton, then to Colonel Baneyev, and off to Moscow by diplomatic courier.

Abbott couldn't be pushed too far, he knew. But Billings was learning how to handle the thick leatherneck. Just talk to him about Marine bravery and his eyes would glaze over. Then come in for the Sunday punch. In this case, the missile codes.

If that didn't work there was always the enlisted chief of Pentagon computer security. He loved to chase spies.

"Get me Sergeant Major McIlheny," Billings called into the intercom. "I want to see him here first thing in the morning."

Chapter 59

Astinof had chosen a young FBI agent, Frank Baxter, to work up the case on Thomas R. Ward, suspected desert murderer and KGB spy. Baxter was to conduct a full sixteen-hour surveillance, from 7 A.M. to 11 P.M., for three days. If additional evidence developed, they would seek a wiretap writ from a federal judge.

At seven o'clock the next morning Baxter parked his Buick Century across from the apartment house on Massachusetts Avenue. At eight forty-five, Ward left the building and took a cab to work, a company called Doric Films, on K Street. The firm, Baxter learned, was owned by one Walter Rausch of Georgetown, a documentary filmmaker involved with both the Democratic and Republican parties. Nothing suspicious there.

Ward went to lunch with Rausch at twelve forty-five and returned at two-thirty. He left work at five-fifty, again took a cab to the Massachusetts Avenue address, then departed at seven and picked up his girl friend, a young brunette—Baxter thought attractive—at her place on New Hampshire Avenue. He took her to dinner at a French place in Georgetown, after which they returned to Ward's apartment, where they spent the night together.

A discreet inquiry at her brownstone revealed that her name was Leslie Fanning. Of all places, she worked at the White House. She was in the Communications Office, a federal euphemism for public relations.

Those first two days were among the most boring in Baxter's young life. The next day, Ward repeated his schedule, but this time he and Les had dinner at Walter Rausch's house. Afterward, Ward drove her back to his own place for the second night in a row.

The following morning, Wednesday, started out equally routine, a pattern that was trying Baxter's patience. If this subject was a spy, he went about his work in a most pedestrian way. Ward left his apartment house alone at eight forty-five and hailed a cab. Baxter's Buick followed the taxi downtown, but instead of going to Doric Films, the taxi turned onto Pennsylvania Avenue. Baxter followed the cab as it seemed to be going past the White House. Suddenly, it stopped at the Northwest Gate of 1600 Pennsylvania Avenue.

"What the hell is he doing there?" Baxter asked as he saw Ward produce identification at the guard shack, then walk the short road toward the West Wing and the Oval Office. He laughed, reprimanding himself for slow reaction time. Of course. Les Fanning worked at the White House. Ward was going to see her.

His deductive victory soon faded. Fanning was still in Ward's apartment house. He had been watching the entrance himself since 7 A.M. When Ward hailed his cab, she had not yet left for work.

Ward obviously had another mission at the White House. But what in the hell was a supposed murderer and spy doing in the White House?

The next morning, Thursday, Baxter was back at FBI headquarters, his report ready. Astinof was waiting in a small conference room, where Baxter handed his supervisor a copy. As Astinof read the results of the first three days' surveillance, his face registered the same boredom Baxter had experienced. Then, abruptly, he raised his eyes.

"What the hell are you talking about, Baxter? The White House? Come off it."

Astinof was staring down his freshman agent.

"Ward was where at 9:15 A.M.? In the Oval Office, in private conference with President Hankins and his chief of staff? Baxter, you can do better than that."

The young agent responded slowly, afraid to disrupt his boss's negative mood.

"It's no bullshit, Astinof. I sat in the car outside the Northwest Gate and saw him go in with my own eyes. I parked the car and called Hennessy. He used to work here. Now he's Secret Service.

"I told him nothing except to check on who this fellow Ward had an appointment with at the White House. I hung on about five minutes. Then he got back on the horn. He said it flat out. 'Frank. Your suspect just went into the Oval Office. He has a private appointment with the President.'

"You think you're surprised? Well, I thanked him and was about to hang up when he said, 'Hold on, Frank. You ain't heard nothing yet. In the four weeks that Hankins has been President, Ward has been in the Oval Office three times.'"

Baxter stared more confidently at his boss.

"That's it. So what do you make of it, chief?"

"Kid, if this is not one of your *Playboy* dreams, it's big. Maybe too big for us. I don't talk to Presidents. Baxter, this goes right up to the director's office. I'll underscore the White House appointments and you hand-deliver it to him personally. You know what I mean. No middleman. Okay?"

Chapter 60

"Listen to this, Bill. 'COUP AGAINST KAMBULA INSTALLS NEUTRAL REGIME. PARTNERSHIP OF EAST AND WEST SEEN.'"

It was 9 A.M. in the Oval Office. President Hankins was summarizing a newspaper story with boyish exuberance.

"Bill, tell Miles to give his CIA people there a merit bonus. Only Kambula and a few friends were killed. The paper says the CIA and the KGB—for the first time in history—worked together to stage the coup. Tell Miles to deny it. I'm sure the Russians will too. But everyone will know it's true, which is just what we want."

Hankins' hand on Fenton's back was affectionate. "Bill, this is the kind of thing that will change history. And nobody can condemn us."

As Hankins was completing his thought, Maude Holly entered.

"Mr. President. It's time for your meeting with Mr. Ward. Shall I show him in?"

Before Hankins could nod, Holly escorted Ward to an armchair next to Fenton. The President took a seat facing them both.

"Tom, congratulations are in order all around," Hankins began.

Ward took the room in. Like KGB catechism, he knew that excess emotion was not congenial to his profession. But he felt exalted sitting in the Oval Office, advising, in some ways instructing, the President of the United States. Lately, he had even started evaluating the projects. It must be the American environment of independence affecting—or was it infecting?—him.

He found that he approved of the African coup. The new government of East and West was surely better than the old regime, a kind of eccentric geopolitical twist that intrigued him. Did he believe it had any permanence? Well, not really. Its "pluralism" was plainly a scrim to convince the world of the Soviets' good intentions before it evolved into an outright Marxist-Leninist state. Surely Hankins knew that.

But as the President started to speak about Kambula, he sounded naive, talking about a "new kind of democracy" in Africa. Considering Hankins' true politics, it made no sense. But not everything in this peculiar, extraordinary land did, Ward was learning.

"I want that vote to be bona fide," Hankins was saying. "Otherwise, the partnership will make us both look dirty. I think the U.S. and the Soviet Union are big enough to let one little African state determine its own destiny. Don't you?"

Ward grinned superficially, not knowing how to respond. It was best, he decided, to let Hankins bask.

"Well, Tom, what else do we have to discuss today?"

"First, Afghanistan," Ward said, propping up his agenda. "When will all CIA aid to the rebels be cut off?"

Hankins glanced over at Fenton. "Bill, tell Miles no more guns. Just some food for the refugees. Particularly, cancel the new anti-helicopter missiles. Check on it personally."

The President turned back to Ward, his mood still enthusiastic. "Tom, it's being done. Next?"

"Mr. President, the Soviets want to bring the MIG-31, the Fox-hound, into Nicaragua," Ward continued. "It has the look-down, shoot-down radar taken from the F-15. That's what made the Israeli jets so deadly against the older Syrian MIGs. Can you keep the information quiet in the CIA and all news of it out of the press?"

Hankins tipped his neck backward and roared.

"You people are funny. This is not the Kremlin. There are leaks everywhere in the United States. Sometimes I even worry about this room. No, the press will have the news the day the planes arrive. But it's not necessary to bring in MIGs to begin with."

Ward's face was registering surprise.

"Tom, don't worry about it. I've cut all military aid to Central America. The Israelis are taking up some of the slack, but I'm pressing Jerusalem to cut it out. Just be patient. You don't need MIGs to win there."

Ward had been watching Fenton. He was reacting to Hankins by fidgeting with his glasses, then shifting anxiously to the edge of his chair.

"But, Mr. President. Surely that's a small request Tom is making,"

Fenton spoke out. "I know Miles can keep it hushed in the CIA. And if we don't alert the press, they'll never know about the MIGs until it's too late."

Fenton seemed desperate to please him, Ward sensed, almost as if the Soviet General Secretary were hovering in the room, judging his every word.

"No. We'll leave it like I said," Hankins repeated. "No MIGs in Nicaragua now. If you bring them in, Delafield will stir up Congress, and they'll vote aid to the reactionary regimes."

Fenton might bristle, but Ward knew he couldn't afford the luxury of dissent. The young emissary simply nodded agreement. He had other points to make, but he sensed Hankins' truculence. Things could wait for another day.

"Mr. President. The Soviet Union appreciates your gestures of peace and friendship. That's really all I have to communicate today," Ward said, now on his feet, extending his hand.

Ward turned to the chief of staff. "And, Bill. Thanks for your interest in our projects."

With that, the confident thirty-three-year-old from Poland, via New York and Moscow, exited the Oval Office, having delivered the Kremlin's wishes directly to the American Commander-in-Chief.

☆ ☆ ☆

Fenton remained in the Oval Office for a moment, pensive.

Like Ward, he had settled for discretion, but he was seething about the MIGs.

How arrogant Hankins had become. Did he really believe he could do his own political theorizing? Particularly when Ward's instructions had stood the test of the Kremlin's best dialectic analysis?

As he started out of the Oval Office, Fenton looked back at Hankins, wondering what had happened to the intellectual humility he had once so admired.

Chapter 61

It was 1 A.M. in the unattractive corridors of the Pentagon as a sergeant and two corporals moved through the halls toward their objective.

U. S. Army Sergeant Major Charlie "Mac" McIlheny had never expected to handle such a mission. Nam had been the strange war of his youth, always with the miserable doubt about who was actually on America's side. Now he and two of his best men were out to covertly check out whether one of their own was, in fact, devoted to the enemy.

Defense Secretary Billings had personally given McIlheny the assignment that morning. Billings hadn't revealed all the details. Just enough need-to-know to accomplish the job.

McIlheny was a security expert on the Pentagon's computer system, the complex software and hardware layout that insured the secrecy of the missile launching codes. If the codes were tampered with and rejected by the silo computers at any of the SAC bases, the "birds" wouldn't fly. Only the right numbers made modern war possible.

The sergeant's job was part of the $50 million a year the Pentagon spent on computer security, to keep "hackers," with their intrusive homemade "virus" programs, and their "worms" and their "trapdoors," from disrupting the vital flow of computerized information from the National Military Command Center and other posts controlling the worldwide nuclear arsenal.

As a safeguard, the data was transmitted on special telephone lines encased in metal tubes filled with high-pressure gas. If someone tried to tap the line and alter the information, the loss of pressure betrayed the leak. Any mayhem would have to be accomplished by an insider, an apparently loyal Pentagon staffer with full access and equal know-how.

Nothing could better describe Mac McIlheny. The Defense Secretary had told McIlheny that he suspected that someone in the Joint Chiefs' office was tampering with the missile codes and was assigning him to thwart the unfriendly hacker. Secrecy was essential, Billings insisted. No one, not even General Abbott, was to know. Of course, the Chairman of the Joint Chiefs was trustworthy, but he might idly mention the investigation to an aide, who could be the culprit.

The Pentagon was reasonably quiet that night, populated mainly by guards prowling the endless corridors. Other officers and enlisted men still on duty were unseen, working in the restricted areas on the first, second, third, and basement floors, maintaining the twenty-four-hour continuity of the Chairman's office, the Command and Control function for missile war, and the entire National Military Command Center, the focus of activity during any crisis.

Mac and his men took a secure elevator to the third floor, then traversed two circuitous corridors before coming to a large unmarked door.

"Hi, Lambert. I suppose you want to see my ID?" McIlheny goaded the young armed MP on duty.

"You bet ya, Sarge. And your two sidekicks too. Nobody gets into this restricted area without my say-so."

"Good to see you so gung ho, Lamby. Keep it up," McIlheny said, producing three passes for entrance.

The trio walked through, then down another small corridor, which ended at an impressive set of stained doors, the legend NATIONAL MILITARY COMMAND CENTER emblazoned on its polished surface.

The three men walked into the massive war room, moving confidently toward the rear, where an unsurpassed array of computer hardware choked the far walls.

"Everything all right, McIlheny? Having any trouble with teen-age hackers?" a young lieutenant on duty laughed in greeting.

"Not yet, Grayson." The sergeant major grimaced in response. "But that's why I came tonight—to protect the country from some crazy fifteen-year-old."

The lieutenant smiled and moved away.

McIlheny approached a master computer terminal, turned on the power, leaning his eye into a lenspiece which looked not unlike that of a microscope.

"What's that for, Sarge?" Jackson, one of his corporals, a new military police recruit, asked.

"Security," McIlheny explained. "To make sure it's me entering the system. The computer has a visual record of the bloodlines in the retina of my eye. If anyone who's not on file tries to put the computer on line, it'll shut down and all hell will break loose."

McIlheny worked at the terminal from a penciled set of notes, programming a miniature "worm" into the system. These few hundred bytes hidden among the millions of bits of classified information would never be found in the Pentagon computer swampland, but it could trap the spy.

The next time the traitorous hacker used the system and called up the missile codes, McIlheny's "worm" would wipe out just one prearranged piece of information. The retina check and the log would show who had used the terminal at the time the worm did its work. They would have their spy.

When he was finished, Mac closed down the system and beckoned to his two corporals. They retraced their steps, finally leaving the restricted areas.

"Jackson, Lemoyne," McIlheny said, his tone both confidential and intimidating. "I want you to forget tonight's mission. This assignment comes from the top boss, and if you open your traps I'll pull those stripes off myself and shove them up your little assholes."

He cautiously broke out a smile. "Of course, if all goes well, there's an extra week's leave. By C-124 to Europe. Okay?"

Within minutes, all three men were back in a main corridor, in time to greet a duo of guards on rounds.

"Hi, Sarge," they called in unison as McIlheny approached. "Everything's all quiet. How's by you?"

"Same, Larry. Keep your eyes open. You never know."

McIlheny moved on, confident. Before long he would have an unimpeachable record of who had illegally called up the codes. Nothing would please him more than to trap the God damn missile spy, no matter how much brass he wore.

Chapter 62

The director of the FBI, Frederick Lionel Buchanan, heir to the fiefdom of J. Edgar Hoover, studied Baxter's report. Once, then twice, then over and over.

He had been in office only a year, a holdover from the last administration and eager to stay that way. There had been potent rumors that
Hankins had several replacements in mind. One of them, the director
had heard, was a young congressman from the Boston metropolitan
area. Out of curiosity, Buchanan had checked him out.

The congressman's file had several notations, mainly for social contact with Polish and Czech exchange students, a few of whom were
suspected of espionage in the Boston electronics corridor on Highway 128. Some director for the FBI.

What the hell was happening to the country?

But that wasn't his most pressing dilemma. The director was faced
with a possible criminal case in which the suspect knew the President, apparently quite well. There was no other course. He would
call the President directly and lay it out. Let him judge. Besides, he
had submitted his resignation as director the day the President took
office. It had not been acted on, nor had he heard anything since.
Perhaps it would be savvy to have another conversation with Hankins, anyway.

☆ ☆ ☆

The FBI director was put through to the President.

"Well, hello, Fred. Glad you could call. Any emergencies in national security?" Hankins asked brightly.

"Mr. President, it's really a small matter. One that I wouldn't normally trouble you about. But somehow you seem to be tangentially
involved."

Hankins was interested, perhaps a touch anxious.

"Yes, Director? What is it? I have time now."

"Well, sir. We have a photo of a suspect, temporarily identified as
Thomas R. Ward, possibly involved in a California murder case. I
know the whole thing sounds implausible, but our agent saw the
suspect entering the White House for a private appointment with
you. Can you tell us something about this man? I just wanted your
guidance on the matter."

Hankins' eyes closed involuntarily. Ward involved in a murder?
Oh, God. Things had been going too well, too fast. In the equation of
life, some unwanted factor had to surface.

"Director." Hankins was speaking more precisely now. "First, I
think there's probably been a misidentification. But second, and this
is quite important, young Tom Ward—if it's the same person—is

working with me on matters at the highest level of national security. He's coordinating disarmament talks with the Soviet Union. He's also involved in other matters so secret I can't discuss them at all. I hope you understand the gravity of what I am saying."

"Yes, sir. I do understand," Buchanan offered lamely.

"And, Director," Hankins continued. "This is off the subject, but I hope you haven't been listening to those rumors about replacements for your job. The more I think about it, the more I prefer to establish the tradition of the FBI director as being beyond politics, untouchable by changes in administrations. What I am saying is that I'd like you to stay on as head of the FBI."

The director was silent for a moment. Hankins waited, certain Buchanan was happily absorbing the news.

"Well, thank you, Mr. President. That's a nice vote of confidence."

"And, Director?"

"Yes, sir?"

"On that Ward matter. The only way we're going to protect the national security is to close the case and make sure the file isn't floating around the FBI. Could you destroy all the copies and send me the original report? I promise you it'll be safe in my care. And please, it must be strictly between us. If the suspect actually is Ward, any exposure could drastically injure our relations with the Soviet Union."

"Yes, Mr. President. I understand. The investigation will be stopped—" he hesitated—"as long as you take personal responsibility for it."

"I will. You have my word on that."

Hankins clicked off the phone. As he placed it back in its cradle, he looked pensively at the portrait of Jefferson. This Ward thing was potentially dangerous, the first misadventure in a magic month.

He felt the signals of alarm, then steadied, praising himself for containing the situation with the director. As the President breathed heartily inward, he marveled at the wondrous powers of the Oval Office.

Chapter 63

"I know he's the legal head," Congressman Danny Bradshaw moaned, "but we've got to show him there's patriotic power still left in Congress. That he can't take this country down the road to Moscow."

Bradshaw was one of five men in the limousine, along with Senators Delafield, Feldman, Frank Masoni of California—two Democrats and two Republicans—along with retired four-star general "Tough Willie" Jamieson.

The group had left Feldman's office in the car borrowed from Majority Whip Masoni and made their way from the Hill to the White House. At the West Gate, the car was moved quickly in and the delegation ushered to the Executive Wing.

"Gentleman. He's waiting to see you," Maude Holly greeted them. "Please come this way."

All five had been in the Oval Office before. Some had even entertained fantasies of occupying it themselves, but this was their first visit to President Jed Hankins.

"Welcome," Hankins said, a smile of forced graciousness on his face. "I thought we'd talk in the Cabinet Room, if that's okay."

As Senator Delafield nodded, Hankins sensed that he was the leader. He wondered what political cards this traveling troupe of opponents had to play, if any. For his own part, he had no concessions in mind. Not unless they were required.

The long table of the Cabinet Room served as an arena, with Hankins on one side and the visitors opposite.

"Well, you gentlemen wanted to see me," Hankins opened with apparent ease. "Who will begin?"

The only hint to Hankins' anxiety was a rhythmic tapping of his thin silver pencil on the polished nineteenth-century table. The FBI problem with Ward was bruising his confidence, but he pushed it back, convinced that he had contained it well.

"Mr. President." Delafield nodded toward the tapping pencil. Suddenly it ceased.

"Mr. President," the senator repeated. "We are here unofficially as four members of the Congress, representing both parties, and one senior military officer interested in national policy. Frankly, we're confused and worried by your first weeks in office."

"I'm sorry to hear that, Senator Delafield. But why? What have I done? I'm only trying to insure our security in a very dangerous world."

"That's just it, Mr. President. We think you're doing the opposite. How can you be bolstering our security by cutting defenses to the bone? And that removal of the Star Wars unit from space? Our only hope of gaining strategic parity with the Russians. Is that security?"

"Senator, I know you disagree with my policies, but don't you think you're exaggerating the seriousness of the situation?" Hankins was straining for stability. "Other American Presidents, in our lifetime, have also disarmed when they felt it was necessary."

Maury Feldman was suddenly flushed with anger.

"Mr. President, we're not here to defend any other President. We came here to show you that you've gone astray. You're under some kind of influence—your own, your aides'—who knows? All we know is that you're moving America into a policy of massive appeasement, one that'll invite the Russians to take more, then maybe even face us down with nuclear blackmail."

Hankins listened, aware that he was facing powerful adversaries. An angry confrontation was the last thing he needed. He would have to act the statesman.

"Gentlemen, I can see we have an honest difference of opinion. We all want to keep the peace. You want to do it by deterrence. I agree, but we only have to kill the enemy once. I think a better route is a partnership between us and the Soviet Union. Did you see what happened in Africa when we cooperated? A nation now free of a madman dictator. It can be done elsewhere, I promise you."

"My God, Mr. President. I really think you believe those Russian bastards!"

Senator Frank Masoni, a spare, chisel-faced man, a usually cool Californian in his fifties, was getting exercised.

"They're using you like you were some college kid. How long do you think that African country will stay democratic? Already that Commie leader is preparing the ground for a second coup. I heard it myself from the State Department."

Hankins' silence lasted only an instant.

"Senator Masoni, I surely don't take them at face value. But since I offered them friendship, they've shown a peaceful hand. My trial balloon of a nuclear-free Europe was shot down, but I think it could have been for the best. If they pulled their missiles out of the Warsaw Pact countries at the same time that we—"

"Hold off, Mr. President," bellowed General Jamieson, rising from his chair. The six-foot, five-inch former West Point football end dominated the room with his bemedaled uniform and basso voice. "If you excuse me, Mr. President, that's an uninformed statement if I ever heard one—especially from a man who is supposed to be our Commander-in-Chief.

"You just don't know what you're talking about," Jamieson continued, his voice now more heated. "If we pull our missiles out of Europe, those people are virtually defenseless. Meanwhile all the Russians have to do is take their mobile SS-20 missiles back to their own borders where they can obliterate the whole European continent at will. What kind of stupid thinking is that?"

Hankins glared at the insult, rising abruptly, his long hands trembling, his careful reserve drained. He faced his adversary, then extended a finger almost into the general's face.

"Where do you—a retired general no longer on active service—come off talking to me like that? You're a damn warmonger. That's all you are—a fascist warmonger!"

The room exploded. Delafield was among the first on his feet, shouting.

"Hankins! We came here to talk some sense into you. To ask you about nominating a better Vice-President, someone we can live with. But now I see that you're talking like a God damn traitor! That's right, I said it. What we've all been sitting here thinking. You're acting like a traitor to the United States!"

Delafield's hand stretched out for a glass of water on the silver server in front of him. He lifted it slowly.

"God help us all!" the senator said, flinging the water sharply into the President's face.

Hankins shied back as if facing a runaway horse. With the water dripping from the edge of his nose, he steeled himself, pushing past his anger. He knew he had needlessly triggered the hostility of men who represented a strong segment of public opinion, one that could grow with his carelessness.

"Gentlemen, I'm sorry. Perhaps I provoked you," Hankins said, the watery insult still on his face. "I'm sorry, General Jamieson. I didn't mean that. You've been an outstanding American. Please accept my apology."

The massive soldier looked disdainfully at Hankins, who had now extended his hand. Jamieson ignored the gesture and smashed his fist down on the antique table.

"You may be sorry, Hankins. But I'm not. I'll see you rot in hell. Like Delafield said, I think you're a damn traitor to the country!"

Chapter 64

Traitor? The word stayed in his ear all day, and now the next morning he couldn't shake it.

He should have known his life would come to this clash of obligations—as a dedicated Marxist and as President of the United States. For the first time, Hankins felt uneasy in office, the confrontation with General Jamieson forcing him into a deeply reflective mood.

As Hankins moved through the papers on his desk, Fenton entered the office, a book in hand.

"Mr. President, I've just been reading something interesting."

"What is it?" Hankins asked, happy to be diverted.

"Surprisingly, it's from Solzhenitsyn, someone I usually don't like. In his book *Lenin in Zurich* there's an interesting anecdote about Lenin."

Hankins looked up expectantly. Ever since taking over the Oval Office, he had been increasingly drawn to the first leader of Communist Russia.

"Yes? What does he have to say?"

"Well, the gist is that while Lenin was in exile in Switzerland he spent a lot of time in the Zurich library," Fenton explained. "One day he was there writing a revolutionary pamphlet when an aide interrupted him. 'The Revolution has begun,' he shouted. 'You have to leave for home, immediately.' But Lenin just looked at him. 'Please, leave me be,' he said. 'The Revolution is going on right here.' Then he went on with his writing."

Hankins laughed, first at the quick humor of the anecdote, then in

some embarrassment. The connection with Lenin was flattering. Was
Fenton truly trying to make it?

"Bill, I hope you're not trying to compare me with the great Lenin.
That would be too much," Hankins said, his smile self-effacing.

"I don't know, Jed. You're two different kinds of people, but you
have the same opportunity for greatness—if you decide to seize it."

Hankins too wondered whether he had Lenin's conviction. Could
he override all opposition, as did the great Ulyanov, and convert his
power as the American President into irrevocable history?

He was not sure of himself, but Fenton, this displaced young
preacher with a fiery mind, certainly had Lenin's resolve.

From conversations with his AA over the years, Hankins had
learned one source of that power. Fenton had always been magneti-
cally drawn to Marxism. Not just in college as a semireligious experience, but from boyhood on. After his father died when Bill was five,
young Fenton worked after school, weekends, and summers in the
fields of his family's worn twelve-acre spread in Alabama, his hands
raw by sundown.

The Fentons were poor when the country was living out its rich
postwar dream. The only prosperity he glimpsed was in the dime
movie house or in library copies of *Life*. He shared poverty with his
neighbors, a family of black tenant farmers, and learned to see the
struggle as one not of race but of class. He was dirt poor, as they
were.

From the Baptist Church and the small local library, Fenton gained
two worlds, those of Jesus and Marx, almost as one. Long before
"liberation theology," the scholarly farm boy had seen the need for
the Lord to take retribution from the money changers. From Marx
and Lenin, he deduced that no amount of violence was too much to
right the imbalance.

In the years before federal school loans, the Baptist Church became
Fenton's patron, proud of his brilliance, but never suspecting they
were helping to shape a disbeliever. First the seminary, then a year of
graduate work at Berkeley.

The youth rebellion was old politics to him. Fenton went to Berkeley not to learn revolution but to spread it. He found eager disciples,
then entered Hankins' service in the House, primed to weaken a nation that denied his word.

As Hankins considered Fenton's past, he wished he could have had
such an ideological lineage. But he had come to Marxism much later,

and by a far different route. It was not born out of material need. And, unlike Fenton, to whom Marxism was life itself, it sometimes seemed like another, detached, part of him.

The President stared out the tall windows, looking toward the Rose Garden, thinking of his own personal revolution, the grand transformation that had overwhelmed and remade him more than a dozen years before.

It had not entered his consciousness for some time. But now, as if the moment demanded a surer grasp of his inner motives, he could recall it in exquisite detail.

☆　☆　☆

Jed Hankins had always been as wealthy as Fenton was poor. Even at eighteen, when he received a $5-million trust from his grandmother, outside of his father's control.

In retrospect, Hankins never believed the money had served him well. As a prelaw student at the University of Wisconsin, when that campus was tense with near revolt over the Vietnam War, Hankins decided to immunize himself by playing the rich eccentric. One weekend he parked a loaded beer truck near campus. The dormitory halls reeked of alcohol for days. The following weekend, a tuxedo rental company delivered its entire stock to Hankins' dorm, after which a dozen young men, dressed like Scott Fitzgerald rejects, invaded the local saloons, tipping goggle-eyed waitresses with twenty-dollar bills.

"You know, Jed, for someone who's supposed to have brains, you're awfully stupid."

It was Nancy Rennart, a fellow A student in his philosophy class. "Instead of using your money for something worthwhile, you piss it away on crazy schemes. What's wrong with you anyway?"

He had never considered that anything was wrong with him.

"What do you think it is?" He was enjoying the repartee with this attractive, hot-tempered brunette.

"First off, you're selfish and falsely conceited. Because you get good grades doesn't mean a damn. You haven't the foggiest how the American system really works for some and not for others. Sure, your exploiting son-of-a-bitch grandfather made a billion. But what did you ever do to earn a cent like a real human being? You disgust me!"

Hankins stood transfixed. Where did the bitch come off? Probably some damn Commie. He'd find out.

Nancy Rennart was active in the SDS, Students for a Democratic Society, the campus radical organization. The best way to get to her, he knew, was by attending one of their meetings.

At the SDS rally, Nancy spotted him and seized the microphone.

"I have an announcement. Mr. Fat Cat Capitalist, Jed Hankins, is with us tonight. Tell us, Jed, when are you brave American boys going to win the Vietnam War for us girls back home?"

Hankins rose to derisive laughter.

"I really don't know, Miss Rennart. Like all the young men here, I have a draft exemption. So I can bullshit about the war while the kids who can't afford college are off in the jungles getting killed."

The SDS students jeered, but he could see that Nancy had quieted. Afterward, Nancy agreed to join Hankins for a drink.

"Did you really mean what you said on the floor tonight? Or were you just snowing me so you could get me into the sack?"

"A little of each." Hankins laughed. "Did I really say the right thing to that bunch of Commies?"

"First off, we're not Communists. Oh, maybe some of the kids. But not me. I want to stop the war, but I don't think college kids should be exempt as long as we're fighting. That's why I was touched by what you said."

Intuitively, Hankins sensed her decency, perhaps what he might have been without his money.

Nancy and Jed saw each other regularly. He took to sex with her and she became his political mentor. After a while he was absorbing her sensitivity to others. He hated to admit it, but he was beginning to see things as a liberal. No damn leftist, he assured himself, but at least aware of those less privileged.

One night in bed, Jed asked Nancy to marry him.

"Jed, I'm proud of you. You're learning how to fight your money. But no, I need to discover my life, not play it out in some castle."

At graduation, Nancy walked over to Hankins and kissed him.

"Jed. Keep fighting. Make something of yourself."

☆ ☆ ☆

Jed was completing his last semester at the University of Virginia Law School when he was reminded of Nancy. On a warm spring weekend at Homestead, a group of neighbors had joined him on the terrace.

One of them, Fred Barrows, the local member of the state House of

Delegates, told Jed that old man Gaines, who had represented the district in the U. S. Congress for thirty-six years, had just died.

"Why don't you run for his seat, Jed? You're twenty-five already. Give you something to do. In fact, I'll bet you a thousand dollars you can't make it."

Barrows had touched a nerve, but not so much with the wager. Nancy's parting admonition, "Make something of yourself," now attacked him. She had begun an intellectual awakening in him, but it had been dormant for three years.

"You mean you'll pay me a thousand dollars, cash, if I run and win?"

When Fred nodded, Jed turned silent, thinking of the colonnaded mall of the Jefferson-designed campus at the University of Virginia. Jefferson, surprisingly, had always been his ideal. A man of philosophy and parts who, like him, loved the land of Virginia. He had served in the Virginia House of Burgesses, then in the Continental Congress before becoming governor of Virginia, then Secretary of State under Washington, then Vice-President and President. Could he take a first step to make that kind of something of himself?

Life involved strange junctures. Perhaps this was one.

"Damn it. I'll do it. I can afford it. Like you said, Fred, it's a rich boy's toy. And I ain't nothin' if I ain't a rich boy."

Jed looked quizzically at Barrows. "Who the hell do I see about running? Do I have to buy anybody off?"

"Don't worry, Jed. I'll introduce you to the Democratic Party people. They'll be thrilled to get someone who can pay for his own campaign. The Democrats have had this House seat for a long time. So you might as well be one."

"Good," Jed affirmed. "I begin tomorrow."

☆ ☆ ☆

The squire of Homestead was nominated, and easily elected in November. Even before going to Washington in January, Hankins began interviewing candidates for the job of AA, the key administrative assistant. They all dutifully trudged up to Hankins Farms, but he had been most impressed by a twenty-four-year-old graduate of a Baptist seminary from Alabama.

Bill Fenton was Southern, but with the sharpness of a Harvard boy and without the studied arrogance. Fenton was arrogant, all right, but in a subdued way. He wrote like a charm, an essayist and journalist in one. He promised Hankins he wouldn't have to be troubled with either writing his own speeches or hiring a speech writer. Fenton would do it all.

Hankins never doubted the boast. He hired Fenton on the spot, convinced the young man would play a part in his political career. He could never have known just how much.

Fenton suggested they get a head start. By Thanksgiving, the new AA was commuting the seventy miles from D.C. to Hankins Farms, often staying overnight. During this interim Fenton hired the congressional staff, all with Hankins' carte blanche. Not only was Hankins taken with the young Alabaman, but he was developing an inexplicable blind faith in him. Abstract and worldly wise in one, far beyond Hankins' own opinion of himself.

On his next trip Fenton brought some material back to the farm.

"Jed. I scrounged up some sample legislation, plus recent copies of the *Congressional Record*," he told Hankins. "Maybe you can read up while you're here. We still have six weeks before Congress begins."

Jed rapidly assimilated the feeling of how the legislation was written and, by inference, the compromises that went into its makeup.

On his second trip to the Farms, Fenton brought up a pile of other reading matter. One night, in front of a fire in the library, he produced three books.

"Jed, I've been thinking about your congressional career. The place is full of struggling lawyers who get ahead by playing political games. You don't need that. You're a wealthy man. You need only one more thing to go all the way."

"What's that, Bill?" Hankins asked, curious about Fenton's prescription for political fame.

"You need a congressional specialty. I think you should become an amateur political economist. Study everything there is to know about money and politics. It'll put you head and shoulders above the others."

Fenton had come prepared. "As a beginning I brought you some books, just in case you didn't get to them at college. John Stuart Mill, Adam Smith. And even Karl Marx. Don't laugh. I think an American congressman should know about Marx's theories. Over a billion people live by them."

Hankins did laugh.

"A guy with my background reading the enemy?" Hankins paused.

"Why not? It might expand my mind. I promise nothing, but if I get bored I'll give it a try."

That weekend Hankins dipped into *Das Kapital.* He doubted what he could learn from the Communist economist, but as he read he was surprised that he was enjoying it. Not because of Marx's politics but because much of it wasn't politics. It wasn't even really economics like Smith, which he found too dry. He saw it mainly as a treatise on philosophy, the only subject that had ever captured his imagination.

Marx sounded a little like Darwin, Hankins thought. Marx felt that there were natural laws governing men. This Hankins believed. Man's laws and morality—including religion—had no history of their own, Marx was saying. Rather, there was a historic materialism, an economic determinism, that governed everything.

Hankins found himself agreeing.

By God, yes, he thought. Money is king. Always has been. I'm living in this style, and serving as a congressman, because of my money. Everything I am or will be is based on my money. On that Marx is surely right. In fact, what am I without it?

He could even appreciate Marx's argument that man became human through struggle, against both nature and other men. Without struggle, Marx said, there could be no growth. Maybe that explained himself, Hankins thought. Until this run for Congress, there had been no struggle. Even now. Hadn't he really bought the seat?

"How did you do with the material I left you to read?" Fenton asked on his next trip.

"I read the congressional stuff. No sweat. The economics books? To be truthful, they bore me. But Marx. He's quite a philosopher. I had no idea he had that much to say about man. In fact, I haven't stretched my mind like that in years."

Fenton almost leaped out of his chair.

"Really. What in particular?"

"Economic determinism. Oh, he's absolutely right about that, Bill," Hankins said. "The buck speaks, loud and strong. But where he and I part company is that he wants to make a revolution against the so-called exploiters. I suppose he's talking about me. That I don't like. I don't exploit anyone."

With that Hankins' face turned stonily serious.

Fenton was surprised, and encouraged. There was something lurking unspoken in Jed's philosophical enjoyment of Marx. Like Marx, who had been brought up relatively well to do as the son of a department store owner in Freiburg, Germany, he might be suffering. It might be chronic rather than acute. Unconscious rather than recognized. But suffering nevertheless.

Fenton made a quick diagnosis. It was guilt, the age-old malady of many of the wealthy. They made their expiations in several ways, from charity to religion, even to politics—as with the many rich supporters of the far left, in America and Europe. Jed pretended to have a blameless psyche, but Fenton sensed the buried culpability. He would try to bring it out.

"Jed, you once told me about a fraternity bash with whores that you arranged in college. Wasn't that exploitation of the girls?"

"Oh no, Bill. How could it be? They got a thousand dollars a night each and a good time. Is that exploitation?"

"Jed, I don't think prostitution falls under the heading of a good time for the women." Fenton looked at Jed paternally. "As for that thousand dollars, how much of it do you think stuck to them? It's no different than a factory owner or a plantation head with slaves in the old days. What do the whores have once their bodies are used up?"

Hankins grew sullen. For the next few days he retreated into himself, speaking to no one.

What was he experiencing? His years as a careless rich boy now seemed irrevocably stained by guilt. Fenton was treading on the same sensitive ground as Nancy, but using discipline instead of sweetness to bring it out. Like her, he was stabbing Hankins' psyche deeper each time, pricking the first feelings of pain about his wealth.

Hankins thought of his father and the enormous fortune accumulated by his meat-packing business. He had been a good man, in the main, Hankins told Fenton when asked. But now he was dead, and Hankins had Homestead and more money than imaginable. Whatever happened to the workers and their children? What did they have?

Over the weeks, Hankins devoured whatever Fenton brought him. He was still somewhat skeptical, but he was drawn to the works of Friedrich Engels, Marx's financial patron and collaborator. Like Hankins, Engels was born truly wealthy. When young Engels took over one of his father's textile plants in Manchester, he was shocked at the poverty of the English working class and turned to socialism as a solution.

Jed saw how the newly awakened conscience of a rich man could become a vibrant weapon for change. If only he could follow the example of Engels. Could he too be something other than just rich?

Could he, as Nancy and his father had hoped, make something of himself?

It was quite a lot for young Jed Hankins, erstwhile playboy, to fully absorb. At the end of six weeks he was still not a true Marxist, but Fenton could see the seed of guilt begin to grow in Jed's aroused philosophical brain. That overriding American Puritan pain shaped by his good fortune continued to eat away at Hankins. It grew as Fenton subtly but regularly applied the salt of condescension to Hankins' soul. Fenton knew he couldn't let up if he was to win a convert.

By January they were in the United States Congress. But Fenton's work with Hankins continued alongside the legislation. More books, all-night discussions, heated arguments about civil and human rights, on which Hankins had been brought up as an American lawyer, went on.

One morning Fenton walked into Hankins' office carrying a congressional notice.

"Jed, you just got a note from the committee chairman on education and labor. They're forming a special subcommittee on hunger. Would you like to join?"

The young congressman almost tore the paper from Fenton's hands.

"Let me see that, Bill. It sounds interesting."

For the next six months Jed Hankins, as a member of the House Select Subcommittee on Hunger, traveled to rural Mississippi, to the badlands of the Dakotas, to the streets of North Philadelphia and South Miami Beach, walking past life-worn senior citizens, Indians, and blacks living not much differently than in the Caribbean.

One experience stood out in Hankins' memory. He was in rural Mississippi, walking from shack to shack, when he stopped to talk to the mother of five. Hankins had been there only a few minutes, noting the misery, when it began to rain heavily.

"Let's stay a little while," Hankins told his aide. "I want to look this place over."

Hankins turned to the young mother. "Could I see where your children sleep?"

She seemed hesitant but then took Hankins' arm and led him back into a small cubbyhole that served as a bedroom for the two youngest children. As Hankins entered the room, he retracted in near horror. In the corner, on a small child's mattress, lying directly on the floor, was a baby, perhaps a year old. Hankins moved down on his hands and knees.

"Bill, come over here. I want you to see this."

The two men stared at the girl child, her body covered with ugly red sores. The child was grabbing at her stomach and crying, as if from abdominal pains.

"It looks to me like pellagra," Hankins said. "God, Bill. I thought that was all gone years ago."

"Not down here, Jed. There's no decent diet. There's all kinds of vitamin deficiency disease. Even scurvy."

"I knew all of this from reports," Hankins said. "But it doesn't mean a thing until you've seen it yourself. Does it?"

"No, it doesn't," Fenton said, staring knowingly at his employer. "I've seen it all before. I lived it. Now I suppose it's your turn."

For months afterward Hankins could think about nothing else. The sight of one hungry American child had irreparably damaged his onetime Western idealism, intruding an even deeper guilt into his golden existence.

The six months on that committee had done more to convince him of the failures of capitalism than all the treatises by Marx. By the time Jed had been elected to his second term in Congress, representing the Commonwealth of Virginia, home of Patrick Henry, he was a true Marxist-Leninist.

Several years later, after Hankins had been elected to the United States Senate, Fenton could see in Jed the ferocity of a convert. They were working late in the Senate Office Building one night when Hankins pensively approached his AA.

"Bill, I've been thinking. I've done what I can here in the Senate. I hope to continue, but I'm frankly frustrated. It's all so passive. It's too early for me to run for President, but I want to get more involved, to do something more active—maybe even more dangerous. I would even be willing to risk my life, if the challenge was great enough."

Jed's intensity surprised Fenton. He now knew that he had recruited a powerful ally for Colonel Baneyev, never daring to expect that within a handful of years Hankins would become President of the United States.

Chapter 65

Harry Decker had barricaded the American Embassy. The twelve Marines on duty had set up a hastily constructed defense perimeter with semiautomatic weapons, some Uzis and Brownings, the heaviest they had.

Ambassador Childs was away. As chargé d'affaires, Decker had assumed command. The closed shutters cut out the sight, but not the sounds, of the AK-47 gunfire from nearby Kambula City, formerly Victoriaville, now renamed Temmboville in honor of the Marxist military leader, Jondono Temmbo, who had just conducted a coup against the new junta. On the radio, he was claiming that the city, and the nation, were already in his hands.

"That sneaky Cholkin. He double-crossed us," Decker was complaining to his assistant, John Manning.

"I knew Hankins was smoking the stuff—thinking you could do anything in partnership with the Russians. It's been only two weeks since I made a deal with Major Cholkin. And they've already turned the country into a Red satellite. Son of a bitch!"

Decker was convinced that events had verified what he had said all along, that the partnership was a piece of dirty, now discarded paper. Every five minutes, on the radio, the Marxist officers were claiming they had been forced to disband the junta because of an imminent "sellout" to American "fascist interests." So far, Radio Temmbo reported, 458 "imperialists" had been executed by the new regime, which had been in office for only nine hours.

Decker was preparing to relay the news to the State Department African Desk in Foggy Bottom when a young Marine, his face dirtied by the red African mud, rushed in.

"Mr. Decker, we have an African Army officer outside asking for political asylum. What should I do?"

A bright touch in this miserable affair, Decker thought.

"Bring him in, Corporal. See if we can't salvage a smattering of honor for the U.S."

He turned to Manning. "Get out the Grand Marnier. Let's do it up as we surrender to the fucking Communists."

In a moment a tall, lithe African officer, his uniform splattered with blood and dirt, arrived, breathing heavily through his fatigue.

"Colonel Nandala!" Decker greeted the pro-Western officer, whom he knew from embassy functions.

"Thank you, Mr. Decker." Harry had brought up a large palm-frond chair for the colonel to sit in. "I appreciate this, but I'm afraid that my presence could bring an attack on the embassy. These people have gone mad."

As Decker studied his worn guest, an idea was released.

"That's it!" he shouted to Manning. "The hell with the coded cable. I'm going to get on the horn to President Hankins himself. Let him be the first to hear how his partnership crap with the Soviet Union ended—as pure *merde.*"

Decker turned to Nandala. "And, Colonel. I'd like you to tell your story personally to the President. Exactly what happened. Okay?"

In a few minutes Manning had gotten through. Decker grabbed the receiver from his outstretched hand.

"Operator? Yes. Tell the President that it's Chargé d'Affaires Harry Decker at the U. S. Embassy in Kambula City. Add that there's just been a second revolution here. He'll want to talk to me."

Decker knew his political animals. Hankins was on the phone almost immediately.

"Yes, Mr. Decker. What's wrong? Why the urgent phone call?"

"Sir, sitting here is Colonel Lawrence Nandala of the East African Republic Army. If you recall, he's one of the pro-Western officers in the junta we helped set up with the Russians. He's just asked for political asylum. Why? Well, sir, if it's all right with you, I'd like him to tell you himself. He speaks perfect English."

The African colonel straightened, his disciplined body propping up a disheveled uniform.

"Yes, Mr. President. Why do I want political asylum? Well, sir, everything was going fine with our partnership with the Marxists— until 4 A.M. this morning. While our men were sleeping in their barracks, Temmbo's troops rushed in and sprayed the beds with automatic fire. Then they threw incendiaries to burn the place down. Virtually everyone was killed in their sleep.

"Me? Oh, I couldn't sleep. When the attack came, I was out talking with a guard. They shot him, but I picked up his M-16 and killed a handful of them, then crawled the last mile to the American Embassy. Sir? Do I want asylum? Yes, of course. But I don't want to put anyone in jeopardy."

The colonel listened to the President's response, then answered. "Well, thank you, Mr. President. I appreciate that."

Nandala returned the phone to Decker. "He wants to speak with you."

"Yes, Mr. President," Decker said. "The Russians broke the agreement on us, just as I figured. They've taken the country. What should I do?"

☆　☆　☆

On the other end, Hankins shuttered his eyes. What had gone wrong?

God, the voters will think I'm an ass, Hankins thought.

He silently vilified the Russians, then reconsidered. Surely Moscow knew nothing about this. Probably just another local madman, using the Soviet Union as a front for his banditry. He would phone the General Secretary and straighten it all out. Meanwhile he had to placate his man in Kambula.

"Mr. Decker. Here's what I want you to do. Give Colonel Nandala unconditional asylum. Then stand pat. I'll get on the phone to the Kremlin and raise the roof. Someone will get back to you within a half hour. Is that all right?"

Decker stretched the cord, placing the phone against the barricaded window.

"Decker? Are you there?"

"Yes, sir. I just wanted you to hear the gunfire for yourself. Don't worry, Mr. President. We'll be here when you call back."

☆　☆　☆

The African incident was more than trying, following his troubles with Ward, then Delafield and Jamieson, and the holdup on the VP consent. Trying to move America closer to the Soviet Union and still maintain public support was beginning to wear on Hankins.

But that was his American domestic opposition. Surely the Soviet Union was different. Wasn't it?

"Maude, connect me to the Kremlin by phone," he called into the intercom. "Tell the General Secretary it's urgent."

In two minutes the Soviet leader was on the line.

"Mr. Secretary," Hankins began, his voice hopeful. "I presume you've heard about the coup in Kambula."

"Yes, I know. It's regrettable, Mr. President," the Russian responded. "Some hotheads in the junta took things into their own hands. But what can I do from Moscow, six thousand miles away?"

Hankins listened uneasily, something in the Soviet leader's softly assuring tone releasing the first doubts in his mind. Could the General Secretary have known about the coup beforehand?

"Mr. Secretary, I have an idea on how to restabilize the situation," Hankins said.

"Yes, I am listening."

"It's simple, Mr. Secretary. All we need do is jointly hold up recognition of the new government until they meet our demands. The junta has to be reestablished as before."

There was silence on the other end.

"Yes?" Hankins asked.

"But, Mr. President." The General Secretary's voice had turned saccharin. "I thought you knew. Just an hour ago we formally recognized the new People's Republic of East Africa. Like you, we were not happy about the revolt, but now that a new government has been formed it should be a great ally for peace and freedom. We presume you will also recognize it. Yes?"

Hankins was stunned. They've recognized the bandits who broke the partnership? Are General Temmbo and his thugs the Kremlin's repayment for my support?

"No, Mr. Secretary. I will not. And I'm shocked that you condone the mass murder of soldiers in their sleep."

"Mr. President, I condone nothing. If the United States held up the diplomatic recognition of murderers, half your diplomatic corps would be out of work. As would mine. No?"

Hankins considered the statement. "Don't you think this is somewhat different? That African government was our brainchild, our partnership for peace. And it lasted only two weeks. Shouldn't I have had the courtesy of a call before you acted on recognition?"

It was now the General Secretary's time to ponder.

"Yes, I think that's reasonable. But knowing your sympathies, we didn't think you would mind. Am I wrong?"

"Yes, Mr. Secretary. In this case, you are wrong. I had a personal interest in that little country."

Hankins hung up the phone, waiting only seconds before depressing the intercom.

"Maude. Could you call in the press secretary?"

Mike Richards moved expeditiously into the Oval Office. With him was a female assistant, followed by Bill Fenton, who had just heard about the coup.

"Mike, get on the phone to Harry Decker at our embassy in Kambula, or whatever they call it now. There's been a new Soviet-backed coup. The Russians, I think, have just fucked us."

Richards' assistant, a young woman, chuckled.

"I'm sorry. I have to watch my language when I'm angry."

The President turned back to Richards.

"The Soviet government has already recognized the new rebel group, but the United States has not. I want you to draft a statement. Say that we're holding up our recognition until the old junta is reformed. Mike, make it formal, but strong. Warn the new African government that any harm to our embassy or Colonel Nandala will be considered a most unfriendly act against America and will be answered by force. Be sure it goes out on the Voice of America all over the world. Have you got that?"

☆   ☆   ☆

Fenton had sat through the entire conversation, his head dizzied. What was happening to Hankins? Had he gone mad? Antagonizing the Soviet Union and an African cousin in the Marxist world? He should be cheering instead.

"Mr. President." Fenton spoke up after the press people had left. "Do you think we should be alienating the Soviet Union just when we're beginning such a staunch friendship?"

"I don't know what's right anymore, Bill." Hankins' tone was weary. "I think this job is getting to me. First domestically, now with the Soviet Union. I think it was a cheap trick on their part. Don't you agree?"

"Jed." Fenton had dropped his protocol. "I can't believe they knew about it beforehand. But even if they did, isn't the important thing that there's another Marxist country in Africa? You wanted that. Didn't you?"

"Well, maybe eventually. But that has nothing to do with now," Hankins said, his expression severe. "You don't have the responsibility to the voters, Bill. They can hate you, but I'm the one who takes all the shit. I promised a friendship to the people, not a rape. Now the Soviet Union has made me look like an asshole. And I don't mind telling you I don't like it. Not one bit."

From Hankins' rage—or was it confusion?—Fenton could see that he had to reevaluate the President. He was reacting with anger over what should have been a celebration. But, Fenton reminded himself, he worked in the Oval Office at the President's pleasure.

"I see your point," Fenton said, straining to appease Hankins. "You gave the American people your word, and the Soviet Union has made it seem valueless. Perhaps you should write the General Secretary, explaining that the partnership must be on firmer ground. I'm sure he'll understand."

Hankins beamed. "Bill, I'm so glad you said that. That's exactly my thought. Yes, I'll do just that. Thank you."

"Of course, Mr. President," Fenton said in parting.

But as Fenton exited the Oval Office, only one thought controlled him. Hankins was displaying thin resolve, showing none of the mettle that fashioned true leaders.

He had to contact Colonel Baneyev immediately. The timetable for STAND DOWN had to be moved up.

Chapter 66

Sergeant Pete Fuller didn't want to believe it.

"Rourke, are you telling me the FBI investigation is finished? Kaput? What's gotten into you guys? You spend a fortune finding the photo of the desert murderer and now you're going to kill the whole thing? Something must be up that you're not telling me."

"I can't give you details, Fuller, because I don't know them," Rourke responded, a touch of embarrassment in his voice. "Except that the FBI is out of the picture. Orders right from the tippy top. But hell, that shouldn't bother you. You're a peace officer for the sovereign state of California."

"You know where that'll get me, Rourke. Isn't there anything you can do for me? A small steer in the right direction?"

"I shouldn't, Fuller, but this whole thing bothers me too. All I can tell you is to call a guy named Astinof in our Washington HQ. Nice fellow, a Russian-American. But if you say that I gave you his name I'll drive out to Berdu and give you a big hickey. Okay?"

Fuller's impatience couldn't be contained, but he had no desire to be rebuffed by Astinof on the phone. He would confront the FBI man in person.

Within hours he was on a plane to Washington. The next morning he pushed open the door to the J. Edgar Hoover Building at 9th and Pennsylvania, a large modern edifice a few blocks from the White House.

"Do you have an appointment to see Mr. Astinof?" The FBI receptionist asked.

"No, just tell him that a detective sergeant from California is here. Add that we have a murderer in common. Okay?"

The receptionist's look was coolly skeptical, but when Fuller produced his ID, she dialed Astinof's office. After a few words, she placed her hand protectively over the mouthpiece.

"He wants to know which murderer?"

Fuller knew he had Astinof hooked. "I don't discuss that in the presence of third parties. But tell him that I flew three thousand miles just to see him. If he gives me five minutes, I'll give him a great story."

The receptionist uttered a few muffled sounds into the phone.

"Okay. He says he'll see you, but he only has five minutes. He's in Room 6124," she said, handing Fuller a visitor's badge for his civvies.

Rourke had been right. As soon as Fuller met the Russian-American, he agreed that he was pleasant. But he was also reticent, telling Fuller absolutely nothing.

"This is the picture of the murderer," Fuller said, placing the 11 × 14 color shot on Astinof's desk. "It was taken as he left the Beverly Hills Hotel. You fellows should want him more than I do. I understand he may be a KGB illegal. Astinof, what can you tell me?"

The Washington agent chuckled. "Son of a bitch. How'd you get my name? Sure, I know. Rourke sent you. He wants to nail this man, but all he's going to nail is my hide. Forget the whole thing, Fuller. Go home and catch some crazy hatchet killer of a movie star. Leave this one alone. He lives a golden life. Nobody can touch him."

Astinof had said the wrong thing. The challenge infuriated Fuller. Why was a KGB agent immune to American justice?

"Astinof, did I tell you what my suspect actually did? It wasn't just murder. He picked up a hitchhiker and, seemingly for no reason, first poisoned him with a cyanide pill, then burned his body. Who knows if the man was even dead when he doused him with gasoline and torched him? Why protect a bastard like that? I don't get it."

As Astinof listened, Fuller could see his head swaying, as if in indecision.

"Believe me, Fuller, I can't take you all the way. I sure wish Rourke had kept his Irish trap shut. But now that you're here, I'll give you an address on Massachusetts Avenue. There's an apartment house super there, Vladimir Radofsky. See if he'll tell you anything. I can't. Now get the hell out of here while I still have a job. I hope."

A taxi took Fuller through the gracious northwest residential section of the city. At the address Astinof had given him, Fuller asked the cab to wait and approached the doorman.

"I'd like to see Mr. Radofsky, please. Just tell him that a California detective is here."

Radofsky met Fuller in the marble-floored lobby.

"Mr. Radofsky. I'm Detective Sergeant Fuller," he said, displaying his badge. "I'm after a suspect who I believe lives in Washington. I understand you might be able to help me."

Fuller reached into his pocket, and as the two sat on adjacent Barcelona leather chairs, he showed Radofsky the photo.

"Do you know who this is?"

Radofsky stared at it, then pulled inward.

"I don't think I can tell you anything, Sergeant. I wish I could, but I don't think so."

The super rose to leave, but Fuller politely detained him.

"Just give me a minute, sir. I guess that you're Russian by birth. Well, there's been talk that this man is a KGB agent. Are you sure you can't tell me anything that will put him behind bars?"

"Shouldn't you go to the FBI?" Radofsky asked again. "If this man is a spy, they are in charge of that. No?"

"I've just been there, Mr. Radofsky. And they sent me to you."

"Who did that?"

"Mr. Astinof. I believe you know him."

"Sergeant Fuller. I'm not saying you're a liar. You look like a nice man. But I do all my business with the FBI. Please. I have to check the heat. It's getting cold outside."

Radofsky turned toward the elevator bank, leaving Fuller with the photo still in hand, no closer to the killer than he had been in San Bernardino.

Fuller sat vacantly on the chair for almost two minutes, trying to divine a next step, if there was one. Something was operating beneath the surface, something about which he felt abysmally ignorant. Whatever it was, it was shaping this case. Without him.

He moved slowly, almost lethargically now, placing the photo back in his briefcase, preparing for a despondent trip back home. He had accumulated almost enough psychic energy to get up and leave, when he saw it.

At first he thought it was a molecular trick played by desire. The man coming out of the elevator seemed to have walked off the silver condensations of the photo. A little over medium height, slim-built, with a light skin, strong black hair, a pointed nose. Yes, the nose was unmistakable, the same one that leaped out of the picture every time he examined it.

Fuller stood immobile as the man nodded to the doorman and walked toward a waiting black Mercedes limousine. Astinof was right. Whoever he was, he led a golden life.

The sergeant rushed to the doorman, his hand now cupping a twenty-dollar bill.

"Mac, tell me. Who's that guy with the limousine?"

The doorman evaluated the bribe. "Oh, him? That's Tom Ward. Apartment 11A. Nice fellow."

Fuller rushed to the taxi, still parked at the curb. Slamming the door, he barked, "Cabby. Go after that Mercedes. If you get a ticket, California pays."

He held up his badge, whose reflective flash reached the driver through the rear-view mirror.

☆   ☆   ☆

In the Mercedes limousine, Tom Ward relaxed as they pulled away from the apartment house and headed down Massachusetts Avenue. His thoughts were of Les, and the tranquillity she had brought. He was on the way to her place on New Hampshire Avenue, then to Walter's for a dinner party. Everything seemed in place in his implausible world.

As Ward moved to pick up a newspaper and light the overhead, he could make out a taxi hugging close behind. He vaguely recalled that a cab had left the apartment house simultaneously with the Mercedes.

It had apparently turned right at DuPont Circle with them onto New Hampshire. Both cars were approaching Washington Circle when Ward leaned over to the driver.

"John, instead of going to Les's right away, hang the next left. I'm checking something out."

The Mercedes turned, and with it the taxi.

"John, please. Two more quick lefts. Someone may be too curious about us."

The driver expertly maneuvered the turns, the stability of the Mercedes in cornering contrasted with the screeching taxi straining to keep up.

"We definitely have company. We'll pick Les up later, John. Shake the cab."

John was part of Rausch's apparatus, a trained wheelman. He spun the Mercedes through several turns and was soon across the Key Bridge and onto the George Washington Memorial Parkway in Virginia, headed north, the obstinate taxi still on his tail.

The Mercedes was cruising patiently at 60 mph when Ward leaned forward.

"Now, John," was all he said.

The driver gradually depressed the accelerator. The limousine moved to 70, then 80, then 90, leaving the taxi a progressively smaller yellow dot on the concrete horizon.

"When you get far enough ahead, just take any exit, then double back and pick up Les. Okay?"

Fifteen minutes later, at New Hampshire Avenue, the chauffeur waited while Ward moved hurriedly up the stairs of the brownstone. Les was in the hallway, fully dressed.

"I'm sorry, honey. Got stuck in some traffic. A big accident."

She kissed him, brushing aside the annoyance. "Don't worry. Any time is good."

As the couple walked down the crumbling red stone stairs toward the Mercedes, Ward thought about the taxi chase and its possible implications.

"Darling, they're playing around with the boiler in my place," Ward said. "It's been a little chilly. Is it okay if I stay with you for a few nights?"

Chapter 67

Teshovich decided that this was no time for protocol.

"Comrade Colonel . . . Colonel Baneyev," he called out, charging, quite uncharacteristically, into the *rezident*'s birch-paneled office at the Washington embassy. Baneyev was at his desk, juggling a report with one hand, the other heavily bandaged from the gunshot wound.

"What is it, Teshovich? More of your gossip about the chess matches in Moscow?" Baneyev was stretching, more in character, for a touch of sarcasm.

It was lost on Teshovich, who adjusted his steel-rimmed glasses.

"The State Department just called. The American police have found our missing Oldsmobile in the sound of the Outer Banks—that's a beach resort in North Carolina. In it was a body. It must be Genshikov."

"I know where it is, Teshovich. Call the local police and tell them we'll send someone down to identify the body. Contact the State Department and secure permission for the trip. Also get in touch with Mr. Rousseau in Norfolk. We'll need him. No?"

"Yes, Colonel." Teshovich was impressed that Baneyev had so rapidly thought of assigning their nearest agent, a staff member at the Atlantic Fleet headquarters in Norfolk.

"Withers is surely on the Outer Banks," Baneyev said. "Tell Rousseau to take a week off from his job and spend it there. Be sure to get him a picture of Withers, by an overnight service. Use Rausch's office as a cover."

"Yes, Colonel. I'm sorry about Genshikov," Teshovich added, mustering some sincerity.

"Surely, Sergeant. I am too. But the *muzhik* has probably played his best role in dying."

☆   ☆   ☆

Alexander Rousseau was a refugee from Communism, or so the Department of Immigration and Naturalization believed. Nine years before, on a trade mission to Vienna, he had defected, taking sanctuary in that neutral country before emigrating to America.

The name "Rousseau" had puzzled officials as unusual for a Russian, but Alexander was descended from a French translator who had worked for the francophile czarist court in the late nineteenth century.

Rousseau was a communications engineer by schooling and a KGB agent by profession, one of an estimated four hundred who had come to America mixed in with the thousands of true émigrés from the Soviet Union. Americans, he was happy to learn, had taken his anti-Communism at face value. Over the years, the FBI had caught a half dozen of the émigré pretenders, but most, like Rousseau, were still plying their KGB trade.

His work as a communications technician at the Atlantic Fleet headquarters was below top secret classification, but Rousseau had recruited four Americans in sensitive posts, who—for considerable sums—had passed along the core of the Navy's communications methods and codes, from fleet battleship to submarine to naval aircraft.

Rousseau now had a week to luxuriate in the near-deserted Outer Banks. To those who inquired why he had chosen a summer resort for a winter vacation, the ex-Russian replied that the starkness was reminiscent of his homeland. Besides, he said, laughing, it was much cheaper off season.

He settled into a small motellike resort and contemplated his problem. Withers might be anywhere on the beautiful barrier reef. First, he had to establish a logical pattern of movement. Rousseau examined the site of the car drowning on the inland side, the Sound. Withers was probably operating alone and would have had to walk to his lodgings after disposing of the body. He should be within two miles of that point, and probably less.

What type of place was likely? Surely not a hotel or a motel. His face had already been advertised on national television. Withers was probably alone in a small house, either on the beach or near the Sound.

Rousseau spent endless hours driving, concentrating on likely roads. He had no idea how he expected to find Withers, who would surely not be washing his car out in the open or shopping in a nearby market.

All he could do was drive monotonously through the tranquil area searching for a man who had carelessly dropped his guard.

☆ ☆ ☆

Despite the successful rescue at the Point, Sam Withers was unhappy. While he vegetated at the beach house, Hankins was inexorably stripping the nation of its strength.

The record player, a handful of books, the television and radio were his only releases as he waited for Davidson to reestablish a link to reality. Then one morning he heard the news on the radio. A blue Oldsmobile had been fished out of the Sound. Local authorities were awaiting positive identification of the body found inside.

So, Genshikov had turned, or floated, up. Now, Withers knew, his incognito was in jeopardy. Baneyev would soon be scouring the Outer Banks, perhaps even planning a touch of "wet business."

Sam guardedly stayed indoors, waiting for a sign of KGB activity. The off season had fortunately thinned the area, and there were no mobs of people to protectively absorb his hunter. Whoever came looking would stand out against the winter starkness.

He stood vigil at the window. The first day, he saw only three cars —a Mercedes, a Pontiac 6000, and a small Toyota station wagon. Two had North Carolina plates. The Toyota was from Virginia.

The next morning, a Saturday, there were a half dozen cars as a few homeowners braved the February chill. But none were repeats, except for the Toyota. By late Saturday, Withers was alerted enough to watch the road more closely. At four o'clock the Toyota passed the beach house once more.

On Sunday the small wagon was in sight again at nine o'clock in the morning. Sam rushed to the side window to watch its progress. The Toyota had slowed to fifteen miles an hour and the driver—he could make out a thin man with brown curly hair and sharp-cut features—was openly searching both sides of the road for something or somebody.

Withers was sure it was he.

He remembered the Beretta he had initially bypassed in the attic. Sam raced the stairs and located the 9mm automatic in the splintered toolbox. Alongside it were two clips of ammunition and a silencer.

Perhaps the discovery of Genshikov's body had created an opportunity. He couldn't stay in the beach house, nor any longer patiently wait for John's call. He had to change his venue and, with it, adopt a new mission.

Sam's mind returned to the wounded image of his natural adversary, Colonel Nikolai Baneyev. Why not return to Washington?

Chapter 68

"Well, Sergeant Major McIlheny came through."

Defense Secretary Billings opened his luncheon meeting with Fenton at the Cosmos Club on that optimistic note.

"Good, Bob," Fenton responded, his usually inexpressive face now animated. "Does that mean we can block any retaliation against STAND DOWN, if it comes to that?"

"I think so. But the chain-of-command idea didn't work out. General Abbott gave me some material, but I'm sure he's holding back."

"Think he's suspicious in any way?"

"No, Bill. He's just playing the military-against-the-civilian game—doesn't think the codes would be safe floating around the Pentagon. I could have pressed him harder, but maybe then he'd really get suspicious. I was better off using McIlheny."

"Has Mac given you everything you want?"

"Absolutely," Billings responded. "All the missile codes, in sequence, for the next several months, including the President's and the Cabinet's GO codes. Even my own. As soon as we get the date for STAND DOWN, I'll have McIlheny put his 'worms' into the computers. They'll wipe out the six-digit launch numbers at exactly the right time. None of our Minutemen or MXs will be able to fly."

Billings coughed, awkwardly.

"What's wrong?" Fenton asked. "Did you forget something?"

"No, I was just thinking about retaliation. Bill, if the Soviets go through with a first strike, none of the thousand Minutemen silos will be left anyway."

"Why? Aren't they superhardened like the Russian ones?" Fenton asked, surprised.

"Not the Minutemen. When they superhardened the fifty MX sites in 1987 and '88, they decided it was too expensive to reharden the Minuteman silos. It was a big mistake."

Fenton seemed pleased that the defense establishment was so accommodating, even without his intercession. "What's the next step?" he asked. "Are we covering all contingencies?"

"I thought so, but the list keeps growing. Someone in the Kremlin forgot about *Kneecap*, the President's escape plane—his airborne command in case of attack. The plane used to be parked here at Andrews, but it's been moved to Grissom Air Force Base in Indiana, with another one at Offutt in Omaha, and spares elsewhere. If the Soviets strike, the President will be helicoptered to a small airfield in southern Pennsylvania, where he'll rendezvous with *Kneecap*."

"Are you doing anything about that?"

"Well, we don't want to interfere with the plane itself, Bill. Should the Soviets have to carry out their threat, you and I will be safely on *Kneecap* with Jed, I expect."

"Bob, I'd love to be on *Kneecap* at the end," Fenton said. "We could fly it right to Moscow. But you shouldn't assume that. I don't think the General Secretary is going to have to order a strike on STAND DOWN. But if he does, he'll send at least fifty warheads into Washington. The presidential helicopter will never make it to Pennsylvania."

As Fenton spoke, Billings thought his eyes flashed, as if from some inner messianic light. Could Fenton be unconcerned about dying? Even relish the idea of martyrdom? Billings decided he would restrict himself to politics and leave the socialist hereafter to people like Fenton.

"There is one problem that you should know about, Bill," Billings confided. "But I don't want to worry you. We're working on it, and I think we've got it licked."

Billings read the annoyance on Fenton's face, aware of Fenton's prejudice against the technocrats of the world—that they were never able to keep up with its philosophers.

"What is it, Bob?" Fenton asked.

"It has to do with the Navy's missile subs. They have a different code system," Billings explained. "Their signals come out of ELF, Extremely Low Frequency, transmitters, one in the Upper Peninsula of Michigan, the other near Clam Lake, Wisconsin. As backup, there are two squadrons of TACAMO aircraft which relay presidential orders to the subs in the case of DEFCON 1, a war alert."

"Why is that a problem?" Fenton asked, his hand returning to the nosepiece of his spectacles.

"Because the Navy has a 'fail-not-safe' mechanism. It's the opposite of a fail-safe. Instead of holding back a firing, it virtually insures it in case of nuclear war. Right now, the subs are continuously receiving 'happy signals.' That means everything is okay back home. The U.S. is at peace."

"What happens in case of war?" Fenton asked, fearful of a possible gap in the scheme.

"If war breaks out, the happy signals will stop and commands to launch would be sent to the subs in code. But if the ground centers and the TACAMOs are knocked out, the subs will have to surface and get orders from nearby Navy ships. If no one is in range, or if the ships have no orders from the President—maybe because he's dead— the sub officers are instructed to follow a built-in scenario."

"What's that?"

"If they are collectively sure America has been attacked, they can act on their own and fire their missiles at will."

Billings slowed. "If Hankins cooperates on STAND DOWN, there's no problem. Otherwise, we'll have to block the subs from retaliating."

"So what's the solution?" Fenton asked sharply. "Or is there one?"

Billings ignored Fenton's short temper, allowing himself a self-appreciative smile.

"Yes, I think so. A young officer in Colonel Orlov's office came up with it. It's simple, but brilliant. All we have to do is make sure that, war or no war, the Navy's 'happy signals' keep coming to the subs. The TACAMOs will be knocked out and the subs won't even know there's a war on. I have our people in the Navy working on it."

Billings stared reassuringly at Fenton. "Bill. Take my word for it. It will be done."

Fenton relaxed somewhat, but Billings thought his expression was still troubled.

"Bob, I suppose you're the only one I can speak with frankly."

Billings nodded.

"It's about Jed. I know. Without him, I'd be running a small liberation church somewhere, and you'd be doing what you could in some foundation. But now that we're on the threshold of victory, I'm worried about him."

Billings was surprised. Indecision and doubt were not part of Fenton's makeup.

"Bill, don't worry," the Defense Secretary assured him. "When the time for STAND DOWN comes, Jed will do the only thing he can. He'll acquiesce to the Soviet Union. Why should you think otherwise?"

"I haven't mentioned it before, Bob, but something's gotten into Jed. I think he's been infected with the glamour of the job. Sometimes I think he's competing with the General Secretary. Just yesterday he made a giant fuss over the MIGs coming into Nicaragua.

"I'm afraid he might not have the courage to go through with STAND DOWN. Or, if we wait too long, that he'll be angry with the Soviets over something else. That's why I'm going to ask Baneyev to move up the date. Then I'll bring Hankins in on it. If he won't go along, the Soviets will have to make good their threat of a first strike."

Billings quieted, contemplating the frightening consequences of his work. But, he assured himself, if all parties performed well, there need not be a first strike. It could be a bloodless and permanent victory for world Marxism. America would be reduced to a defeated, nonnuclear power—which was probably her true psychological goal anyway.

Otherwise why wouldn't such a wealthy nation have more heavily rearmed to meet the Soviet threat? People generally get what they *really* want, don't they? he observed.

"Don't worry," Billings finally responded. "Jed's always listened to you. You'll get him to see it our way."

"I hope you're right, Bob," Fenton said, then switched emotional gears. "Otherwise, what's up at the Pentagon?"

"Well, General Abbott has been a doll. He's doing just as we thought. Occupying himself building up the Army and the Marines, for a war he'll never get a chance to fight."

Billings relaxed into the hard-backed dining chairs and permitted himself a slight grin.

"The Pentagon's never been in better shape."

Chapter 69

Sam Withers sat at the window of the one-bedroom apartment on Tunlaw Road in the high-rent district of northwestern Washington, intent on the sprawling Soviet compound across the street.

He had been peering at the iron gates all evening, expectant. This was not the first night of his vigil. Sam had been in Washington for three days and three nights and, except for a handful of hours of sleep, had spent twenty hours a day waiting for Baneyev to leave the diplomatic fortress. It made little difference where the KGB *rezident* went, as long as he exited the compound.

For months, Baneyev had been playing greyhound to his rabbit. But Withers had reversed the game. He had seen blood. The sight of Baneyev's gun slipping from his wounded hand that night on the Maryland shore had enlivened him. His forced flight from the Outer Banks had brought him to Washington to implement a long-delayed plan: to kill Baneyev.

Sam had not told Davidson. He was entrusting the big picture to John, to maneuver the patriotic forces back into contest with the Red President. Sam felt more comfortable with the small frame, the tactical work needed to erode their enemies.

The KGB attack at the CIA safe house in Alexandria had paid off in unexpected dividends. Jim Barber had recovered from his concussion and was back at work. On his way up from the Outer Banks, Withers had called Barber at home, cautiously from a pay phone, to arrange a meeting.

A few hours later Withers and Barber were in cars parked side by side at a shopping center in Silver Spring.

"Jim, I need your help. I'm going after Baneyev. He's the KGB colonel who directed the killing of Mary and who had you and Hopper pummeled."

"Anything you need, Sam. Those Russian cocksuckers are beginning to think it's their Agency and their country. You know why? Because I think they've got one of their own men somewhere in the

White House—maybe pretty high up. Otherwise, none of this would be happening. So what do you want me to do?"

Withers avoided commenting on Hankins. "Remember that apartment on Tunlaw Road where we used to observe the Soviet Embassy?" he asked. "What happened to it?"

"When Fenton found out about it, he ordered Miles to close the place. We have it up for sale now with a broker. Why?"

"I'd like to use it, Jim. Could you get me the key?"

Barber seemed to be weighing his obligations to the Agency. "God damn it. I shouldn't, but I will. One of the girls in the office has it. I'll get it from her and meet you here tomorrow night. Good luck, Sam. Anything you do to hound those no-goodniks is fine with me."

Now, three days later, Withers was still waiting for Baneyev to move. From an old surveillance log that Barber had retrieved, Withers learned that Baneyev used a deluxe Volvo sedan, one of the 760 GL series, in gunmetal gray. There were several exits from the huge Soviet compound, but from the apartment window he could see Baneyev's car on the driveway on his side.

All day he squinted into the sun and shadows, watching the exit. At night he peered through special infrared binoculars that sliced through the darkness. But the car sat where it was, its driver occasionally toying with the ignition or opening the trunk. One afternoon he watched as Baneyev's driver washed and polished the entire vehicle.

Patience paid off, but not as Withers had expected. The Volvo remained immobile, but one night, a little before 9 P.M., Withers saw a man walk out onto the driveway and toward the gate. He had seen many people come and go for three days, paying scant attention, always focusing on the Volvo. But tonight the infrared binoculars picked up a signal. A white bandage on a man's hand. Withers quickly pulled the infrared glasses up to the face. It was the pale, bony cheeks of Nikolai Baneyev.

Sam pulled on his coat and raced for the door, exiting the building just as Baneyev reached the corner. He walked briskly behind him until the colonel turned down Wisconsin Avenue. Baneyev stood there stiffly, waiting for a taxi. Withers held back about fifty feet, the Beretta and the silencer warmed by his hand in his large coat pocket.

He could kill Baneyev right here, but there were a half dozen people nearby. If possible, Sam wanted it done in private. No need to tie the CIA to the public execution of a KGB officer, no matter how professionally notorious.

It was not prudent to be standing near a busy street corner. His face was now a national institution. Withers raced up the hill to where his old Ford was parked. He would lose minutes, but it was the only way he could safely follow the colonel.

He was in luck. Just as his car reached Wisconsin Avenue, Baneyev was hailing a taxi. Withers followed, holding a half block back, concentrating on the cab to see where Baneyev got off. The taxi drove on, block after block, until at DuPont Circle, where several major thoroughfares merge, it stopped and Baneyev got out to cross the street.

Withers was tied to his car while his target was vanishing, moving rapidly by foot in the opposite direction. Without preliminaries, Withers made his decision. Taking the Beretta out of his jacket pocket, he screwed on the silencer and laid the gun across his crooked arm. Instantly, he found the colonel in his sights. The target was convenient, only forty feet away. The street lights illuminated Baneyev, but where Withers was double parked no one could see the flash of the gun. It had to be now.

Sam moved the gunsight a millimeter to the right, tracking Baneyev as he walked toward the Metro entrance, the Russian unaware that his brain was only seconds from being shattered. Withers started the pressure on the squeeze, the one that would avenge Mary.

But the tension suddenly drained from his trigger finger. A teenage girl and her boyfriend were crossing the gun sights, heading toward the same Metro station. Sam could still see Baneyev, but he was no longer a clean, isolated target.

Withers held his breath, sighting continuously, hoping for a split-second break in which to fire. But then it happened. The young couple were now fully in his sights and Baneyev had disappeared behind them, down into the Metro escalator.

"Damn!" It was all Sam could muster as he slumped his head into his hands, his gun now fallen uselessly into his lap.

For an instant he dreamed of vengeance.

Chapter 70

On his Leesburg farm, John Davidson forced his back into the worn green leather wing chair and pondered strategy. If he were to extract maximum leverage from Fenton's mistake in kidnapping McDowell, he would have to employ directness.

He dialed 202-456-1414. The White House.

"May I please speak directly to the President? This is John Davidson, retired head of counterintelligence for the CIA."

"One second, sir. I'll give you his assistant."

"Hello. This is Maude Holly, the President's secretary. Can I help you?"

He needed to mobilize her energies.

"Ms. Holly. This is John Davidson, former chief of CIA counterintelligence. I'm retired, but if you tell the President that I have urgent news about national security, I believe he'll see me. I'd like about twenty minutes, this afternoon. Can you arrange it?"

"Mr. Davidson, if you want to see the President personally, the best I can do is three weeks from today. And that's not definite. I'll have to confirm and get back to you."

For Davidson, information was weaponry, the implement of survival. Giving it away was painful, but he had no other option if he wanted to see the President.

"Just tell him it involves Bill Fenton and a breach of national security. I think he'll see me."

"One minute, Mr. Davidson." Holly was gone from the phone for only seconds before she returned, her voice now less diffident.

"Yes, Mr. Davidson. The President will see you. Three o'clock this afternoon."

Davidson had not been to the White House for many years. This visit, especially the idea of face-to-face negotiations with his young adversary, appealed to him.

Promptly at three, the President was waiting for him in the Oval Office.

"Mr. Davidson. We haven't met, have we?"

It was Hankins at his most gracious, moving across the room to greet Davidson, a sign of generational respect.

"No, Mr. President. We haven't. I left the Agency when you were just entering the Senate."

"Well, that gives us a chance to get acquainted now. Sit down. What's on your mind?"

"Mr. President. I've come here on behalf of the Agency."

He could see Hankins' forehead stretch upward in surprise.

"Oh, I don't mean that they have sent me. Rather, that I took it upon myself as a former Agency man. The point is that I don't think you should proceed with the nomination of Mr. Fenton as director of the CIA. In fact, I believe you should withdraw his name immediately—before it causes you acute embarrassment."

"Why should I ever be embarrassed by Bill Fenton, Mr. Davidson?"

"Well, my friends in the FBI tell me they've given damaging information to the Senate Select Committee on Intelligence, something involving his year at Berkeley. But that's not what's troubling me. I have to tell you that, even before his confirmation, Fenton has used the Agency to commit a felony. To be exact, the kidnapping of an American citizen."

Davidson watched for the response. Hankins' jaw fell involuntarily.

"Kidnap? What did you say?"

Hankins was clearly surprised. Even so astute a pol as he couldn't have faked the reaction.

"Fenton ordered the kidnapping of an American?" the President repeated, incredulous.

"Yes, sir. And not just anyone. He directed the CIA to abduct the man who was held captive the night of the attempt on your life. Doug McDowell, the television newscaster."

Davidson thought the President would choke. Hankins reached over and poured himself a glass of water from a silver canister, sipping it while he coughed spasmodically.

In a moment, Hankins had regained some of his composure.

"When did this supposed abduction take place?"

As Davidson told the story of the kidnapping, McDowell's imprisonment in the CIA safe house in Alexandria, and the gunfight with the KGB, he could see the perspiration enlarge on the President's brow. His nerve endings seemed to be seeking outlet, perhaps in some primitive political wail. Instead, Hankins sat immobile, his face as stone.

"What happened to McDowell after that?"

Davidson had no intention of revealing his part in the rescue at the Point.

"The Russians took him to their summer place on the Chesapeake. But he was lucky. A Russian guard fell asleep and McDowell went down the drainpipe and stole one of their small boats. He's back at work at the network."

Hankins became silent. To Davidson it seemed a ploy to stretch out the time, to quiet the President's anguish before it crippled his maneuverability.

"Has McDowell told anyone what happened?" Hankins finally asked.

"No, sir. He's an old friend of mine. He assumes I represent the whole intelligence community, in or out of office. He came to see me right afterward and is waiting to hear from me now. I believe he wants my advice on whether it's better for the national interest to publicize the incident or keep it quiet."

Davidson stared impassively into Hankins' eyes.

"What do you think I should do, Mr. President?"

As he waited, Davidson speculated on Hankins' next move. Would he call on the politician's best friend, the brave bluff?

"Mr. Davidson. It's a horrible story, but I believe you. All I would have to do is phone Mr. McDowell to check it out. Mr. Fenton would probably tell me the truth as well. But I needn't do that. You do know there is an easy way out for me, with only a minimum of embarrassment?"

"What is that, Mr. President?"

"Simply to fire Mr. Fenton and brush him aside for misconduct. He comes out a villain and I emerge as a dedicated public servant who will not tolerate CIA abuse. What do you think of that idea, Mr. Davidson?"

"That would be fine with me. Are you willing to do that?"

Hankins laughed, his bluff quashed in one retort.

"No, not really. I prefer not to have a scandal this early in my administration. I just wanted your response."

The President paused. "So what is it you want me to do, Mr. Davidson?"

"What I said the moment I came in here. Withdraw Mr. Fenton's nomination as head of the CIA."

"And if I refuse?"

"Then I suppose I'll have to advise Mr. McDowell to tell the press everything. Unless, of course, Mr. Fenton is planning on kidnapping him again. Or maybe me as well."

"There's no reason to be sarcastic, Mr. Davidson."

Hankins was pensive for only a moment.

"You know, Mr. Davidson. I think you're right. The public doesn't want any more discord. They had enough in the Nixon administration. I'm much better off if I just withdraw the nomination. And chastise Mr. Fenton as well, privately. You know, there's something about the White House that can distort a man's soul—make him think he's a Tartar prince. I resist it, but I'm afraid Mr. Fenton didn't. I assure you, he won't be the last person in this building who'll try to abuse his power."

Hankins leaned forward, adopting what Davidson gauged to be his most sincere look.

"We both want to do what's best for our country. Don't we, Mr. Davidson? By the way, what do you think of Matthew Miles as CIA chief instead of Fenton? He's a career man. In fact, he's told me he worked closely with you for years."

"I think he'll do, Mr. President. He always impressed me as a competent professional."

"Good. Thank you for that recommendation. Coming from you, it means a lot to me."

"And, Mr. President," Davidson said with emphasis. "Please never mention what we've discussed with anyone, especially Mr. Fenton. I would consider that a breach of confidence."

"Absolutely, Mr. Davidson. I understand."

The President rose from his chair, thrusting his long arm at the ex-CIA man.

"Good, it's done. Mr. Fenton's name will be withdrawn. And Mr. Miles will be offered to the Senate for approval. Mr. Davidson, you have done a yeoman's job for your nation today. And I thank you."

Davidson lifted himself off the sofa to shake the President's outstretched hand.

"Just one thing, Mr. President. I hope you don't mind if occasionally I come to see you—if I have any other information of value."

Davidson could see Hankins straining to disguise the grimaced corners of his smile.

"Of course not, John. I hope I can call you that. Any time. As long as it's in the national interest."

☆ ☆ ☆

"Are you fucked out of your mind? I warned you that this was not Moscow! Ordering the CIA to kidnap a newsman, then turning him over to the KGB. You want us thrown out of here on our asses a month after we came in? What in the hell possessed you, Bill?"

Fenton was standing in front of the President's desk in the Oval Office as Hankins reviled him.

"Why? Why do such a thing, Bill? And without talking to me?"

Hankins' tone had suddenly softened. Fenton sensed that Jed had spoken those last words almost as a lament, afraid to totally antagonize the man who had brought him this far.

Fenton restrained his anger, knowing he couldn't reveal the truth to Hankins—that he had to kidnap McDowell because he had somehow stumbled onto STAND DOWN.

But Hankins was right on one thing, Fenton acknowledged. He had acted idiotically. He should have insisted that Baneyev kill McDowell outright, in Washington if necessary. But Baneyev believed McDowell was fronting for someone, and had to find out who. Now, because the newsman had escaped from the Point, he had to be reproached by Hankins, like a schoolchild.

Whatever story he concocted had to be plausible, even appease Hankins somewhat.

"I don't blame you for being angry, Jed . . . Mr. President. I know it was foolish, but I was only trying to protect you."

Hankins was surprised, his stare inquisitive.

"Me? How?"

"That phrase STAND DOWN that McDowell mentioned on the air. That's Baneyev's new code to replace Oval Red. It stands for your relationship with Tom Ward and the link to the Kremlin," Fenton lied. "When I heard it on television, I suppose I did go crazy. I knew it would jeopardize you and I figured . . ."

"Bill. I appreciate that," Hankins interrupted. "But you were wrong to do anything without first talking to me. And we're lucky I've been able to keep it hushed up. But I'm afraid I had to pay a stiff price."

"What was that?" Fenton asked.

Hankins angled his eyes away from Fenton.

"The price was your nomination to head the CIA."

Fenton fell into silence. Not head the CIA? After all these years of painful discipline. To come so close? He glowered at Hankins, who turned away from the visual pressure.

"You might not have made it anyway, Bill. The Senate was holding it up—I think because of Berkeley. I'm going to have to go ahead with Miles instead. Naturally, you'll stay on as my chief of staff. I hope you understand."

"No, Jed. I don't. In fact, I can't believe you're saying this. After everything that's happened between us personally."

"This is not personal, Bill. You, above all, should know that. It's what you and I must do to keep our program on target. Otherwise, you'll be exposed. That wouldn't be pleasant for anyone. Would it? And you're not going anywhere. Just a change in roles."

"Who's the blackmailer?" Fenton almost screamed at the President. "Who's threatening to expose me?"

"Bill, you know I can't tell you that. It would only escalate everything. Please trust me. I've contained it. Now we can move on to bigger things. You know how much work we have to do in this country."

Fenton started out of the room, at first petulantly. Then he turned back, his expression suddenly conciliatory.

"Mr. President, I accept your decision. Naturally, I don't like it, but I wouldn't consciously do anything to hurt you or delay our work. We have a mission together. Nothing must stand in our way."

"That's great, Bill. I'm so glad that you see it that way. Exactly. Nothing must stand in our way."

Fenton smiled artificially, knowing that his meeting with Baneyev could not be delayed another minute.

Chapter 71

Marge Coulton was waiting at the Taft Memorial just below the Hill when Fenton approached and kissed her.

"I'm glad you could get away," he said. "It's very important."

Fenton was satisfied with their cover. As supposed lovers, they could meet at the campanile at any time and perform virtually any indiscretion without arousing suspicion.

"Marge, I must meet personally with Baneyev. Can you arrange it?"

"Of course I can, Bill, but do you think it's wise? Your position in the White House makes you exposed."

"Marge. Are you worried about our work, or me? Our affair is only supposed to be a cover. Remember?"

"Bill, you shouldn't kid me. You know how I feel. I just never know about you."

What Coulton couldn't appreciate was how little he was affected by either the opposite, or his own, sex. Fenton had never understood the physical passions; the rarefied gratifications of the mind seemed his only release. But Marge had to be placated. Keeping directionless people like her and Hankins from frustrating his plans drained half his energy these days, it seemed.

Fenton could afford no compromise. Hankins had lost his revolutionary resolve and was reverting to the pettiness of most American politicians, a regression that risked everything. The President no longer understood the boldness needed to change the world in a narrow time slot—the animal prowess of a Fidel Castro or a Khomeini. Fenton now knew that Hankins didn't have it. Probably never did.

He leaned toward Marge, his arm warmly enveloping her shoulder.

"Dar . . . ling." The strain of the word prompted a stutter. "Please, Marge. Don't worry. I'll be careful. Just set it up."

"All right, Bill. The Metro stop at the end of the Orange Line at New Carrollton is relatively safe. I'll make it for eleven tomorrow night. You'll recognize Baneyev. He's a muscular man, but with a thin, white face. His right hand was hurt in an accident last week. It's bandaged. Use the name 'Taft.' And, Bill, be careful. Remember, the Metro shuts at midnight."

He needn't tell Marge that a code name wasn't necessary, that he had already met Baneyev, in the distant past.

"Don't worry, Marge. I only need a few minutes with him. I'll be careful."

☆ ☆ ☆

Baneyev stood in the shadows at the edge where the platform dropped off. Fenton's train had just come in silently on its rubber cushions at one minute before 11 P.M. The Metro station was virtually empty.

Fenton walked briskly up to the KGB *rezident* and extended his hand. Baneyev touched it with fingers of his left hand, holding up the injured one in explanation.

"Colonel. Good to see you again. You remember me?" Fenton said.

"Yes, I remember you well, Mr. Fenton. In fact, I hear much good about your work. Not only here but from the Center in Moscow. But what is the urgency of this meeting? Couldn't it be done through Ms. Coulton?"

"No. Only the Center should know what I have to tell you. Incidentally, my nomination as CIA chief is being withdrawn by Yearling. Because of that McDowell incident."

Baneyev pushed out his lips in surprise.

"Colonel, I came here to tell you that we no longer have six months for STAND DOWN. We have to move much more rapidly. A matter of weeks."

"Why so hasty? Is something wrong?" Baneyev asked, his white face now almost translucent.

"It's Yearling."

"Why? Isn't he with us anymore?"

"Don't worry. He's still one of us. But he's becoming a little corrupted by American politics. He was outraged by the practical course the Soviet Union took in East Africa, then he yielded to blackmail on my CIA appointment. Before anything else happens, I think we should move up the date for STAND DOWN. I'd like to propose March 15."

"But that's only two weeks from now."

"I know. But my end will be ready. The codes will be in place in time. And our disarmament is proceeding even faster than I had hoped."

Fenton could see it was all a surprise to Baneyev, who had been dispatching reports to Moscow forecasting only total cooperation from the American White House.

"Will the President actually be against STAND DOWN?" Baneyev asked, his bandaged arm swinging aimlessly at his side.

Fenton waited until another train had loaded and left the platform. He realized he might be presenting too negative a picture. It would be catastrophic if he inadvertently dampened the Soviet desire to move ahead.

"No. Of course not. Hankins is a devoted Marxist. I'm sure he'll agree that STAND DOWN is the only way for total victory. Leave him to me. I just think the sooner the better. Do you understand?"

Baneyev stared at his American colleague. "I understand thoroughly. I'll radio your urgency directly to the Kremlin. Good night, Mr. Fenton. I hope you don't mind if I don't shake your hand."

As the men parted, Baneyev walked toward the other side of the station to begin his trip back to the embassy.

☆   ☆   ☆

In the shadows of the return platform, Sam Withers waited. He had followed Baneyev once again from the compound, this time in the Metro.

Withers had no idea what Fenton and Baneyev had discussed. But he had to make sure that Baneyev did not live to follow out the directives of the Kremlin or the Oval Office, both of which were now fused into one in Withers' mind.

Chapter 72

Colonel Lev Orlov peered out of the chauffeured Chaika as it traveled out of the city on one of the new six-lane highways built to military specifications. The road's destination, as well as his own, was an installation thirty miles outside Moscow—SNADF, the Soviet National Air Defense Forces headquarters.

As the car approached the base, Orlov was surprised that the SNADF headquarters looked peculiarly empty. Then he realized why. Its surface buildings were only service units for the real city, which lay buried below.

He had come at the personal invitation of General Mikhail Boritsky, the Deputy Minister of Defense, who had hinted that Orlov was to receive a private briefing on the preparations for STAND DOWN, now only a week away.

At the gate the Chaika was stopped by four guards armed with AK-47 submachine guns. They closely inspected his papers, then waved him in.

"Enter, Comrade Colonel. Minister Boritsky is waiting."

The guards motioned his car to a parking area, where a young captain met Orlov and escorted him to a small concrete structure about thirty-five feet square and only ten feet high. More like a bunker than a building, Orlov thought.

It was. The bunker was basically a reinforced elevator shaft, with two sets of stairs running down on either side. This was one of a dozen such entrances and egresses scattered around the four-square-mile base. As he entered, the young escort captain caught Orlov's eyes wandering about.

"Yes, Colonel Orlov. These walls are superhardened. Each is ten feet thick, made with a steel structure reinforced with special blast-resistant concrete. It would take twelve direct hits to seal us in. That is improbable. Too wasteful for Americans with their small arsenal of accurate MXs. Their less accurate Minuteman missiles could hit randomly around here and still leave us safe below. Come."

Orlov and the captain descended in stages. At the first level, a hundred and fifty feet down, they entered a series of well-lit tunnels with dozens of rooms partitioned off for storage, supplies, and offices. They walked about two hundred feet to the left, to another bank of elevators.

"By staggering the elevator shafts we prevent a single direct hit from sending the shock wave down to our lower levels below," the captain explained. "This way the damage is blocked at any one of the higher levels."

Orlov was impressed. The next elevator descended three hundred feet farther, where they switched again. The second level was the beginning of a city, with giant storage areas, hospitals, weapons rooms, communications areas, even theaters and large barrackslike areas, each of which held hundreds of people.

In Moscow, Orlov had visited the main underground headquarters of the Kremlin, a unit some nine hundred feet below the surface. It was equipped with an electronic center from which to wage war, and excellent living quarters for five hundred people, the top echelon of the government bureaucracy. It was impressive, but SNADF was a true city of the future—a place for men to run the world after the holocaust they had created.

"How many people can exist here underground?" Orlov asked.

"This is only the second level. We have three more, down to the Command and Control Center sixteen hundred feet below ground. In all, Colonel, I would say that eight thousand military personnel and government officials could withstand a nuclear attack here. With proper functioning of our decontaminated air supply, they could last for a very long time. We have food and medical supplies for over a year."

Just from reading the secret memoranda, Orlov knew that facilities now existed to house 110,000 preselected people—the elite of Marxist society—in hardened underground units throughout the country. There were seventy-five such nuclear shelters near the Moscow ring roads alone. No one had ever discussed it, but it made sense eugenically. If the nation was ever destroyed, which he doubted, those who survived would be of the highest intellect, able to procreate a superior race of Marxists to control the remaining world.

Within minutes, the fourth elevator transit had deposited them at Level A, the heart of the city.

The escorting captain now turned Orlov over to a major, who briskly moved him toward a large metal double door guarded by armed soldiers.

"In here, Colonel Orlov. If you've never seen this command center, you're in for a surprise."

It mimicked Hollywood, at least what Orlov had seen in films of fanciful missile command centers in James Bond pictures. In some ways, it was a more grandiose version of the Houston Space Center.

In the center of the room, raised to a height of thirty feet, was an electronic map of the world, some ninety feet across. At a wave from the major, the map zoomed in, filling the area with a map of the United States, from California to New York.

The map was dotted with legends, showing all the United States missile sites for Minutemen and the MX, every SAC bomber base, fighter interceptor stations, and the five main American command headquarters, plus two alternate SAC centers at March Field, California, and Barksdale Air Force Base in Louisiana.

"Very impressive, Major." Orlov nodded in approval.

The electronic map changed. In giant proportions, Orlov could now see a schematic of Whiteman Air Force Base in Missouri, one of the six Minuteman sites. Every one of the launching pads, silos, and command buildings near the little town of Knob Noster, fifty miles east of Kansas City, was marked with an X.

"We have two SS-24 warheads targeting each Minuteman silo," the major explained. "Our missiles are accurate to a CEP, a Circular Error Probable, of 250 feet over an 8000-mile range. We have them tied in electronically on a continuous basis—missile to target. No preparation is necessary, except the decision to fire."

The electronic screen shifted to what looked like another missile base.

"These are the MX silos at Warren Air Force Base in Wyoming," the major continued. "They're the only American missiles accurate and powerful enough to destroy our superhardened silos and command posts. But they have only fifty of them. To be sure they are taken out, we have assigned four warheads to each silo. Because of their small number we can afford that redundancy."

The major's glance at Orlov was knowing. "Fortunately for us, the Americans have no mobile missiles to worry about."

Orlov suddenly craned his neck up toward the glass-enclosed command unit atop the six-story-high room. Another officer was waving, apparently for Orlov to be brought up.

"Welcome, Colonel Orlov." It was Boritsky himself, outfitted in a brown uniform with numerous red and gilded trappings. "Welcome to Command Center," he said as soon as they had walked up the flights of stairs.

"Orlov. I wanted you to see our follow-up to your excellent work in America. We lost 22 million in the last war. You're too young to remember, but I must tell you that we'll never go through that again. This time, in a matter of days, we shall be defeating our new enemy, the American imperialists—maybe without losing a man."

The Minister General lifted a gold phone. In an instant the electronic map displayed the outlines of the Soviet Union, from the Baltic to the Pacific Ocean, a stretch of six thousand miles and eleven time zones.

"Your boss, Vassilin, keeps reminding me that espionage and subversion are cheaper, in money and blood, than all the missiles in the world. He may be right. But without our enormous missile strength and our defenses, the threat we'll soon be making to America would be like whistling at wolves. Let me show you what we have planned for STAND DOWN."

As he spoke, the map closed in, revealing a color representation of what looked like a missile base.

"Colonel, the time for STAND DOWN has been set. It is March 15, 3 P.M. Washington time, 11 P.M. Moscow time—just one week from today. The night before, your operative, Fenton, will get President Hankins' response to STAND DOWN. Baneyev will receive it at the embassy and relay it directly to us by radio. If it is positive, then STAND DOWN will move into action. At 2:30 P.M., the General Secretary will offer his terms to President Hankins, then accept his formal surrender a half hour later. If all goes well, we will need none of this. But otherwise . . .

"You see that, Orlov." The Minister was pointing to a close-up view of a launch pad between two short rail tracks, with additional missiles on line.

"That is our antisatellite launcher at Tyuratam, one of five operational in the country." Tyuratam, Orlov knew, was the Soviet space center near the giant landlocked Aral Sea in southern Russia, the locale of an enormous military push into space which had begun in the early 1980s.

"A day in advance of STAND DOWN, these interceptor antisatellites will be launched and placed in orbit. Then, at our command, they will be ready to attack the American early warning satellites which track our missiles from a synchronous orbit 22,000 miles up. At the same time, our High-Energy Ground Laser station at Sary Shagan will double-target the same satellites, reaching them almost instantaneously. Without their satellites, the American defenses will be blind. Meanwhile, our satellites are in place, including our new laser detectors in low orbit continuously monitoring the position of all thirty-seven American missile submarines. Watch."

The screen reverted to a projection of the entire world surface, on which were dotted the names of America's nuclear submarines, with their exact underwater locations digitally noted alongside. In the vicinity of each American submarine were the markings of nearby Soviet attack subs and naval units with the direction, range, and time needed for nuclear-tipped AS-15 2000-mile-range cruise missiles—fired from Bear-H bombers or from Soviet naval ships—to reach their targets.

Boritsky offered Orlov a self-satisfied grin as he waved again. The screen now showed twenty-six ICBM missile launch bases throughout the Soviet Union, from Derazhnya near the Polish border on the west to Zhangiz Tobe in Central Asia, to Svobodnyy in the Far East close to the Chinese border.

"We need only 2500 warheads—only one eighth our strength—to take out all their Minutemen and MXs, the White House, Camp David, the Pentagon, and other command posts, plus the Air Force bomber and fighter bases," the general explained.

"Orlov, your Americans are totally unprepared for modern war. None of their command posts are hardened against a nuclear attack. The main SAC bunker is only forty-six feet below the lawn at Offutt AFB. The NORAD Cheyenne complex was built into the Rockies, but they made a big mistake. Instead of going into the base of the mountain and having its full height above to protect them, they built only 1400 feet below the peak. Our SS-24s will shear it like wool off a sheep.

"Their air bases are vulnerable as well," Boritsky continued. "The old B-52s can't get off the ground in time to avoid a submarine missile attack. We can reach them all in ten minutes. Those already in the air —B-52s or B-1s—would never get through our superior air defenses. And offensively, we have over 500 modern bombers to their 100 B-1s. They might be able to launch their cruise missiles, but most of them are ancient instruments. The Pentagon cut back their original plan of 5000 cruise missiles to 1725 because they are already outmoded, totally vulnerable to our new SAM-12 ground-to-air units.

"And, unlike us, they have never built—even appropriated money for—an adequate air defense system against bombers and low-flying cruise missiles. Even their antisatellite weapons are not deployed. Their Congress forced the Pentagon to stop testing them back in 1985."

Orlov had a question. "Comrade Minister. What about our defense against missiles?" he asked. "Is our ground-based system as good as their Star Wars—or former Star Wars?"

"The Americans made much of their Star Wars," Boritsky replied.

"True, it was an excellent system, but long before it was deployed we had an effective ground-based antiballistic missile shield. It began around Moscow and has since been extended to fourteen other major cities, including Leningrad and Kiev. The Americans are screaming that we have violated the 1972 treaty. I don't know about treaties, but I do know that not to defend oneself against nuclear attack is madness."

As Orlov listened, he confessed to himself. He had never really understood his American charges. Even though the 1972 treaty, signed in the Nixon détente years, allowed one city in each country to be protected by ground-based ABMs, the Americans had never built any. Moscow was the first city in the world to prepare for nuclear war, and the experience had taught them well, Orlov could see.

The electronic chart now displayed a view of an ABM installation, one of nine ringing Moscow in two circles. The first was at the periphery of the city, with a second ring where he was now, thirty miles out. The original system was still in place, consisting of sixty-eight above-ground launchers for Galosh ABM 1-B missile interceptors at four complexes, with six TRY ADD guidance radars in each group. They were tied together by several target-tracking radars south of the city.

The second layer consisted of more advanced ABMs capable of destroying most American missiles. Buried securely in silos, these long-range Galoshes could hit their targets outside the atmosphere, before they could endanger Moscow with fallout. The silos were reloadable and could handle large numbers of ABM missiles.

To make the system nationwide, Boritsky explained, they had been forced to build outlawed types of inward-looking radar scanners, like the one in Krasnoyarsk in Siberia. When tied into others, it provided the superb radar tracking needed for a complete ABM network.

"We're secure in our defense and ready to attack, Colonel. But to ensure total destruction of America, we're assigning five thousand warheads to do the job," Boritsky explained. "Even the Pentagon admits that the SS-18s can take out eighty percent of the Minutemen. Our fifth-generation missile, the SS-24, will make that number a hundred percent."

Boritsky seemed to be smiling. "You know, Orlov, we have to thank our American friends for that. During détente, they sold us the machine tools to make micro ball bearings—from their plant in Vermont. Without that, our missiles would never have their devastating accuracy. Meanwhile, the American Minutemen cannot destroy our superhardened silos. Some of the older ones can't even reach our SS-18s in southern Asia. The MX can do the job, but, as I said, they have only a pitiful fifty of them."

Boritsky suddenly stopped in his explanation and turned to Orlov, his expression that of a student to a teacher.

"Colonel, you're an American expert. Tell me. Why wouldn't such a rich and successful country want to defend itself? For us it is good. But I don't understand. Do you?"

Orlov had tried to understand. America, he was convinced, had a Puritan, guilt-ridden, suicidal streak, a wish to compensate for all the past success by perishing.

Unlike Russia, or Israel, they also had a way of complicating their defense issues—as if to talk themselves out of life. Maybe it was because they had never died massively in war as did the Russians, or in the gas chambers as did the Jews, Orlov thought. Spared so often by their two oceans, their demise possibly did not seem credible. But now, of course, it was a childish notion.

The colonel looked at Boritsky sympathetically.

"It's a long story, Minister General. Another time perhaps."

Boritsky shrugged.

"America will be in no position to retaliate once our barrage of SS-24s is completed," he continued. "Even if they could, they'd never find our mobile missiles—the ten warhead SS-24s on rails, or our single-warhead SS-25s on trucks, hidden in the forests. We have an entire arsenal of them, while the Americans are still arguing about their Midgetman. Fifteen years ago, the Americans had a mobile MX system like ours on paper, but they scrapped it."

Boritsky again looked toward his American expert, seeking elucidation. When none was forthcoming, he merely shrugged.

From his lofty glass-enclosed perch, the general waved toward the electronic screen, which was soon filled with giant color portraits of fifteen American politicians, with Hankins at the apex of an organizational chart.

"This is their STAVKA, Orlov, their table of command, those in the succession for the presidency. First Hankins, then the Speaker of the House—there is yet no Vice-President—then the president pro tempore of the Senate, the Secretary of State, then Treasury, then Defense, down to May Ellen Miller, Secretary of Education.

"We must knock out their leadership so they can't use whatever resources they have left—if any. Each has a GO code to launch the missiles if they succeed to the presidency. But none of them will take a breath in time. Our first missiles will kill all fifteen. Congress then has to name a successor, but there will be no Congress. As you know, Orlov, there is no other succession by American law. It will be instant decapitation—a wounded country with no one to run it."

Orlov was aware of the flaws in the American succession, but he had a question for Boritsky.

"Don't they have an escape system for their leadership, as we do?" Orlov asked.

He was referring to the complex escape units provided to the Politburo and its alternate members, about thirty leaders in all. In addition to several aircraft, the system included a secret sealed train, a submarine command center, and a naval destroyer equipped to handle the running of nuclear war at sea.

"The Americans have only four converted Boeing 707 command planes called *Kneecap,* on which the President and his people are supposed to escape and continue the fight. But we know just where they are. They will never leave the ground."

Orlov was receiving a lesson in modern military strategy and enjoying it. He had assumed, but never exactly known, just how well prepared the Soviet Union was for World War III.

He was about to ask Boritsky a question when the general waved his hand. The electronic map went blank.

"Some coffee, Colonel?" Boritsky asked. "We have had enough war talk. Now let us talk peace—and surrender. That is your specialty. No?"

"Yes, sir. I suppose you could describe it that way. I've tried to make America more amenable to our control. I think we have made some good progress."

Boritsky laughed. "Colonel, you are too modest. With Yearling in the White House, STAND DOWN is practical. Either through their surrender or their annihilation. I much prefer to limit the bloodshed."

The general stared inquisitively at his American specialist.

"What is your opinion, Colonel? Do you think Hankins will go along?"

Orlov knew his answer would soon be tested by events. What did he really think?

"As the soothsayers say, Minister General, do not hold me to it. But

I firmly believe he will. He is with us ideologically. He may find it distasteful to surrender his country's independence, but he knows our overwhelming power. He also knows how much he has diluted America's already weak position. I think he'll scream and yell. And curse in the dark. But, yes, he will surrender."

"On that note, I toast you, Colonel Orlov." Boritsky had risen to his feet. "With young men such as you, the great Soviet people are assured of victory."

As Orlov drank down his coffee, he could almost feel the Order of Lenin resting warmly on his small chest.

Chapter 73

Ward's taxi had let him off at the Northwest Gate of the White House. Staying over at Les's place the night before had been prudent. He had no idea who was investigating him but caution was the best strategy.

It wouldn't do to appear upset at this morning's meeting with the President. Hankins' office had called him at Doric Films only minutes before, asking that he come to the White House immediately.

The guard knew Ward but insisted on the formalities. Inside, he was ushered into the Oval Office by Ms. Holly. Fenton was seated facing the President, who was standing behind his desk, obviously restraining a temper.

The President perfunctorily inquired about Tom's health. Ward could feel the tension but couldn't imagine its source.

Hankins came rapidly to the point.

"Tom, I called you in because I need word on the MIG-31 situation in Nicaragua. I can't get a straight answer out of the Kremlin. Now that I've cut off all aid to the Central American countries, I anticipate nothing but victory for the socialist forces."

"Yes, sir. Then what's the problem?" Ward asked.

"Tom, I'm frankly worried that it could all go down the drain if the Soviet Union sends in MIGs now. Delafield will rouse up the people, and I'll have a real fight on my hands. I need to know what's going on in Moscow. Do you have any information?"

Ward felt diplomatically sandwiched. He had the information, just delivered to him by Rausch. The number of MIG-31s, replacement parts, even the names of the Polish and Bulgarian ships and their arrival dates in Corinto, the Pacific coast Nicaraguan port. But telling Hankins would only heighten his antagonism.

"No, Mr. President," Ward lied. "I've passed along your concern about the MIGs, but thus far I've heard nothing."

"Damn Russians," the President muttered. "Sometimes talking to them is like talking to this picture of Tom Jefferson. No, I think old TJ is straighter with me than they are."

Ward glanced across at Fenton. A grimace, a sign that the aide was suffering intellectual pain, marred Fenton's expression.

"Mr. President." Unable to contain himself, Fenton rose from his chair and paced in front of Hankins' desk. "Could you be exaggerating the negative impact of the MIGs?" he asked. "Maybe it'll have a good result—show that the Soviet Union is determined about Central America no matter what the American public thinks. You know the Americans haven't the guts to do anything about it. They'll just wail, like they always do. Then find a scapegoat ten years later to blame for the area going Communist."

"No, Bill. I'm not exaggerating." The President was shaking his head vigorously. "If the Soviets don't raise a fuss down there, the American people won't do a damn thing. They like to sleepwalk. In fact, they're only hoping that it's a bad dream. But if we put a gun in their faces, like in the Cuban missile crisis, they'll react. Never confront the American voter. Sweet-talk him and lull him to sleep, I say. Bill, I know of what I speak. I've won six elections that way."

Hankins abruptly shifted to Ward.

"Tom, tell Moscow again. If they leave Central America to me, it'll work out. If they don't I'm afraid they'll fuck it up."

The buzzing intercom interrupted.

"Yes, Maude. Please tell him I'm in a meeting. He knows? He wants to see all of us? All right. Show him in."

Matthew Miles, chewing on his empty meerschaum, entered the Oval Office, his Midwestern cheer subdued.

"Mr. President. I'm afraid I'm the courier of lousy news. Satellite observation and gossip at the Russian Black Sea ports have just confirmed it—there are eighty-six MIG-31s on Polish and Bulgarian freighters on their way to Nicaragua. The pilots have been trained and are waiting for their planes. When we release this news, Delafield, Feldman, and their boys are going to scream holy murder."

The President pushed back into his enveloping leather chair and started to laugh.

"Is there anything wrong, Jed?"

It was Fenton, forgetting his protocol again as the lanky President fell into the grip of what looked like a hysterical attack. Or at least one of childishness. What had gotten into Hankins? Ward wondered.

The President finally recovered from his laughing fit, wiping the last tear of frustration from his eyes.

"I've almost had it with the Soviet Union, Tom. Please tell that to the Kremlin. And underscore that America is not Czechoslovakia. I still share their goals, but I must tell you I sure as hell don't like their methods. Relay that exactly. Okay?"

Hankins caught Miles's eye.

"Matt, the Soviets have forced me into a lousy position. Our only strategy now is to keep it real quiet. Shred every damn memo on the MIGs at Langley. If it leaks, it could be very embarrassing."

As the meeting started to break up, the President was still shaking his head, the last muffled guffaw of nervous laughter in his throat.

Chapter 74

"Good evening, Ms. Larsen," the White House guard greeted Meg that evening at five past ten, a few minutes after Hankins had left the Oval Office. "The President is expecting you."

Standing at the entrance to 1600 Pennsylvania Avenue, Meg Larsen congratulated herself that life had reached the level of her highest fantasies, her network earnings plus the income from Rausch making the dreams of finery a reality.

And now the intimacy with Jed Hankins was providing the stimulus of power. As she entered the presidential mansion Meg asked herself again: did the work for the KGB trouble her?

The answer was always the same. Not really. Spying and warfare and empires were boys' games, played out in the schools, the streets, the courts, the world's athletic fields and officer clubs, government houses and corporate boardrooms. They had been doing it for thousands of years—the Greeks, the Romans, the Spanish, the British, the French, the Germans. And now the Americans and Soviets. They would be doing it long after she left.

Why worry about such male obsessions? Women were always the losers, either as mistresses, or wives, or mothers, or overfaithful employees. She had no intention of aping men's power ploys. Meg had a girl's game to play. More pleasing really, and far more innocent, she was sure. Hers only required money—to spend. Who could begrudge her the enormous pleasure it brought?

Now she had a magnificent client, in every way. Jed Hankins found her attractive. Actually irresistible, she thought immodestly as her work expanded into the White House itself. Although, Meg had warned Rausch, she cared more for Hankins than she did for the job. She would only pass along information that wouldn't injure the President.

It wasn't her politics, she assured Rausch. She didn't really understand what Hankins was trying to do in the White House, and didn't much care. But he had been generous, and loving, and sexually pleasing. So Rausch had to understand that, here, money took second place.

But Meg had not told Rausch the entire truth. She was priming him not to expect any White House intelligence so she could hold open her options. Learn what she really felt about Hankins, then proceed accordingly. Either to make a fortune from her relationship with the President or to find some other—equally rewarding—compensation.

The assignations began in the evening, generally after nine. There was little chance for scandal. Both were unmarried and the White House guards had sworn discretion, an oath broken only under the persuasive whip of New York book publishers.

Moments later a Secret Service agent had escorted Meg to the door of the upstairs family quarters, then retreated.

As she entered, Meg again noticed that it had the disorderly air of a bachelor's apartment.

"Meg. Come here."

She turned just as Hankins grabbed her about the waist, placing the other hand on her dress, over a breast, and kissed her as one would a lost lover.

"Jed—I hope I can call you that, Mr. President. We just saw each other Thursday. Surely you can't have missed me that much."

Meg's smile explained how much she enjoyed this powerful man's admiration.

"Much more," Hankins laughed, holding her closer.

He sounded young and impetuous, but Meg could see the weariness in his dimmed eyes. She had seen that look before, but only in older men, enervated by the years. What was troubling him? Meg thought of asking, then checked herself. She had made a beautiful accommodation with Hankins. Was it to be marred by her excess concern, even affection?

"What's wrong, Jed?" Meg finally asked. "You look absolutely exhausted. Maybe a little depressed?"

"I know, Meg. I think that when a man reaches high places he expects there's some divine touch involved. When he learns that's nonsense, he becomes mature, and a little saddened. Let's say I'm growing up."

"Do you want to talk about it?"

"No, not really. Now I want to savor you."

Hankins gently moved Meg back two steps, as if leading in a dance. She stood erect for his benefit, the dark brown silk dress outlining her full body, her long hair slung, seemingly casual, in front of her shoulders, each side touching the soft outlines of her breasts.

"Just like I thought. Magnificent," Hankins said, awed by female mysteries only vaguely perceived. "A pageant of beauty. But not like a little girl, modest about her appeal. A mature woman—prepared, confident—gorgeous."

Meg laughed, moving the two steps quickly toward him, kissing his cheek, this time innocently, gracefully.

"Jed, you're too much. But I love it."

They chatted only fleetingly, both awaiting more intimacy.

"Come, lovely. I have a surprise. Do you like history?" Hankins asked.

"I suppose as much as the next girl. But right now?"

"Now above all," Hankins said, the game relieving some of his tension. "Come with me."

He half walked, half pulled Meg, awkward at that speed in her heels, down the corridor of the White House's second floor.

Hankins stood before a large door and knocked.

"Is there someone in there?" Meg had become curious about the escapade.

"I sure hope not. It's the Lincoln Room. There's a wonderful early Victorian high-backed bed inside. I've heard that John Kennedy used it on occasions like this. What do you think?"

Meg laughed. "Boys will be boys. Why not? As long as the old man doesn't mind, wherever he is."

"No, I don't think so. Lincoln had propriety, and I don't believe he played around. But he would have liked you."

"Again, you're too much," Meg said, removing her high-heeled shoes. This time she led Hankins softly by his hand, almost reverently on her tiptoes, into the gracious Victorian room, its large bed inviting.

☆ ☆ ☆

"Do you want to talk about it now?" Meg asked.

Her nude body was carelessly draped in bleached White House sheets, Hankins at her side, lying back, his eyes open to the tall ceiling. The lovemaking had again been ideal for Hankins, the enthusiastic woman lending her youth, and considerable skill, to the sport, yielding with neither calculation nor reluctance. Only with unbridled fun, for the love of it. It was the best antidote for his political malaise.

"Well, maybe I'd like to, but it's so complicated, Meg. And so much of it involves national security."

"Jed, I don't care about details, and I'm not going to let anything out of the Lincoln Room. You can be sure of that. Maybe it'll help if you get it off your chest."

That was the one integer missing from the equation of his presidency, Hankins realized. There was no one, truly, to speak to. Fenton would listen, but Hankins had always known that, for all his power, he was only a player in Fenton's Machiavellian schemes.

He hadn't cared, for their purposes had melded. It was still that way, but Bill's dogma was so parochial that conversation between them was now like all political relationships, filled with deceit or trade-offs. Other Presidents had wives to counsel with—Reagan, and Truman and Carter, even FDR. Could Meg be that kind of help?

"It's the frustration of the job, Meg. I know what I want to do, but everyone keeps interfering—those who share my views and those who would like to see me dead. The presidency is a strange business, and I still don't fully understand it. Sometimes I have enormous powers. Other times none at all. Just as if I were a private citizen watching events control me."

"What particularly, Jed? Why this sadness tonight that you didn't have last Thursday?"

What sense in revealing? Hankins asked himself. Surely, a rapid catharsis, some sympathy, then the fear that the secret was gone. What did he know about Meg except that she was beautiful and ambitious? Perhaps a spy—for the fascist Davidson, or Delafield. Then his frustrations would only multiply.

"Meg, we've never spoken about politics. What are yours?" Hankins asked.

"Politics? I'm not against it, but I leave that to people who know more, and care more. Like yourself."

"I appreciate that, Meg. But what I mean is—what are your sympathies? Are you liberal, or left, or conservative? Or what?"

He could see Meg straining under the idea.

"I never really thought about it. But when I vote, which is rarely, I just press the Republican levers. Is that what you want to know?"

"But why Republican?" Hankins asked, enjoying this uncharacteristic discussion with Meg. "Why not Democratic? Or even Communist? You know, they're on the ballot for President too."

"No, I didn't know that. But I don't like Communism. No beauty, no humor, no sensitivity. But why Republican? Well, my father was a poor Scandinavian in an Irish Democratic city, but he voted a straight Republican ticket. He was mad about politics, like you. Always said that the Democrats were a bunch of Bolsheviks. He even hated FDR and Jack Kennedy. So, I suppose I've followed in his footsteps."

Meg waited, staring at Hankins' now immobile face.

"How about you? You're a Democrat," Meg said, laughing. "My father must have been wrong. You don't look like a Bolshevik. Not with your money."

"Appearances are deceiving, Meg. Haven't you been reading the criticism? They say I'm a dangerous leftist determined to hand the country over to the Soviets."

He could feel Meg pushing aside the draped sheet, approaching, her eyes now peering into his, her white breasts pressing firmly against him.

"Well, are you?"

Hankins laughed. The woman pleased him, raising strange points of intuition in his head. He somehow felt he could trust her.

"Meg, I can't tell you everything, but yes, I am a leftist. Does that shock you?"

"Not really, Jed. I've always assumed that you were somewhat left. I can't say that I agree with what you're doing, but I won't lose any sleep over it."

"Meg, you're refreshing. You worried about my depression, or whatever it is. Well, the truth is, I'm trying to be good friends with the Soviet Union, to stop the Cold War and build a real friendship. But they seem determined to run me, to push me around. As they did just yesterday."

"What happened?"

"It's about Central America. I've stopped all aid to the area, but it seems that's not enough for them. I've warned them not to send MIGs to Nicaragua—that it would inflame the public and the right-wingers like Delafield. I thought what I said meant something in Moscow. Well, I've just learned that there are two boatloads of MIGs headed for Nicaragua. When they land, all hell's going to break loose, and I'm going to look like an idiot."

"Jed, does anybody else know about this?"

"No one except Fenton and a couple of administration officials. Why?"

"Because I think your best bet is to play ignorant, and shocked. Make believe you know nothing about it, so when they land you can be angry at Russia, without doing anything about it."

Hankins leaned over and kissed her. "That's just what I was going to do," he said, "but now I know it's the right thing. You've got a canny head on your shoulders. But, Meg . . ."

"Yes, Jed?"

"It'll only work if you say absolutely nothing, to anyone, particularly at the network. Can I trust you on this?"

Meg could feel Hankins' eyes on her, as if worried that he had said too much. She knew Rausch would appreciate this information, whose worth she quickly calculated at $5000. What would she do with the money? Perhaps add a few thousand more and buy the lynx coat that had tantalized her. But then her eyes met Hankins' and she saw the boyish trepidation in his face.

"Jed. You can trust me on this. On your life," she said.

"Good, good," Hankins responded.

Meg sensed that the President knew she was speaking the truth.

Chapter 75

Doug McDowell was uneasy, perturbed by the state of his own indecision. But Samuels had been definite. If he discussed the Hankins matter with anyone it would mean immediate dismissal from the network, the loss of one of the best jobs in television.

A six-figure salary and the freedom to discuss virtually anything on the air—but apparently not President Hankins—was a heady mix for a man still not thirty-five. He was career-oriented; he didn't doubt that. But the tortuous events of the last nine months were beginning to change his perceptions.

Perhaps there was more to life than an insincere handshake and self-satisfied bank deposits. McDowell had to settle this with himself. Either stifle any dissent about Hankins, once and for all. Or make that one bold step.

McDowell didn't want to plead patriotism. He had seen too much evil wrapped in the thin scrim of nationalism. But this was a case of simple political fraud. A Communist pretending to be a loyal Democrat, secretly leading the nation down a vulnerable course—perhaps even worse. He now knew, finally, that Samuels, and the network, could go to hell. He had been kidnapped twice, insulted, fooled, and intellectually raped. He was going to join the small army of the concerned.

His best lead into the conspiracy was Hankins, a man he had met several times in his capacity as a journalist. But without network backing, Hankins was probably not a fruitful avenue for investigation.

But Meg. She had been involved in the news of Mary Withers' death, and then in the suspicious circumstances of his own kidnapping. Could his well-turned-out assistant be part of some larger scheme? Perhaps not a major player, but he had to begin somewhere.

That evening at five o'clock, Meg Larsen left the office at L Street

and retrieved her Jaguar from the building garage. McDowell had left
the office fifteen minutes earlier and was waiting outside, parked halfway down the block in his silver Audi. When Meg appeared, he followed discreetly behind as she drove out New Hampshire Avenue,
then onto Route 29, all the way to Silver Spring. She drove the car
into the garage of her apartment building off Georgia Avenue.

While Meg was upstairs, McDowell waited across the street, immobile in the front seat of his Audi, hoping she would emerge once more
that evening. He laughed that he was playing cub reporter, a stage he
had skipped in his career. He normally had no patience for such
details, leaving the workday trivia to Meg. Now he had to learn a
whole new pattern.

Almost an hour passed, the car radio alleviating some of his boredom, until he saw her. Meg's Jaguar was coming out of the apartment
house garage. The elegant lifestyle was obviously inconsistent with
her network salary. Could the money be coming from a source other
than a conveniently deceased aunt?

McDowell's first instinct was embarrassment. What if Meg should
catch him tailing her? His red hair and freckled complexion were
easy signposts. He'd die. But he pushed away the self-consciousness,
reminded of Hankins' perfidy.

The Jaguar was heading back toward Washington, McDowell following at a decent interval, trying to obscure his head behind the
wheel. The car kept moving south and west and had soon entered
Georgetown.

It was now six-fifteen. The winter light was dimming, the thin
cover of snow slicking the roads. Meg's car turned smoothly through
Georgetown's picturesque streets, until it slowed, then came to a stop
on one of the old community's finest blocks. A line of minor mansions
were stretched out in front of him. A large black and white colonial
house toward the middle of the block was the most impressive.

Fortunately McDowell saw the Jaguar slow in time. He came to an
abrupt halt half a block before. From where he was parked, he could
see her clearly. Meg left the car and walked to the lamppost on the
corner. She searched in her purse for an instant, then did a seemingly
inane thing. She slashed what looked like a crayon once across the
pole.

McDowell watched unbelieving as Meg returned to her car and
pulled away. The entire episode had taken only one minute.

What was that all about? He had no time to ponder, for Meg was now driving more quickly. She picked up the same route as before and was headed north and east, back toward Silver Spring, McDowell supposed.

He was right. He followed her to the city line, then directly to her apartment house. Meg parked the car on the street, but instead of entering her building she moved toward a pay phone across the road.

McDowell watched as Meg stood in the lighted glass compartment, immobile, the receiver still in its cradle. Her expression was frozen, her body calm. Three or four minutes later the phone rang. McDowell couldn't hear, but he could see Meg pick up the receiver and begin to speak. He looked at his watch. It was exactly seven o'clock.

The conversation lasted five minutes. Meg then crossed the street and disappeared into her apartment house. McDowell felt relieved that his suspicions were not an acute case of paranoia. Meg had made some sort of clandestine connection.

But with whom?

☆ ☆ ☆

"How are you this morning?" Meg asked, opening the next day at the network with her usual brightness.

McDowell winced. Typically, he perked up at her ebullience, even at the sight of her pert physique. But now, after the prior night, things were different. He still had no idea of what she was involved in, but the thought of Meg being a spy, perhaps for the KGB, tore at him.

"Oh, I'm fine, Meg. How about you?"

"Couldn't be better," she answered, and the more he stared at her, the more truthful it seemed. Meg's usual glow radiated stronger, her pinkish cheeks suffused with health, the gray-green eyes shining. Even her hair seemed to have gained in sheen.

McDowell was aware that ideologues often blossomed in danger, but this was a new contentment for Meg. He couldn't account for it.

His surveillance of her continued. The next night she returned to Georgetown and made the same crayon slash, followed by a phone call. It was from a different pay booth in Silver Spring, but the time was the same. Exactly at seven o'clock.

The following evening, when McDowell and Meg worked until 9 P.M., he was struck by an uneducated hunch that she might change her routine.

"Mind if I walk along with you?" McDowell asked Meg as they stood together on the sidewalk outside the L Street building.

Some of his motivation was real; he still found her attractive. But he could sense that he was learning to dissemble, paradoxically to use subterfuge to protect what little innocence he had left. Where was she headed tonight?

"That's nice of you, Doug. But I have a date," Meg said, kissing his cheek. She waved, then moved toward a standing taxi. "See you."

Fifty feet in the opposite direction, McDowell jumped into another cab.

"Like in the movies, Mac. Follow that taxi. Here's twenty dollars in advance."

The surveillance was short. Within minutes Meg's taxi pulled up at the West Wing entrance to the White House. He watched, stunned, as she got out and approached the guardhouse, apparently offering her name and ID. His taxi waited as Meg Larsen walked into the Executive Mansion to visit, he was sure, President Jedidiah B. Hankins.

McDowell had found the source of Meg's cheeriness. But he doubted that she was receiving phone calls in a pay booth from the President of the United States.

☆ ☆ ☆

Twice now Meg had marked the lamppost in Georgetown with a slash, then returned to Silver Spring to take a phone call at 7 P.M. If not the President, with whom was she communicating?

The next morning at nine McDowell walked into the seat of government for this unique city, the District of Columbia Building at 14th and Pennsylvania, across from the National Theater.

In Room 7 he approached a Board of Elections clerk.

"Could you please tell me where to find the Single Member District register for this area in Georgetown?" McDowell asked, showing the clerk the street intersection where Meg had marked the lamppost.

Within moments McDowell was poring over a list of all the registered voters on the block, searching for a name that would spark meaning. Perkins, Salzmann, Giannini, Lenox, Kensell, Tilden, Rausch.

Rausch? None of the names meant anything except Rausch. Walter Rausch? The producer of the convention documentary? Meg had interviewed him several times, once on camera. Could Rausch be her contact in Georgetown, the recipient of the graphic crayon messages?

That night McDowell dropped his surveillance of Meg and switched his attention to Rausch. Was there anything in his behavior that could tie them together?

McDowell drove from the studio to Georgetown and circled the block, searching for the lamppost signal. It was there, a single red slash, Meg's mark. She must have passed by during her lunch hour.

He parked the car at the end of the street, but close enough to observe the cast-iron stoop of Rausch's colonial mansion. McDowell waited in the Audi from five past six until six-forty, when he observed Rausch walking down the stairs. He decided to follow on foot, keeping a discreet distance behind.

When Rausch reached Wisconsin Avenue he entered a pay phone, dropped in some coins, and dialed. He began talking almost immediately. McDowell glanced at his watch. It was exactly seven o'clock.

It required less than the skill of an investigative reporter to figure it out. Walter Rausch was contacting his colleague, Meg Larsen, who was tied to him in some covert operation.

Could it actually be the KGB?

The situation was getting beyond his competence. He would have to reach John Davidson.

Chapter 76

In Clint Low's office at Operations, the clandestine division of the Agency, things had been devastatingly inactive. The only movement seemed to be men leaving, pushed into early retirement or transferred to nonsense work. All that was missing was the "going out of business" sign. He had lived through the 1970s, but they were innocent liberal purges by comparison.

That morning Low found his desk the way he had left it the night before. Except for a single piece of paper. It was neatly placed in the center of his desk, face down under a clear plastic paperweight.

Low picked it up, curious. Marked DUPLICATE. DO NOT RECOPY, it was from the Central American Desk and seemingly not intended for

him. He was about to move it into his Out box when he decided to
read it.

The memo was headed: MOVEMENT OF MIG-31s TO NICARAGUA.

Information received from sources in Black Sea ports, verified
by satellite pictures, indicates that 86 advanced MIG-31 fighters,
the Foxhound, have been dispatched by the Soviet Union to Nicaragua on Polish and Bulgarian freighters. An inventory list of
planes, spare parts, and ships involved follows below.

Who had placed the memo on his desk? It was surely no clerical
error. No, he had a friend somewhere in the Agency. But who? Barber was equally disgusted with the Administration, but he was too far
down the organizational pyramid to get his hands on such material. It
rested higher up, possibly someone who knew that he was in contact
with Davidson.

Whatever, Davidson could use the information in his guerrilla campaign against Hankins. He would make another trip to Leesburg tonight.

Low was feeling useful again after a month of despair. Why
couldn't everyone see that Hankins—or someone close to him in the
Oval Office—was a damn Red, out to destroy not only the Agency but
the nation? Were the people anesthetized?

He sometimes attributed it all to television. To the fear of any
hostilities, to see bodies mutilated on the screen, something the Soviet
public were never allowed to view despite their enormous casualties
in Afghanistan. To Americans, war of any nature, no matter how
brief or how small, had become the ultimate horror. Low was sure
that if the press had come along on the Grenada invasion and shown
even one American boy dying it too would have ended up as an unpopular move.

The child's chant in college came back to him. "Better Red than
dead." It had real meaning now. Hankins' appeasement had received
no great public acclaim, but there was a kind of resigned acceptance.
A cheaper, less painful way to face a dirty future. Not for him, but
was he already a breed apart? A political dinosaur at forty-eight?

That evening Low left his house in Arlington and took Leesburg
Pike to Davidson's farm. After alerting Davidson with the flashing
signal, they met in the shopping center. Davidson received Low's
missive joyously. As did Dulles, his Labrador, who relished the late
night rides in the back of the Volvo wagon.

"So the Communists are moving in modern jets to take all of Central America?" Davidson said. "Clint, we've got to make this public immediately. It'll make Hankins supposed 'hands off' policy look like the fakery it is. It's just what I need. Something to rub in Hankins' eyes. Maybe even something to wake up the public. Thanks, Clint."

☆ ☆ ☆

The following morning, Davidson decided, he would visit the Cosmos Club, then contact Doug McDowell. But he had to protect the newscaster from suspicion that he was carrying on a vendetta against the Oval Office. He would ask McDowell only to be a courier, to carry the information directly to Delafield in the Senate. The cagey ex-general would know how to get it on the air.

Chapter 77

"Tom, I feel like a charity case at the White House. As if the President hired me only because I was Marc's closest aide."

Ward and Les Fanning had just awakened in the double bed in his Massachusetts Avenue apartment. Lightly, he kissed her cheek.

He could see that Les had not been the same since Governor Daniels' death. Her manner was more subdued; she was more intimidated by daily life. Les had accepted the White House job to stay close to the center of politics—her right had Daniels lived. Now, she was complaining, she felt ill at ease in the Administration.

"Jed treats me so formally, like I was glass," Les explained. "I suppose it's survival guilt with him. He's alive, young, and President of the United States. Marc is just dead."

This woman's presence was something undecipherable, Ward decided. Never before had Captain Peter Semanski considered another person as almost as important as himself. Until he met Les, existence had been so reassuringly rational. Political direction. Advancement in the system. Actions. Rewards. Even failures. It was linear, clear and gradable.

He had never been an ideologue, never fantasized about the day of Marxist omnipotence. But he was proud of his professionalism, of doing his job in an orderly if somewhat detached way. He pursued his goals, one at a time, and liked being rewarded for excellence in what he did. It was a strange but seductively attractive line of work.

But existence now seemed less coherent. His liaison with Les spelled happiness, more than he had ever known. But it was not understandable. Perhaps, he thought, it was all too Western for him.

"Les, you're too smart for me to con you," Ward said, knowing that, for all her femininity, she resented being treated less than straightforwardly.

"There's no sense claiming that Hankins is Daniels, or that you'll ever again get such satisfaction from politics. But life can go on. You have a good job at the White House. And I hope it's important that you have me."

Les leaned closer, her body confirming confidence in him.

"It is important, Tom. But ever since Election Night, I haven't slept well. Do you think I did the right thing?"

It was almost four months since he and Hankins had conspired to withhold the truth—that Daniels had died a crucial half hour before the polling booths closed in California. But this was the first time Les had mentioned a word about it.

It was strange that Hankins owed his presidency to Les. She never said as much, but it was evident that, like Daniels, Les had never admired Jed Hankins. And now, only weeks into his administration, she seemed to like him less.

"You must understand, Tom, that I'm not proud of what we did," Les was saying. "It sort of bent the Constitution. Maybe Marc and Hankins would have been elected anyway, but maybe not."

Ward looked at Les, who seemed to be husbanding a secret, even from him.

"Tom, you know I never fully believed Jed when he told me he would act in Marc's place."

"Then why did you go along with his idea?" Ward asked, surprised.

"I've thought about that a lot, Tom. I think it was because of you. I trust you. You made it seem like a plausible act, and"—Les hesitated —"and I must confess I've sort of fantasized that you were privy to some information, maybe secret information, that I didn't have. That if you felt it was important I should naturally go along. As if—I know this sounds stupid—as if you were in the CIA, or somehow closer to the government. But now, I just don't know what to do."

Do? Ward's body snapped involuntarily. Did Les mean she was con-

templating doing something? Perhaps exposing the truth? It could
mean Hankins' impeachment. For him, it would be equally definitive.
Having to choose between Les and the Soviet Union.

Circumvent the question, Ward told himself.

"Les, you don't seem to like Hankins. Is there anything specific he's
done?"

"Well, yes and no. The unspecific is that he's always so polite to me,
and I think so false. Maybe now that he's President he has to be
careful. But I don't know. Personally he just seems so cold. You know
how I am, Tom. I like warm, easy people."

Les looked at Tom, suddenly uncomfortable in his tortuous double
role.

"You know, like you."

"I know, honey. But surely that's not the whole thing. What else
bothers you?"

"I suppose it's his politics too. A lot of people seem to like his peace
initiatives and all that disarmament. But Governor Daniels was never
one of them. And neither am I."

Les pondered for an instant. "I guess I don't think he's very patriotic. But I know that's not fair either. I suppose he's doing what he
thinks is right for the country. It's just that Marc would never do it
that way—be so soft on the Communists. Do you understand?"

He understood only too well. It had taken these months for Les's
critical faculties to revive. She had been in a defensive shell, leaning
on him for energy, for life. Now she was becoming her own person
again. And she didn't like what she saw around her at the White
House.

Ward cradled Les closer. What he was about to say had serpentine
motives. Some were to save, at all costs, the conspiracy he had helped
engineer. But another was to protect Les. It was part of a grand
delusion he had not yet interpreted—how to keep them together, forever. Maybe in some godforsaken neutral land, or on a distant planet
where the forces they represented didn't have to scorch each other to
death.

"Of course, I understand, Les. And I appreciate what you're going
through. But you must know that, in some strange way, I've taken
your place. I've sort of assumed the job with Hankins that you had
with Daniels. I'm not his assistant, but he calls me in to ask my
advice, and often takes it. I don't really know why, except that you

once told me I had good political instincts. I suppose Hankins agrees."

Ward knew what he had to say required exquisite care.

"Les . . ."

"Yes, Tom, what is it?"

He waited.

"I don't want to upset you, but there are things I can't tell you right now. I need you to trust me, implicitly. Later, I will tell you—everything. I swear it. Until then, could you please try to forget what happened on Election Night?"

Les looked up, a smile pressing through the pain.

"Tom, I don't know why you're asking me, but I'll be patient with you. You tell me when you can. Whatever it is, I promise I'll understand."

Ward knew she meant every syllable. But if she really knew the depth of his deceit, could she understand?

He doubted it.

Chapter 78

Colonel Baneyev could not make up his mind. He listened to the tape again, trying to arrange the pros and cons into some useful pattern. But the conclusion kept eluding him.

Rausch had delivered the latest batch of tapes from the bug implanted in Tom Ward's bedroom. Clever, he thought. It had been hidden in a hollowed-out rear bedpost next to where the couple made love.

Much of the conversation was titillating domestic pornography, which Baneyev found more stimulating than the artificial type in X-rated movies. In some ways, he did not believe in pornography. It overexercised him. But in his job as electronic eavesdropper on several prominent members of Washington's permissive society, he was inundated by it. Even afraid of becoming addicted to it.

Between the love gushes and anatomical directions in Ward's tapes, Baneyev had heard an alarming word. Leslie Fanning, one of the three people in the room the night of Daniels' death, had now raised the question of "doing" something with her crushing knowledge.

Hers were the only weak hands. Fenton and Hankins would be silent. The Center trusted Ward as much as they did himself. But Les Fanning could destroy the new administration and, with it, the hopes of STAND DOWN.

It was true, he had to admit, that Ward had successfully calmed her doubts with false promises. But as the Hankins administration continued its pro-Soviet policies, her antagonism and remorse were bound to mount. There was no assurance that Ward could always contain it.

What did Teshovich think? He touched the intercom.

"Sergeant, can you come in?"

Then, instantly, Baneyev reconsidered. "No, Alexei. Forget it. It's not important."

It would not do to call Teshovich in on every decision. As if his wisdom were necessary to the Wisconsin Avenue operation. In any case, he knew what the young man would say.

Yes. There was no more hesitation in his mind. Leslie Fanning would have to die.

Chapter 79

"Damn! Would you look at who's on television? I can't escape the SOB."

President Hankins was in the Oval Office, the console of three television receivers turned to the early morning news programs. With him were Bill Fenton and Ms. Holly, having coffee as they reviewed the agenda for the upcoming day. Hankins walked over and raised the volume on one channel.

A reporter was standing on the steps of the Capitol on this sunny winter day, his microphone in the ruddy face of Angus Delafield.

"Senator Delafield. I understand that you have some private information that could drastically change the Central American situation. Can you tell us about it?" the newsman asked.

"Here it is," Delafield said, waving the paper close to the camera to display the Agency seal. "A secret memo from the CIA Central American desk.

"Right now, eighty-six MIG-31 Foxhounds are in the bellies of Soviet satellite ships, scheduled to land any day in Nicaragua, at the Pacific port of Corinto. The pilots are trained and the planes will be stationed at the giant new military airfield at Punta Huete. Not only is the President doing nothing about it, but he has known about it all this time and has kept it a secret from the American people."

Delafield stared into the camera lens. "What I'd like to ask is, what's going on in this country? I don't know who leaked this one but, as far as I can see, only the leakers are watching out for the American people. That's all I have to say. For now."

Hankins' head dropped toward his coffee cup, then pulled up, his eyes fiery.

"God damn CIA!" Hankins' voice registered above the din of the television. "Even with our own people in charge, it's still a fascist sieve. That's what it is. A stinking Trojan horse in the Administration!"

The President turned to his assistant. "Maude, get me Miles on the horn."

At that instant the phone rang.

"It's the CIA director," Holly called out.

"Mr. President, I suppose you're watching the same damn show I am." Miles's casual Midwestern tone was now clipped. "I don't know what happened, sir. I stood there, right over the shoulder of the desk chief, while he shredded the memo. I suppose some son of a bitch made an uncontrolled copy."

"I'm not blaming you, Matt. But what do we do now?" Hankins asked, his tone deadened.

"As far as the Agency is concerned, I obviously have more housecleaning to do," Miles responded. "On the MIGs, I'd play it by saying that Delafield has hurt national security. We were secretly negotiating with the Soviet Union to take back the planes, but now Delafield's exposure has made that impossible. A matter of face for the Russians."

"I'll do that, Matt. It sounds reasonable. But please. No more leaks."

After Hankins hung up the phone, he caught Fenton's eye.

"I know, Bill. This wouldn't have happened if you were in charge of the CIA. Maybe not. Meanwhile, Delafield is having a field day."

☆ ☆ ☆

Fenton had been silent during the entire uproar, content to hold back his glee that the news about the MIGs had leaked. Now Hankins would have to stop his asinine shadowboxing and face the fact that the Soviet Union had become the dominant power in the world.

And in less than a week STAND DOWN would make that preeminence permanent.

Chapter 80

"Tom. I'm so pleased you could come to the house tonight. Here, give me your coat."

Rausch had asked Ward not to bring Les along for this combined business and social evening. Just the two of them and the Hungarian maid, who was part of Walter's apparatus.

In the dining room, all ten Chippendale chairs were in place. But the settings were absent except for two, one at either end of the impressive eighteenth-century oak table. It was set formally, with heavy Georgian silverware and Walter's antique Wedgwood china. Ward had seen it used only once before, at a dinner for the governor of Virginia. Alongside was a sculptured silver champagne bucket of enormous weight.

The cast of the room was somewhat strange, Ward thought. Just the two of them amid such old finery and emptiness. Why?

"Please, Tom. Eat hearty," Rausch insisted as they began.

During dinner, served impeccably by the brunette Hungarian maid, reputedly his mistress, Rausch spoke only of Washington gossip and simple things. There was no mention of work as the two colleagues devoured a tureen of duck soup, a fine veal roast, and Austrian pastries.

When the meal was over Rausch offered Ward an Upmann Havana cigar. The men relaxed with the smoke for a few minutes.

"Why don't we go into the study for our liqueur?" Rausch asked.

Seated in front of a quiet fire, they looked not unlike two English Edwardian gentlemen, surely not plotting world revolution. At a wave, the Hungarian maid brought in a fine cognac, a seventy-seven-year-old Moullon.

"Tom, first, I want you to know how much the Center thinks of your work," Rausch began.

There was, Ward suspected, a touch of uncommon insincerity in Rausch's manner. One that was usually direct.

"I have been asked to pass on some extraordinary news," he continued.

"At age thirty-three, you've been promoted to a full major in both the SB and KGB. They tell me it's almost unprecedented. I no longer outrank you, my friend. It means that on your return you'll be given a driver and a car, and privileges that go with the rank. In any case, that means little here. You are far from underprivileged. What is most important is recognition of your work for the Soviet Union. It is appreciated."

Ward felt uncomfortable. It was good news, but did it merit such an extravaganza?

"Walter, it's nice of you to put on such a feast to celebrate my promotion. But you know how I feel. No sacrifice is too much for the cause."

Ward had meant it as a platitude expected of KGB officers, but he sensed that Rausch took it as sincere.

"I'm so glad you said that, Tom," Rausch responded, breaking into a full smile. "I told Baneyev you'd react that way. That nothing—nothing—is too much to ask of you."

Ward was now certain the sumptuous repast had its price. The Center wanted something of him, probably something excessive. What could it be?

"I'm listening, Walter. What is it?"

"I'm going to give you a piece of paper, Tom. Orders directly from the Center. It's not good. But it is beyond our criticism."

Rausch held it back for a second. "Here."

Ward could see Rausch's eyes edge away as he handed him the dispatch. It was written on code paper in Walter's clear block letters.

Ward instantly absorbed the words. He bent over, placing his head between his knees.

"Tom, are you all right?"

Rausch placed his arm around Ward's bent shoulders.

"It's cruel, I know. But these are hazardous times," Rausch said. "We have little right to our own lives. No?"

Ward pulled his head back up and read the dispatch again. It was only a few lines, but it would reorder—no, destroy—his existence.

LES FANNING IS ONLY ONE OUTSIDE APPARATUS WHO KNOWS DANIELS' DEATH WAS COVERED UP PRIOR TO CLOSING OF POLLS. NEW EVIDENCE INDICATES SHE IS WEAKENING. COULD INCRIMINATE YEARLING BEYOND REPAIR. IRONMAN IS TO KILL FANNING. SOONEST. THE CENTER.

Kill Les? Ward had no voice. He had not come to dinner expecting such finality.

"Tom, I know it's horrible." Rausch seemed truly moved. "But someone must do it. I have a thought. I'll break cover and speak to Baneyev personally. I can't stop the order, but maybe I can convince him to get someone else for the job. One of our professionals, someone without feeling. Les would prefer it that way, too."

Rausch lifted Ward's head. "What do you say? That's a better way. Am I right?"

Ward was trying to push through, to first decipher what Rausch had said before responding.

Someone else kill Les? No. Then he would have no control. He had to be the one to do it. Or to stop it. In his hands, there was some hope. Later, he could think. Now, the energy was needed to fend off Rausch's idea yet retain him as an ally.

"Walter, I appreciate that. But you must see that this is something only I can do. I will insure that it is painless. Leave that to me. I have been well trained."

Rausch seemed pleased, if somewhat surprised, that Ward had finally taken it so bravely.

"Good. Then we will speak no more of this unpleasantness. To your promotion, Major Semanski. And many, many more."

Chapter 81

From his rented Ford parked on New Hampshire Avenue, Sergeant Fuller could see into the second-floor apartment window of Les Fanning's brownstone. Her face, occasionally the top portion of her body, surfaced as she looked out the window at the heavy rain or moved between the kitchen and the living room.

There was no sign of Ward. He hadn't shown for three days at his own Massachusetts Avenue apartment, where Fuller had run a virtual round-the-clock stakeout. Boredom had finally paid off. Fuller decided to give it up. Ward had obviously moved somewhere else. But where? He had taken down the limousine's plate number, but that had been a dead end. The stretch car belonged to a leasing service that refused to divulge the client's name.

Fuller's frustration was increased by Radofsky, who had tried to close off the apartment house to him. The super was convinced that Fuller would spoil the FBI's investigation with his provincial police work and had warned neighbors not to speak to the California cop. Almost everyone listened to Radofsky, slamming the door in Fuller's face.

But down the hall, in 11J, one matron felt obligated to talk.

"You mean that man with the pointy nose in 11A?" she asked Fuller. "Oh, he seems okay. But he has a girl friend. You can't tell if she lives here or what. Always coming in with clothes to put on, then leaves again with a bag. Then comes back. I don't like the whole thing. Her name? Les. Les Fanning, I think. You won't believe it, but she works in the White House. Some business. A hussy like that with the President."

Fanning's address was in the phone book. Fuller, who maintained an unlisted number in California, believed people were too free with their addresses. But of course it made his job easier.

Fuller had arrived at the stakeout of Les's place on New Hampshire Avenue just two hours before. He could barely see through the rain, except near the street lamp, which was shining a soft circle of light in front of the brownstone stairs.

It was 10:20 P.M. If patterns repeated in life, it was that men hid out with their girl friends. It made no sense, but life was like that. Even in desperation, men liked their comfort, or their sex, or both. He knew that this time, if he waited him out, Ward would show.

It happened that very minute. At first Fuller didn't realize it because he was diverted by a near accident. A taxi stopped on his side of the street and a man got out. Fuller couldn't see his face. The man started to walk across the street toward the brownstone, but he was unsteady, not even looking as he went. Maybe drunk, Fuller thought.

A car suddenly turned the corner and came right toward him. The

man started to run out of the way but, as he did, he slipped on the wet
pavement, landing on his side just as the car screeched to a stop not
more than ten inches from his head. The man got up, waved the car
away, then started up the stairs, still groggy. As he stopped to ring
the bell, Fuller saw.

It was Ward. Wet, a morose expression on his face, brushing the
dirt off his coat, a tan British "warm." But it was Ward. Like all men,
he had returned to his natural habitat.

Fuller knew that it was too late to take him now. Ward was already
entering the building, and as Radofsky had reminded him, he had no
warrant. But he intended to snare Ward later, probably at the point of
a gun. Then hold him, either illegally or in a Washington jail, on some
trumped-up charge.

Astinof at the FBI had warned that nobody could touch the man in
the picture. He would change their minds.

☆ ☆ ☆

"My God, Tom. What happened? I saw it out the window. You
were almost hit by that car."

Les was seeking to calm herself. "Take off your coat. You're soak-
ing. Sit in front of the fire and I'll get you a brandy."

She stepped back and stared at Ward's face, which was strangely
discolored.

"Tom, you look terrible. What in the world happened at Walter's?"
Les was suddenly laughing softly. "I told you it was dangerous to go
anywhere without me."

Ward kissed her, but without a word. Once his coat and jacket were
off, he started to circumvent the room, his hand searching out every
cranny. Ward upended table lamps, forced his hand into the back of
bookcases, probing. Finally, using a small table as a ladder, he stood
up and felt about in the chandelier fixture.

Les stood by, her eyes displaying bewilderment.

"Tom, what in the world are you looking for? What's going on?"

He took Les's hand and led her to the couch, where they sat in
front of the fireplace.

"I was looking for recording devices—bugs. I found out that they
were bugging my apartment, and I was afraid they were doing the
same here. But I think the room is clean."

"Who is 'they'? What in the world are you talking about, Tom? I
swear, honey, you sound a little crazy."

"I wish that's all it was. Les, you remember a few days ago, you were worried about what had happened Election Night?"

Les nodded.

"I told you to trust me. That I would tell you everything at the right time. Well, this is the time. I have a lot to get off my mind. A lot."

He knew there was no beginning that would soften his story, a sordid tale that he had shaped into a life. An agent hired as an ideologue to kill and lie. Whatever was needed to advance the cause of two theoreticians.

One from Freiburg in Germany, whose father ran a small department store and who practiced much of his revolutionary trade in the bookish confines of the British Museum in London. The other a Russian, also from a solid bourgeois family, who had studied to be a lawyer and who envisioned a different kind of world. They had never met, but their names were now hyphenated together everywhere, like a modern married woman. Marxism-Leninism. Lives and honor were sacrificed in their names.

And now his own assignment—to kill Les. What could he possibly tell her that could explain him?

"Darling, few things are what they appear to be," Ward began, forcing himself to look at her. "Only one thing in what I'm going to say is constant. It's that I love you. Having said that, I must tell you that everything else, since we first met, has been a lie."

Small tears were forming in Les's eyes, but she was still holding his hand, even drawing it a little closer.

"Before we met at Walter's party, I didn't know you existed. You weren't part of my assignment. But as things went on, your importance in American politics, and the job I was given, made your friendship vital to my work. I would have stayed with you whether I wanted you or not. But I did want you. So my job became easy.

"The lies were many. I am not a simple American with little politics. I am a totally politicized person, but a stranger to your ways. Les, I am the worst in your eyes. My real name is not Tom Ward. I am Polish. Major Peter Semanski. I am an agent of the Soviet Union."

Les's hand was now limp, dropping away from Ward's. The tears that had been slowly forming became incessant. Unable to speak, she looked at Tom with puzzlement, then crossed the room, staring into the mirror over the fireplace, finding him in the reflection.

Finally Les spoke.

"To think that I trusted you. Even, I suppose, committed perjury for you by protecting Hankins. All because I somehow thought you knew something—something that would benefit the country. In my fantasy, you were a patriotic hero, perhaps CIA. And . . . and all this time you were KGB. What an idiot I've been."

Les turned away from the mirror and addressed Ward to his face.

"Why tell me this now, Tom? You could have continued the masquerade and gotten away with it for a long time. Why risk exposure by telling me?"

"Because you're in danger, Les. The dinner at Walter's was a macabre play. He's KGB as well. By listening in at my apartment, they heard that you were worried about what you had done on Election Night. They're afraid you're going to talk."

Ward pulled Les gently over and sat her down in a chair. At her feet, he explained everything—Oval Red, Hankins' treason, Rausch's apparatus, Baneyev, his own role as Tom Ward, supposed American and Kremlin contact with the Red President. He held back nothing, except the two murders—one committed on orders, the other, he presumed, in self-defense. She would never understand either, he knew.

As Les listened, her tears started to dry. Ward could see that she was steeling herself to the truth, her mind perhaps moving back to the magnificence that had been, only a half hour ago.

"Tom, I can't handle it all. Just tell me. In what way am I in danger?"

"That's what the dinner at Walter's was all about, Les. Nothing is too much for them to ask. Walter gave me my new assignment."

"Yes?" Les asked. "And?"

"And, darling, I am to kill you."

He gagged as the words left him, but he couldn't take them back.

Les placed her hand over her mouth and started to cry in muffled gasps, lacking the strength to let it all out. Ward rose from the floor and placed a sheltering arm around her. But she moved it away.

"Rausch said that if I wouldn't do it he would get Baneyev to use a professional. But I pretended I had to do it myself. To save you the pain."

Les's sobbing was now staccato, her eyes on him like an imploring child.

"Tom. Are you going to kill me?"

Ward brushed aside any fear of her anger and grabbed Les in his arms, kissing her on the cheek, holding up the palms of her hands, kissing them as well.

"I would first kill them all and myself, Les. Why do you think I've told you everything? Because I am finished with them. Now I have to find a way to protect you, and maybe me as well. If there's still some chance for us together. But now only with the truth."

She was still sobbing haltingly. "What shall I call you? Is Tom dead? Are you back to Peter? Is it . . . what . . . Semanski? It's so strange for someone you've loved to have two names, two lives."

"I'm still Tom Ward. And I will be from now on. I'm going to defect, Les. Seek political asylum. Then I'll find a way to protect you."

Les broke out in a laugh, the irony of the situation suddenly striking her.

"Defect? To whom? Have you forgotten? Your people are now in charge at the White House. At the CIA too, from what you tell me. If you approach the authorities and ask for asylum, they'll only turn you over to Baneyev. And they'll get me as well. No, Tom. For the first time since I've known you, you're not thinking."

Tom's laugh was spontaneous. "I always suspected you were smarter than I, Les. You would have made a great agent."

Suddenly, he could see the stirrings of a new reality in Les's eyes. Not as natural as before, but at least with a residue of affection.

"Les, there must be someone who can help us. Someone who'll take us in. As soon as we've disappeared, Baneyev will be after us both. I could leave, but they mean to kill you, with or without me. Think. Is there someone you know—maybe from the Daniels campaign—who would risk helping us? Perhaps to get away to Canada, or Europe?"

Then he answered himself. "No. Out of the country is no good. I have no passport. They made sure of that."

"Tom, let's get something straight." Les seemed to be regaining her alertness. "I'll go with you, as much to save myself as anything else. But don't think for a minute that I've forgiven you, or even trust you fully. Let's just consider it a necessary partnership. Love is something else. We'll worry about that later—if at all. Do you understand?"

"I understand, Les. Any way you want it is all right with me. Now, put on your thinking cap."

"I know someone we can trust," Les said. "At the end of the campaign, a former CIA man, John Davidson, came to see Governor Daniels. He had some big secret about national security. They couldn't tell me then, but it must have been about Hankins. After Davidson left, the governor said that Davidson was a real patriot. I spoke with Davidson just before he went home. We were chatting about his dairy farm. It's in Leesburg, right off the Pike. Why don't we go there? I don't know what else to do."

Ward reached over to kiss Les, but she motioned him away.

"All right, Les. Leesburg it is. We'll go in your car."

Chapter 82

Fuller felt lucky. He had been waiting only an hour in the miserable dampness when through the misted car window he could make out Ward and his girl friend coming down the brownstone stairs. Ward was carrying a bag, on their way across the street toward a blue Honda station wagon, parked only two down from him.

The detective sank deep into his seat, convinced Ward knew someone was after him. The bag was a sign he intended to make a break for it, possibly to the airport. Perhaps he could arrest Ward there. The California badge was not holy in Washington, but the old detective's bluff might work. For now, he would track them and see where they were headed.

Fuller followed as the Honda turned toward Georgetown, then over the Key Bridge. It was difficult tailing in the rain, the wipers obscuring the subtleties of vision. But Fuller knew it was equally difficult to notice a tail, to distinguish the blurred lights behind as belonging to any specific car.

Once on the Virginia side of the Potomac, he could tell that they weren't headed toward National Airport. The car was traveling in the opposite direction, west into Virginia. Perhaps Dulles Airport. He had come in that way himself. But when they finally turned off onto VA 7, Leesburg Pike, he realized Dulles was not their goal. But where?

Fuller held back a couple of cars, in the center lane, hoping not to alert them. After another twenty minutes of painfully slow driving, the Honda hugging the right-hand side, there was still no sign of change. Just more rain and concentration on the wet pavement.

His mind was off the Honda only for seconds. But when he glanced again to his right the car was gone. Where? He pushed the accelerator to catch the fleeing little wagon, but after two miles at 80 mph, there was still no sign of Ward and his girl friend. He must have taken his eyes off the road just long enough for the Honda to leave the Pike, unnoticed.

Fuller exited the Pike, quickly turned a double left, and got back on, driving in the opposite direction. He scrutinized his odometer, then repeated the two miles before leaving the Pike himself. This fellow Ward was not stupid, Fuller could see. Even if unaware of a tail, he hadn't turned on his right directional blinkers as a habit of caution.

Fuller now had to scour the countryside for a blue Honda station wagon. Was it possible in the damn rain? On the right side of the Pike, he picked up a small road headed south. He had gone only a few hundred yards when he saw a house up ahead.

Where was he? The only sign was a farmer's ID. DAVIDSON'S COWS, it said, atop a well-drawn picture of a smiling calf. If this was where they had come, what were they doing at a dairy farm?

Fuller parked the car where he had stopped, doused the lights, and walked out into the mud, his collar up and without boots. His foot pressed a deep imprint into a pile of soggy cow dung. He cursed a little, then walked on. No one had ever promised a cop a rose garden. Or even a decent job.

Through the rain, he could make out the outlines of the large white farmhouse, the cloudy illumination from its windows shining on the driveway. There were two cars parked side by side. One was a dark green Volvo station wagon. The other was the Honda. He had found Ward and his girl friend.

But first, Fuller decided, it made sense to get back into his car. Put on the heater and dry out as he tried to develop a strategy on how to take Ward back to California.

Chapter 83

Presidential Chief of Staff William Fenton could not sleep. He had not been home to his small apartment in a middle-income housing project in the old southeast behind the Capitol. The leather couch in the cranny adjacent to the Oval Office was his bed, unmade, without sheets, just a resting spot for his frenzied mind.

Contradictions. It was 2 A.M., and all he could think about was contradictions. The hours of tossing had produced one conclusion: he had fallen into an intellectual trap in his view of Hankins. As a Marxist-Leninist, Fenton had been taught to understand and use contradictions. Instead he had reacted to them. They had used him.

Fenton decided to get up. He smoothed his wrinkled pants, put on his jacket and tie, and wandered out to the West Gate. No one except the guards was in sight. In the dim light, the White House looked austere, even forbidding.

"Working real late, eh, Mr. Fenton?" the guard offered, touching his cap in an informal salute.

"Yeh. Time to go home," Fenton responded.

Coatless, he strolled out on the street, closing his jacket collar over his neck in the cold. He was not headed home but down Pennsylvania Avenue. About six or seven blocks south toward the Capitol, then over to the east, he recalled, there was an all-night eatery he had occasionally frequented when he was a Senate AA. It was a working-man's place. Nobody would recognize him there. Or care if they did.

"What'll yah have, dearie?" The waitress handed him a menu, which Fenton promptly returned.

"Just some coffee, black, and toast. No butter, please."

He stared at the dirty white tile walls and at the floor, probably unmopped in days, and thought about his dilemma.

Hankins' peevishness at the Soviet Union was a contradiction. Jed should not have reacted angrily, as he did on the MIG-31s and Kambula. He was proudly jousting as the President of a sovereign United States, forgetting that his true obligation was to strengthen the worldwide Soviet revolution.

But Hankins had reacted humanly, and pettily, instead of dogmatically.

That contradiction was a failing on Hankins' part. But now, Fenton was coming to realize, it was he, Fenton, who was personally endangering STAND DOWN. By reacting to Hankins' anger, instead of using it. By resisting contradictions, as Americans always did.

STAND DOWN was the culmination of his dream, the capitulation of America to the Soviet Union. Americans would call it "nuclear blackmail," but it was simply the recognition of superior determination and proper use of national resources to ensure victory. Theoretically, America was even better equipped for victory. But it had no resolve. No backbone. That was one of the reasons he hated the country. A nation of spoiled children.

With America's surrender would come peace, the hegemony of Russia over a worldwide collective. But to make that dream come true, Fenton would have to make sure that on the day of STAND DOWN Hankins would be his ally. His friend. His tool. Not a peevish and truculent American politician.

But how could he use the American Marxist President when that President had the delusion that he had to maintain some American "sovereign" power?

Fenton sipped the hot coffee slowly through his teeth. He had the answer. It was not the same one he would have come up with even hours before. But he was sure it was the correct one.

"Anything else, dearie?" the waitress asked.

"No. The check, please."

Fenton knew where he had to go. By taxi, to Bethesda. He had to wake Marge Coulton in the middle of the night.

☆ ☆ ☆

At 3 A.M. Marge Coulton woke when the bell rang, hard. Her apartment was upstairs in the two-family house, reached by a private entrance.

Marge looked through the closed bedroom window at the clouded outlines of a man in the street below. As she focused, she could make out Fenton's ministerial face and his tortoise-rimmed glasses.

She moved quickly to her dressing table, straining to smooth out her sleep-matted hair. She knew Fenton had not come calling for sex, even at this hour. But perhaps she could attract him, find his defenses lower at this time of night. Smoothing her nightgown, Marge slipped on a robe. Her hair. If only it wasn't so stringy. She ran a comb through it anxiously, then stopped. It was hopeless, she decided, to try to look good for Fenton so quickly. More than that would be needed to divert him from his true passion, anyway.

Marge walked down the stairway to let him in.

"Marge, please forgive me. I wouldn't bother you if it wasn't urgent," Fenton said in greeting.

Upstairs, Coulton served him a cup of coffee, thinking how much she admired this resolute man.

"I'm sorry I woke you," Fenton apologized. "But I have to reach Colonel Baneyev right away, and you're my only contact."

Marge was suddenly hesitant, almost disapproving.

"Bill, I got hell the last time I arranged a meeting. Baneyev got feedback from Orlov in Moscow that you were being reckless. Baneyev said not to do it again, unless it's extremely urgent. What's up?"

"It's not something I can talk about, Marge, but believe me it's urgent. You've got to make contact for me. Everything depends on it."

"When do you want to see him?"

"Tonight. Otherwise, I wouldn't have woken you. It's now three. No later than five this morning. Every minute could be crucial. Do you have any way of reaching him quickly?"

"It'll take at least a day for a drop. But there is one emergency way," Marge responded. "Are you sure it's urgent?"

Fenton nodded, twice.

Marge picked up the phone and dialed a local number. It rang at the bedside of Colonel Baneyev, in bed with his wife.

"Nicky." His sleepy wife poked his side. "The phone."

He struggled over to the receiver. "Yes. Who is this?"

"Mr. Taft," Marge answered. Then hung up abruptly.

Coulton turned to Fenton, who looked confused.

"Don't worry, Bill. It's a foolproof system. The FBI tracks all incoming calls to the Soviet Embassy, but they can't trace a call that quickly. Now, Baneyev knows to reach me. We have to go into town, to a pay phone near the post office. He'll call us there from his safe phone in exactly forty minutes. What time is it now?"

She looked at her watch. "Three-eleven. Okay? We've got about twenty minutes before we have to leave. Want some more coffee?"

Marge couldn't reproach herself for this last try at Fenton. She took off her robe and moved closer to him, pressing her body into his. At first his eyes opened wide, surprised at her quick change of demeanor. Then, perhaps as an aftereffect of no sleep, his discipline vanished.

She led him into the bedroom.

☆   ☆   ☆

The meeting was set for four forty-five in the morning at a marina on the Anacostia River in the southeast quadrant of Washington. The dock was empty, the early morning air foggy and chill. Fenton had borrowed Marge's car, which he parked in the near-empty lot. He could see Baneyev's silver Volvo, already there.

At the end of the dock, he could make out the strange, thin visage of the colonel, his milky skin reflecting the glow of a small stern light from a nearby boat.

"Colonel, thank you for coming."

Fenton could see the annoyance on Baneyev's expressive face. He would have to make his case strongly.

"Yes, it's a major emergency, Colonel. Otherwise I would never have risked it."

"What, Mr. Fenton, could be important enough for a meeting before five in the morning? Please tell me."

"It's the MIGs for Nicaragua. Where are they right now?"

"You know as well as I do. They are in the freighters on their way. In fact, they will arrive later today at Corinto. Why?"

"I was afraid of that."

Fenton's hunch that he hadn't been acting impetuously, scurrying about in the middle of the night, was being borne out.

"Colonel. You must radio Moscow immediately. The ships have to be turned around. The MIGs have to go back to the Soviet Union."

"Mr. Fenton, you sound like a madman. We have made a mutual alliance treaty with our friends in Nicaragua. We have appropriated the money, secured the ships, placed the planes aboard. They have been at sea for over two weeks and will arrive in about five hours. And now, at five in the morning, in a deserted boatyard, you want me to rush back to the embassy, call the Kremlin to tell them to turn the ships around and send them back? They will think me as mad as you."

Fenton knew he couldn't make his case too strongly.

"Colonel, a lot more depends on what I'm telling you than MIGs for Nicaragua. The fate of STAND DOWN, of ultimate victory, is involved. When we met before, I warned you a little about Hankins. But, frankly, I was holding back. The truth is that he feels affronted. The MIGs are a symbol that he's being treated like a satellite already. He's convinced that Central America will fall to Nicaragua and the guerrillas, with or without the MIGs."

In the dim light, Fenton could make out the surprise clouding Baneyev's face.

"He may or may not be right," Fenton continued. "But that's not the point. It's what's in his mind. I never understood that until tonight. If those planes land tomorrow, we'll probably have lost him for STAND DOWN. But if he sees that his warnings to Ward have been listened to—that the General Secretary respects him—then I think I can get him to do anything. Otherwise, I guarantee nothing. Do you understand?"

"Mr. Fenton. You are never unclear. We have come far with your help. I presume you know the President better than anyone. I don't believe Moscow felt it was all that important. But if you say so . . ."

"Colonel, it's all-important. Please tell that to Moscow. We have only one week before STAND DOWN."

"I will see what I can do, Mr. Taft. I'd better hurry back. Whatever happens, we have only a few hours left on the MIGs."

As Baneyev returned to his silver Volvo, Fenton thought about March 15. The Ides of March. Psychologically the darkest days of winter, before the warming rays of April. It was opportune. If Baneyev succeeded, America would never know another free spring.

☆　☆　☆

At 5:30 A.M., Baneyev's car stopped in front of the iron gate, the entrance to the Soviet Embassy compound on Tunlaw Road.

Across the street, Sam Withers was rising from three stolen hours of sleep, beginning another twenty-one-hour vigil. His last surveillance in the Metro had failed, but perhaps Baneyev would offer him another chance by leaving his lair.

Sam poured himself a cup of black coffee and moved to the window to observe in the dawning light. He could not believe his luck. There was Baneyev's silver car, ready to back out of the compound! Withers began the motions of strapping on his gun, beginning his movement toward the door, when he stopped, as if in a quick-freeze double take.

He stared again. The embassy gate was opening. Baneyev's car was going in. He was returning from a trip, not going out! Withers cursed. He had slept through a middle-of-the-night liaison from which Baneyev would never have returned.

Disgusted with himself, Withers loosened his gun and returned to the window.

Chapter 84

"Mr. Davidson, we would have called first, but your phone number is unlisted. We're lucky we found the place at all. You told me it was off the Pike, but without that cute sign of yours, I wouldn't have found it."

"Come inside, young woman, and bring your friend," Davidson responded warmly to the drenched couple at his front door. "Let's adjourn to the fireplace. You can tell me what this is all about as soon as you dry out."

Les Fanning was welcomed by the ex-CIA man, who remembered the pleasant young woman from their chat at Governor Daniels' suite in Phoenix, in happier times for the Republic. With their soaked outer clothes off, Ward and Les stood by the fire, hot drinks in hand, as Davidson curiously awaited an explanation. He only knew that Les had been working at the White House since the Hankins inauguration. The slim black-haired man with her he didn't know at all.

Why had they come to visit on such a miserable night?

"Mr. Davidson, I want you to meet a friend of mine. He's . . ." Les was struggling for the right identity.

"Mr. Tom Ward," she finally said. "He's been working with President Hankins." She stopped again. "Sort of unofficially."

"Les, I've got to interrupt you." Ward spoke up sharply. "Mr. Davidson, to save us time I'll drop all pretense. I am Major Peter Semanski of the KGB. I've been assigned to the United States as an illegal, under the name of Tom Ward. For the last months I have been the major contact to President Hankins from the Kremlin."

Davidson, veteran of the unexpected, smiled. So this was the young man he heard had been dispatched by the Center to deal with the Red

President? He might also be part of Walter Rausch's apparatus, which
Barber and Low were now investigating.

"Mr. Ward—or Major Semanski. What on earth are you doing here,
telling me this? You must know I'm an enemy of both the Soviet
Union and the present American government."

"Les has told me. That's why we are here. I want to defect, but I'm
in an embarrassing position. I have no American official I can turn to.
If I try for political asylum, Fenton will turn me right over to
Baneyev at the Soviet Embassy. I'll either be killed or sent to Moscow
in irons. Les thought you might be able to help."

Ward looked at Davidson, hopeful. "I'd like to defect to you. We
don't know what else to do."

"I'm honored, young man. But what can I do? I'm only a private
citizen."

Les had been silent during the whole exchange, listening impatiently.

"Mr. Davidson, don't you understand? We need help! Desperately!
We need someplace to hide out and someone to give our information
to. It must be important. Because of it, Tom was assigned to kill me.
That's why he's defecting. Mainly—am I right, Tom?—to protect me
from the KGB. Now they'll be looking to kill us both. Do you understand now?"

Davidson was embarrassed. He had been handling the couple like
casual Sunday-after-church visitors.

"Miss Fanning. I can't imagine what you could know that would
warrant killing you. But I'm willing to hear. Let's sit down. Start all
over again and tell me everything."

From his parked car at the end of the broken asphalt road, Sergeant
Fuller could see into the window of the farmhouse. The trio were
standing against the fireplace, the room lit only faintly by the glow.
He couldn't make out their faces, but it was obviously Ward, Les
Fanning, and an older man, probably the Davidson in the cow sign,
whoever that was.

Until someone moved, observing from the car was all he could do.
They stood for a while, then sat down and seemed to be in animated
conversation. Fuller watched patiently for fifteen minutes, until all
three rose together. His eyes followed them out of the room, then
through the front door.

By focusing on the spot of light thrown off by their torch, he could see the trio move across the grass. The rain had stopped and in the moonlight Fuller could tell they were entering what looked like a cow barn.

☆ ☆ ☆

"Les, I think this should do nicely," Davidson said. "At least until I can figure out a more permanent place to hide you."

Davidson was showing the couple a small apartment in the upper rear of the barn, reached by a side ladder. It was a finished room with a small kitchen and a bath.

"It was built for my maid, but she passed away after being with me for forty-one years. I never got used to the idea of hiring anyone else. So I do what little cooking an old widower needs. But I think the room should do, at least for now."

Les seemed touched by his soft hospitality. "Mr. Davidson. We have to thank you for so much. For this room. And for hope."

"Don't be premature, Les. But your story of what happened on Election Night is the best news I've had in months. It's absolute grounds for an impeachment. But I don't want to put this country through another trauma unless I have to. And we don't even have a Vice-President. First I'm going to use a little political blackmail on Hankins. Meanwhile, we have to protect you from Colonel Baneyev. Les, now you're precious not only to Mr. Ward but to the Republic as well."

Davidson turned to Ward.

"And, Major Semanski, I admire your courage in defecting. Or at least in wanting to. But I've thought it through. You're much more valuable to us if you still appear to be with them. A double agent of sorts. You'll have to invent a story why you haven't killed Les yet. Perhaps she's away at an aunt's place in Colorado and will return on the weekend. Or whatever. Assure them you'll do it then. With your record, and with you personally present in Washington, they'll believe you. You can stay here tonight. Then tomorrow morning you should get back to the city. What do you think?"

The prospect of spying on his former colleagues was not appealing to Ward. But anything that would advance his new life and protect Les made sense.

"It's fine, Mr. Davidson. I don't mind working for you, but I must

ask one thing. I won't betray my contact in the Washington apparatus. You can have me, but only me."

As an intelligence professional, he hoped Davidson would be em-
pathic.

"I understand, Major Semanski. We'll leave it at that," Davidson
agreed.

Davidson waved his hand in a parting gesture. "Good night," he
said, moving out of the room and down the ladder.

From his car, Fuller could see the disembodied light leave the barn.
As it reached the front door of the farmhouse, Fuller could make out
only one person. The other two had apparently stayed inside.

With his police revolver and handcuffs, Fuller started toward the
barn, hugging the sides of the trees in case the older man was watching from the window. In less than two minutes, Fuller was at the
barn door. It was unlocked and squeaked as he entered. He could hear
voices upstairs, but no one seemed to be aware of his presence. Moving through, he stared at the sleeping cows, who, unlike horses, were
lying down, most with their eyes closed. Those that were awake ignored his soft progress across the straw-covered floor. He passed the
stalls and kept moving toward the ladder at the far end of the barn,
the source of the animated voices.

Fuller could hear Ward and his girl friend talking. The sound was a
little muffled, but he could make out the conversation.

"Tom. I feel like a character in an old Barbara Stanwyck movie,"
Les was saying. "Do you think there's any decent end to it? Won't
Colonel Baneyev find us here right away?"

"I don't think the KGB will be looking for us so soon, Les," Ward
commented as he unpacked their bag. "As Mr. Davidson said, they
trust me. They shouldn't become suspicious for forty-eight hours, but
I'll be back there tomorrow morning. So far so good."

Ward became pensive. "You know, Les, you made the right choice
in Davidson. Now I remember hearing about him in Moscow. He
was legendary in the KGB, an adversary to reckon with, everyone
said. They call him 'The Baptist.' He seems so simple—and old—but
I'm sure he knows just what he's doing."

Staring at Les, seated at the edge of the bed, undressing, Ward weighed the unpredictable turn his life had taken. So rapid, so over-whelming and inexorable. And all for a woman, the one area in which he felt invulnerable. Or was it all Les? Hadn't he been yielding to the attractiveness of a life without rigidity, with passions not generated by an addiction to danger? Or to an ideology? Whatever, he was here.

"Les, it may sound like a rationalization," Ward said, "but in a strange way my horrible assignment may give us our only chance to escape together. I was learning to enjoy this country and having my doubts about the Soviets. But what triggered my leaving was you."

Les got off the bed and in her underclothes approached Ward, both arms circling his neck.

"Tom darling. I know it's a nightmare, but it's better sharing it with you."

Ward kissed her, then moved to touch her body, leaning Les down slowly toward the bed.

Fuller had been climbing the ladder and was now at the landing, futilely trying to hide his large frame behind a four-by-four, staring at the couple through the open door to the small apartment. Gun stretched in front of him, he walked toward the room, a measured step following another.

Eeewww. An old floorboard groaned beneath his shoe.

"What's that?" Ward asked.

He didn't wait for an answer. In a reflex, Ward jumped off the bed and was racing across the room toward the sound. But before he reached the doorway Fuller was inside, his gun leveled at Ward's head.

"Don't move, Ward!" Fuller then waved his gun at Les, whose half-dressed body was quaking. "Get over there with him."

Les stared at the scene. Here, in the almost sweet solitude of an escape, Baneyev had found them so quickly.

"Don't kill him!" she called out. "He wasn't running away. He was going to kill me like you wanted!"

"I don't know what you're talking about, lady." Fuller's expression was dazed. "Nobody wants to kill you. I'm only after Ward here."

Tom was confused. "Aren't you one of Colonel Baneyev's men?"

"Baneyev? I heard you mention that name while I was listening. Who is he? Your KGB chief? No, the only Russian I know is Astinof, and he's no colonel. He's with the FBI."

"Then who are you?" Ward asked. "And what do you want with us?"

"I don't want your lady friend. Just you, Ward. I'm Sergeant Pete Fuller of the San Bernardino sheriff's office. You're wanted on suspicion of murder in California. At the FBI they said you couldn't be touched—that your connections went all the way. Well, I don't give a damn. I don't work for the federal government.

"Now, nice and easy, I'm going to put these cuffs on you. Just turn around and walk backward to me. I'll hold the cuffs out and you just move into them. Okay?"

Following instructions, Ward moved backward toward Fuller. He had come within two steps of the detective when the room was filled with the same sound—a creaking floorboard.

Eeewww.

Instinctively, Fuller turned toward the noise. As he did, Ward swung his body against the detective in a rapid, sweeping motion. As the two men collided, the sergeant fell to the ground, on his back. From that awkward position, he fired two shots at Ward. The bullets scattered wildly, one shattering a lamp on the bed only inches from Les's face.

Fuller was quick. He was still down on the floor from Ward's impact, but he hadn't lost his gun. On his back, he faced the gun up toward Ward.

"All right, Ward. Good try. But no luck. Now, just stand there while I get up. We'll do it all over again."

The sergeant started to stand, but when his head had risen only inches off the floor, he could make out a .45 pistol targeted at his forehead.

"Mr. Davidson!" Les exclaimed.

"I wouldn't ignore any sounds in this old house, Officer," Davidson was explaining to a prone Fuller. "They're an easy giveaway that someone is approaching. As soon as you crossed the perimeter, I was alerted by my sonar system. I've been behind you all this time, just waiting for the chance."

Ward took Fuller's gun, helping the detective to his feet. It was now the law officer's turn to be confused.

"What are you? A whole gang of Communists? What's going on here?"

☆　☆　☆

Davidson knew how inopportune the intrusion was. He needed Ward to return to the White House. It was important not to alert the Administration that conditions had changed in any way. This zealous police officer could spoil everything. A murder charge was something Ward could face later.

"No, Officer, you have it wrong. As a matter of fact, you've walked into a counterplot. An attempt to save our country from the Communists. Would you like to hear more?"

Fuller stared up at the gun pressed into his temple.

"You know, Mr. Davidson—I suppose that's who you are—when a .45 is against your head, you're liable to listen to almost any argument, no matter how strange. Go ahead. What do I have to lose?"

Chapter 85

Milt Samuels stretched his round frame and touched the intercom.

"Barnett. Do me a favor. Call Doug McDowell in Washington and tell him to get his skinny ass up here to New York. I want to see him this afternoon. No ifs or buts."

After his confrontation with McDowell, Samuels had spent days in introspection. He had finally made a decision about the impetuous commentator, the only rational action under the circumstances.

Samuels prided himself on the logic of his life.

From his origins in the old ghetto of Williamsburg in Brooklyn, he had not so much fought his way out as skillfully glided away from what he feared was an encircled community. It was not that Samuels was ashamed of being Jewish. Rather, he was chauvinistic, proud of it —privately. To him, Jews were bright, alert, sensitive, often intellectual. It was just that Samuels knew he had to avoid the Jewish "subway academy" of CCNY if he were to make the smooth transition to the power he envisioned.

He searched for a school far removed from Williamsburg, settling on the College of William and Mary, an outpost of ancient Southern civility, ironically in colonial Williamsburg, Virginia.

After graduation a spare, polished Samuels joined the network, where his intelligence, logic, and skilled manipulations brought him from writing news copy for the local radio station to president of network news thirty years later. He was now able to relax his stomach line and occasionally even his diction. Even add a few Yiddishisms to his speech.

In any case, he had found a true home, working for worthwhile causes and kissing ass for the Old Man in such a sensitive way that the network chairman had almost come to view him as an equal.

Now, all the goals achieved, that punk redheaded kid, Doug McDowell, an "Irisher," as his mother would say, had come into his office with a crazy story about the President being a Communist. It had upset his entire, scrupulously constructed life.

He had mentioned it to the Old Man, who had reacted perhaps worse than he had. Just turned on his heels and uttered a profane comment as he walked out of the room.

"Do what you want with the kid, Milt. Fire him. Crucify him. Or send him to an affiliate in Wichita. But keep the asshole quiet and out of my sight."

He could keep McDowell out of the Old Man's sight but not, apparently, out of his own mind. Ever since the frantic visit—he could still see McDowell's bloodshot eyes darting about in their sockets—he had been trying to decipher the truth. He had dismissed McDowell's kidnapping story as nonsense then, so why was he rehashing it now?

It was simply that McDowell had never impressed him as crazy or as a fabricator. Just an ambitious young kid who had adopted liberalism as the norm of his time and profession. So why would a liberal suddenly turn into a right-wing fanatic and invent a convoluted tale about Communism?

He'd soon find out.

☆　☆　☆

McDowell had been avoiding limousines lately. And keeping Meg ignorant of his plans. Should he fire her? Well, perhaps. But now, playing detective, it might be more fruitful if he kept her around, even under occasional surveillance. He wondered what Davidson was doing with his information on Meg and Rausch. The old spy had sworn him to secrecy.

The taxi soon arrived at the National Airport. The forty-five-minute flight seemed interminable. Why was he being summoned to the Tower? For peremptory execution? Had Milt already heard that he was snooping about, even if he was keeping his mouth shut about Hankins?

The plane landed at La Guardia without incident and McDowell taxied to the Tower, where Samuels met him in the outer office.

The news chief's hand was outstretched, his face exhibiting none of the scorn he had shown the visit before.

"Glad you could make it, kid. Come in. How about a drink? I've got some fantastic Puligny Montrachet."

McDowell was nonplussed by the reception. Was Samuels imitating the Japanese corporate tradition, one of strained, extra politeness before the professional ax fell?

"Doug, I know I was abrupt with you the last time," Samuels said as soon as they were seated. "That's why I want to talk to you about it once more—now that your clothes are pressed and your breath doesn't smell. You're feeling better, aren't you? All recovered from that escapade?"

McDowell just smiled. "Sure, I'm feeling great, Milt. Back in harness. Haven't given the whole thing a moment's thought since we last met."

"Bet you haven't. Don't bullshit me, kid. You probably don't sleep nights over it. You know how I know? Because it's beginning to affect me, and I don't know a thing about it except what you told me."

"Then why did you ask me to come back?"

"Because maybe I was too hard on you, Doug. Maybe I closed the door too quickly. Do me a favor. Look me square in the eyes and answer me—with just one word. Yes or no."

"Sure, Milt. Whatever. Go ahead."

"Those days you were missing. Were you kidnapped by the CIA, turned over to the KGB, then incarcerated in their damn summer estate at the Point? Then you escaped? Yes or no?"

"Yes . . . but?"

"Oh, shit, kid. What's the 'but'? But you made it up? I asked you, yes or no. Straight. No bullshit."

"Yes, damn it, Milt. The only 'but' is that I lied about escaping."

"What do you mean you lied about escaping? Did they kill you instead?"

"Now the thing is making you crazy, Milt. No, I was freed by two friends. CIA guys."

"Oh no, kid. The story keeps getting bigger. Can't you stop the baloney and see that I'm interested in getting to the bottom of it?"

McDowell was surprised, curious about what had turned Samuels' mind.

"Really, Milt?"

"Yes, really. I still don't believe a word of what you said. Well, maybe a little. But I owe to myself—not to you or the network or the Old Man, or even to the country, but to myself—to find out the truth. Do you understand? I didn't work my ass off all my life to walk away from the biggest story of the generation, if there's the slightest possibility it's true. Maybe you've come in here with another Watergate. I'm not about to turn down a Peabody. *Versteht?*"

Samuels got up and strolled the long room, as if McDowell were not even present. Then he spoke to the wall, assuming McDowell was alert, all ears.

"Here's the deal I'm going to make with you, kid. You've got your documentary, or at least the chance to pretend there's one. Contact Hankins and tell him that you want to spend some time with him. That the network is going to do a personal profile on his amazing career and his first weeks in office. Some of the decisions were historic, tell him."

"Milt. I thought I was too obsessed to handle a documentary on this?"

"Don't get fresh with me, McDowell. You are. But I didn't say there would actually be a documentary. Right now, that's just our cover story so that you can gain entry. Maybe once you're there your obsession about his being a Commie will be valuable. At least you'll work harder, and maybe—just maybe—we'll get a documentary out of it. What do you say, Doug?"

"What do I say? Great is what I say, Milt. I'm convinced that the Kremlin is running this country by remote control. And I appreciate the chance to prove it to you."

"Good, Doug. And don't worry. I'll confirm everything. Just have the Oval Office call me. I promise I won't tell them you're crazy. Now get the hell out of here before I change my mind."

☆ ☆ ☆

Keeping Meg away from information was becoming a part of his regular routine, McDowell noticed. He had never before called the Oval Office from a pay phone, for example.

McDowell went down to the lobby of his building and from a booth dialed the Press Office of the White House: 456-2100. He was put through to the assistant to the press secretary, Mike Richards, but McDowell told her that he had to speak to the President personally.

When Hankins heard from Maude Holly that it was McDowell, he picked up the phone immediately.

"Doug, pleasure to speak with you. I think the last time we met was the July television debate. Am I right? Yes. What can I do for you? You know, everyone here is embarrassed by what happened in that CIA snafu. We'd like a chance to make it up to you."

McDowell was pleased that he could capitalize on Hankins' guilt.

"Well, I appreciate that, Mr. President. The reason I'm calling is that my network news chief wants to do a full documentary on your life and career, and these first historic weeks of the Administration. I've been assigned to write it. The best way to start, I think, is a few days in the White House. Any chance of that?"

"Terrific idea, Doug." Hankins' response seemed genuine. "In fact, maybe I've got something even better for you. I'll be going to Camp David soon. How about coming along?"

"Sounds good to me, Mr. President. Sounds perfect."

Once Hankins got off the line, McDowell checked his travel arrangements with Holly. She invited him to join the President on the helicopter, but McDowell demurred, hoping to avoid Fenton as long as he could. No, he told her, he preferred to drive up. That way, he could return on his own.

As soon as he hung up, McDowell dialed the Cosmos Club.

"Could you connect me to Mr. John Davidson?" he asked. "If he's there, you'll find him in the library. Tell him it's Doug McDowell."

☆   ☆   ☆

John Davidson's incipient ulcer was acting up less in the last few days, settling down with the political atmosphere.

Jed Hankins was no less powerful in a constitutional sense but, seated in the Cosmos library, dozing off intermittently as he read still another biography of Winston Churchill, Davidson felt the stirrings of hope. He was now armed with the facts of the President's Election Night conspiracy and looked forward to its early use as a persuasive tool. That would require another personal visit to the White House.

"You're wanted on the telephone, Mr. Davidson."

He wondered who would be calling him at the club.

"Oh, Doug. No, no problem calling me here. Yes, I'm sure this line is clear. Go ahead."

"Mr. Davidson, things are breaking quickly," McDowell began, his voice emotional. "Milt Samuels at the network called me in. He's interested in doing a documentary on Hankins. I'm sorry, but I had to tell him about the kidnapping. Samuels doesn't buy all my suspicions, but he's hedging his bets. I'll be spending a few days with Hankins at Camp David next week. I called because I wondered if there is something you might want me to do there."

Access to Hankins for several days at Camp David? That might be valuable, Davidson thought. Then he remembered Ward.

"Yes, Doug. There is. Learn what you can. But also, a friend of ours, Tom Ward, may be there too. He's an adviser to the President, but you can trust him. He was one of them, but he's totally on our side now. Remember, if you need anything, ask Ward. Just tell him you're working with me."

Davidson paused. "If you need to reach me, call here, or even at Leesburg. The number is unlisted. Please write it down."

He waited. "703-658-4771. That's probably not a clear line, so use it only if it's urgent."

Davidson held the phone in his hand for a second longer. "And, Doug. Keep your paranoia up. It might come in handy."

Chapter 86

"Gentlemen, I can't tell you how I'm going to do it. Only why. We all agree that Terry Maynard as Vice-President would be as much a threat to American security as President Hankins. All I can tell you is that I have the lever to make the President drop that nomination. And substitute another person more to your liking. Who do you believe the Congress should ratify as VP under the Twenty-fifth Amendment? I think I can persuade the President to accept your recommendation."

John Davidson, dressed in his three-piece herringbones, was addressing seven members of the United States Congress, an ad hoc bipartisan group hastily convened by Senator Delafield immediately after Davidson had called.

Around the hickory conference table in Delafield's suite in the new

Senate Office Building was a worried group of anti-Communist Republicans and Democrats, still wincing under the blows of Hankins' administration.

In addition to Senators Delafield, Feldman, and Masoni, there were four men from the House—Democrats Danny Bradshaw of Kentucky and Orvil Hoopes of Georgia and two Republican congressmen. They had all come to hear the former CIA man.

"John, most people here know you, or of you. And those who do trust you." It was Senator Angus Delafield, acting as chair.

"But for those less acquainted, I want to say that John is not a bluffer. If he says he has a 'lever,' as he calls it, to convince Hankins to negotiate with us, we should believe him. And move to the business of picking our own VP. It's a golden opportunity."

From the end of the table, a short man with a wizened face raised two skinny fingers of his left hand for recognition. The congressman from Georgia, Orvil Hoopes, was respected by his colleagues, who had followed his parliamentary intrigue for thirty years.

"Mr. Davidson, I've heard a lot of stories 'bout you," Hoopes began in his rural Southern twang. "Some, I don't mind saying, are good. T'others, a mite seamy. But that's beside the point. What I want you to tell me is this. If you got enough on Hankins to twist his pecker, how come we can't take him all the way to impeachment? Use your damn lever like a rope and swing the son of a bitch by his executive neck. Maybe you got some treason on that boy. Ha? And, Mr. Davidson. You're a CIA spook. Tell me. Is that no-account a real Red? I swear it won't go no fu'ther than this here table."

The legislators loved Orvil's way of defining every argument in colorful patois. Davidson smiled with them, but he had no desire to lend himself to Hoopes's legendary manipulations.

"Senator, we both have one purpose. To save the Republic from its enemies. You gentlemen are elected officials, so you have to do it a special way. I'm just an old private citizen with a lot of quirks. One of them is doing things my way. I'm not looking for vengeance, or name-calling, or public trials and executions. Forbid, we've had too much of that in the last twenty-five years. I have no desire to contribute to the public skepticism about America's elected leaders—not unless I have to. I just came here today to ask you to give me the name of a Vice-President you can trust to protect the Republic. That, sirs, is your business. What I do with the name is mine."

"Yahooo!" Hoopes's rebel yell startled his colleagues.

"Son of a gun. This man talks Princeton fancy, but he's got the balls of a Southerner. Mr. Davidson. I salute you. And I'll give you a name for VP. First off, he's got to be a Democrat. We won the damn election, even if our candidate died on us. Secondly, it's got to be somebody who cares about the plain folks. Thirdly, he's got to be somebody who can chew a Commie rat up without salt and eat him for breakfast.

"I 'pose there are only about three people in the whole damn country who fill that bill. And I only know one of them. My good friend Hawley Briggs, three-time governor of Arkansas. No better American ever lived. Nor will. Not since the likes of HST. He's my first and last vote for VP."

Hoopes leaned forward, his face lit. "And I forgot to say. When Hawley's riled, he's got the temper of a pig in heat. Maybe he'll scare that Commie Hankins to death. Then all our problems'll be over."

His nomination of Briggs struck the table with one reaction. A good choice.

"Orvil, what makes you think Hawley will accept?" asked Republican Senator Maury Feldman, probing for a flaw in the idea. "You know, he was a presidential candidate, even if on the wrong side. Will he think the VP office grand enough for him?"

Hoopes stood up to his full five feet five to respond.

"Gentlemen. Hawley's a good Methodist, same as me. But I'll tell you this. For a chance to sit in Harry's chair someday, he'd travel to Rome and kiss the mighty ass of the Pope. On that I rest."

The meeting was virtually concluded with that remark, but Davidson coughed his way to recognition.

"I respect your choice of Mr. Briggs, and I hope to come back soon with the President's own nomination of him. I ask only that everything said here be kept confidential until you hear from me. Then I would appreciate almost instant action in the appropriate committees. I believe the Senate Rules—Senator Feldman—and the House Judiciary—Congressman Bradshaw. Without secrecy, all could fail. Can I count on that?"

Davidson went around the table and received a nod from each one in turn.

Delafield banged his palm on the table like a gavel.

"Gentlemen, I commend you all. And, Mr. Davidson, thanks."

Chapter 87

Fenton pressed his fingers deeply into the President's large chair, then relaxed his slender body into the leather, pretending he was in power. The day following his meeting with Baneyev, he was in the Oval Office by seven forty-five, before Hankins arrived.

What momentous things he would do for American society, he fantasized. Remake it into a nation in which sacrifice was the goal of a decent life.

Fenton didn't delude himself that he could ever be elected by the people. Nature had not endowed him with the graces of a public political animal. But when America was a Soviet Republic, the Party alone would decide who was fit to rule. In that equation, he, not Hankins, would be the most powerful of Americans. If STAND DOWN was successful—and this morning he was endowed with new optimism—who knew? Maybe that chair would soon be his.

Fenton's predawn meeting with Baneyev had already borne succulent political fruit, spread all over the morning paper. He opened the front page on Hankins' desk, the headline face up, in bold, inch-high type, proclaiming Fenton's coup, with all credit to the President.

Just what he had hoped for. This was the surer route to Hankins' political heart, the necessary ingredient for STAND DOWN.

The headline told it all.

PRESIDENT HANKINS' PROTEST TO SOVIET UNION IS SUCCESSFUL; SHIPS CARRYING MIG-31s TO NICARAGUA TO RETURN TO RUSSIAN PORTS.

Fenton was still in the chair, in reverie, when the President arrived moments later. He leaped out, Hankins pretending not to notice.

"Bill, that's great news, isn't it?" Hankins said, picking up the newspaper. He glanced through its columns, relishing every word.

"I received a call from the General Secretary early this morning," Hankins said, his eyes flooded with success. "He wanted me to know that they were turning the ships around right in the ocean. And taking every last MIG back to the Soviet Union. I haven't felt this good in weeks."

Fenton was sure that at countless breakfast tables across the country this morning Hankins' name was the object of praise. His soft line on the Soviet Union was paying off, people were saying. The Soviet Union, in response to Hankins' protest, had responded civilly, calling back their MIGs. The American recipe for success, Fenton laughed. Dignity without sacrifice.

On the morning television, commentators were playing up the concept of "super détente," a phrase invented by press secretary Mike Richards, and already threatening to become a journalistic cliché.

"Bill, on days like this it's great to be President. I feel like a real leader. Doing what I believe in and having the people accept it."

Hankins' smile was luminescent. "Bill, it was a good thing I wrote that letter to the General Secretary on your suggestion. I think now he understands."

Fenton couldn't have been happier. Not only had he chosen the right course in approaching Baneyev, but he now realized that Hankins would do anything for the Marxist cause—as long as he could explain it to the American public or could find excuses they would accept.

Hankins was not necessarily wrong. There just wasn't time for that. Vassilin's intelligence people had given the President six months of uninterrupted power, but Fenton didn't believe Hankins could maintain a strong enough mental state for anywhere near that length of time.

The MIG affair had brought him and Hankins back together, at least temporarily. Now he had to take the President all the way to STAND DOWN on March 15, less than a week away.

"Next week we're going to Camp David for three days," the President suddenly reminded his aide. "I'm looking forward to it. How about you?"

The presidential retreat in the Catoctin Mountains of Maryland had become Hankins' second favorite home, after Homestead. The cool mountain air was contagious, as was the relaxed sense of being only seventy miles away but still isolated from the madding Washington crowds.

Fenton was pleased. Camp David was his setting of choice for STAND DOWN, the ideal place to reach Hankins philosophically. Absent the steady stream of presidential visitors, he would have Hankins virtually to himself, to plead the case for this final, irrevocable solution to the Cold War.

Despite the rustic setting, Camp David had been turned into another White House. The General Secretary would be only seconds
away by a special printout computer hot line, and equally reachable
by transatlantic phone. A special red telephone kept the President in
direct contact with the National Military Command Center at the
Pentagon.

The military aide to the President, Navy Commander Janet Kelly,
one of the first female graduates of Annapolis, would be at Camp
David as well, carrying her omnipresent black attaché case, the nuclear Football. Only she, the special warrant officers, and the chief of
the White House Military Office knew its combination.

But Fenton was confident that it was now his Football. Only yesterday Billings had told him that McIlheny had successfully planted the
computer "worm" that would nullify the President's Command and
Control codes at the right instant. On March 15 the American missile
offensive would be crippled for those few crucial hours.

It was only a fallback position, Fenton reminded himself, certain
that Hankins would soon be joining them as a willing protagonist in
STAND DOWN.

"Jed . . . Mr. President. I'm looking forward to Camp David too,"
Fenton finally responded. "It'll be a chance for us to think through
some of the important moves for the coming months. And, incidentally, for you to relax. Yes. A good idea."

"Great. By the way, Bill, we're going to have some company there.
Tom Ward called this morning. He has some business to do with us,
so I invited him to Camp David. Do you mind? You know, I find him
a very pleasant chap."

"Not at all, Mr. President. Not at all."

Hankins' expression tensed.

"And, Bill, there'll be one more guest coming along."

"Who's that?"

"You know him. The television newscaster, Doug McDowell. His
network is doing a whole hour on my administration, and he needs to
get some color."

"McDowell?" Fenton asked, his tone rising with tension. "But, Jed,
how could you do that? He must still be boiling about—that unfortunate incident."

Fenton's voice betrayed only a portion of what he was thinking. A
newsman at Camp David at the time of STAND DOWN? He had to
persuade Jed to cancel McDowell's invitation.

"Don't worry about that, Bill," Hankins assured him. "McDowell and I talked it all out. He's convinced it was a big mistake. This is a chance to make up for it. Get in his good graces and get some favorable publicity for the Administration."

Publicity? My God, Fenton thought. More provincial American political claptrap. He was almost tempted to tell Jed about STAND DOWN now. But he knew it was premature. He needed the isolation —what he would have left—that was available only at Camp David.

The intercom ring interrupted.

"Yes, Maude. Who did you say? John Davidson?"

Hankins placed his hand protectively over the receiver. "Bill, I hope you don't mind. I'd like to take this call now."

Fenton stood immobile. He had just been dismissed. What did that meddling old fascist want with the President, anyway?

As Fenton turned to leave, he could hear the beginnings of a conversation.

"Mr. Davidson. Surely. Any time. Yes. Make an appointment with Ms. Holly. Yes. I look forward to it too."

What could the two of them have to talk about? Fenton asked himself again as he exited the Oval Office, considerably less elated than when he entered.

Chapter 88

Hankins was surprised to hear from John Davidson again. The old spy had left the door open, supposedly in the interest of "national security." But more likely, Hankins thought, his game was closer to blackmail. What had Bill Fenton now done that Hankins would have to atone for? And at what price?

"Mr. Davidson? Returning so soon?"

Hankins greeted him with mock cordiality as Maude Holly escorted the ex-agent into the Oval Office and onto the couch near the fireplace. The President sat in a facing armchair.

"I had hoped your appetite for intrigue would have been satisfied for a while longer, Mr. Davidson."

"Mr. President, when you've been in this business as long as I have it becomes genetic. I hope you don't mind."

"Of course not, John. Always a pleasure to see you."

Hankins studied Davidson's sure composure. The CIA man's eyes seem suffused with self-satisfaction, like a poker player who has just drawn to an inside royal flush. It unnerved Hankins.

"So what's on your mind today, Mr. Davidson?"

"I believe we've reached an important crossroad, Mr. President. Some valuable information has just come to me, something that jeopardizes your whole administration."

"Yes?" Hankins asked, his full eyebrows rising.

"I have evidence that your election was fraudulent—that you withheld knowledge about Governor Daniels which might have given the race to the Republicans. Is that true?"

Hankins was wary. What knowledge about Governor Daniels?

"In all sincerity, Mr. Davidson, I don't know what you're talking about."

"Let me refresh your memory. The night of the election, Daniels went into his hotel bedroom at ten past ten to lie down. You and Miss Leslie Fanning were in the living room, watching the election returns. At ten-thirty Les looked in to see how the governor was sleeping. She couldn't wake him and called you in. You told her that the candidate was dead. When she rushed to tell the Secret Service you stopped her. Told her the election could be lost in California if the news got out. Then you convinced her to keep his death secret for a half hour until the polls closed. That's the thirty minutes that permits you to sit in this office right now."

Davidson paused. "You know, Mr. President, that's an impeachable offense."

So that was it. The night Daniels passed away. So much had since taken place that Davidson's story seemed a page torn from someone else's history. He had isolated it from his mind, fearful it would inhibit his ability to move America into the world Marxist orbit. But now it had returned, uninvited.

"That's quite a story, Mr. Davidson. Where did you hear that tale? In the men's room of the CIA Club? If you have such a thing."

"No, sir. Directly from Miss Fanning. She drove to my house in Leesburg the other night. I had met her during the campaign and I suppose she trusts me. The guilt had been eroding her, and she confessed to everything. I'm afraid the story is quite true."

Hankins leaned over, pressing the intercom, his extended finger displaying a slight tremor.

"Maude, would you please ask Les Fanning to come in?"

"No, she's not at work today," Davidson interjected. "Nor will she be. She's under my protection. To get her, someone would first have to get at me."

Hankins stared at his strange adversary. Where did this pale sexagenarian fit into the profile of world politics? Could he actually be blackmailing an American President down to a finale?

"Mr. Davidson. In this supposed story about Election Night, were there other participants? Any other witnesses?"

"No, she was the only one," Davidson lied. "Miss Fanning specifically told me that you and she were alone in the room."

It made sense, Hankins thought. Les was protecting Tom Ward. But at least Davidson didn't know anything about Ward and his connection to the Kremlin. He took Davidson's measure again.

"Mr. Davidson, you've subtly threatened me with impeachment. Do you think that you, or your friends, have the votes in the House? I don't think you could get a majority for impeachment even if I brought the defenses down to a broomstick and let the Soviet Union take most of the world. Don't you think I'm right?"

"Unfortunately, I agree with you. But we're not talking about impeachment now, unless it's necessary. Simple public exposure of your conspiracy on Election Night could lead to anything."

"So what do you want from me, Mr. Davidson? What is the payment this time?"

"The vice-presidency. I want you to withdraw the name of Terry Maynard. I don't believe he'll advance the commonweal any more than you have."

Hankins sensed the blood returning to his face.

"Is that all? Why, surely, John. I'd be pleased to remove his name. I have several other men, all equally good Americans, in mind."

"No, Mr. President. Not one of your people. I've come equipped with a name. Some prominent members of Congress have recommended a man they trust. They want Hawley Briggs in the number two spot."

"Hawley Briggs?" Hankins frowned. "He's an old windbag. And a Red-baiter to boot."

So far, Hankins considered, he had held the Administration together with spit and persistence. He might have to continue these unfortunate accommodations, but his real power was still intact. As long as he was Commander-in-Chief.

He would pay the blackmail. Davidson was right. He could fight the impeachment in the House, perhaps even win the vote. But if the case ever got to the Senate a trial would result and that would only invite more investigation. He might not be as lucky next time.

"Mr. Davidson, you win at poker again. Mr. Briggs it is. I'll call the appropriate committee chairmen today and change my nominee."

The humiliation of yielding to this meddlesome old spy was cutting him, but Hankins knew he had to brave it through.

"Is there anything else I can help you with, John?"

"Just one more thing, Mr. President. I must ask you to keep our conversation confidential until the Congress acts on Governor Briggs. Particularly from Mr. Fenton. I'm afraid he's too friendly with Colonel Baneyev at the Soviet Embassy. I wouldn't want anything to happen to Miss Fanning."

Before Hankins could respond, Davidson added, "The same holds true for this old carcass. And, Mr. President, I've given taped copies of Miss Fanning's statement to Senator Delafield and one unnamed person. Should anything happen to Miss Fanning, or to any of us, the information will immediately be released to the press. Do you understand, sir?"

Hankins stared unremittingly at his opponent, thinking how convenient it would be if he could rid himself of Davidson, and Les, and Delafield, all at once. But he knew that wasn't his game. Bill's maybe. That's why Davidson was right. He couldn't confide this to Fenton.

"I understand, Mr. Davidson. I understand. Perhaps more than you think."

Chapter 89

It was 10 A.M., March 14, twenty-nine hours before STAND DOWN.

The giant Sikorsky H-3 helicopter, THE UNITED STATES OF AMERICA painted across its frame, stood immobile on the White House lawn, its pilot, a U. S. Marine major, awaiting the President and his party.

Bill Fenton was the first in, dressed in his blue serge suit and a full-length topcoat, eccentric garb for the rustic Camp David life. Tom Ward, the next to board, had come prepared with a woolen plaid shirt, heavy sweater, and down jacket. The temperature at Camp David, two thousand feet up in the Catoctin Mountains of northern Maryland, often touched zero at this time of year, he had heard.

Hankins soon arrived, braving the cold with only a woolen shirt and a bulky ski sweater. Running alongside, straining to keep up with the President, was Commander Janet Kelly, her navy skirt flapping in the frigid breeze, her gloved hand clutching the black attaché case that symbolized the difference between American sovereignty and surrender.

Hankins returned the salute of the Marine at the helicopter with a nod, then boarded the stairs, giving Commander Kelly a pull aboard.

"Let's go," Hankins instructed the pilot.

The helicopter took off and flew northwest across Maryland, beginning the seventy-mile trip to the mountain hideaway. In half an hour all four passengers would be out of the Washington maelstrom and settled down to the ease of Camp David.

☆   ☆   ☆

Bill Fenton knew he was approaching a personal Armageddon. In the Weathermen at Berkeley, he had dreamed of brazen schemes to advance world revolution. As a teenager he had even thought of joining Che Guevara in the hills of Bolivia. But his nature had moved him in another direction and fate had tied him to Hankins. Now the helicopter was taking him to Camp David, where, in just over a day, the world would be reordered to his liking.

But it would not happen without resolve. Tonight he would offer Hankins the arguments for action, the reasons for accepting STAND DOWN.

So far, except for the freakish McDowell incident, security on the project had been perfect. Not even Ward, in the seat next to him, was supposed to be aware of the impending crisis. Could Moscow have entrusted him with the truth? Fenton didn't know but, if so, it was surely secure in the hands of this KGB captain. Or was it now major?

"You've never been to Camp David, have you?" Fenton said, turning toward Ward.

"No. But I understand it's quite a place. Even a bowling alley and skeet shooting. A regular resort."

"Yes, it is. There shouldn't be too much business these next few days," Fenton dissembled. "Just routine stuff. Why don't you just enjoy yourself?"

Ward laughed. "That's not supposed to be my job when I'm with the President, but I'll try."

☆ ☆ ☆

As the helicopter passed over Frederick, Maryland, the last sizable town before Camp David, Ward peered out the window. He had achieved an agent's glory as the Kremlin's covert contact with the American President. Now he had to adjust to a new perspective, that of a "double," an unannounced defector working against the Soviet Union and their allies in the White House.

Ward glanced over at the President, in conversation with Commander Kelly, then at Fenton. Could either Hankins or his aide be suspicious of his new role? No. There was not even a nuance of change in their behavior toward him.

Nor, he was certain, did Rausch suspect anything. The story about Les being in Colorado was received with disappointment, but Rausch agreed it made little sense to follow her across the country. He could kill her when she returned.

He was now an agent for John Davidson, which he had to assume was the same as being one for the United States. But he wasn't working for the present American government. He was truly out in the cold, operating for a third faction, a cabal of men representing the people who had led America before Hankins.

But if Fenton and Hankins succeeded in converting America, either into a Communist satellite or a Finland of the West, a mute partner in the Soviet conquest of the world, he would be out. Permanently.

☆ ☆ ☆

The President stared down at the landing pad as the helicopter approached Camp David.

"It's quite a place, isn't it?" he asked Commander Kelly.

"Oh yes, sir. For me it's California and Florida. My only real chance to relax. We should have a quiet three days, don't you think?"

"Yes. Just simple routine, Commander."

Hankins hoped his prognosis was accurate, for he had been strung to his limit. First, the anxiety over the MIGs, then the exhilaration of the planes being sent back to Russia, a victory of his own strategy over the inflexible Kremlin strategists. Then the FBI revelation about Ward and the crazy kidnapping of McDowell. Could either one erupt at any time?

Now the disappointment of Davidson's blackmail on Maynard. But why should he care about the Vice-President? Of course, he would have preferred Maynard to Briggs, but it was an impotent office, a stand-in. Nevertheless, he wouldn't tell Fenton until it was necessary. He shivered at the thought of his controlled outrages.

It was true. Sometimes he couldn't handle the crosscurrents of his own mind. That's why Fenton was so valuable. But there were things he hadn't told Fenton, or anyone else. Not even Meg. He had come to worship the purpose and the power of the job, as if he were a legendary Charlemagne. But he sometimes ached internally as well, not as cavalierly certain of his political course as he pretended.

Was he sacrificing something good in America by his allegiance to Marxism-Leninism? Fenton would surely argue that doubt away, but it still disturbed him. Was there a residue of chauvinism, some American jingoism—or was it national pride—left in him? If so, should he purge it? Or nourish it?

The President looked down at the copter pad and the flag again, relaxing at the thought that three days in Camp David would restore his mental tone. He expected no crises, no more maddening confrontations.

"Commander." The President had turned back to Kelly, who was as one with her ominous black case. "How is the Football this morning? Everything in order?"

Kelly smiled, tapping the side of the leather box.

"Yes, Mr. President. I checked the combination myself this morning. It's ready to go if you need it. But I hope you never have to."

"So do I, Commander. So do I."

Chapter 90

Doug McDowell had driven his Audi up to Camp David, a two-hour journey from the District. He had never been to the Catoctin Mountains before but he immediately felt at ease in a place somewhat reminiscent of every boys' camp. Rustic, with chilled, refreshing air, and cabins set beneath tall trees.

The difference, of course, was the sense of the military. Run by the Navy, Camp David was protected not only by Secret Service agents but by the U. S. Marines, whose men, McDowell noticed, were unobtrusive but subtly omnipresent. Armed guards strolled casually throughout the perimeter, a handful bunched only at the ten-foot cyclone fence that controlled the entrance to the camp fortress.

"Welcome aboard, Mr. McDowell."

A young Marine lieutenant was checking McDowell's ID against a security folder, which included a publicity photograph of the commentator.

"The President's office told us to expect you this afternoon." The lieutenant looked at his watch. It was four forty-five.

"We were expecting you a little earlier, but I'm sure the President will be glad to see you any time. You're in Sycamore Lodge, the small cabin a few hundred yards down the road, on the left. You can see it from here. Just leave your car. If you get in the jeep, we'll load your baggage and take you down."

"By the way, Lieutenant," McDowell said, "one of the President's advisers, Tom Ward, asked me to look in on him later. Which cabin is he in?"

"Walnut Lodge. Not far from you, just about a hundred yards farther down, on your right."

The Marines unloaded McDowell at Sycamore in moments. The inside of the cabin was decorated in pure mountain hominess, replete with checked curtains and stained wooden furniture. A country stone fireplace dominated the main room. Through a square timber archway was a small bedroom and bath. Quite sufficient, and cozy, for the three days he expected to spend.

McDowell put away his things, then noticed a note on the small table desk. The stationery bore the presidential seal. Studying the handwriting, he guessed it was the President's own.

> DOUG, IF YOU CAN MAKE IT TO BIRCH LODGE, MY OFFICE, BEFORE 5:00, PLEASE COME RIGHT OVER. ASK FOR MS. HOLLY. IF NOT, PERHAPS WE CAN BEGIN TOMORROW AFTERNOON.
>
> BEST,
>
> JED HANKINS

McDowell was surprised by the informality of the note, a further attempt, he was sure, to mollify him after The Incident.

He looked at his watch. It was five minutes to five. A bit late, but worth the chance. The training of a newsman was showing. Always press for the story.

From a Marine guard patrolling near the cabin, McDowell learned the direction of Birch Lodge and began the walk, about ten minutes away, at a slow pace. Once out of sight, he quickened, and soon saw the stone cottage. It was larger than his own but, from pictures he had seen, still smaller than Aspen Lodge, the President's residence.

McDowell entered the paneled hallway, his eyes searching out Holly in the outer office. But the two desks were empty. The clock on the wall read 5:07. Ms. Holly and her assistant were out, possibly at the dining lodge. Ahead of him, a large, highly polished walnut door was closed.

He was turning to leave when he heard voices emanating from behind the door. It was the sound of two men talking, one of them agitated, occasionally shouting.

Doug moved into the shadows of a corner, close enough to overhear, yet hidden to anyone casually entering. He could make out Hankins' voice, speaking in loud, outraged tones.

"Damn it, Bill! That's madness. Pure madness!"

"No, Jed. It's not mad. It's rational, reasonable. In fact, essential."

He recognized the second voice as that of Bill Fenton.

"You want me to do what?" The President's tone was increasingly histrionic. "Are you crazy? Capitulate to the Russians? Why on God's earth should we do that? Isn't our help for them enough?"

"Jed, we can't count on a long term in the White House," Fenton was answering. "Let alone a second one. You can see yourself what happened with me and the CIA nomination. Our past is too riddled for us to rely on the American system. We could end up impeached, maybe even assassinated. STAND DOWN is our best chance to come out ahead."

The sound of Hankins pacing the small office came through the door.

"Bill, what do you think? I'm God?" Hankins called out. "If we go ahead with this, one of our military maniacs is still going to shoot a missile off toward Russia when we're challenged. It'll all end up in ashes, with everyone dead."

"No, Jed. No one has to lose a single life. As Commander-in-Chief, you'll simply order our military to stand down while you accept Soviet terms. Tradition is on our side. The military has never violated a presidential command. And the Soviets won't press their advantage. There won't be an occupation. Just a treaty that will make America a nonnuclear power, along with a tacit agreement that the Soviet Union will be supreme."

From his place in the hallway, McDowell could hear everything that was being said. From what he had heard, it sounded like nuclear blackmail. But when? It didn't appear to be some distant theoretical scheme but an actual tactical plan. He pressed closer to the door, afraid to miss a word of the stormy argument.

☆ ☆ ☆

Inside, Fenton was offering Hankins his most intimidating professorial look.

"Jed, the Soviets are going to win over the years anyway. You know that. The Americans are too soft for modern warfare. They're paralyzed with fear. It's a nation without nerve, spoiled by its own riches. History tells us what happens to such countries. They perish—of their own anxieties."

As Fenton spoke, Hankins' eyes were registering terror.

"And what if I refuse? What if I don't accept their nuclear ultimatum? What happens then?"

"Why do we have to talk about that, Jed? It's ugly. The Soviets are ready to do what's necessary. To make a first strike. They've become invincible. I'm sure the American military could put up some defense, even kill some millions of them. But the Soviets will win in the exchange. They'll recover and occupy what's left of America—if there's anything left. Do you want that, Jed? Is that why we started all this a dozen years ago? To see how many people we could kill?"

Fenton could sense that Hankins was now listening more intently, struggling to absorb the arguments. It was a chance to capitalize on Hankins' tortured contradictions. Instead of playing on his allegiance to the Soviet ideal, he had to reach out for Hankins' vestigial American patriotism. To assuage any guilt about betraying his own nation.

"Jed, you'll really be doing this for the American people. You know as well as I that the United States' worldwide defeat is inevitable, just as it was in Vietnam. All we'll be doing is hurrying it up. And making it painless. This way there'll be no nuclear holocaust. No millions dead as on the television shows. Just a quiet, orderly surrender. The whole Cold War will come to an end with a whimper. And, Jed. I tell you a lot of Americans will accept it. Not be happy about it, but accept it. They haven't the stomach for any long struggle. Not even a cold one."

Hankins stared at his chief of staff.

"Bill. You're very persuasive." The President's tone was quieter now, more modulated, less angry. "What you're saying makes sense. I agree the Americans are going to lose. They're an indulgent people. But why must I be the one to bring about their defeat? Why should history remember me as the Benedict Arnold of the twentieth century?"

Fenton knew when to play to Hankins' vanity, to his developing sense of political immortality.

"No, Jed. It won't be that way at all. The new history of a socialist America will show you in the opposite role. You'll be the glorious father of a new era, the American Lenin. Your face will be on statues, postage stamps, honored in books and legend. No, Jed. Quite the opposite of Benedict Arnold. You'll be the great antifascist hero of a Communist America."

Hankins had silently placed his face down, almost touching his chest, his gaunt cheeks in his hand. The President remained quiet for almost a minute, then raised his head only a few inches to speak, in a quavering whisper.

"Bill?"

"Yes, Jed?"

"Is it truly the right move?" Hankins asked.

"Jed, it's the only possible move. A quick, bloodless surrender, now. Or a painful, murderous death later on. The American people have ordained it themselves. You're only the agent of history."

Hankins' eyes were now locked on his aide, really his partner.

"All right, Bill. I'll do it." He waited, gathering in strength. "When will the General Secretary be making his nuclear threat? The one I'm to accept without retaliation?"

"At three o'clock tomorrow. He'll call a half hour before to give you time to think it over. A gentleman's proposal, I presume."

Fenton placed his arm around Hankins' bent shoulders.

"I know it's hard, Jed. But you've made the right decision."

Fenton then turned his face upward, directionless, seeming to address the room itself.

"A glorious decision!" he called out.

☆ ☆ ☆

From the hallway, McDowell had heard it all. He had eaves-dropped on the biggest story of his life. But he realized that he was no longer a newsman, the impartial observer of events. He had suddenly become a soldier in the army of survival. He had to reach John Davidson, immediately.

Chapter 91

Had it been anyone else, Davidson would not have believed it.

"One more time, Doug. What are they planning to do?"

Dizzied from the conversation between Fenton and Hankins, Mc-Dowell still had the presence to retrieve his car, leave the camp, and drive seven miles downhill on a twisting road to Thurmont, a small village on Route 15. At the first pay phone, McDowell stopped to dial Davidson's home in Leesburg. This was no time to worry about a tap.

"Yes, John. You've got it right. It was a wild argument. Hankins fought him but finally gave in. It's called STAND DOWN, the very words I put on television. It's set for tomorrow at 2:30 P.M. The Soviet General Secretary is going to call Hankins and demand American surrender."

Davidson's throat contracted. "Surrender? Did you say surrender?"

"Yes. Simple nuclear blackmail. Hankins will be given a half hour to think it over. Three o'clock is H-Hour. If he doesn't agree, they'll make a first strike. But Hankins has already agreed to give in. It seems like a fait accompli. Hankins is going to tell the American military to stand down, then he'll sign a treaty dismantling American missile capability everywhere. The country will become a giant neutralized Finland, with no foreign power. Probably later, a Communist satellite. As Fenton said, the Cold War will end with a whimper."

"Thank God you were there. I don't know what I can do, Doug. But I'll try something."

Davidson paused. "Doug. If someone wanted to reach you at Camp David, how would we arrange it?"

McDowell's response was rapid. "John. I'm staying in a guest cottage—Sycamore Lodge—about two hundred yards from the gate. I'll crack one of the small windowpanes. That will be the contact signal. Okay?"

"Good. Doug, Sam Withers is coming out there."

"Withers? But why?"

Davidson's end of the line was momentarily deadened.

"John, I can't believe you intend . . ."

"Doug, please don't get involved in this. Just help Sam to get to Tom Ward."

"John, I won't be part of any assassination attempt. You're not planning that, are you?"

"Please, Doug. This is not your kind of thing. Just hand him over to Ward. Remember. The nation is at stake."

Davidson hung up, then patted Dulles compulsively as he thought.

He picked up the phone and dialed feverishly, first hitting the wrong buttons, then redialing again.

It rang and rang. But no answer. It was his fault. He had told Sam not to install an answering machine in the beach house. Someone might recognize his recorded voice. Damn.

He dialed another number, now inside the 703 area code. It answered immediately.

"Clint, this is John. Things are bad. I've got to reach Sam Withers right away. I called him, but there's no answer. Any idea where he is?"

"As a matter of fact, yes. Barber told me that Sam is at the Tunlaw Road place."

"What the hell is he doing in Washington? Tailing Baneyev? Do you have the number? Good. Sorry I can't talk now, Clint. Thanks."

The phone rang at the apartment facing the Soviet Embassy in Washington. The old Agency lookout, Davidson now remembered. Still no answer. Davidson decided to let it ring. Five, six, seven times. Finally someone lifted the receiver.

"Hello." The tone was gruff, unrecognizable.

"Who is this?" Davidson asked.

At the other end, he heard the voice rapidly change.

"John, it's me. Sam. What's up?"

"Thank God. Sam, listen carefully. You have to leave immediately. Drive up to Camp David in Maryland. You know where it is? Good. Get settled somewhere close by tonight. Then tomorrow morning, before dawn, you have to break through the Marine perimeter. You have to finish what you started at the convention. That's right. Take out Hankins. By 2:30 P.M. tomorrow. We have no other choice. He's going to surrender our nuclear capability—what's left of it—to the Russians. Understand?"

"Yes, John. Crystal clear."

"One more thing. Your newsman friend, Doug McDowell, is at Camp David interviewing Hankins. He's come fully over to our view. You'll find his cabin not far from the gate. It's got a cracked window-pane. He'll put you in touch with Tom Ward, one of Hankins' advisers. He was KGB, but he's with us now. Good luck, Sam."

"John, thanks for the chance. I'll be right on my way."

Davidson wasn't confident that he could manipulate the situation from his small HQ. But he would have to be dead not to try. Now his mind turned toward political realities. There was no Vice-President to take Hankins' place. Hankins had already agreed to Hawley Briggs, and officially nominated him. But could a VP be approved by Congress in less than a day? He would find out if the federal inertia could be moved—even if the nation was at stake.

If Sam completed his mission, Briggs would then be President and face up to the Soviet leader. If not, he would have to bluff it out by confronting Hankins at Camp David with the new VP and the military chief, General John Abbott.

Davidson went to the phone again. This time he dialed the office of Senator Delafield, an obsessively late worker. His assistant, Kitty Shumberg, answered.

"Mr. Davidson, I'm sorry. Senator Delafield is in a meeting. No, I really can't disturb him. Why don't you leave your number? I know he has a late dinner engagement right after the meeting, but I'm sure he'll get back to you sometime tomorrow."

Davidson cast his eyes heavenward. He had to engage her mind, quickly.

"Miss Shumberg. Please listen carefully. This is John Davidson, former head of CIA counterintelligence. Angus and I are compatriots in a very urgent matter. Just go into the meeting. Interrupt it, no matter who's there. Tell him John Davidson is on the phone. And add this line: 'The Republic is falling.' He'll understand."

She gasped.

"I'll try. But aren't you being a bit melodramatic, Mr. Davidson?"

"Miss Shumberg, you take charge of getting Senator Delafield to the phone. I'll take care of the melodrama."

She moved, as if on fire. Delafield was on the phone in thirty seconds.

"John, what's up? I think you've petrified Kitty."

"That was my intention, Angus. Listen carefully. All may be lost. One of my men at Camp David has just called. Fenton has persuaded Hankins to go along with a nuclear blackmail plan the Russians have been putting into place. It's called STAND DOWN and it goes into effect tomorrow at 3 P.M."

For the horrified senator at the other end of the line, Davidson filled in the details, including Hankins' Communist past.

"John, what do you want me to do? What about the military calling a missile alert?"

"They have no authority, Angus. I know McDowell is telling me the truth, but it's not legal evidence. What we need is a Vice-President. Hankins has already nominated Hawley Briggs. Angus, you must get Briggs approved by the two committees and ratified by both houses of Congress and sworn in by early tomorrow afternoon. Can you do it?"

"No, John. It's impossible. But, God damn it, I'm going to try."

Delafield was seized by a thought.

"But, John, even if we make it, Hawley will only be the number two man. He can't order a nuclear alert. We'd have to have him succeed to the presidency first. How in the hell can we do that?"

Davidson's speech was becoming rapid. "With Briggs, we can try to face Hankins down and declare him mentally disabled. It's not fully legal, but there's a chance that Abbott and the military will buy it."

The old CIA man paused. "I've also started the wheels going on another way to make Hawley President right away."

"John, you don't . . . ?" The senator trapped the rest of the sentence in his mouth.

Chapter 92

Withers needed a place to sleep. It was 11 P.M., the evening before STAND DOWN. Sam had driven up from Washington in his old Ford and parked the car at the camp site in Catoctin Mountain Park, the quiet neighbor of Camp David.

The area was deserted. Sam walked on the unmarked trails, a thin layer of snow covering the unused camp sites. There were small public bathrooms with cold running water, but no tents, no lean-tos, nothing large enough to protect him from the chilled night air. It would drop to below twenty degrees, Sam thought. March was still winter in the mountains.

He kept walking until he saw an old building at the edge of the creek. It was a restored water-powered sawmill, a kind of museum without an attendant. It was perfect. No witnesses to the beginnings of his journey.

Sam pulled down the hood on his down jacket and lay on the floor, curling up to preserve his body heat. Inside his ample pockets, he felt for the items he had brought along. A package of hard biscuits, a compass, a map of the area, a pair of collapsible binoculars, a pencil-thin flashlight, sharp wire clippers, extra bullets for his 9mm Beretta, now mounted with a silencer.

He laughed at the thought of these small details, and at the spate of books that would surely follow his assassination of President Hankins. They would do a poor job of reporting what happened, and why. He had seen it in the Kennedy assassinations and Withers expected no greater accuracy in writing about him. But it didn't trouble him. In fact, he would be disappointed if a colorful new legend was not created around the man who killed the Red President.

Sam replaced the gun in his pocket and set the alarm on his wristwatch for 5 A.M.

Chapter 93

It was 11:30 P.M., the eve of the Ides, in the Dirksen Senate Office Building on Constitution Avenue. The huge stone structure was eerily still, as was most of the American government.

But tonight a handful of men were in action. The members of the Senate Rules Committee were filing into the empty building, displaying their IDs to the surprised guard on night duty. The clerk of the Senate had been alerted by Senator Feldman and the committee hearing room had been opened for business, including the appointment of a stenographer to record the proceedings.

The senators sat in the large chamber facing empty seats, the austere walls and grand federal symbols looking down on the assemblage of tired legislators, who had thrown on anything to make this emergency muster. Most had been roused from their homes, a few from their beds, one from a local restaurant. With a phone number supplied by an AA, one senator had indelicately been called at the apartment of a young female secretary.

Several senators were annoyed at this nocturnal draft, but all except four finally yielded to the call. Those who complained the loudest were picked up by a borrowed Senate limousine.

"I feel like a damn British officer impressing seamen in the eighteenth century," Feldman told Delafield.

No sooner had the Rules Committee been called to order by Feldman than the patriarch of the Senate, seventy-nine-year-old Kendall Gaylord of Maine, stood. He addressed Senator Delafield, who had roused him from bed at 10 P.M. with the message that in one hour he had to meet—if he cared about the Union.

"Damn it, Angus. This is pure nonsense. We take months to discuss a budget that's killing us, and you say we've got to name a new VP in an hour in the middle of the night, or we're going down some kind of a drain. What kind of talk is that? We've survived lots of bad Presidents. One more's not going to kill us. Sure, Hawley's a fine man. But he's waited over sixty years to become VP. He can wait another few days. What in the hell is going on?"

Delafield was now privy to the whole ugly dimension of Hankins' treachery, but he couldn't reveal it to anyone, even to Feldman. Davidson had insisted on that. But Delafield knew the urgency. Without a Vice-President to confront Hankins in a matter of hours, there would be no semblance of legitimacy to their plan.

"Kendall, please trust me," Delafield implored. "I'm sorry I can't paint you a complete picture. Except to say that the national security is at stake as it's never been. Go along with us. I promise you won't regret it. The President has nominated Briggs. And we feel we need him—now."

Senator Gaylord wasn't the only one to complain. But when the carping was completed, Feldman banged the gavel, which seemed to echo doubly in the cavernous room.

"All right, gentlemen. It's time to vote. The motion before the Senate Rules Committee is President Hankins' nomination of Hawley Briggs, former governor of Arkansas, as Vice-President of the United States. How many vote aye?"

Feldman counted the raised hands.

"Ten in favor. How many vote nay?"

Again he counted. "One. The ayes have it. This committee has approved Governor Briggs to be the next Vice-President of the United States and so recommends him to the full Senate to give its consent under the Twenty-fifth Amendment to the Constitution."

Then, under his breath, he added. "With God's help."

Over at the Rayburn House Office Building, Danny Bradshaw of Kentucky was orchestrating the same scene in the House Judiciary Committee. Bradshaw would do anything to hobble Hankins, but he was facing more opposition than had Delafield in the Senate.

Some congressmen were angered that Hankins had dropped Maynard. Nobody knew why, and the President had refused to answer any inquiries, even from his closest legislative friends.

"How do we know that Briggs—should he ever become President —is going to follow Hankins' policy?" asked Congressman Larry Matthews, representing an affluent northern California district.

Bradshaw listened, smoldering inside. He decided to push party discipline to its limits.

"Damn it. I'm talking to men in my own party. Don't you trust your own President? If he says he wants Briggs, then he's got his reasons. Who are we to deny him?"

The final vote on the committee was close, in favor of Briggs, but by only two votes. But the House Judiciary had spoken along with the Senate.

"Congratulations, Danny," said Delafield, who had raced over to the House Office Building with his Senate victory in hand.

"You've pulled off a miracle. Now I need another one from you. I want you to get to the Speaker of the House tonight. I don't care if you have to wake Tompkins up at his Watergate apartment. Cajole him. Threaten him. Kiss him. Bribe him. But get the Speaker to arrange for the Judiciary's recommendation to be voted on by the whole House tomorrow morning. Feldman's doing the same with the Senate president pro tem. We've got to have Briggs approved and sworn in by early afternoon. The latest. Okay?"

"Delafield, I think the sun in Vietnam fried your brains. It can't be done."

"Will you try?"

"You know God damn well I will," Bradshaw said. "Anything to crush the nuts of that bastard in the White House."

Chapter 94

It was still dark when Withers woke at 5 A.M. Even in the dim moonlight he could see that he was alone. On the floor of the sawmill, he spread out the map and put on the flashlight. Using his fingers as calipers, Withers estimated that he was less than three miles from the main Camp David compound, and from Aspen Lodge, the President's weekend White House.

In 1970, Don Hughes, Nixon's director of the White House Military Office, had demonstrated how easy it was for an undercover agent to walk, unannounced, into Camp David and up to the front door of Aspen Lodge. Posing as a plumber, he had placed a dummy bomb in the President's personal toilet, the device rigged to explode when it was flushed. An ignoble presidential end.

Withers knew that security had since sharpened, and that breaking into Camp David's 143 acres—which had been cut out of the 10,000-acre park that surrounds it on all sides—would challenge him.

As he started through the Catoctin wilderness, Sam found the winding mountain trails hard to traverse, especially in the weak pre-dawn light. He strapped the compass to his wrist and checked his direction with the flashlight every few hundred feet. He was afraid of losing his way on the serpentine paths and end up, not in Camp David, but in some uncharted area. Instead of him getting Hankins, the elements would get him.

Sam walked for forty minutes until he estimated that he was near the perimeter of Camp David. As he sat down to rest, a large search-light on a watchtower scoured the grounds next to him with a bright arc. Sam moved swiftly under a tree branch as the light moved over his head. He hoped he had not been seen. Camp David obviously lay just ahead. And in it, his quarry.

He dropped onto his stomach and started crawling, moving away from the giant searchlight. For almost ten minutes Withers used his elbows and knees for locomotion, pulling his small frame along until he could go no farther. In front of his face was a wire fence, the outside defense line of the U. S. Marines. He took out the pen flash-light and moved it cautiously up the fence. It looked to be eight feet high and topped by a concertina barbed wire.

Was it electrified? Sam doubted it. Otherwise a multitude of little animals would be fried, as would any innocent civilian who got lost in the mountain park. Too much like the private sanctuary of a mad dictator. To check, Sam looked for the plastic insulators attached to wiring, but the fence seemed clean. No electricity was coursing through its metal veins.

Sam crawled back into the woods and brought out a pile of ever-green branches. He heaped them on the ground, then moved into the pocket underneath. The primitive camouflage might protect him from the harsh searchlights. With his wire clippers, he began to cut. First one, then two, then a dozen small rungs of the perimeter wire fell away.

The sweeping searchlight kept glancing off the evergreens. If any-one was close enough, he could see a large animal, actually a human one, burrowing his way inward. But just as Withers had cut almost through the fence, he could hear the underbrush rustle with the sound of boots coming toward him.

"Quiet night, like always, Jim." One of the guards, a tall young Marine, was talking to his sidekick, a shorter man. "See anything?"

"No. But it's getting colder. I'd sure like to get my hands around a beer."

Sam waited until the two Marines had walked away, then resumed his wire cutting. After the last rung had been removed, he pried his shoulder into the hole, pushing to enlarge the opening, bending back the remaining wire. Finally, he pulled himself through.

He was just rising off the ground to begin a quick run through the cleared "no man's land" into the forest on the other side when he tripped. He tried to hold his balance, but he was falling, indelicately on his face, to the ground.

"What's that?" The tall Marine had turned in Withers' direction, his M-16 at the ready. "Did you hear that sound?"

Withers picked himself up and was racing into the woods when the Marine started firing. Sam could hear the insistent meter of a rifle squeezing off a volley of shots in his direction. But the searchlight had not yet made its way back. The Marines were firing blindly in the dark.

Just as Withers was about to enter the woods, it happened. An M-16 missile moved too close, sinking its lead into the fleshy part of his left upper arm.

"Jesus!" Sam was tempted to cry out, but he pushed his padded arm into his mouth in time. The blood was coursing through the down jacket. To keep it from dripping on the leaves of the forest floor, Sam placed his mouth to the hole above the wound, sucking up the blood, all the while running deeper into the forest.

"Over here! I think whatever it was went this way. Let's take a look."

The young Marine joined his partner, and the two young men bent down to examine the snowless leaves, looking for any sign of blood, animal or human.

"No, nothing here. Either I missed or it was just my imagination," the tall Marine said.

In the woods, Withers was doing what he could to treat the wound. It hurt badly, but he could still move the arm. There were probably no broken bones, but he had to stop the bleeding. Fortunately, it was his left arm, not his trigger hand. Otherwise his mission would be aborted. Over before it began.

Sam took off the down jacket and ripped out a piece of the flannel lining, wrapping it tightly around the wound as a combined dressing and tourniquet. He knotted it, then put his coat back on.

With his arm pulsing, Withers marched another half mile until he saw signs of civilization pressing in. He passed garbage cans, a few wooden utility cabins. Ahead he could see the back of a large building. Aspen Lodge, the home of the President.

The blood loss was reaching his head, his eyes blurred by weakness. Sam felt faint. He had to find McDowell's cabin. If he couldn't reach it and rest, the assignment to kill Jed Hankins would become academic.

☆ ☆ ☆

Supporting his weight by grasping the trunks of small trees, Sam painfully made his way for another quarter of a mile until, through the vegetation, he could make out a small road. Facing it were a handful of cabins, apparently for the guests. First one, then a second. At the third, he slowed. A small pane in one window was broken. McDowell's signal.

Up ahead, about two hundred yards, he could see the main entrance to the camp, blocked by a metal gate ten feet high and patrolled by a half dozen Marines, each armed and at the ready. He was sure there were others hidden for an emergency. Two Marines were pacing up and down, about a hundred feet from him, but they were facing in the opposite direction.

No one saw him approach the door. Withers knocked softly, then again. A crop of red hair was visible through the glass.

"Doug. McDowell." Withers could manage only a whispered call. "Open up, please. It's me. Sam Withers."

McDowell opened the door, then pulled back at the sight of the down jacket, lacerated by tree branches and badly bloodstained in the upper left arm.

"What happened, Withers? Come in."

As Sam's first step crossed the threshold, his head reeled and his legs lost their tautness. He was angling toward the ground when McDowell caught him, half dragging his limp body into the cabin. He helped the staggering Withers onto the bed, where a few sips of water brought him around.

"How do you feel?"

"Okay. Just weak."

"Let's get that jacket off. I want to look at the wound."

McDowell tore the shirt away around the bullet hole, washed it with an impromptu mixture of hot water and rubbing alcohol, then dressed it with a bandage torn from one of his clean undershirts.

"Well. It's better than nothing," McDowell said, staring inquisitively at the wounded Withers. "So, Sam. What's your plan?"

"Best you don't know. Davidson told me you'd put me in touch with Tom Ward. Where can I find him?"

"He's just down the road in another cabin. But you can't go anywhere for at least a few hours."

"I've got to," Sam mumbled, his strength ebbing just in speaking those few words.

McDowell knew he had inherited an ugly dilemma, one in which action, or inaction, offered disastrous results either way. If he washed his hands of the affair, as would the contemporary neutral observer-journalist, he might lose a country. But to cooperate with Withers?

"McDowell?"

"Yes, Sam, what is it?"

"I was going to ask Ward, but you're probably right. I need sleep. Maybe you know. Where will Hankins and Fenton be this afternoon at two-thirty? In their office at Birch Lodge?"

By answering the question, McDowell would no longer be able to play Pilate. The intentions of Sam Withers, and he supposed John Davidson, would become his own.

"No, Sam. They won't be at Birch," McDowell said, all hesitation dropping away. "Last night I heard Hankins say that he'll be at Aspen Lodge all day. I suppose John told you. Hankins is going along with Fenton, but he's petrified about STAND DOWN. Wants all his calls today, including those from the General Secretary, to come right into Aspen."

"Good. Right now, all I need is a little rest," Withers said, his voice trailing off. "Doug, could you tell Ward everything you know about STAND DOWN and let him know I'm here? John tells me he can be trusted. Then, please come back and wake me. Not later than two o'clock. Okay?"

"Okay. Meanwhile, I'll lock you in."

"Good luck," the newsman muttered as he moved out of the cabin. No one had to tell him that the small man had come to Camp David for only one purpose. To kill President Hankins.

Chapter 95

"Good morning, Mr. President. How are you feeling?"

Bill Fenton entered Hankins' bedroom in Aspen Lodge at 9 A.M., satisfaction etched into his stark features.

"I've been better, Bill."

Hankins was dressed, but his breakfast was uneaten on a tray near the window, its vista a deceivingly tranquil mountain scene. He hadn't slept more than two hours during the night. The first moments of disturbed sleep were tolerable, his mind rationally exploring the pros and cons of the upcoming submission to the Soviets. But as the night progressed he moved in and out of sleep, his dream transposed into a nightmare.

He had seen the landscape of Hankins Farms. First, it appeared to him as it actually was. Then it transformed into a darkened, hideous camp of some kind, closed in by high barbed wire. Possibly a prison, over which a giant Red flag flew. The horses in the stables were whimpering, seeking to escape brutal masters who were flogging them incessantly with whips.

At first the waking was a relief from the nightmare. Then Hankins faced the greater torture of reality, of his upcoming confrontation with the General Secretary.

"Jed, please don't worry yourself," Fenton was saying. "In a few hours it will all be over. We'll have won."

"I thought the game was being played the other way, Bill. It's the Russians who are blackmailing us, not vice versa."

Hankins sensed that Fenton was surprised by his negative remark but was reining himself in.

"I know you're worried about the correctness of what you're doing, Jed. But you shouldn't be. Soon you'll have changed the world for the better—permanently. Everything you've worked for. You should be pleased with yourself."

Hankins felt shamed that this young man, so obviously his intellectual superior, had such an effect on him. A magnet that moved him in virtually any compass direction.

"Bill, I'm sure history will vindicate you. But right now, I must tell you, I'd as soon forgo the honor."

Hankins gauged his aide, his inferior in rank but his master in fact. So many times he had felt Fenton manipulating him, scheming to capitalize on his lifelong weakness. Now Hankins could finally describe, even understand, his own failing.

It was a deep lack of confidence tied to his delusionary desire to achieve greatness. If only to prove to himself that he was something more than a rich boy, scion of someone else's success.

Hankins looked up at Fenton, aware that he was uncomfortable, anxious to retire from the room.

"Just a few more hours, Jed," Fenton said, starting toward the door. "And it'll all be over. If you don't mind, I have a few things to look after."

Hankins was now alone in Aspen Lodge, staring out the window, his eyes searching out the farthest point in the wooded landscape, his mind miles beyond even that. A Navy mess boy freshened his coffee. Fenton had left him a pouch of documents, perhaps to pretend that this was like any other presidential day. The papers dealt with a multitude of problems, some as small as the appointment of a new postmaster for Jackson Creek, Montana.

Others were as important as a report from his legislative liaison. The House and Senate committees had met in extraordinary sessions at eleven-thirty last night and had approved Hawley Briggs as Vice-President. The swiftness of the action surprised Hankins, but he decided to say nothing to Fenton. Perhaps he hadn't heard the news.

Hankins sat with his coffee and weighed the eccentric rules by which one played this game of nuclear blackmail. The idea was to win without any loss of life. It was accomplished strictly with the threat of annihilation. But behind it, of course, there had to be the power to make the consequences real and frightening. In this game, nations were lost, not lives—unless one side failed to play by the rules. Because of the moral codes of the West, the deadly contest could only be initiated by the Russians. Witness STAND DOWN.

But even in these last minutes Hankins knew he was still a factor. To accomplish STAND DOWN without losing millions of their own people, the Soviets needed his cooperation.

A prideful thought struck him. What would the Russians do if, at this very last moment, I backed out? And refused to go along with their blackmail?

God knows. Hadn't he taken American defenses down too far? Star Wars was no longer regulating the heavens. He had even given orders to empty the nuclear weapons from the B-1 bomb bays. Wasn't it too late, much too late, to resist?

It was only today that he had reached the point of revelation. He had so misread his friends in the Kremlin. Kambula was an early warning, a symptom of what he should have recognized. He could see now that the world struggle had never been a battle merely of megatons, but one of resolve. And in that—like many of his compatriots—he was surely no match for the Soviet Union.

As a Marxist, the President knew he should be elated by STAND DOWN. Within hours he would be instrumental in the final victory of the cause.

But whose?

Instead of jubilation, Hankins could feel only a cold pain in his stomach.

Chapter 96

It was early afternoon, at 1:45 P.M., when Tom Ward stretched his frame out on the single bed in Walnut Lodge, his mind moving in circular waves, each thought paradoxical to the next. He had been invited to meet with Fenton and Hankins at Aspen Lodge at two-fifteen. No one had told him the purpose of the meeting, but Fenton had hinted at its "historical" value.

His new role as a double agent was confusing. As Major Peter Semanski, it had all been coherent. But he was now Tom Ward, a Soviet defector without asylum, in a nation he was coming to appreciate, but whose leader had himself joined the enemy.

He could tell that Fenton had a sensitive antenna for the scent of betrayal. It was essential he handle himself carefully at this meeting if he was to survive. And, in surviving, protect Les against Baneyev's killers.

Ward looked up at the sound of a knock on the door. Was it already time for his meeting?

"Who's there?"

"Mr. Ward, you don't know me," a voice came through. "I'm Doug McDowell." A few seconds passed. "Davidson sent me."

Ward was startled, then smiled at Davidson's extraordinary reach. Even here in Camp David.

As Ward opened the cabin door, he recognized the man in front of him. It was the network commentator, but absent his television personality, a muddled expression masking his features.

"Come in. Why the visit?"

As McDowell searched out a chair and sat down, Ward studied him.

"You say Davidson sent you. To do what?"

"We don't know each other, Ward, but I have news. Not too good, but Davidson said I should bring it to you."

"Hold off, McDowell." Ward needed to slow down the agitated commentator. "First off, what are you doing at Camp David?"

"I came down here to interview Hankins for a network documentary, and—actually—to do some investigating. But it seems like ancient history. In a few hours the whole thing could be pointless."

"Why so? What's happening that's so important?"

"Can I trust you?" McDowell asked.

Ward laughed. "Mr. McDowell, that's an unprofessional question if I ever heard one. If you couldn't, I surely wouldn't tell you. But if trustworthy means am I on the same side as John Davidson—the answer is yes."

"I sure hope John is right. Here goes."

In rapid, bold strokes, McDowell described the Soviet plan for STAND DOWN, every detail of the nuclear blackmail he had overheard the night before.

"Incredible," Ward said, reacting strongly to the news. "I know Fenton is easily capable of this. But I'd never have expected Hankins to go along."

"He tried to resist, but Fenton seems to control him. Is it blackmail?" McDowell asked.

"Nothing so simple. The two are tied in some hypnotic union, with Hankins, I'm afraid, the subject."

"I have other news, too," McDowell added. "Davidson dispatched Sam Withers, a CIA out in the cold, to come here. He's in my cabin, wounded. I think he's here to kill Hankins."

Ward was used to the patterns of covert action, but Davidson's bravado surprised him.

"Is that so? When will it happen?"

"Before two-thirty. If he makes it. I've got to go back and wake him by two. He's pretty weak and Aspen Lodge seems to be well guarded. I don't know about you, but I don't like the idea much. Although, at this point . . ." McDowell's voice trailed off in thought.

"I don't know what to do," McDowell picked up. "It's almost two o'clock. I suppose Davidson is at work in Washington. But what can we do here?"

"I'm sure Davidson told you. I was KGB, but I've decided to defect," Ward explained. "Apparently at the wrong moment. Both Hankins and Fenton still think I'm with them. In fact, I'm supposed to be at Aspen Lodge at two-fifteen. Now I know why."

"Is there anything you can do there?" McDowell asked.

"The only way I can help is to get Hankins to stand up to Fenton and the Soviets," Ward responded. "To refuse their blackmail. But I have no idea if it'll work."

Ward stared inquisitively at the newsman. "How about you? What will you do?"

"Honestly, I'm getting a little panicky. I'd feel a lot better if I heard from Davidson. I'll try to get him on the phone."

McDowell's fingers were soon anxiously dialing.

"Operator, please get me John Davidson in Leesburg, Virginia."

He rummaged through his inside pocket for the unlisted number, but before he could locate it the operator spoke up.

"Sorry, sir. No outside phone calls."

"No calls? Why is that?"

"Mr. Fenton's orders, sir. The only open line is for the President."

"Damn it," McDowell groaned, then hung up. "Fenton's closed off the phones."

Ward moved off the bed, donning his jacket.

"Nothing more we can do here, McDowell. I've got to get to the meeting. Good luck to both of us."

Chapter 97

"It's time."

Sam Withers woke in Sycamore Lodge, the strength revived in his body.

"It's two o'clock," McDowell was saying, gently shaking Withers' uninjured side. "How do you feel, Sam?"

Sam touched the wounded arm. "It's still stiff, but it doesn't hurt as much. Thanks for your help."

Withers could sense McDowell's discomfort, but not a word was said about assassination.

"I went to see Ward and filled him in on everything," McDowell said. "He's been invited to the meeting at Aspen. He'll do what he can. I'm going to get a bite to eat now. Hope you don't mind."

After McDowell left, Withers extracted the Beretta and checked the clip. He was soon at the cabin door, peering out onto a chilly afternoon, a deceptive peace enveloping the rustic atmosphere.

Withers slipped out unobtrusively, but instead of moving down the main street he turned back into the woods, toward where he remembered seeing Aspen Lodge. He walked several hundred yards through thick underbrush. Then he saw it. A sizable one-story ranch-style house with rough loglike siding, not much different than the country home of any affluent American.

Sam walked around the perimeter, keeping a safe hundred yards away. Thus far he had spotted four Marines walking guard, but each was trying to remain anonymous, seeking even here to create the illusion of a civilian President with little to fear.

As Withers circled from the distance, he strained his eyes to see inside. At the back, there was a large plate-glass window overlooking the countryside. That was obviously the living room of the lodge, a large area with a mammoth stone fireplace and beamed ceilings. He could make out two figures, Hankins and Fenton, both standing and talking.

Withers knew this room was his target area. He would have to close in on it within the next fifteen minutes.

He looked at his watch. It was a few minutes after two, no time for error.

Chapter 98

The activity in front of the Capitol building was frenetic. The green helicopter with the insignia "U. S. Army" painted on its frame had landed on the pavement directly in front of the Capitol steps. Six Army men with Israeli-made Uzi submachine guns jumped out and stood guard around the plane, its rotors whirling, poised for an immediate take-off.

John Davidson was waiting near the bottom Capitol step, studying his watch. It was 2:10 P.M.

It was now an equation of minutes, Davidson knew. At two-thirty the first counter in the blackmail scheme would be put in place, presented to Hankins by the Soviet General Secretary. A half hour later the President was to relinquish the national pride.

He thought of Sam Withers at Camp David. Had he gotten past the perimeter guards? Would he take out Hankins in time?

Joint Chiefs Chairman John Abbott was standing alongside Davidson, holding his Marine cap in place in the wash of the rotors. Inside the Capitol, in the President's Room of the Senate, Delafield and Feldman were with Hawley Briggs, who, Bible in hand, was waiting for the Chief Justice of the Supreme Court to arrive and swear him in as Vice-President. Only minutes before, both houses of Congress had ratified Briggs by the simple majority vote required by the Twenty-fifth Amendment.

"Where in the hell is that man?" Senator Delafield's foot was rhythmically beating the floor. "I told him that it had to be by 2 P.M."

He surveyed the assembled small group. "If he doesn't come in a few minutes, is anyone else empowered to swear in a VP?" the senator asked.

Feldman, Briggs, and his aides looked blankly at one another. That piece of democratic trivia elicited no response.

They didn't need it. Seconds later, the eighty-two-year-old Chief Justice, wheezing as he walked in on the arm of an aide, moved up to Briggs.

"I understand you're in a hurry to take that job, Hawley. Why, I don't know," the Chief Justice said defiantly. "I turned it down twice twenty years ago." Everyone smiled nervously.

"But here goes. Raise your right hand and place your other one on the Bible."

For an eternal minute, in the slowest of tempos, the Chief Justice recited the oath to defend the Constitution.

"I do. So help me God," Briggs responded. He clutched at the forearm of Delafield and the two men raced down the thirty-six steps of East Plaza of the Capitol, newsmen and photographers in professional pursuit.

At the bottom, Davidson, General Abbott, and all except one soldier were already in the helicopter.

"Let's hurry!" Davidson yelled above the whir of the rotors.

He was calculating the timing and the alternatives. If Sam was successful, the new President—Hawley Briggs—would be aboard their helicopter. Otherwise the Vice-President and the Chairman of the Joint Chiefs would try to defy Hankins at Camp David and seize executive control. He hoped that wouldn't be necessary. The military might refuse to obey anyone except the President, the man who had already agreed to STAND DOWN.

Delafield moved rapidly inside the helicopter, but Briggs's way was blocked by a half dozen news people.

"Where are you going with your armed guard, Mr. Vice-President?" a reporter yelled out.

"Can't say. It's top secret. But I'll fill you in later. Good-bye."

The soldier elbowed a path through the newsmen for Briggs, and the two of them mounted the steps. An instant later the doors were closed.

The helicopter took off, its nose pointed northwest toward Camp David.

"Let's make some time, Lieutenant," Davidson leaned over and whispered to the Army pilot. "Your job—and everyone's—is at stake."

Chapter 99

Sam Withers studied his watch. It was two-seventeen. Time to move in on the back of Aspen Lodge. From his position, he could see the front of the building, its entrances guarded by Secret Service men.

Only by circling away, then coming in straight at the back window did he have a chance, if only for brief seconds. Just enough time to fire two shots. One to pierce the plate-glass window, the second to kill Hankins. Then a race through the woods and, maybe, to leave Camp David the way he had come in.

Withers dropped to the ground and, with his elbows and knees slithering over the damp grass, began his infantry crawl. He covered the first hundred feet more slowly than he had hoped, still missing the perfect rhythm of the movement. It was more painful than he had expected, the wounded left arm pulsing with each push of his elbows.

At two twenty-five he had reached a large tree at the back of Aspen, some eighty feet from the house. He could see a Marine guard patrolling not far from him. The timing was vital. Davidson had stressed the two-thirty deadline. There was no second chance. Hankins had to be dead before the opening move of STAND DOWN.

He removed the Beretta from his pocket and checked the magazine clip. It slid gracefully in and out of the stock. It was fully loaded but he would need only two 9mm shells to complete his job.

Withers took the collapsible binoculars out of his pocket and surveyed the scene. It was clear. The President was close to the window. Another man—he assumed it was Tom Ward—had entered the room and was standing unobtrusively near the stone fireplace. Fenton was at the side of the room, facing them both, but he could make out only his face in the shadows.

As he started his last movement toward Aspen, Sam could feel the pain of each half swing of his elbows, then the determined drag of the knees toward the objective—a seemingly passive scene behind the plate-glass wall, one that reminded him of a giant fresco.

Now, only two more slithery movements and he would be close enough to shatter the glass and avenge everyone.

Withers had started his elbows outward again when he suddenly slowed. His knees refused to follow on. He could, inexplicably, feel himself fading. The gun was getting soft in his hands, his eyes unfocusing.

This time it was not simple weakness from his wound. Sam could sense a large hand grasp the back of his neck and twist. Then a sharp blow to his temple.

Just as Withers moved into black unconsciousness, the last sight to reach his eyes was that of two large Marines, one with gun drawn, standing over his now stilled body.

Sam cursed himself. Once again, he had failed to kill Jed Hankins.

Chapter 100

The phone rang at two twenty-eight.

Maude Holly was on the line, relaying a call to the living room of Aspen Lodge, where the President, Fenton, and Tom Ward were waiting expectantly to hear from the Kremlin. Ward had already been briefed on STAND DOWN, but the Secret Service men had been ordered to stay outside. No other witnesses were wanted to this piece of history.

The President was surprised. The General Secretary was early, by two minutes. Hankins picked up the phone, listened, then handed it to Fenton.

"Bill, it's not Moscow. It's for you."

"Mr. Fenton, we didn't want to bother the President. This is Captain McLaughlin, Camp David Marine detachment. We just caught someone trying to infiltrate Aspen. His name is Withers, Sam Withers, a former CIA man. He had a loaded Beretta on him. I'd say he was coming to kill the President. We have him in the MP headquarters. You want to come down and talk to him?"

"Okay, Captain. That's no problem," Fenton dissembled, determined not to disrupt Hankins with the crucial phone call only minutes away. "Just hold everything on ice until I get down there. Thanks." Fenton hung up and moved away from the desk.

"What was that all about, Bill?" Hankins asked.

"Oh, nothing. A mechanical problem in the helicopter. But they're working on it."

A minute later the phone rang in Birch Lodge. The call from the General Secretary first came in to Holly. The hot line teletype wire would not do today, the General Secretary told her. He wanted to speak directly to the President, on the phone.

The line rang in Aspen Lodge at exactly two-thirty.

Hankins passively listened to it ring, once, then twice, as if seconds gained would somehow alter history. Finally he lifted the phone.

"Yes, Mr. General Secretary. I hear you clearly. Yes, I know today's an auspicious day. We should make the most of it. I agree."

The General Secretary's tone was precise, an effort to avoid any misunderstanding of his intentions.

"President Hankins. Our full might of 71 nuclear submarines, 22,000 nuclear warheads, and 650 Blackjack, Backfire, and Andropov bombers armed with cruise missiles and nuclear devices is poised, ready to annihilate your nation. Our SS-18s and SS-24s are targeting every one of your silos and command posts. The 24s are accurate within 250 feet and none of your hardened installations, or your command personnel, will survive. I must add that we have two warheads aimed directly at you in Camp David."

He paused. "But it's not necessary for any of this mass devastation to happen. As a progressive American, you surely understand the inevitability of world Communism. Instead of destruction, we offer you a partnership in the socialist community. Just instruct your military to stand down."

Hankins' eyes closed. He was not sure it was of his own volition. He was hearing the inevitable, but his mind refused to register that the moment had actually come. The General Secretary was still speaking.

"We shall accept simple terms. The elimination of your nuclear capability, on your shores and overseas. The immediate end of your interference in world affairs. Recognition of the dominance of the Soviet Union, and an eventual transformation of your political system into a duplicate of ours. A democracy of the Party. I have no time to discuss this further. Now, I must move forward to implement this threat—if we must. But I am counting on you, on your record, on your sensitivity to world geopolitics, to accept our terms. Unconditionally."

Without offering Hankins a chance to respond, the General Secretary concluded his remarks.

"I will call back at three o'clock for your answer. For the sake of all humanity, and the future of world socialism, I hope it will be positive."

With that he hung up, leaving Hankins with a dead phone in his hand. The President turned to his longtime aide.

"Bill. He's actually made the threat."

Hankins was stunned by the expected.

"I knew it was coming, but I had hoped it was only a gesture of strength. A warning. But no. I truly believe that unless I surrender they intend to destroy us."

Hankins turned away from the other two men and walked to the window, now speaking to himself, even to some unseen posterity.

"It's mad! That's what it is. Mad!"

Hankins faced Fenton again, his gaunt features now more drawn, his expression shifting to rage.

"Bill, they're not civilized!" Hankins screamed. "How in the hell did I ever get involved with those fucking barbarians? Nuclear holocaust if I don't give in! Those cocksucker bastards. What's been wrong with my mind? Why didn't I see it before?"

Then suddenly his rage turned on Fenton.

"Bill, you're the one who got me into this! Into a position where I don't even know if I can fight back. God. Hundreds of years down the drain. Maybe thousands of years of the future. Didn't you know that they were madmen? Didn't you? God damn it! Didn't you know?"

Hankins stopped and dropped to his knees. Without assuming a position of prayer, he looked up.

"Oh, my God. What have I done? What have I done?"

Watching, Fenton had turned ashen with contempt. He rushed over, straining to pull Hankins up off the rug.

"Stop it, Jed! Damn it, stop it! Since when have you had a God other than power? This is no time to break. You started something. You had a plan to Communize America and help the Soviet Union take the world. Now that it's happening, you're shitting in your pants! This is not a damn furlong race for two-year-olds, Jed. This is the real world and the Soviets are winning it. Damn it. Join it. Or die!"

Hankins looked at his partner of fourteen years as if he had never seen him before, his eyes exuding hatred.

"I see it all now, Fenton. I was the rich patsy, the tool to fulfill your mad dreams of becoming the American Lenin. You know your rich people. Oh, you do. Play to their vanity. Chisel away at their guilt. Give them a purpose other than money. And you did, you son of a bitch. You're no better than those barbarians. You turned me into a traitor to my own people. But no more, Fenton. This is the end."

"The end of what?" Fenton asked. "What do you think you can do, Jed?"

"Hang around and watch me."

The President picked up the telephone.

"Maude. Get Commander Kelly in here with the Football. That's right. On the double."

"Oh, that's funny, Jed. The Football? Didn't I tell you? Billings has been working on that for a month. We've deactivated all the authorization codes—the missile-launching numerals and the GO codes for you and the Cabinet. Commander Kelly's little Football is worthless."

Hankins bounced the phone impatiently in his hand.

"Fine. Then I'll do it through regular command, by telephone. They know my voice. I don't care if the generals have to manually arm every missile."

He lifted the red telephone, connected directly to the National Command Center at the Pentagon.

"Hello. Who is this? Major Clemens, this is the President. Quickly, get me General Abbott. He's not there? Then get me his deputy, General Atkins. And set up an immediate conference call with CINCNORAD General Landsdowne at Cheyenne Mountain and General Hollaran at the SAC Command Center at Offutt. And, Major, make it quick. This is a national emergency!"

Fenton was paralyzed for an instant, then his eyes responded, fired.

"Jed. I really believe you intend to fight back. You're the one that's mad. Everyone in America will be dead! Sure, you'll kill some Russians, but it'll be the end of America. And the Soviets will survive and win."

As the President stared at Fenton, he could see his aide's harsh expression suddenly fade. He was now looking benignly at Hankins, his voice more conciliatory. As if, Hankins thought, Fenton was trying to regain his hypnotic hold over him.

"Jed, please try to think calmly," he could hear Fenton say. "Wouldn't it make more sense to give in now instead of triggering Armageddon? Maybe later America can win back some measure of independence. A kind of Finland. Isn't that better than mass suicide? No one will remember your brave gesture—only the nuclear death. Try to think straight. In a few minutes the General Secretary will be calling for your answer."

"Bill. I can tell you right now what it's going to be. As soon as my military men get on the phone I'm going to order a full alert of what we have left and threaten the General Secretary with that. I'm gambling that he only wants STAND DOWN if I go along—as you told him I would. Some of our missiles will get through. The few MXs we still have on line will destroy his hardened underground headquarters in Moscow. Maybe the General Secretary doesn't want to die himself. We'll see."

Fenton's expression transformed again, this time to a mass of hostility.

"I didn't want to do this, Jed, but I've had an ace just in case. Baneyev gave me Withers' whole file on you. It proves you were working for the Soviet Union long before you got into the White House. Jed, do you want the public trial, the infamy as a traitor? Hang up the phone and go along with the General Secretary. I swear I'll never tell him that you were thinking of opposing STAND DOWN. You'll still be the head of a new socialist America."

Hankins laughed, his head thrown back.

"Bill, you're really as mad as they are. We're talking about surrender or 150 million dead, and you think I'm going to be influenced by a lousy dossier. Screw you and the file."

Hankins turned back to the phone. "Major. Damn it. Hurry."

"I'm telling you to stop it, Jed," Fenton warned. Reaching deliberately into his pocket, he extracted a small German PPK, a three-and-a-half-inch-long Walther automatic.

"Drop the telephone, Jed. Nobody is going to order any alert against the Soviets. Drop it now, or I'll shoot. Your dying is not going to help America. There's nobody here who can pick up the pieces in time. The Russians already have their bombers in the air, and their nuclear subs and ICBMs are ready to launch. Drop the phone, Jed, or you'll be the dead last President of the United States."

Chapter 101

The Army helicopter carrying Vice-President Briggs and the others touched down on the landing zone at Camp David at exactly two forty-nine.

From his cabin, Doug McDowell had seen the commotion near the helicopter pad and raced toward the area, arriving just as the giant helicopter door swung open. Briggs, Delafield, Abbott, and Davidson jumped out, followed closely by the Uzi-armed soldiers. General Abbott moved out in front of the group.

"Welcome to Camp David." A young Marine captain saluted Abbott, who waved him on.

"Follow me, Captain," General Abbott ordered. "Things are hopping at Aspen Lodge."

Davidson noticed McDowell standing at the edge of the group and motioned him over to join them.

On the double, with Davidson and Briggs struggling to keep up with Abbott and the younger men, the group ran the distance from the helicopter pad to Aspen Lodge, racing through the rustic compound like some strange army on maneuvers.

Chapter 102

"Jed, I'm asking you for the last time. Put down that phone. Don't believe I won't do it."

"Oh, I believe you'll do it. I see it now. You'll do anything for your Marxist obsession."

Hankins moved back to the phone. "Yes, Major. General Atkins coming on? Good."

The miniature Walther automatic started upward in Fenton's hand.

"Jed, don't talk to General Atkins. I warn you. For the last time."

Ward had been watching the entire scene without speaking. His plan to influence Hankins had been needless. The President had confronted Fenton on his own, but Ward realized that if Hankins didn't yield Fenton was going to kill him.

Ward stared into Fenton's PPK, his body apparently immobilized. But his hand was moving slowly toward a large Ming vase on a table alongside him. Ward could feel his outstretched fingers strain, then touch it. Turning his hand inward, he quickly gave the vase a backward flick of the wrist. It moved off the table, crashing to the floor.

Fenton jumped at the irritant, turning his gun toward the noise. In that instant Ward's body left the ground in a smooth leap toward the outstretched gun.

Out of the corner of his eye, Fenton saw the balletlike move. When Ward was only inches from the automatic, Fenton turned the gun back toward him and fired. The 9mm bullet ripped Ward in the center of his throat. The blood gushed out, staining the floor as he tumbled into the fireplace well.

The President watched, motionless. Fenton, his eyes now distorted, stretched the pistol outward, pointing it at Hankins' heart. The two men stood immobile for several seconds, their eyes meeting.

"Sorry, Jed," Fenton whispered, then fired.

The bullet struck the President directly in the heart. Hankins uttered only one word—"God"—then collapsed to the floor, the receiver of the red telephone lying next to his outstretched hand.

From the phone came the sounds of a man's voice, shouting.

"Mr. President! This is General Atkins. What's happening there? What's going on?"

Fenton stood in the center of the room, surrounded by the mayhem, the small automatic still in hand, his consciousness seemingly gone.

Chapter 103

Commander Janet Kelly, summoned minutes before by Hankins, had just returned the salute of the Marine guards outside. Entering Aspen Lodge, nuclear Football resolutely in hand, her mind was rehearsing the combination to the black bag. Why had Hankins asked for the Football?

Once inside the foyer, Kelly was startled by what sounded like the report of a gun. She clutched the Football and raced toward the living room. As she entered, she stood fixed, her eyes first concentrated on Fenton's outstretched arm, then shifting to the sight of Tom Ward's body falling into the fireplace well.

Before Kelly could look back at Fenton, she heard another shot. She turned to see the President fall to the ground, then wheeled back toward the front door, her screams now filling the lodge.

"Someone! Come quick! The President's been shot. Hurry! The President's been shot!"

As the commander reached the door, her frame was hit by an oncoming soldier, a large man rushing into the lodge.

"Oh, General Abbott. Thank God! The President's been shot! He's on the floor—over there!"

Several soldiers and Marines who had followed behind Abbott ran in and examined the two prone men, bloodied by bullets.

"The President's dead!" the Marine captain shouted. "Right through the heart."

"This one's finished too," called out a soldier examining Ward's body. "Cut down right in the neck."

Fenton was standing, fixed in his assassin's spot, the automatic still in his hand, his eyes vacant.

"Take him away, will you, Captain?" Abbott waved the Marine officer toward Fenton.

"All right. Everyone in uniform please leave. Except you, Commander Kelly. We may have to play a little Football."

Abbott reached down and picked up the red telephone.

"Hello? Atkins? This is General Abbott. Hold on for orders. This is an emergency." He replaced the receiver on the desk.

At that instant the other telephone rang. Hawley Briggs, who had just arrived with Davidson, lifted it.

"The General Secretary? Yes. I'll take the call."

It was precisely 3 P.M. Washington time, 11 P.M. in the Kremlin.

"Hello. Camp David? This is the General Secretary. May I speak with President Hankins?"

"I'm sorry you can't," Briggs responded calmly.

"Why not?" the General Secretary's voice was gruffer than usual.

"Because he's dead. He's been assassinated."

The line seemed to have expired for a moment. When the General Secretary resumed speaking, his voice did not skip an emotional beat.

"Is that true? Then to whom am I speaking?"

"This is President Hawley Briggs. What can I do for you, Mr. Secretary?"

"You may not be aware of it, but President Hankins and I were in the midst of very delicate negotiations. I have asked for a surrender of your nuclear capabilities. The alternative is total nuclear attack. Were you aware of our demands? They were made at two-thirty. Hankins was to respond to us now, at 3 P.M. Washington time."

"Yes, Mr. Secretary," Briggs answered. "I was aware of your demands."

"And your answer?"

"The answer is no. Absolutely no. We shall face STAND DOWN with a full nuclear alert."

"But how? How can you do that? You're not prepared to match our nuclear threat. Even your B-1s carry only useless conventional bombs. No?"

The General Secretary seemed somewhat disoriented by the rapid change in the scenario.

"I'll put General Abbott on to answer all your military questions, Mr. Secretary. He handed Abbott the phone.

"Yes, Mr. Secretary," the brusque former Marine colonel began. "Yes, our defenses were heavily crippled by your people—in our high offices—but we military are onery. If you know what that means. I took the nuclear weapons off the B-1 bombers as Hankins ordered me. But I kept them handy, just in case. When Vice-President—President —Briggs called this morning and said there was a national emergency, I ordered them reloaded. For an hour now, 92 of our 100 B-1 bombers, loaded with nuclear bombs and over 1000 cruise missiles, have been in the air from our European and American bases, headed in your direction. They should be coming into your radar range pretty soon.

"Also our happy signal is no longer being transmitted to our nuclear subs. Hankins beached most of them, but the rest are awaiting my orders from the TACAMO planes, all of which are aloft. The Looking Glass command center is in the air over the Midwest as well, with the deputy CINCSAC on board, alerted. Incidentally, I have two of our few remaining MXs targeted. One on the Kremlin and the other on your National Air Defense Forces headquarters outside

Moscow. I don't know who'll survive the exchange, Mr. Secretary, but I don't think it'll be me—or you."

"But your missile communications from Camp David are in disarray," the General Secretary protested, his strident voice weakening in its timbre. "Your launch codes are incorrect. Am I right, General Abbott?"

"No, Mr. Secretary. You're not. I spotted that little computer game weeks ago. I was just playing along with Defense Secretary Billings. The Football is also fine, with the GO codes in place and ready to be used if President Briggs orders. Commander Kelly is standing right alongside me now. Shall we start our mutual assured destruction, Mr. Secretary, or will we both—as you say—just stand down together?"

At the other end, the phone erupted into a hearty laugh.

"General Abbott, please put the President back on," the General Secretary asked, his voice brimming with warmth.

"President Briggs. Congratulations on your new office. Please understand that we were just probing for your vulnerabilities. Testing your mettle, as it were. I've heard that your God protects little babies and Americans. Perhaps. But we Russians have a saying too. Fairy tales of one generation can become the nightmares of the next. In any case, Mr. President, I will now recall our alert. Can I presume you will do the same?"

"Yes, Mr. Secretary. And in the future, please remember that I'm a reasonable man. But I cannot be pushed. It will be to your disadvantage."

"I can see that, Mr. President. By the way, I look forward to seeing you in Geneva at the disarmament talks. We have a lot to chat about. Yes? We must continue to work, always, for good will between our nations. Especially for universal peace. Good day, Mr. President."

Chapter 104

John Davidson was pleased to be visiting the White House under more salubrious circumstances. He had been invited to the mansion just a few days after Hawley Briggs was sworn in.

What could the President want? Not to give him a professional assignment. At Camp David, Davidson had refused Hawley's offer to return as head of the CIA, a reaffirmation of Daniels' pledge. Davidson preferred to keep his private status, with its more challenging freedom.

"Come this way, Mr. Davidson." He smiled at his escort. It was Les Fanning, the new executive assistant to President Briggs.

"Les, I'm sorry about Tom." Davidson touched the edges of her hand. "But in the end he made his own decision—for us. I'm glad to see you're back in harness, where you belong. And thanks for your help."

"No one deserves thanks more than you, Mr. Davidson."

Les placed her head into the doorway of the Oval Office. "President Briggs. John Davidson is here."

The President rose from his desk and moved out into the center of the room to receive Davidson.

"So glad you could come, John. Let's sit near the fireplace. Like you, I'm past fifty. And Washington ain't Arkansas in March.

"John, I asked you here to tell you a few things and ask you some. First, I can't complain. Sommerville has resigned. Baneyev is being expelled from the country and, thanks to you and Doug McDowell, the FBI has rounded up Rausch, Meg Larsen, Marge Coulton, and the whole Washington KGB apparatus. Of course you know about Fenton and Billings. Last night they both committed suicide in their cells. The first decent act for their country.

"John, I know you don't want the job yourself, but I need your advice on the CIA. I've brought your old friend Al Springs back as CIA director. But I'm wondering about Matt Miles. Was he in cahoots with Fenton and Hankins? Or is he okay? What I'm asking is—should I keep him on in a high Agency position?"

This was the second time in only months that an American President had asked him about Miles. Davidson knew why. Miles, who had long been under suspicion by conservatives in the Agency, had been accepted by Hankins as the authentic Soviet mole.

Davidson thought back twenty years to the time he had placed Miles in that position. To play the mole. It had paid dividends many times, again just these last months. He had to preserve Miles's double identity, if he was ever to use him again.

Davidson assumed a thoughtful pose. "Yes, President Briggs. I think Miles is a competent professional and, overall, a credit to the Agency."

"Good, John. I'll go with what you say. Incidentally, I'm awarding you the Medal of Freedom. And the same for that newsman, Doug McDowell. He's waiting outside now to see me. I'm also awarding presidential commendations to Clint Low and that stubborn cop, Sergeant Fuller. Your friend Sam Withers, though, is a more difficult case. I'm sure he deserves a medal too, but what I've done instead is grant him a presidential pardon. I'll get heat for it, but I suppose that's the least I can do. As for his CIA job, well, we'll have to wait and see."

"What about Defense?" Davidson asked. "Who'll be taking over?"

"I've reappointed General Abbott as Chairman of the Joint Chiefs —he's learned the value of strategic arms. And Willie Jamieson is going to be my new Secretary of Defense, as Governor Daniels intended. They're hard at work rebuilding our capabilities."

The President's tone suddenly turned more confidential.

"John, you gambled and won. Now, we've got to follow up on your theory and make sure the American public never learns how badly they were betrayed, and how close we came to extinction. The circle of people who know what Fenton and Hankins did is small. I want to keep it that way. I've eulogized Hankins as the victim of a madman who was jealous of his power. I suppose, in some way, that's close to the truth."

Briggs paused. "Those of us who know what actually happened have to take it with us to Judgment. I've gotten that pledge from Delafield and Abbott, and McDowell and Les Fanning. I can count on you for the same? Right, John?"

Davidson smiled at Briggs's resolve in adopting his insistence on secrecy, that the treachery of President Jedidiah Hankins would never unfold in the pages of history.

"Hawley, it's just one more in my inventory of untold and untellable stories. I promise. No one will ever know that you were nominated for the presidency by seven frightened congressmen and a decrepit ex-agent. Trust me."

"John Davidson," the President roared contentedly. "You're a son of a gun. A real rooster. But believe me, it's been a pleasure anyway."

THE END

ABOUT THE AUTHOR

Martin Gross, author of *The Red President*, is a writer, editor, and educator.

He was the founder and editor-and-chief of *Book Digest* magazine and is the former president of a book publishing firm.

His three previous books—*The Doctors, The Brain Watchers*, and *The Psychological Society*—all nonfiction, were trenchant social commentaries that resulted in Congressional hearings and subsequent federal legislation.

Mr. Gross is also the author of over 100 magazine articles, his work appearing in such publications as *Life, Look*, and *The New Republic*. For several years, his nationally syndicated column, mainly covering Washington affairs, appeared in major daily newspapers including the Los Angeles *Times*, Chicago *Sun-Times*, and *Newsday*.

The author was a longtime member of the social science faculty of the New School for Social Research and Adjunct Assistant Professor of Social History at New York University. He has received awards from the National Education Association and the American Heritage Foundation.

For a time, he was active in politics and served as an alternate delegate to a national political convention, a vital background for *The Red President*.